YOUR MONEY'S WORTH

Seattle Elementals, Book 1

Connie Suttle

SubtleDemon Publishing, LLC

Published by: SubtleDemon Publishing, LLC, P.O. Box 95696, Oklahoma City, OK 73143

To Walter, Joe, Sarah, Lee, Larry, Dianne and Mark
Thank you

Copyright (c) 2016 Connie Suttle

All rights reserved

ISBN-10: 1-939759-40-5
ISBN-13: 978-1-939759-40-5

This is a work of fiction. Names, places, incidents, and characters are the product of the author's imagination and are fictitious. Any resemblance to actual events, locales, persons, living or dead, is coincidental.

Cover Art by Renee Barratt @ The Cover Counts

Acknowledgements

As always, this book is the result of collaboration. If it weren't for the support of my editor, my cover artist and my beta readers, it would be less than it is. All mistakes, as usual, are mine and no other's.

About the Author:

Connie Suttle lives in Oklahoma with her husband and a conglomerate of cats. They have finally banded together to make their demands, which has proven disconcerting to all humans involved.

You may find Connie in the following ways:

Facebook: Connie Suttle Author

Twitter: @subtledemon

Website and Blog: subtledemon.com

Other books by Connie Suttle:

Blood Destiny Series:

Blood Wager

Blood Passage
Blood Sense
Blood Domination
Blood Royal
Blood Queen
Blood Rebellion
Blood War
Blood Redemption
Blood Reunion

* * *

Legend of the Ir'Indicti Series:
Bumble
Shadowed
Target
Vendetta
Destroyer

* * *

High Demon Series:
Demon Lost
Demon Revealed
Demon's King
Demon's Quest
Demon's Revenge
Demon's Dream

* * *

God Wars Series:
Blood Double
Blood Trouble
Blood Revolution
Blood Love
Blood Finale

* * *

Saa Thalarr Series:
Hope and Vengeance
Wyvern and Company
Observe and Protect*
* * *

First Ordinance Series:
Finder
Keeper
BlackWing
SpellBreaker
WhiteWing
* * *

R-D Series:
Cloud Dust
Cloud Invasion
Cloud Rebel
* * *

Latter Day Demons Series:
Hot Demon in the City
A Demon's Work is Never Done
A Demon's Due
***

Seattle Elementals Series:
Your Money's Worth
Worth Your While*
* * *

BlackWing Pirates Series:
MindSighted*
*Forthcoming

Part 1: The Christmas War

Chapter 1

R ock smashes ice.
    Fire melts rock.
    Water quenches fire.
Ice freezes water.
—*The elemental demon version of rock, paper, scissors*

* * *

Birmingham, Alabama
December
Shelbie Foster

Be smart, Shelbie, I mentally berated myself. It wouldn't do to show how terrified and shaky I was to anyone else. My stalkers were in the grocery store parking lot, waiting. I hoped more weren't inside the store; that could ruin my plan and cause human deaths.

Stopping at the tiny post office inside the store and struggling to slow my breathing, I parked my shopping cart beside me and pulled the package from the reusable grocery bags I'd brought in. I'd hidden it that way to keep my watchers from knowing it existed.

"I'd like to mail this, please," I set the package on the counter in front of the clerk, forcing my hands not to shake as I did so. The sealed box didn't weigh more than six pounds.

"Overnight?" the clerk asked while setting the box on her scale.

"Oh, no. Cheapest and slowest," I attempted a smile.

"All right." Postage was printed while I watched, then slapped on a corner of the box. "That'll be ten dollars."

I handed her a twenty; she gave me change. "Thank you," I said and turned toward my grocery basket. I'd leave with groceries, to make my trip look authentic. In the back of my mind, I knew it wouldn't matter what I purchased. I'd never make it home to eat it anyway.

* * *

Seattle

December

Cassie

He was a pig. My boss, that is, but calling him a pig was probably an insult to pigs everywhere, including the wild, dangerous kind. If I didn't need my job, and I mean really need my job, I'd have left months ago. That's when my boss' wife left him and he turned his lascivious attentions to me.

Geoffrey Gruber, the man who'd made my life hell for nine months, was short, squarely built, balding and a pig. A nearsighted pig on top of that. His nearsighted gaze was focused (unfortunately) on me, most of the time.

I'd met his wife when I started working for Geoffrey—she was nice and probably on a short list for sainthood somewhere, just for putting up with him so long. She was now in the process of divorcing him and when he wasn't complaining about what she might get out of him in the divorce, he was making sexual innuendos, most of them aimed in my direction.

Chapter 1

I cursed the day I was promoted to be his personal assistant. I'd read an article somewhere that said some married men didn't know how to be alone—that they needed someone. It was the reason many widowers married again shortly after the death of their spouse. My opinion was this; if Geoffrey Gruber required someone to herd him around, he should get a border collie.

"The copier is out of toner," Annabelle Taylor, Geoffrey's associate at Gruber, Taylor and Worth, said as she sailed past my desk. With hair loosely swept into a bun, thighs swishing in a too-tight pencil skirt and too many buttons undone on her blouse, she looked ready for a role-playing event as the sexy schoolmarm.

Annabelle had a personal assistant, but Jeremy had been hired strictly as eye-candy for Annabelle. I figured if he had half a brain, he'd realize that. As it was, he was great at sharpening pencils. Changing a toner cartridge was outside his personal skill set.

That meant I did his work and mine, too. Couple that with Geoffrey's unwelcome attentions and my anxiety meter ran constantly on high.

"Oh," Annabelle tossed over her shoulder, "Parke Worth, old man Worth's son, is coming in tomorrow to take over his father's part of the business." I knew, just as Annabelle did, that Parke Worth had inherited two-thirds of the business. She and Geoffrey shared a third between them.

Harmon Worth, Parke's father, had died unexpectedly a year earlier, leaving a gaping hole in the business. Worth had been the best attorney of the three, so I secretly found it humorous that Geoffrey's wife had hired someone better than her soon-to-be-ex to handle her part of the divorce.

Parke, Harmon's only son, worked at a law firm in D.C. when his father died and had cases to tie up before returning to Seattle and his father's business. I'd never met him—or Harmon. I'd arrived during the gap in between. I figured, too, that Parke was returning two weeks before Christmas so he could spend time with family.

I hoped Parke wasn't as insufferable as Geoffrey or Annabelle. If he were, I'd be forced to look for another job. I knew as well as anyone that nobody wanted to hire a paralegal or personal assistant over the holidays, and there was no way I'd survive without a paycheck.

"I'll get the toner cartridge changed immediately," I called out while hauling the supply cabinet key from a desk drawer. Standing stiffly, I realized I hadn't moved for nearly three hours while preparing a brief for Geoffrey's latest case.

Annabelle's office door closed with a snap and no acknowledgement. I hadn't really expected a thank-you, and likely would have fainted if she'd said it. Five minutes later, with a new toner cartridge installed and a cup of coffee in my hand, I returned to my desk to find someone sitting there.

I froze. He wasn't magazine-cover handsome in any traditional sense, but that didn't keep my radar from pinging. This guy intrigued me.

A lot.

"Hello," I said, setting the coffee cup on my desk and smiling at the man who'd commandeered my workspace.

"Have you drank from that?" he nodded at my disposable cup.

"Not yet," I said, wondering why he'd asked.

"Thanks." He lifted my cup and downed half of it, scalding heat and all.

"Uh," I was temporarily at a loss, "you're welcome?"

"Good answer. I'm Parke Worth. Sorry for stealing your coffee," he said, setting the cup down and standing before extending his hand. I took it and afterward I could have sworn it made my hand tingle before he let me go.

Chapter 1

"That's all right, I can get more. Coffee." I pointed vaguely behind me, hoping it was in the general direction of the break room. "I just made a fresh pot," I babbled. "If you need more."

"No, I just needed something to drink," he shrugged. "Is Geoffrey in?"

"He's in court this afternoon. Annabelle is in her office." She'd also told me Parke was scheduled to arrive the following day.

Not today.

"Does she have an assistant?" Parke asked, turning to look down the hall toward Annabelle's office.

"She does. His name is Jeremy. You may have to explain who you are," I said. "Twice."

"Doesn't he have a paralegal certificate?" Parke asked with a frown.

"I doubt he can read one, let alone qualify," I replied. "He's nice enough," I added with a shrug. I had no idea why I was telling Parke the truth—that was out of character for me.

"How long has Jeremy worked here?"

"Three months. The paralegal Annabelle had before that quit. He was good." I bit my tongue before admitting that he was gay and Annabelle tried to sleep with him. He turned her down and left the next day.

"I see," one of Parke's eyebrows lifted. "What about the secretary pool?"

"Efficient for the most part."

"Good. You'll let me know if that changes?"

"Of course, Mr. Worth."

"No, call me Parke."

"Of course, Parke."

"Better, but don't sound like a parrot. All right?"

"Of cour—right. Parke it is."

He laughed and walked down the hall toward Annabelle's office.

* * *

"Is that brief done?" There was never a hello from Geoffrey; he either ogled or demanded. There was no in between with him.

"Yes, Mr. Gruber. It's on your desk."

"I'll look at it tonight and hand corrections to you tomorrow. Have you started a file on the Griffin case?"

"Of course, Mr. Gruber. I sent an e-mail to you and the information for a cease and desist to the secretary pool. You should have it first thing tomorrow morning." He walked past me, giving me a lewd once-over before heading to his corner office.

The moment he walked inside, I heard a crash and ran, skidding to a halt in Geoffrey's doorway.

There Geoffrey was, breathing hard and staring at Parke Worth, who now sat in his chair. Geoffrey had just knocked his award from the Civic Improvement Club off a bookcase; he'd swung his leather valise around to fend off a potential attack from the intruder.

"Surprised to see me?" Parke swung his feet off Geoffrey's desk and dropped them to the floor.

"Why, no—er, I mean yes. Yes, I expected you tomorrow. That's what the e-mail said," Geoffrey sputtered.

"Surprise," Parke flung out his hands and wiggled his fingers. I wanted to giggle at that point but managed to stifle the urge. Geoffrey would make my life a much larger, hotter hell than it already was if I laughed.

"Have you," Geoffrey began with a huff.

"I've spoken with Annabelle and fired her assistant. Jeremy insisted on calling me Mr. Parker and lied on his application, stating he had a paralegal certificate."

Chapter 1

I wanted to tell Parke that Annabelle had added that tiny fabrication, but didn't. I had a feeling Parke already guessed it. The people at the D.C. law firm were likely sorry to see him go—that's how efficient he was.

"What do you want?" Geoffrey sputtered. His flushed face and near-stutter told me how flustered he still was.

"I want a meeting tomorrow at two," Parke said. "To discuss all the cases currently being handled by the firm. If there are any of my father's old cases that haven't gone to trial yet, I'll take them back. Don't worry," Parke held up a hand, "I'll give anyone who did any work on those cases an amicable split when they settle."

"You act like they're already settled," Geoffrey huffed.

"They will be."

Parke didn't sound as if he were kidding. "I also intend to ask the Seattle PD to look into my father's death. I don't believe it was accidental, like everyone thinks."

"Wh-what?" Geoffrey was definitely stuttering, now.

"What I said," Parke stood and stretched. "Tomorrow. Two. Meeting." He stalked out of Geoffrey's office, brushing past me as he walked through the door.

Had I imagined the wink as he did so? Shaking my head, I eventually followed him out of Geoffrey's office.

* * *

Unable to decide whether it was a good thing or a bad one that I'd arrived early for work the following morning, I dealt with six of Geoffrey's tantrums before nine. The copier wouldn't work. The coffee was too hot. The dry cleaner lost two shirts. The judge on the case the day before was an asshole. At least I'd worn two-inch heels; they were better suited for running after Geoffrey the pig.

Annabelle had a meltdown, too, when she couldn't convince HR to alter their hiring practices just for her. I understood that to mean she wanted another Jeremy. Why she thought she could slide that past Parke was a question I couldn't answer.

The question that intrigued me most was this; why had Harmon Worth allowed Geoffrey and Annabelle to buy into the firm to begin with? Their win-loss ratio wasn't stellar by anyone's standards. Resigning myself to the fact that I'd probably never know the answer, I went back to reviewing the cease and desist before placing it on Geoffrey's desk for his signature.

"Cassie?" Parke's voice interrupted my proofing session.

"Yes, Mr. Wor—Parke?"

"I want you to clean out your desk."

I froze. "But," I began. I was ready to beg for my job. I needed it. Had taken far too much of Geoffrey's excrement to just let it go.

"No, bring your things to my office. You're working for me, now. I already notified HR; they're looking for Geoffrey's replacement."

My shoulders sagged and I wanted to weep—whether from relief or happiness, I couldn't decide. "Does he know?"

"I sent a text."

That made me freeze again. Geoffrey hated texts. If I knew him at all, he'd find a way (the more devious the better), to make me pay for my defection. Now, I didn't care. Working for Parke had to be a hundred times better than working for Geoffrey.

"I'll be there in half an hour," I said, offering Parke the most professional nod I could.

"Perfect. Will you arrange for lunch to be delivered to my office? I have a pile of cases to go through."

"What would you like?"

"Roast beef sandwich?"

"I'll find one for you."

* * *

Chapter 1

I didn't hear the explosive complaints Geoffrey and Annabelle exchanged that afternoon; I was far away in my new office with a door, and actually had a lunch hour on my own outside the firm (at Parke's insistence) while he ate a roast-beef au-jus with fries at his desk.

Want Starbucks? I sent a text to Parke on my way back to Gruber, Taylor and Worth.

Why, yes. Triple capp, please, lots of foam.

It's yours, I texted back.

Ten minutes later, I set the cup down on the only bare patch I could find on his desk, which was covered by case files.

"You've been sitting too long," I ventured to say.

"What?" He blinked at me. "Yeah. You're right. I think I'll go to the boardroom and drink this while looking at the view."

"It has a great view," I agreed. "Your father had such good taste, choosing this building." It did have a wonderful view—of Elliott Bay. You could see the ferry traveling across the bay to Bainbridge Island and back on clear days.

"I miss the old man. Mom does, too." Parke stood and stretched before lifting his cappuccino. "Will you call Daniel Frank for me? Ask him to give me a call the moment he can. Cell-phone number only."

"Of course, Parke."

I watched him walk out of his office, heading for the opposite side of the building where the boardroom (and the view) was located.

Chapter 2

P^{arke}

What the hell is she doing here?

That question plagued me. She'd apparently moved to Seattle between the time Dad died and before I came back. Otherwise, she should have checked in.

Unless…

"Parke here," I answered my cell on Daniel Frank's second ring.

"You have another job for me?" Daniel never wasted time.

"Yeah. I need a background check on Cassie Randall," I said.

"Who is she?"

"My new personal assistant. Check her paralegal certificate and anything else you can get. I'll text her address and social as soon as I'm off the phone. All correspondence through my cell, please. Have you got anything on Dad's death?"

"Looking into it. You're right, it does look fishy, and not in the usual sense."

"Dad would never have drowned, that's bullshit," I agreed. "He went fishing all the time and the waters weren't rough that day."

"Are they asking you to step into the Chancellor's shoes?"

"Hinting at it. It's mine for the taking—you know the succession runs in the family unless the position is refused, and then it's a conclave or a war to determine who gets it."

"Why haven't you taken it before now?"

"I had things to tie up in D.C. and I'd like to get these mysteries solved, first."

"Your dad and this Cassie girl?"

"Daniel, she's demon. I know it by looking at her. She's got a shield up so strong a bullet couldn't crack it, and that tells me she's hiding something."

"Takes one to know one," Daniel mumbled.

"Yeah. You wouldn't read this one, Dan. I think I may be the only one who can."

"Because you're Harmon Worth's son."

"Yeah."

* * *

Cassie

Stopping by the post office after work to collect my mail, I found only bills there. Those I didn't mind so much. At least I could pay them on my current salary, although sometimes it was a stretch. Living in Seattle wasn't cheap, but anything was better than Birmingham, Alabama.

My tiny, efficiency apartment waited when I got home, where I still hadn't changed the last tenant's name on the mailbox downstairs. Brian Erving was so much better than Cassie Randall—that way, nobody knew for sure who occupied the small, cheaper condo with no view.

Fog rolled in while I ate dinner and cleaned up the excuse I had for a kitchen. Sure, I'd had a chance at better not that long ago. The strings and conditions that came with better weren't worth it.

Parke had hinted to Geoffrey that his father's death hadn't been an accident. It made me curious, so I powered up my laptop and went looking for information on Harmon Worth's accident.

That's when I learned that Harmon hadn't invited Geoffrey and Annabelle into the firm—he'd had a partner six years earlier who'd died, leaving his third of the business to the family, who, without consulting Harmon first, sold that third to the first takers they could find who had ready cash—Geoffrey and Annabelle.

Harmon Worth, Dead in Fishing Accident, the next article's headline read. After reading the article, which claimed that a gust of wind capsized Harmon's boat, leaving him in cold water to drown before being nibbled on by fish in the bay, I went looking for last year's calendar.

With a sigh, I shook my head. I was beginning to think Parke was correct about his father's death, but there wasn't any way I could tell him what I thought I knew—he'd know something about me, then, and that would start a chain of events I wanted to avoid at all costs.

* * *

"I proofread the letter to Rachel Johnson, but you may want to read through it before signing," I handed a folder to Parke when he arrived at work the next morning.

"I was just going to ask for that," Parke smiled and took the folder. "If she agrees to these terms, then the companies can merge happily."

"And fun will be had by all," I said. "I guess that's what happens when two toy companies get together."

"You'd think so, anyway," Parke nodded. "Have you heard from Geoffrey or Annabelle this morning?"

"No. Were you expecting a call? I was here early and haven't left my desk."

"Yes. I offered to buy out their share. It's no surprise they don't want to give it up, but I need their answer anyway."

I couldn't help thinking that buying out Geoffrey and Annabelle would be the best possible thing to happen to the firm, but didn't voice it aloud. "I'll be on the phone for the next hour or so—will you see I'm not disturbed?" Parke asked.

"Of course."

"Will you check the status of the Hillman case, too? Geoffrey is supposed to be handling it, but I can't find any updates in the last six months."

"I will."

"Thanks." I was waved out of Parke's office, so I left, closing the door behind me. I knew the Hillman case and had asked Geoffrey regularly whether he'd called Frank Hillman about it. Hillman wanted to sue another company for infringement on some of his software designs, but Geoffrey was dragging his heels.

If something wasn't done within four days, the statute of limitations would kick in. Hillman would be furious and unable to file another lawsuit. I knew exactly where the file was, too—in my desk. I'd planned to ask Geoffrey about it (again) when Parke pulled me away to work for him.

I wrote up everything that needed to be done on the Hillman case while Parke had his hour on the phone. When he buzzed to tell me he was done with his telephone conversations, I took the file and the information I'd gathered into his office.

"I tried to remind Geoffrey several times about this," I explained nervously when I handed the file to Parke.

"I understand." Parke opened the file and quickly read all my notes. "We'll have to hurry to get all this done before the deadline," he said, looking up at me. "Will you get Hillman on the phone? I'll handle what I can if you'll get the ball rolling with the court clerk."

Chapter 2

"Right away," I said.

As long as the case was filed before the deadline, it would go forward. Geoffrey seemed content to let it die. I had suspicions about that—the software company Hillman wanted to sue had money behind their name. It probably wouldn't be the first time that something like this had happened.

By the end of the day, we had a case filed with the court clerk and notice would be given to all parties involved. Hillman, after Parke spoke to him, was more than happy to get something done on the case. Feeling like a load of bricks had been lifted from my shoulders, I left the office at six-thirty—at Parke's insistence.

* * *

Parke

"What have you found, Daniel?" I asked. The call was on the hands-free in my car while I waited at a stoplight.

"That's not her name. No idea who she was before, but I'm working on it. Her paper trail is good, too—somebody with experience managed that. To my knowledge, there are only three who might accomplish that—the Feds, Gray Barker or Lance Thorne."

"I doubt it was the Feds. Put some pressure on the other two— tell them they won't appreciate a visit from the Chancellor's office."

"You thinkin'?"

"Yeah. It may be the only way. I'll have plenty of enemies once I make the move, but the spot's there if I want it."

"When?"

"First of next week."

"Anybody else know?"

"Mom. Louise. That's all. They've been begging me to do it. Maybe it's time."

"Your mother and your sister won't sell you out, I know that much," Daniel agreed. "Look, I'll contact Gray and Lance. If they know anything, I'll promise to keep it quiet."

"I'd prefer that," I said. "Until we have all the facts, I don't want to make any moves."

"I want to meet her. I want to check this shield that she has."

"Be careful. I don't want to spook her."

"I can be discreet."

"I know that. You haven't seen her yet, that's all I'm saying."

"Looker?"

"You know it."

"I'll check out her place this weekend."

"You do that. Don't scare her or I'll see you in the gym."

"I'll be discretion itself."

"Good."

* * *

Cassie

Friday. FridayFridayFriday. I felt like singing the word on my way to the office that morning. While Parke was a breath of fresh air after working for Geoffrey, the week had still been stressful. It didn't help that Geoffrey glared every time he saw me—even from a distance.

Saturday and Sunday would be my chance to relax and breathe. I could do laundry and cook something besides a hurried breakfast or dinner. Maybe I could read a book or two, or watch a movie.

Any or all those things would take my mind off being alone. Sure, I had friends. They'd helped me get away. Contacting them would place their lives in jeopardy. I wasn't about to do that.

For now, they were safe. I just wished a few people thought I was dead or gone forever. It wasn't their habit to forgive, if they ever

Chapter 2

caught up with me again. At least they hadn't found me—likely because Seattle was the last place they'd look.

* * *

Parke

"What are you doing? Working?" Louise looked ready to sail, wearing a crew-neck sweater, wool slacks and boots. I sat, shirtless and wearing pajama bottoms, at the desk in my father's office.

"I can fritter my time later, sissy," I told her. "If I take the Chancellor's seat, I have to catch up on a few things."

"Including the squabble between the shifters and the werewolves?"

"Look, you can't go around eating the deer shifters. It's just not done. Find real deer, not were-deer for Pete's sake," I said, offering my sister a grin.

"Or moose or elk," she nodded before giggling.

"Finals done?" I asked.

"Turned in the last paper yesterday. Now, we can do Christmas and I don't have to go back till January."

"I remember those days," I sighed.

"Bridgett called Mom yesterday," Louise said.

"You had to ruin the mood, didn't you?"

"Why don't you tell her she doesn't have a chance in hell and to go marry somebody else?"

"I did. She thinks I was joking. She believes everybody wants her, including me. Anybody who says otherwise is just teasing or playing hard to get. Her ego is like a black hole, sucking everything into it."

Bridgett was a sore spot with all of us. Why she thought I was her personal property when we'd never gone out and had nothing in common still mystified me.

"Mom says it wouldn't be terrible to have a Water Demon in the family," Louise pointed out.

"Over my dead body will it be that particular Water Demon."

"That's what I wanted to hear," Louise snickered. "I can't stand her."

"Daniel may be in the area this weekend," I said.

"You're dangling that carrot in front of me?" Louise became defensive.

"I know how you look at him."

"He's—he's," Louise tossed up a hand as she floundered for a word.

"Cool?" I asked. "Rugged, maybe? What are those other terms that make women swoon?"

"He's a grump," Louise snapped. "One hundred percent. Nasty and snarky, too."

"I don't recall those things," I flipped open another file folder of complaints against rogue werewolves.

"Because you're a guy and belong to a secret club or something. All I get from Daniel is go away, little girl. You bother me."

"He does not say that."

"It's what he means."

"Want me to ask him about that?" I read complaints instead of looking at my sister.

"What? No!"

"See—all your imagination," I said. "You shouldn't put words in someone else's mouth, baby sis."

"You sound like Daddy."

"I'll need to sound like Daddy if I take the Chancellor's seat."

"Breakfast," Mom called from the floor below. Shutting the file, I stood, grabbed Louise by the arm and led her toward the stairs.

* * *

Chapter 2

Cassie

I ended up going to the market before I could cook breakfast. I'd wanted an omelet, but found I was out of eggs. To top it off, it was raining, so my walk was in a Seattle downpour. Clutching my cloth grocery bags to my chest, I struggled to keep them from getting soaked.

By the time I got back home, the bags were soaked, anyway. The egg carton had to be tossed in the recycle bin—it was nothing but soggy cardboard by then. After drying off the milk carton and everything else I'd bought, I set about making my omelet. That's when I saw it—or him, I should say.

I caught only the barest shadow, but I knew. Somebody was watching. If they'd intended to make me uncomfortable, they'd achieved their goal. I was shaky the rest of the day.

Should I move? Would it do any good? Those thoughts circled my brain so often I couldn't even read a book or watch television. Later, when it was time for bed, I couldn't sleep, either.

Sunday was a rerun of Saturday. Shakes, no appetite, no sleep. By the time Monday morning came, I was hoping someone would run over me on my way to Gruber, Taylor and Worth.

* * *

"Cassie, are you ill?" Parke dumped an armload of case files on my desk and actually looked sympathetic.

"I think I have a stalker," I said, staring at my hands, which trembled in my lap. "If I don't show up for work someday, well," I shrugged.

"What the hell happened?"

"I—saw somebody. Outside my window on Saturday," I quavered. I would not, would not, cry in front of my boss.

"Do you know who it was?"

"No."

"Do you need to take a day off?"

"No." I almost shouted the word. I felt safer at work than I did at my tiny condo.

"Look, I need to make a call, but after that, we should talk." Parke lifted his pile of folders and walked into his office, shutting the door behind him.

* * *

Parke

"Daniel, did she see you?" My voice was clipped. Hard.

"I don't know. She was in the kitchen, doing something, but she looked up, just before I could get out of the way. Why? What happened?"

"She's terrified. Says she has a stalker. Now, what does that tell you?"

"That I messed this up."

"Yeah. Did you get anything from Grey or Lance?"

"I have an appointment with Lance tomorrow. He'll be in the area, or so he says."

"I want to be in that meeting."

"When are you putting the word out?"

"It went out this morning, before I left for work."

"Then you'll have the authority of the office to back us up, then," Daniel sighed. "Look, nobody knows I'm there. Ever. It's the way my shield works. I can't say why she saw me anyway."

"What are you doing for dinner tonight? Want to come by the house?"

"Sure. I'll take your mother's cooking over a restaurant any day."

"Good. Be there at seven."

Chapter 3

C*assie*

Parke had three calls in a row, so our meeting didn't happen until lunchtime. "Come on," he growled, standing beside my desk. "We're going out for lunch."

"But," I said.

"No. You're coming. We'll talk about this."

I had no choice but to grab my purse and follow him toward the elevator.

Half an hour later, we sat in a tiny back room of a Mexican restaurant, where margaritas and menus were placed in front of us. It didn't take a genius to know who owned the place.

"Now, tell me why one man outside your window terrifies you," he began.

"I can't."

"Yes, you can."

"You'll have me locked up."

"No, I won't."

"You say that now," I huffed, looking away. A painting hung on the wall, depicting a bullfight, but rather than what you'd expect to see, it appeared the bull was just about to get his revenge on the bullfighter.

Good for him.

"Tell me, Cassie. I'm your employer and I have a right to know whether my employees are in danger."

"Since when?"

"Since I hauled my ass back to Seattle. Start at the beginning. Tell me everything."

I don't know why I did—how in hell was he ever going to understand this mess? "My father sold me," I quavered. "To Ross Diablo in Birmingham."

* * *

"Let me get this straight—he's aware of the law and he did it anyway?" Parke shook his head.

I'd learned just as much as Parke had—he was not only a truth demon, he was the new Chancellor of everything paranormal or supernatural.

"Ross paid him two million. He wanted a fire demon in the family. This was his way of getting what he wanted." I shivered. That wasn't all Ross wanted, either. A fire demon blackmailed and under your command?

Scary.

I wanted no part of that, so I'd run away.

Now, Parke knew exactly what I was. How dangerous I was. Dangerous enough for somebody to hand out two million like it was candy.

"How was he threatening you?" Parke asked.

"He said he'd kill my baby sister. She's only twelve and hasn't come into her ability, yet."

Chapter 3

"Is she a fire demon?"

"No. Neither are my parents. My great-grandfather on my mother's side was a fire demon."

"Sherman Phillips?"

"How did you know?"

"Dad knew him," Parke shook his head. "I know he was murdered," he added.

"Yeah. Just like your dad," I sighed.

"You know something?"

"I think I do," I nodded. "But I can't prove anything—or do anything—until the full moon."

"Which just happens to be at Christmas."

"Yes."

"You're coming home with me tonight," Parke said.

"No, I," I began.

"Mom and Louise are there. We'll feed you. You'll sleep. End of story."

"But what about Ross?"

"Let me think about that, all right?"

"You don't have to fight my battles," I said.

"I'm the Chancellor. Someone breaking the law makes it my battle."

"But what about the paper he made me sign?" I wanted to cry. Ross had threatened my sister if I didn't sign, so I'd signed it.

"Under duress. Was the copy filed?"

"Yes." I felt hopeless at that point. Ross made sure to do everything the law required to keep me under his thumb.

"I'll take a look."

"You won't find anything. I've gone over it so many times I have it memorized."

"What's your real name?" His eyes compelled me to answer. I'd never met a truth demon before. Now I knew why information bubbled out of me anytime he asked. It made me uncomfortable.

"Cassandra King."

"Where's your little sister? Still with your father?"

"No. I—uh, got her away, too. I really don't want to say where. It'll place lives in danger."

"Dad always said Ross was shady, but nobody ever filed a complaint to warrant an investigation."

"Too afraid," I snorted and hugged myself. Just the mention of Ross' name scared me. Sure, I was a fire demon. My little sister wasn't. She showed all the signs of being an ice demon, like my parents. Ross could hurt her—or kill her—and I wasn't sure I could stop him. If I did, it wouldn't stop Ross' family from labeling me a killer and demanding that the Chancellor have me hunted and destroyed. They'd gotten away with too much to think otherwise.

No matter how you looked at this, I was screwed.

"So a rock demon wants a fire demon. Huh." Parke was lost in thought. "What about your father? Where is he in all this?"

"He's not the greatest," I mumbled. "You know what they say, too—rock smashes ice."

"And fire melts rock. Water quenches fire. Ice freezes water."

"The demon version of rock, paper, scissors," I whispered.

"Only a lot deadlier," Parke agreed. "Truth can hold one or more of those talents, which make us the ideal candidate for Chancellor."

"What?" I began.

"Can't say. We'll keep that for a surprise," he flashed a grin. "I intend to sort this out. In the meantime, you will come home with me, tonight. I'll have someone clear out your apartment and bring your things. Ross Diablo will have to break down my door to get to you, now."

"I don't think this is right. I can't place your life in danger," I said. "Somebody got to your father."

"And with your help, we'll get to the bottom of that. By the full moon." His narrowed, darkening eyes and the tightness of his mouth told me how determined he was. If a demon's eyes go black, unless you're a stronger demon, then all hell is about to break loose.

Literally.

* * *

"This is nice," I ran my hand over the soft leather of the dashboard in Parke's car. He drove a Mercedes, which didn't surprise me at all.

"You drive?" He turned and asked as we made our way out of the parking garage and onto a foggy Seattle street.

"Not since I got to Seattle. No car," I said.

"If I wasn't so worried about you being out alone, I'd find a loaner for you."

"That's all right," I waved a hand. "I can walk. It's good exercise."

"That's another thing. No going walking by yourself—not until we get this managed," he said. "There's a gym at the house. You can walk or run on the treadmill while watching TV or a movie."

"Does it suck to be you?" I asked as innocently as I could.

"Sometimes." His frown kept me from talking the rest of the way to his house.

* * *

Parke

Daniel was already working on the mystery of Cassie King— I'd asked him to the minute she and I'd gotten back from lunch. I have no idea whether she suspected I was investigating her—the answer was probably, but she was too scared to ask me about it.

It took a special person to make friends with a truth demon. You had to come to trust us—that we wouldn't ask for anything too personal. That had ruined many of Dad's relationships—he knew too much, simply from asking questions.

He'd made a promise to Mom, years ago, that he wouldn't insist on a personal answer if she wasn't comfortable giving it to him. That, I believe, saved their marriage. She only had to say no and he'd back off. He believed her, though, whenever she said she loved him. That was always enough.

Daniel would give me the information he had after dinner. Mom would insist that Cassie join her and Louise for television—it was an after-dinner ritual. You got an hour to sit, talk and listen to something that didn't matter in the background.

"Here we are," I said, turning in to the driveway.

"Holy cow," was her only response.

* * *

Cassie

The house—if you could call it that—was huge. Bill Gates sort of huge. I understood Parke's great-grandfather had started the dynasty and each generation kept building onto the thing until it looked as if a moat might be the next addition.

Yeah, holy cow was out of my mouth before I could stop it. No wonder he didn't mind bringing me home—I could be lost for days inside his freaking house. He'd never have to see me unless he wanted something. It was just as well; being near a truth demon made me nervous.

"It's home," Parke shrugged as he drove into a garage that held six other cars. In Birmingham, I'd been lucky to own one.

Chapter 3

"Your home," I pointed out. "You boss. Me employee. Me sleep in broom closet."

"My mother would kill me if I suggested anything of the sort. Out of the car. Into the house. I've had your things brought over already."

By that time, I was getting the idea that whenever Parke Worth waved a hand, people (demons included) scurried. It was probably the same with his father. Parke was my boss, as well as the new Chancellor. I scurried, just like everybody else.

* * *

"Oh, my goodness," Mrs. Worth's smile nearly blinded me when we walked into the kitchen. "Parke, why didn't you tell me how pretty she was?"

"Mom, that's considered sexual harassment in the business world," Parke said. "You can say it all you want. I can't."

"We're having pot roast," Mrs. Worth waved me into the kitchen. "Call me Kate, please, and can you mash the potatoes?"

"I sure can," I smiled at her. "On both counts."

While it surprised me that Kate did most of the cooking, with help from Louise, Parke's (very pretty) sister, she explained it while we worked. "I have a full-time staff, but I like my cooking better," she laughed. "And I like to cook, so I just let the staff clean and carry, now. Both are demon—Harmon hired them years ago. They're like family."

In half an hour, we had dinner on the table. Kate's pot roast was excellent; I hadn't had anything that good since I'd left the South behind. Another man joined us for dinner; I met Daniel Frank, the firm's investigator, in person for the first time.

That's when I learned what Daniel really was—an ice demon with an unusual shielding ability. He could get in and out of places without being seen—by most people. "Only a handful have ever been able to see past the shield," he said. "I know who all of them are."

"Up to now," Parke pointed his fork at Daniel.

Louise watched Daniel whenever he wasn't looking in her direction. The moment he did, she dropped her eyes and toyed with her food. It didn't take much to figure out what was going on, there.

Louise, the rock demon, wanted Daniel, the ice demon.

Really bad.

I was surprised to see such diversity in one family, and mystified that Parke was the only one to inherit his father's truth demon skills. At least as I understood it. He did say he had other skills. Perhaps his sister did, too.

Daniel, though—the more I watched him, the more I understood. Rock breaks ice. He wasn't sure how to deal with a powerful woman. He wanted to be the strong one. I wanted to tell him that as long as he loved her and she loved him back, it didn't matter. Besides, I could imagine Louise turning to jelly if he just touched her.

"What do you think, Cassie?"

"What?" Parke caught me off-guard.

"About the recent election?"

"The incumbent is a bumbling fool," dropped right out of my mouth. "That's not fair," I pointed out. "I don't like discussing politics with anyone. It's too personal. Everybody is entitled to their opinions."

"I keep telling him that," Louise huffed and went back to pushing carrots around her plate.

"Don't worry, I feel the same way," Parke said. "Sorry. I didn't mean to upset you."

I wanted to tell him that he shouldn't ask those questions, when he knew it might upset someone. Perhaps he was feeling me out, to determine whether I should keep my job or not. I know it had happened in the past—I'd read articles on the subject. It wasn't exactly legal, but plenty of people had been fired for less.

"Cassie, what's troubling you?" Kate asked.

"I need my job," I said. "Please excuse me." I rose and left the table, although I had no idea where to go—for now, I only knew where the kitchen and dining room were.

* * *

Parke

"Way to go, big brother," Louise snapped the moment Cassie was out the door, heading for the kitchen. "Can't you turn that shit off during dinner?"

"I'm ashamed of you," Mom said and stood to follow Cassie.

"Fuck," I mumbled and scrubbed a hand across my face. It didn't take much to realize that Cassie found it difficult to trust anyone. I'd just blown a huge hole in my efforts to make her comfortable with me.

"Man, that's a fire demon," Daniel rumbled softly. "What the hell are you trying to do? Alienate her?"

"She was miles away, so I thought I'd draw her into the conversation," I said. It was a lame excuse and Louise was right, I should have turned the truth shit off during dinner. The truth was—Daniel was right, too. Fire demons were quite rare. A female fire demon hadn't existed in recent records until Cassie showed up. I already had Daniel working on that conundrum, in addition to everything else.

I knew what Mom was thinking, too; Water demons were a dime a dozen. Adding a fire demon to the family would be the biggest coup ever. No wonder the bastard in Birmingham wanted her. Demon families often went looking for missing pieces to add to their arsenal, especially if they planned to make a grab for power.

Ross Diablo had been on Dad's radar, but he'd never overtly done anything wrong.

Until now.

Cassie was at the crux of everything, and I'd made her think her job was on the line. She was afraid to disagree with me, too, most likely. What troubled me most was this—I wanted her to trust me. To see me as a friend, at the very least, if not something more than friends. Obviously, I'd have a longer way to go to make that happen, now.

Chapter 4

assie

Kate followed me into the kitchen, where she found me having a panic attack. "Cassie, he didn't mean it that way," she soothed. "Your job is safe, I guarantee it. He can't help himself when it comes to politics. Just to know you agree with him on this one makes him feel as if he can talk freely around you."

"He's a truth demon. Why would he worry about that?" I flung out a hand and struggled not to cry.

"Truth works both ways. He has to guard his carefully. Remember, anything he says can and will be used against him."

She smiled as she paraphrased that part of the Miranda speech. "He's the Chancellor, now, and he'll be looking to protect himself even more than he did before. I know you're traumatized and I wish that weren't so. In a way, so is he, because so many things have been building up since his father's death. All of it just landed in his lap."

"Along with my problems." I breathed a shaky sigh and nodded. Parke had a difficult job and I was making it harder. That didn't mean I wanted to go back to the dinner table and pretend nothing happened. "May I see my bedroom now?" I asked, embarrassed by how shaky my voice was.

"I'll show you. It's on the west end, with a nice view of Elliott Bay."

* * *

Parke

I knew I'd hear it from Mom after I concluded my meeting with Daniel. That encounter could wait. "What did you find?" I asked Daniel after closing the door to Dad's study.

"Talked with Barker and Thorne, since Barker couldn't make the original meeting I scheduled. Barker had a hand in getting her away. He says your girl was a law student at the University of Alabama in Tuscaloosa. I had somebody go through her school records. She finished the fall semester last year. Never showed up for the spring semester. One year away from graduation with top grades."

"What about her father or her little sister?"

"Found a reward listed on Demonnet—for both girls, no questions asked."

"Put up by her father?"

"Nope. Just a number listed, which connects to voicemail. I figure somebody in Diablo's employ listens to the messages."

"How do you know it's not her father, then?"

"Word has it her old man is in Mexico, living in a beach condo. I guess that's how much he cares about his kids."

"Two mil goes a long way in Mexico, I hear," I growled. "What happened to Cassie's mother?"

"The records say she disappeared over ten years ago. No word on her whereabouts."

"Too bad Cassie's father isn't here. I'd ask him a few questions about that."

Chapter 4

"Tough to grab him in Mexico."

"I'm sure he knows that. I'll wait to get Cassie's view on this. I don't want to upset her again tonight."

"You think Diablo's aiming for the Prince's seat in Alabama?"

"Could be, although Prince Jasper is an idiot if he can't see Diablo's building an army."

"I'll check on that," Daniel dipped his head. "Anything else?"

"You don't have to bow to me. The old man earned it. I haven't."

"Goes with the job," Daniel grinned. "You'll just have to get used to it."

* * *

Cassie

The clothes I'd had at the condo hung in a closet far too big for them. My shoes, set neatly beneath hanging jackets, skirts and slacks, looked sadly insufficient.

Everything else was in drawers built into an island in the closet, which also held a comfortable chair and a small table. If there'd been a minibar, it would have been far too tempting. I didn't drink much or often, but I needed something to calm my unsteady nerves.

Digging through one of the two drawers holding the rest of my things, I found my pajamas. When I left the closet and made my way toward the huge bed, someone knocked on my door.

I expected Kate to be on the other side. I was prepared to hug her if she had a glass of wine for me. Dumping my PJs on the bed, I went to answer the door. Parke stood on the other side, two cups of hot chocolate in his hands.

"Wh-what?" I stuttered. He was the last person I expected.

"Come on, I stole your coffee that first day. Then you offered to buy me Starbucks, even when I didn't deserve it. Let's sit together, hash this out and drink cocoa."

"I'm not comfortable doing that," I hugged myself.

"I know. Just sit with me. We'll talk. The last thing I want to do is upset you and make you uncomfortable. Trust me, your job isn't on the line and won't be."

I had little choice, so I showed him to the sitting area, next to the fireplace in my suite. The house was his, after all.

"Want a fire?" He nodded toward the logs. "I think I can get one going."

"Just set the vent," I said. "I can take care of the rest."

"Will you show me? I've never seen a fire demon work." He opened the flue and stepped back.

I'm not sure what he was expecting—perhaps somebody with the control of an infant. Holding up a finger, I allowed the fire to burn from the tip of my nail. Then, leaning over, I touched my finger to the ready pile of logs. They lit immediately. I drew my hand away and held it up, allowing the flame to die. I'd never had a burn my entire life. Fire knows fire. It failed to affect me. It was also how my parents determined what I was at a very early age—I hadn't been burned after placing my hand on a hot stove.

"Outstanding," Parke breathed.

Lifting a cup of cocoa from the small table where he'd left both cups, I sipped. It was good. We sat. Parke drank from his cup. "I'm sorry," he said. "Sometimes I don't realize that I'm grilling somebody. It's habit, I guess."

I wanted to ask why he did it, then. I didn't. We were back to employee and boss, again. *Cassie, I see the pain in your eyes*, his voice whispered in my mind. *I hate that I'm the one responsible.*

"I thought telepathy was a myth." I rose and wiped moisture from my cheeks.

"There are a few who can do it," Parke sighed. "That's one of my secrets, Cassie."

Chapter 4

"Then I'll make sure it stays secret," I snapped.

"Hey." He was behind me before I knew it. "Cassie, please trust me. That's all I'm asking. I swear we'll sort this mess out. I promise."

"I don't know that it can be sorted out," I whispered.

His arms wrapped around me. His lips touched my temple. *I promise*, he said before dropping his arms and walking swiftly out of my suite.

* * *

Louise knocked on my door the following morning, to tell me breakfast was ready. I'd spent a restless night, worrying about all the complications in my life. I did and didn't appreciate the contact with Parke the night before. I was afraid to read anything into it—that I might come to see it as more than he intended.

Sure, I'd been on a few dates—with humans. I'd read all the information on demon/human sex. It generally isn't a good idea to get too involved, so I'd held back—and held any seriously-interested humans at arm's length.

That didn't mean I never wanted someone in my life. Far from it. The hard truth was this—who (besides Ross Diablo, who only wanted me to complete his collection and to do his bidding) would want to take on poor Cassie King and all her problems? I'd love to tell (voluntarily) someone all my troubles and have them offer moral and emotional support. To help me find a way to get my baby sister to a safe place where Ross could never touch her. The only safety she had now was that Ross had no idea where to look.

I wanted to weep, too, over the fact that Christmas was coming soon and I couldn't mail her a package without worrying that someone would find me and trace the address. If Mom were still alive, she would have helped us. I knew she was dead—she'd disagreed with Daddy when Ross first offered for me over ten years ago. I had no idea where her body lay, but Ross had been more than adept at hiding his tracks.

Dad capitulated after that and became distant from Destiny and me. Destiny was so tiny, then. Was still young. At times, I couldn't help but hate my father. He hadn't even tried to save us. The offer of money and the threats from Ross worked with Dad. We may as well have been dead, too—we could have run wild and he'd never have noticed.

I was fourteen and took over with Destiny, with help from one of Mom's friends, a Water Demon who'd guessed what Ross was up to. She'd take care of Destiny while I was in school; I took care of her after I got home. Between Aunt Shelbie and me, we'd managed to raise Destiny.

Shelbie was the only other person who knew where Destiny was and I knew she'd die before she told anybody that secret. After all, she'd been the one to make the suggestion in the first place. Her friends and her foster-daughter's lives depended upon her silence.

* * *

"Mom and Louise will drop you off at the office," Parke said when I sat down at the kitchen island for breakfast. He was right—it wouldn't do for me to ride to work with the boss. Workplace relationships were frowned upon at Gruber, Taylor and Worth. Everybody would assume a relationship, whether there was one or not, merely because I was driven back and forth by Parke.

"I'll pick you up tonight at six," Louise offered a grin.

"I—thank you," I allowed my shoulders to sag. Already I owed Louise and Kate a lot—having me in their home was turning into a huge chore for them.

"It's no bother," Kate said, rubbing my back. "It's easy to get bored, and there's only so much shopping you can do." She offered Louise a smile. Louise laughed.

Chapter 4

* * *

Kate and Louise dropped me off at the Starbucks three blocks from work; I grabbed a latte and walked the rest of the way. "Your boss is already in his office," Annabelle snarled as she stepped out of the elevator. "If I were you, I'd try harder to get here before he does."

She was on her way to court; her designer briefcase was in her hand as she brushed past me. I watched her walk through the glass doors of the building as the elevator doors closed, shutting her out. Parke knew exactly when I'd be there, and I was still half an hour early. Annabelle wanted to fuck with Parke by fucking with me, first.

At least nobody else was on the elevator to see me smile before sipping my latte.

"Parke's already in his office," Geoffrey snapped as I walked past him in the hall on the way to my office. That's when I knew Geoffrey and Annabelle had some sort of scheme worked out.

* * *

"Here's the latest on the Hillman case," I dropped a file on Parke's desk. "By the way, Geoffrey and Annabelle are plotting. Do you like fried fish?" I asked.

Parke blinked up at me, confusion showing in his dark eyes. "I love fried fish. Dad always brought home his catch. I learned how to clean them when I was twelve."

"I'll make some for you, sometime. Southern style," I smiled. "Hillman left a message on voicemail. His adversary has offered to buy him out directly."

"Without going through me?" Parke lifted an eyebrow.

"It's a way to avoid punitive damages. We both know one of Hillman's assistants went to work for Fli-Bi-Net. Six months later, they have software eerily similar to Hillman's."

"How much did they offer?"

"Ten million."

"Chump change," Parke snorted. "We can triple that in court and he'll still have his company."

"It's personal for Hillman, now. He loves his company."

"This is a lucrative case," Parke said. "Why did Geoffrey sit on it until the statute of limitations almost ran?"

"I have a theory, but I can't prove anything," I said.

"Bring your coffee, shut the door and we'll discuss it," Parke grinned.

* * *

Parke

"I have deposit records for one of Geoffrey's accounts," Daniel pushed a folder toward me. "Five million, shortly after your father's death, not long after Geoffrey took the Hillman case. Then another five million from the same source one year later. I've traced the money to a subsidiary of Fli-Bi-Net."

"So Geoffrey did take money to hem and haw while the statute of limitations ran. What did he expect to do when Hillman filed a malpractice suit?"

"Word has it the beaches are nice in Mexico."

"Fucker," I growled. The firm would end up paying for Geoffrey's criminal behavior. So far, Cassie had been right all the way about him and Annabelle. All we had to convict him was the deposits Daniel had uncovered, and there were ways of explaining that away.

"At least Hillman will have his day in court. You file charges against Geoffrey, the firm takes a black eye. I'm sure he considered that when he did it," Daniel observed.

"Yeah. Something about this bothers me—a lot more than it should."

Chapter 4

"Your dad always said if you can't prove it, it didn't happen," Daniel quoted.

"I remember."

"They'll try to get to you and Cassie," Daniel said.

"I know that, too. Both of them jumped Cassie this morning, telling her she should be in the office ahead of me, even when she was half an hour early. I planned it that way, but that still upset her."

"Fuckers."

"Agreed. Do you have somebody on the Alabama situation?"

"As of this morning. They're digging into any possible ties between the Prince and Ross Diablo."

"I like the way your mind works," I said.

"Your dad taught me to be suspicious of everybody until you know better."

"He told me the same thing."

"What are you going to do about Bridgett?" Daniel asked. "Word has it she may show up at your house if you don't call her soon."

"She needs to recognize the truth when she hears it. There's a reason I haven't talked to her since Dad died; before then it was only over the phone. Yes, I know she was at the funeral," I held up a hand. "I don't have time for her and even less desire to listen to her talk about us as the perfect couple. I'd rather marry a badger—a real one and not the shifter kind."

"Look, I need to go," Daniel stood and stretched. "There's research to do and feet to hold to the fire."

"You do that," I said. "I have some things to take care of, myself."

* * *

Cassie

I set Parke's triple capp on his desk when I got back from lunch. He frowned—I'd left the building on my own.

"I just got off the phone with Bridgett Moss-Murphy," he said, lifting the cup and nodding his thanks. "She thinks I'm kidding when I say we don't have a future together," he added.

"I have no idea who that is," I said.

"Somebody who thinks I'm her property, although we've never gone out or even had a hot dog together. Her Dad knew mine; that's all she has to go on."

"What are you going to do about it?" I asked.

"Get engaged."

"But you just said," I stuttered.

"To you."

I had to mop up my spilled latte before I could demand an answer.

Chapter 5

*C*assie

"Look at it this way," Parke grinned. I sat in the guest chair inside his office, trying not to shake. "Even if you signed that paper Ross Diablo has, he can't prevent you from accepting a better offer before the marriage. It's in the Demon law, modified in 1937 to reflect that the female gets to choose her mate, especially if a better offer is put forth. It's her decision to make."

I could see that Parke was looking at this as a challenge—one he was determined to win at any cost. "Then, we'll post the upcoming nuptials on Demonnet, get married and Ross will be left holding the bag."

"But," I tried to interrupt his planning of the rest of my life.

"You'd rather marry Ross?"

"No," I shook my head violently.

"Then this is easy. It gets Bridgett of my back, Ross Diablo off yours, we can bring your sister here—Mom would love to teach a fledgling ice demon—and we continue to investigate Ross while he's not looking."

"I don't think he'll give up that easy," I shook my head at Parke. "He hates to lose."

"You think he'll challenge the Chancellor and the Council of Princes?"

"Three of those are Princesses," I pointed out.

"Same thing," Parke shrugged. "Come on—if you can't stand me after the obligatory five years, then we go our separate ways."

So many things were wrong with this picture. "What about," I said.

"There's a suite attached to mine, with its own bath. You can have that. No shagging unless you want to."

"Shagging?"

"Slang for sex. In Britain."

I felt trapped. Smothered. I'd never had a life that was my own. I'd had to earn my scholarships and work weekends and summers to pay for college and law school. The only thing I had was the house in Birmingham—Daddy paid for that, at least. It was bad enough that I'd had to give it up just to protect my sister's life.

"Cassie, don't do that—your eyes are going dark. Cassie, sweetheart, come back, okay? My office isn't fireproof."

That brought me out of my panic. I could burn the place down if I wasn't careful. I'd always been careful. Always.

"I want to finish law school," I whispered, once I knew I was back to myself.

"That goes without saying. Your grades are too good to just waste them on a paralegal's certificate."

He'd investigated that. Lovely. Daniel had likely done it for him.

"Look, I'll have Louise drive you home. I think you need the rest of the day off."

Chapter 5

I rose to leave his office, my legs unsteady beneath me as I walked toward the door. Geoffrey almost fell inside Parke's office the moment I turned the knob.

"What the hell?" Parke almost exploded.

"I just wanted to tell you in person that Annabelle and I have no interest in selling our share in the firm," Geoffrey huffed.

At that moment, I prayed he was telling the truth. I had no desire for him to cause more trouble because Parke intended to marry me.

* * *

An hour later, I settled into Louise's Porsche and shut the door. Too many things threatened to bring on an all-out panic attack and that wouldn't do. Louise didn't bother me with small talk—Parke already told her what he intended. It surprised me that she wore a look of sympathy as she drove me away from Gruber, Taylor and Worth.

We'd just gone past the space needle ten minutes later when a car ran a red light and broadsided us before bursting into flames. Our airbags deployed so we weren't hurt—it takes quite a bit to harm a demon, after all.

"The driver's still in the car," Louise shouted as she hit the buckle on her seat belt and tumbled from the car. I was out of my seat half a second later. "Let me," I said as we raced toward the driver's door.

Fire knows fire.

Without hesitation, I gripped the door handle and yanked, tossing the door into the street before melting through the seat belt with a touch and hauling the unconscious driver away. Louise, right beside me by that time, pulled both of us along—her strength as a rock demon evident.

The car exploded behind us, knocking both of us to our knees. We bent over the driver, though, so he wasn't injured further by the blast. Police sirens sounded nearby as we laid the driver—a young man—on the street and checked for a pulse.

Yes, I'd taken first aid during my undergrad studies. It came in handy now. "He's alive," I said.

By that time, a crowd had gathered. "I'm a nurse," a dark-haired woman knelt beside us. She checked pulse and respiration. The victim woke while she tended him.

"What happened?" he mumbled.

"You ran a red light," the nurse explained. "You and these two ladies, here, are lucky to be alive. If this one hadn't pulled you out of your car, you'd be toast. The fire department is on the way, but there's not much to save, now."

"Wow," he lifted a hand to his forehead. His clothes were scorched in a couple of places, but his skin wasn't burned.

"What's your name?" the nurse asked.

"Cliff Murphy," he said automatically.

"Come with me," Louise grabbed my arm and steered me away.

* * *

It took an hour to fill out an accident report and convince the police we were all right. By that time, Parke and Daniel had arrived. Daniel wasn't happy; Parke looked angry enough to kill. At least his eyes were clear instead of tinged with black.

"Cliff Murphy is Bridgett's half-human cousin," Louise whispered in my ear as we walked toward Parke's Mercedes. "I haven't seen him in years, so I didn't recognize him right away."

"What does this mean?" I asked. I was shaky enough as it was; now it looked as if I were embroiled in even more intrigue.

Chapter 5

"It means that Bridgett was having him tail my new fiancée and Cliff fucked it up," Parke growled behind us. "Then you end up saving the bastard's life after he tries to kill you and my sister."

"Is she crazy? This Bridgett person?" I blinked at Parke.

"Extremely jealous, exceptionally possessive and seriously nuts," Louise confirmed. "Mom always said maybe it would calm her down if Parke married her, but he and I have been against that from the start. She's always nice around Mom, but I've seen the other side of her a few times."

"Are you sure you're all right?" Parke asked as he opened the back door of his Mercedes so Louise and I could climb in.

"Might be stiff tomorrow, but otherwise okay," Louise confirmed.

"You'll let me know if I should call Doc Xavier?" Parke asked.

"We will."

Louise slid in first—I waited for her to get comfortable before moving to sit on my side of the back seat. "Wait," Parke gripped my arm.

"What?" That's all I had time to say—Parke pulled me against him and kissed my hair. *So glad you're both all right*, he said mentally before letting me go.

Louise was grinning when I sat beside her and fastened my seat belt.

* * *

Kate fussed over both of us when we arrived at the house. Eventually, we were settled in the library with hot tea and blankets while Kate and Parke ignored our assurances that we were all right and called the demon doctor anyway.

Doctor Xavier listened, poked and prodded before saying we'd probably be sore and achy for a few days. He handed Parke a bottle of pain relief designed specifically for our race and explained that it would help.

Louise shot Parke an *I told you so* look after the doctor walked out with Kate. "I don't care," Parke stuck his tongue out at Louise. She giggled. I tried to hide a smile. "Here," Parke handed each of us a pill. "Take that and I'll help you get to bed."

Louise grumbled while Parke held her arm as we walked up steps to the second floor. Her bedroom, as it turned out, wasn't far from mine. She was dropped off first, making a face before shutting the door on Parke.

"She always was an independent sort," he grinned and took my arm.

I wanted to make a face at him, too, but I didn't. I figured most people shouldn't glare at their intended shortly after becoming engaged. "I think the medication is starting to work," I mumbled instead.

"Good." Even I couldn't predict what happened next—I was lifted and carried to my room, undressed carefully and covered up in bed by the time I fell asleep.

* * *

Parke

"Vernon Murphy has called three times." Mom handed my cell phone to me when I made it to the kitchen.

"What does he want, besides his baby girl as wife to the Chancellor?" I snapped. "It won't happen."

"I think it's more serious than that," Mom said as I hit redial on my phone.

It was.

"Vernon?" I asked when he answered the phone.

"I'm sorry, Parke," he said right away. "When Cliff showed up at the house, Bridgett shot him and took off."

Chapter 5

"What?" I exploded.

"She thinks she killed him. Granted he's had a tough day, but bullets don't kill half demons as easy as they kill humans. Our doctor says he'll be all right. Cliff says Bridgett paid him to follow your new fiancée. I'm sorry about the accident. Grateful your girl saved Cliff's ass—he's not fire-proof."

"So what does this mean?" I asked. "Other than an attempted murder charge against Bridgett?"

"I'm asking you to be lenient; you know she had her heart set on you. Yes, I know you kept saying no, but she doesn't really understand that word. Cliff says he's willing not to press charges."

"She's indirectly involved in an attack on my sister and my fiancée," I snapped.

"Your eyes, Parke," Mom warned from nearby.

"Your father," Vernon began.

"My father would have been more than pissed that his daughter was placed in danger," I shouted.

The line went dead—Vernon hung up. At that moment, I wanted to punch something. The last thing I remembered was Mom yelling at me to go outside.

* * *

Cassie

"Oh. My. Gosh."

Parke's Mercedes looked like a pretzel. I didn't see (or hear about) the damage done until the following morning after breakfast. "Parke did that after Vernon Murphy called and asked him to look the other way when Bridgett shot Cliff. She was pissed that he messed up his tailing assignment and caused the accident, which implicated her." Kate shook her head as Louise and I surveyed the damage.

"Parke had a conversation with the Prince of Washington State this morning, and there's a warrant out for Bridgett's arrest. She meant to kill Cliff. If he'd been completely human, he'd be dead," she went on.

I wasn't sure what Louise thought, but I was grateful to be learning all this after the fact. And the pretzel that used to be a car? That was rock demon work if I ever saw it. "So Cliff is still alive?" Louise asked.

"Yes, although he's staying with his human mother at the moment. She says she's had enough of demons for a while."

"Half-demons are rare," I said. Louise nodded her agreement. They were protected by Demon law, just like the rest of us.

"He's lucky to be alive—twice over," Kate huffed. "If you hadn't pulled him out of that car when you did," she shook her head. "I always liked Cliffy. Who knows what Bridgett threatened him with to go after both of you?"

"I thought you liked her," Louise said dryly.

"Hmmph," Kate muttered. "Come on, let's get out of this wind. It's cold."

It was cold out, and less than a week before Christmas. Doctor Xavier was right, too—I ached from the accident. Cliff had been driving quite fast when he plowed into us. Humans would be either dead or seriously injured from the impact.

The Worths were down two vehicles, too.

"Want to get in the hot tub?" Louise asked as she and I hobbled into the house after Kate.

"I think I have a swimsuit. Somewhere," I shook my head. "Where is it? The hot tub?"

"On the south side in the solarium," Louise said.

Chapter 5

It took nearly half an hour for me to get back upstairs, find my swimsuit, put it and a robe on and then find the hot tub. Louise was already soaking in it when I finally reached the solarium.

An indoor pool waited there, too, but that wasn't my goal. Hot water bubbled around Louise's shoulders and I wanted some of that. That's where Parke found us, soaking aching bones and muscles in frothy water.

"Hey," he sat on the flagstones surrounding the spa, rolled up his pants, removed his shoes and socks and stuck his feet in the water.

"How are you feeling?" he asked, tucking loose hair behind my ear.

"Hot water makes a big difference," I leaned my head back to look at him. "I saw your car," I added.

"Hmmph," he said. "Could have been worse. I was pissed."

"Remind me not to piss you off," I said.

"You don't have anything to worry about," he said and leaned down to kiss me. I was shocked. Louise snickered.

* * *

Parke

"I sent them upstairs," I said. "What do you have?"

"This," Daniel handed his tablet to me. "Whatever Ross Diablo intends to do, the Prince of Alabama is in it up to his teeth."

"How did you get this communication?" I asked. Somehow, Daniel had gotten his hands on an e-mail from Ross to Prince Jasper Bridges of Alabama. The gist of the communication was this; I'll find her before he can marry her, and then we'll see who's in charge.

"I have friends—and ways," Daniel shrugged.

"This is sounding like a coup," I said. "Why the hell does he want her so badly?" I frowned at Daniel.

"I suggest you start calling your supporters now," Daniel said. "I've got eyes on both, but my people have been instructed to be discreet—no contact."

"Understood," I nodded. "I'll make calls. Meanwhile, arrange for a flight to Vegas, with a quick turnaround. We'll see who gets the girl."

* * *

Cassie

Two pain pills, six hours and a rough flight to and from Vegas meant a ring on my finger and my last name changed to Worth. Something was happening, but Parke wouldn't tell me what it was.

He kept saying not to worry about it and in my foggy, medicated mind, I believed him.

Chapter 6

The next day, our photographs were all over Demonnet; Parke in his tux, me in a rented gown, with Daniel, Kate and Louise smiling around us. There were photographs of us together. Photographs of us signing the marriage license. Photographs of Parke kissing me (I barely remembered that).

If that didn't piss Ross Diablo off, then nothing would. If I knew him at all, he'd be on his way to Seattle with his extensive family behind him.

Parke worked from home while handing Geoffrey a plausible excuse, while I was still officially recuperating from my automobile accident. Christmas was only a few days away, I was married and expecting the end of the world at any minute.

"Baby?" Parke kissed my temple, waking me from a brief nap in my new suite.

"Huh?" No, I'm not at my most articulate when I'm waking.

"I need your help on a few things. Feel up to doing your paralegal thing for me?"

"Sure." I sat up and shoved hair out of my eyes. "Let me get dressed."

"Nah, your jammies are fine. Come on, Mom's making coffee."

* * *

"I like this," Kate beamed as she set a tray of coffee and sandwiches on a corner of Parke's desk. He and I were doing business as usual, except we were doing it from his father's old study at home and I was wearing my cat PJs.

Writing up briefs and typing letters into the extra laptop Parke scrounged from somewhere was almost automatic; it gave me time to think, once the coffee cleared my head.

I thought about Ross. Then the Demon Prince of Alabama, who appeared to look the other way at all of Ross' antics. My mind then wandered to Geoffrey, Annabelle and—eventually—Bridgett. I even had some theories swimming through my head as Parke handed me another missive to type for his signature.

In order to test my theory, I had a mission to plan. Also, now that I was married, I had to find a way to include Parke without having him lock me up for lunacy.

I had to wait for the full moon, just as I'd told him in the past. That was Christmas night. I wasn't looking forward to it.

The printer pushed out the latest letter; Parke grabbed it, read it swiftly then sat down to sign it. "I've hired a few people," he informed me while I stuffed letters in envelopes. "I'll be doing a lot of work from home from now on, as the Chancellor. I have two competent attorneys hired for the business, and they'll hire two paralegals. We'll find a law school for you in the spring, and if you agree to keep working as my paralegal until you pass the bar, then I'll let you have plenty of hands-on experience."

Chapter 6

"That's what I had in mind when I took the job at Gruber, Taylor and Worth," I said. "I wanted to keep my hand in it, hoping I could finish law school eventually."

"I think you've done an exceptional job, even when you had to work around Geoffrey," Parke grinned. "Frank Hillman is certainly grateful."

"He deserves better than what Geoffrey was giving him," I huffed. "That's why I kept everything up to date, hoping Geoffrey would do the right thing."

"You did a wonderful job, sweetheart," Parke rose and walked toward me. He leaned in to give me a quick peck. "It feels really good to be able to kiss you," he said, kissing me a second time. "Mom and Louise don't care about the law. Louise is studying Veterinary Medicine. Now I have somebody who'll understand when I say Writ of Replevin."

"I know that term and plenty of others," I said.

"Talk dirty to me," Parke pulled me close.

"Animus nocendi," I said. "Compos mentis."

"Oh, yeah," Parke deepened his kisses.

* * *

I think if we'd been anywhere besides Parke's father's old study, he might have asked for more than kissing. I'd started thinking it might not be a bad thing. I hesitated to tell him I'd never had sex with anybody—that could be embarrassing.

Still, he probably ought to know. We'd gone back to work after ten minutes or so of kissing and petting.

"Dinner," Kate walked in at seven, when we were wrapping things up for the day. I was glad to be fully dressed, even if I was still in my pajamas.

"I should change," I said.

"I'll come with you," Parke offered.

"I expect you at the table in fifteen," Kate warned. Parke grinned and hauled me out the door.

We made it—barely. Parke insisted on helping me dress.

"I get to help you, sometime—it's only fair," I shook a finger at him after he zipped me into the only nice dress I had.

"I would welcome it," he laughed. "Having somebody pick out the right tie sounds like heaven."

"Wear that black Armani and the burgundy tie for the Hillman case," I said as we walked out of my suite. "You look amazing in that."

"You think I look amazing?" he lifted an eyebrow.

"Pretty much all the time," I said.

"I'll settle for that from my girl," he grinned.

My breath caught—I was his girl. It was finally beginning to sink in. It made me wonder whether Geoffrey and Annabelle knew. If any of my theories were correct, it was possible.

* * *

Daniel arrived for dinner; he and Parke had a private meeting afterward. Kate, Louise and I had wine and talked in the family room, while an old rerun of CSI played in the background.

"Tell me about your sister," Kate said.

That question made me glad I had a glass of wine in my hand. "Cute. Perky. Smart," I sighed. "I haven't seen her for a year." I gulped my wine. "Aunt Shelbie gave us money to get away, but I sent most of mine with Destiny."

"Dark hair, like yours?" Louise asked.

"We look like sisters," I agreed. "Dark hair, blue eyes, et cetera and so on."

"It's uncommon to have two girls in the family. Two boys are more likely," Kate said. That's the way it was with Demons—I figured it had something to do with genetics, way back when Demon

Chapter 6

wars were more common. Males tended to be more warlike. It's just the way things were.

"The tree is going up tomorrow," Louise said, changing the subject. "I love Christmas."

* * *

Parke

"I have this—I really don't want to tell Cassie."

"Shelbie Foster is dead?" I frowned at the information Daniel handed to me. "This isn't good. Shelbie's the only one—besides Cassie—who knew where Destiny King is."

"I hope that's still the case," Daniel said. "But we don't have any guarantees."

"What do we have on the murder? I'm assuming that's what this is?"

"No doubt about that," Daniel nodded. "I have photographs of the crime scene, but we probably should keep those away from Cassie."

"I'm worried about her reaction if we tell her Shelbie's gone. She'll imagine the worst."

"I'm imagining the worst, too," Daniel sounded grim. I agreed with him.

"My worry is for the girl. Did you get any information from Lance Thorne?"

"Not about that. I'll contact him again. If he knows anything, we may be able to get to Destiny first, and get her away. If they already have her, Lance may know that, too."

"Get him on the phone. Put the call on speaker. I want in on this conversation."

* * *

Cassie

Aunt Shelbie was dead—I could feel it. It woke me in the middle of the night—somehow my mind had received the message, just as I'd received a message ten years earlier that my mother was gone.

Some people called it clairvoyance. I had no idea what to call it. My sorrow for Shelbie was intensified by my fear that Destiny was in terrible danger. Half my night was spent in sleepless terror while I huddled in a chair and fought tears away. By morning, I didn't need anyone to tell me that my little sister was in the hands of the enemy.

* * *

"What the hell?" Parke exploded when I opened my bedroom door to him. I wasn't showered or dressed and looked like I'd been crying for a week.

"Aunt Shelbie's dead and Ross has Destiny," I mumbled, working to hold back fresh tears. Somehow, they'd managed to fly from Alabama to California in a matter of hours to snatch Destiny away from Shelbie's friends. I worried they were dead, too.

"You have the sight?" Parke stood, unmoving, while I wiped tears away. "That's an unusual gift in a demon. Why didn't you tell me?"

That's when he took a step forward. I was wrapped in his arms quickly. "Daniel and I got word a few minutes ago that Ross found Destiny," he whispered against my hair. "I didn't want to tell you about Shelbie until after breakfast. I see you already knew. I'm sorry, sweetheart. I wish you'd come to me last night."

"What could you have done?" My voice trembled as I pulled away from him.

"I would have held you," he said simply. "You could have listened to the phone conversations I made, sending the Prince of California and his people after Ross' Demons. We're on their trail,

Chapter 6

but they're headed in this direction. I told Prince Alfred to keep them in his sights, and Prince Edmund and his crew are waiting to Join Alfred's team when Ross and his thugs cross into Oregon. As long as Ross is headed this way, I think he'll keep Destiny alive. He doesn't think anybody knows he's on the way here, but he has to have a bargaining chip, baby, just in case. He knows I'll tell Edmund and Alfred to back away if a young Demon's life is at stake."

"She's scared," I mumbled against his chest when he pulled me close again.

"I know."

* * *

Parke

Cassie was terrified for her sister. I couldn't blame her—if Louise were in the same situation, I'd be scared to death, too. Especially if she were surrounded by demons who could kill her easily.

I didn't tell Cassie what else I knew—Prince Jasper of Alabama was with Ross. I had no idea who wanted to take me down, but it didn't matter. At the moment, they didn't know I knew anything. It also didn't take many brain cells to determine that this would come down to the full moon on Christmas—and that sent a shiver up my spine.

If Ross and Jasper were in contact with rogue werewolves, and made promises that they could hunt any shifter they wanted afterward, why wouldn't the rogue wolves stand with the regime poised to take over the Chancellor's position?

That meant we had two days. I needed to make more calls—and fast.

* * *

Cassie

"We're postponing Christmas," Kate sighed and set a cup of coffee in front of me at the kitchen island. Parke was served next—I looked awful after crying for hours; Parke's face was drawn with worry. He'd gotten a call on his cell while I dressed for breakfast, and he'd moved into his suite and shut the door to take it. The call worried me—Parke looked grim when he came back moments later to escort me to the kitchen.

Celebrating Christmas, too—if any of us were still alive—was the last thing on my mind. Destiny came first, and I was terrified and angry at the same time. If Ross intended to kill her, he may as well take me on as Fire Demon—I didn't intend to let him get away with this.

"Sweetheart," Parke said, "I'm afraid Prince Jasper has allied with Ross and both are coming this way." I stared at him, stunned for a moment, before white-hot anger slammed into me.

"Cassie, sweetheart, your eyes are going dark," Parke cautioned.

"Huh?" I turned toward him and forced my anger down.

"That's better," he shook his head. "Save it for the full moon—I think we'll need it."

* * *

The following day and a half, I swung between terror and fury. Parke received regular updates on Ross and Jasper's approach—they were timing everything right to arrive in Seattle just before the full moon rose.

It was anybody's guess where they'd choose to make their stand, but it made sense that they'd go for a spot where a small demon war would go unremarked by the human population.

At least by their standards.

I know Parke worried about it too—probably more than I did because he was the Chancellor. Another day, perhaps, I'd ask him whether his father had ever faced anything this serious in his tenure as King of the Demons.

"Come with me," Parke arrived in the kitchen, where I stood staring at refrigerator shelves, pondering whether to eat something. My stomach rebelled and argued against every selection inside the roomy appliance.

"Where are we going?" I asked, shutting the fridge door.

Parke took my left hand and lifted it to his lips. *I'll never forgive myself if we die without consummating our marriage*, he informed me telepathically.

"Huh? Parke, I uh," my face went from merely hot to blazing.

"What?" He stopped in his tracks and turned to look at me.

"I've never," I hung my head. Why did I feel shame over this? Aunt Shelbie always said I should find a nice human and get on with it, but I hadn't. Now, I was about to show Parke everything I didn't know.

"What?" His hands gripped my shoulders and repeated his question. At least there was a different inflection, this time.

"What I said." I refused to look up. A gentle finger tilted my head up, instead. "I'm glad you told me. I know to hold back, now."

"Hold back?" I stared at him in shock.

"You mean nobody ever told you that you go to Prelim before you—I guess not." He shook his head at my confusion.

"I know about that," I huffed. I'd just never put it into practice.

Prelim. Yes, we have another form—like shapeshifters have another form. It's called Preliminary or Prelim, because it's an interim stage before your demon type fully manifests itself.

In that stage, we're taller. Thicker skinned. Many think it's our most beautiful form. It always terrified me to get that far, because my fire demon always wanted to come out to play. I'd learned to shut down those thoughts shortly after I learned what I was. After all, I didn't want to burn the house and the neighborhood down because I had no control.

Nowadays, I was the queen of control. If you needed a light for your fire or a cigar, I could do that easily. Containing the full fire demon might be another problem.

"I'm afraid I'll hurt you," I said, blinking worriedly at Parke.

He huffed his response, grabbed my hand again and pulled me toward the front door.

Oh gosh, he wasn't kidding.

He intended to do this.

Not that I didn't want him—I did. Because I'd never done this before, I was terrified—for both of us.

I saw the back garden for the first time that afternoon. At the center, surrounded by trees and plants that would be thick with blooms come spring, lay a huge, rock-lined bowl.

It was the first time I'd ever seen a Demon hollow. I'd heard them mentioned, but many demons didn't have the luxury. That meant a pond, ravine or quarry had to serve, depending on the type of demons involved.

Sure, they could have sex with humans, but only in human form. A human didn't call out the prelim like a demon partner would. If you wanted sex in the back seat of a Chevy, you had to find a human. Two amorous demons in a Chevy would destroy the vehicle.

In seconds.

"Don't worry, I'll take care of you," Parke turned me toward him. Leaning in, he kissed me. That kiss deepened.

Set it free, he urged as he continued to kiss me.

"Afraid," I whispered against his mouth.

Don't be.

Chapter 7

assie

I had no idea. None. I'm sure my mother would have explained things—if she'd lived. Shelbie always waited for me to have sex with a human before describing the finer points of demon sex.

Parke had set me on fire.

Literally.

Tiny flames burst at times through my Prelim's skin, licking about Parke's hands and body. Yes, at first I was afraid I'd hurt him. It made him laugh instead, as he gripped my body harder against his and gave me a fanged kiss that nearly melted my heart.

The rock of his rock demon showed through at times as he held me so tightly that anyone else would have lost their breath. It exhilarated me, instead. When he pulled me onto the rocks at the center of the hollow, I went with him willingly.

The moment we joined, I keened from the pleasure of it.

I never knew.

I never fucking knew how good it would be.

Gripping stones about me while Parke continued to lavish me with his attention and his body, I crushed the rocks into dust because the sensation was so intense.

Yes, that's my girl, Parke encouraged. *Break them all. I'll find more.*

When I came, I felt as if I'd exploded, taking Parke with me. I saw stars, I remember that much, while Parke shouted my name and told me he loved me.

* * *

Parke

If I were resolved before, I was more than determined, now.

Nobody was going to take Cassie away from me. I'd die before I'd let that happen. I think Daniel knew it too, the moment I stalked into Dad's old study after getting Cassie back in her bedroom and encouraging her to soak in the tub for a while.

"You look like your dad," Daniel ventured.

"What?" I turned swiftly in his direction.

"That look he got at times when somebody needed to be put down," Daniel shrugged.

"Several someones need putting down," I growled.

"We have a fight on our hands," Daniel pointed out.

"You think I don't know that?"

"Save those dark eyes for later," Daniel warned.

* * *

Cassie

If I weren't terrified again, I'd find Parke and ask for a second round of sex. As it was, Destiny's captivity worried me. When would we learn where Ross and his horde intended to meet?

Yes, he was likely to offer Destiny in exchange for Parke stepping down.

That was an offer Parke couldn't accept.

Chapter 7

Destiny would die if something weren't done quickly. If Ross had enough demon power at his back, not to mention rogue werewolves and anyone else willing to join the fight, we could all go down.

I knew Parke wouldn't go down without a fight.

I intended to fight beside him. Ross and his horde might kill us, but we'd let him know what we thought of him before we fell.

I dressed in my best and sturdiest jeans, low-heeled boots and a sweater before leaving my bedroom to search for Kate and Louise. I found them in the kitchen, having cocoa while they waited for Parke and Daniel.

Kate offered me a wonderful smile when I appeared—it caused my cheeks to heat. I had no doubt that Parke and I had been noisy enough for anyone inside the house to hear earlier.

Louise surprised me by hugging me and kissing my cheek. "Welcome to the family—for real," she grinned as she stepped back.

"It's tradition in the best families," Kate laughed. "Humans used to hang out bed sheets. Demons destroy their hollow."

"Not to mention the noise," Louise ducked her head and snickered.

"I'll never live this down," I sighed.

"No, sweetheart—this is only the beginning," Parke dropped his arms around my shoulders from behind. "You were perfect."

"We've had word," Daniel said, ignoring Parke's admission with difficulty. "They're making their stand near the base of Mount Pilchuck."

"Pilchuck?" I pulled away from Parke's embrace.

"You know something?" Parke demanded.

"You may get your fried fish sooner than I thought," I said. I didn't bother to explain. Parke nodded before turning toward the door. Daniel, Kate, Louise and I followed him out of the house.

* * *

I'd had poor Christmases in the past, after my mother's death—Daddy no longer cared or celebrated the holiday. Shelbie, who'd died trying to protect Destiny and me, was the one who'd done her best to see we had a Christmas. As we drove along the winding road to our destination, I realized that this might be my worst—and last—Christmas.

After we passed Granite Falls, I wanted to panic. The full moon danced in and out of sporadic cloud cover, while tall firs stretched their branches into the night sky, as if reaching for the brightly shining orb.

I knew who lived where we were going—when I'd been hired into the secretarial pool at Gruber, Taylor and Worth, I'd processed property-tax payments for Geoffrey and Annabelle.

Both had homes in prestigious sections of Seattle. They also owned homes on Mountain Loop Highway, past Granite Falls and not far from Mount Pilchuck. There was only one, however, whose second home would be suitable tonight.

Annabelle's.

I didn't tell Parke that I knew where we were going. He'd likely guessed I knew already. I wasn't sure he knew everything about his erstwhile partners, however. That information could wait until later.

We had demons to fight, first.

* * *

Parke

I drove our van to the rendezvous spot. Daniel knew who waited for us but Mom, Louise and Cassie had come, thinking only to stand with me. Cassie's unquestioning loyalty squeezed my heart. She wanted to stand beside me and fight, even if we went down.

I hoped that wouldn't happen, but was prepared in case it did.

Chapter 7

The Prince of Washington State was the first to approach as I stepped out of the van, Daniel and the others following quickly. Cars were parked everywhere, most belonging to allied demons, a few to werewolves sent by the Grand Master.

It was their job to deal with the rogue wolves while my crew and I handled the demons. I prayed we'd survive to raise a glass together afterward.

Many of the werewolves were changed already, some of them howling at the moon high overhead. I didn't care. Let the rogue wolves know they would be challenged.

"Chancellor," Prince Dexter of Washington State offered a respectful head bob.

"Prince Dexter," I acknowledged. "Is everything in place?"

"Yes. Prelims only past this point," he confirmed. "It's less than a mile away."

"Good. Gather the troops. You, Daniel and I will lead."

"Yes, Chancellor."

* * *

Cassie

I went to Prelim for the second time in less than six hours. This time, pleasure wasn't waiting for me.

Just the opposite, in fact.

"You, in the center," Daniel waved an arm at Louise. She growled at him but did as he asked. Kate, Louise and I, making up the only women in what appeared to be a small demon army, followed Daniel's directive.

I didn't intend to stay in the center long, once I caught sight of Ross.

I'd never let my demon out to play, before. I'd always held it in check. My mother—and then Aunt Shelbie—always said to practice my control. It helped us live among humans.

Tonight, all their advice would be tossed aside. I'd live or die according to my skill and ability as a fire demon. Ross, likely used to fighting, had the advantage, I think. That didn't quell my determination. If he hurt Destiny, I would attack.

When I fell, I intended to do damage on the way down.

That's when it hit me, and in my desperation to reach Parke, I attempted telepathy. Whether it actually worked or not, he heard me.

Parke, I need to get on the far side of this, I whispered into his mind.

Baby? He and the rest of us were running, now. *How?*

No, he wasn't asking me how I was speaking to him like this. He was asking how I could get on the far side of this fight.

Throw me, I said. *If I go full demon midflight, I won't get hurt when I hit the ground.*

Parke cursed. I understood that he was terrified I'd be hurt anyway. This was an opportunity we couldn't let pass, though. Too many lives hung in the balance.

Please, I begged. *Your rock demon can throw me far enough, I know it.*

Get up here, he growled.

On my way.

I increased my speed, while Kate and Louise expressed their displeasure at my outrunning them. In seconds, I ran beside Parke. That's when I was able to see the full rock demon for the first time; he turned while he ran.

He was magnificent. At sixteen feet, his stride lengthened as he scooped me off the ground with one hand. *Be safe*, he said and hurled me far into the night.

* * *

Waiting until the last possible moment, my fire demon blazed into existence, flying like a fireball through thick stands of trees.

Chapter 7

Yes, I'd seen the army crowding around Annabelle's house as I flew overhead—Ross and company were waiting for us.

I hit the ground with an explosion, while trees and anything else flammable bloomed with fire about me. I could hear Parke's army coming at a run, their demon feet hitting the ground and shaking it with their weight and speed. Recklessly, I released every bit of fire I had and ran toward Annabelle's luxury cabin in the woods.

* * *

Parke

Daniel knew what to do. His job was to get Destiny away if possible, before Ross and Jasper had a chance to harm her. He and I hoped that his shield would suffice—he needed to stay hidden to grab the girl. Once she was in his arms, she'd be protected by his shield, too.

I'd ordered him to deliver Destiny to Mom and then return to fight. Mom knew to get the girl to safety—I didn't intend to let her fight.

Louise, on the other hand, was an adept fighter. Dad made sure both of us were trained by the best.

The wild card, of course, was Cassie. When she asked me to toss her to the far side, I imagined she intended to set a fire to keep the enemy from running.

Fine by me—one way or another, this would end tonight.

I smelled smoke before I saw flames licking the tops of tall firs—Cassie had done just as I suspected. It meant she was alive and well, too, which eased my mind.

We were almost upon Ross' army when the commotion began; a werewolf from our side chased after the wild boar that brushed past Daniel, on his way down the hill. Something had spooked the animal, but I was concerned that we might need the wolf.

I shouldn't have worried—the boar squealed in seconds before grunting and expiring—the wolf knew his business, at least.

Daniel employed his shield and disappeared before my eyes— he was ready to retrieve Destiny—if she still lived.

Meanwhile, the crackle of flames grew louder, amid the sounds of Ross' army racing in our direction.

He was bringing the fight to us.

All the better.

* * *

Cassie

Ross' army outnumbered ours—that was easy to see, but what he wasn't expecting, and what also surprised me, was that everything was burning or melting in my path. Like a volcano, I melted rock as I raced down the mountain, getting an occasional glimpse of Annabelle's cabin, its outdoor lights shining like a beacon in the clearing ahead.

I was running toward it faster, now, as the ground leveled out somewhat, although there was still a downward slope. Molten rock flowed about me, running as fast as I did, as if it were in competition with me.

I didn't care. A rogue werewolf yelped—his paws were burned by heated ground as he ran from my approach. More yelps sounded, until the entire pack of rogues ran toward Annabelle's cabin—they had no desire to take on a racing fireball.

They weren't fireproof. No animal was.

After tossing carefully-formed flames toward the Olympic-sized swimming pool at the back of Annabelle's property, I sped toward the horde of demons, who in turn were racing toward Parke and his army.

I saw a few running at the back of the pack—some had turned to watch me chasing after them.

Chapter 7

Why were they running away? I didn't slow my pace. If Destiny weren't alive by the time I reached Ross, then I intended for both of us to go down fighting.

Shoving the first demon out of my way, I barely heard his scream as I reached for the next one running before me. His scream joined the first. I could hear the edge of Ross' army crashing into the forefront of Parke's. I knew he was there—he wouldn't have it any other way. The King of the Demons was doing battle. I hoped he survived.

Tearing my thoughts away, I grasped another running demon by the throat. His scream cut off as he began to burn, his body lighting like fireworks on Independence Day.

The next was the first water demon I encountered. I ran through his wall of water, thinking that all my plans to destroy Ross were gone. Water quenches fire; the old tale rushed through my thoughts. Demon water sizzled, hissed and then turned to mist as other demons on both sides of me shouted and scattered.

Was I still burning?

You bet your ass I was.

Chapter 8

P^{arke}

Dexter fought beside me like the experienced demon he was. He was always Dad's best supporter and a good advisor. He gave me the same loyalty and allegiance he'd offered Dad.

I'd let him know how much I appreciated that, provided we survived the night. So far, I hadn't seen Daniel go past with Destiny.

Tucking that worry into the back of my mind, I watched as Ross and Jasper's army flowed toward us, chased by a huge (and growing) fireball.

With the forest surrounding us as wet as it was following recent, heavy rains, it surprised me that Cassie was having such an effect. *Are those screams I hear?* Louise's voice filtered into my mind.

She and I had telepathy. I'd heard Cassie, too, but that could be the bond we'd formed earlier in the hollow. Something to explore if we survived. Grasping an ice demon by the throat and throwing him forcefully to the ground, I watched as his ice shattered into shards of glittering, frozen crystals. Another one down—too many more to go.

I hear screams, too, I replied to Louise's question. *No idea what that means.* I punched a water demon in the face, breaking his body into a rain of droplets as I stalked onward.

* * *

Cassie

I could see Ross ahead—there was no mistaking his Rock Demon. He towered over the rock demon next to him—likely Jasper, Prince of Alabama. Rock demons were common as Princes and Princesses—they held a tremendous amount of power on their own.

I suspected, too, that Ross was wading through his army to get to Parke. That was his intention—to take Parke down and force everyone else to bow to his will as he took the Chancellor's seat. With the army he'd gathered, he could stand against any who thought to come against him.

I was working my way through that army as swiftly as I could, refusing to think of the lives I was taking—focusing instead on the ones I might save.

Surprisingly, Ross didn't have Destiny with him. Tossing out fireballs on either side of me, I heard more screams as I worked my way through the crowd toward Ross' broad back.

* * *

Parke

I had no idea where Daniel was. Dexter had dropped back to fight a rock demon who'd attempted to blindside me. From the noise coming from behind, I understood that Dexter was teaching the fool a lesson.

The wolves, too, had dropped back to attack the rogues who'd attempted to flee the coming fire. That's what it appeared to be, now—half the mountain was ablaze. I could survive a normal fire. A

Chapter 8

fire demon's fire, however, looked to be another story. A worry nagged at my mind—*could Cassie turn this off, once it had gone this far?*

* * *

Cassie

Where was Destiny? A horrible fear gripped my heart that Ross had already killed her before this battle started. After all, what incentive did he have to keep her alive past this point? Fury possessed me.

I didn't think I was capable of running faster, but I did. Ross would die, if I had anything to say about it.

* * *

Parke

Cassie was almost behind Ross and Jasper. I was close enough to see the fear in their eyes.

That's when the booming shout came, and to my horror, I recognized the voice.

Bridgett was here.

* * *

Cassie

From the corner of my eye, I caught movement, and then saw enough to stop me in my tracks—a bitch of a water demon held Destiny against her, my sister looking frail and small against the taller demon's scales.

The worst part?

The water demon held a huge gun at Destiny's head. I'd only heard of the guns built specifically to destroy demons before—that's why they were referred to as demon killers. This demon had somehow acquired one of the rare weapons and now threatened my sister with it.

"Stop now or the girl dies," the water demon screamed. I knew who she was; she would have no sympathy for my sister or me.

The flames of my tears dripped to the ground as I stared at the scenario before me. Every piece of the puzzle fell into place the moment Ross approached Bridgett and draped a heavy arm about her shoulders.

* * *

Parke

I understood how my father died the moment Ross placed an arm around Bridgett's shoulders.

How easy would it be for a water demon to capsize a fishing boat?

Too easy.

I suspected she had other help, too, but that could wait.

Bridgett held a gun to Destiny's head while Cassie stopped in her tracks. It had come to this, and I had no doubts that Bridgett intended to kill Destiny and Cassie.

"Move and the girl dies," the Prince of Alabama's voice was as gravelly as his outer Demon skin.

"Let her go, Jasper. Making a threat against a child relieves you of the title of Prince."

"I'll have your title instead," Jasper threatened.

"You mean Ross didn't tell you?" I growled.

"Tell me what?"

"That he's using you as his stepping-stone. You won't get the Chancellor's seat—he intends to take it."

"That's a fucking lie." Ross pulled away from Bridgett and walked several steps in my direction. He thought to intimidate me.

"I'm a truth demon, remember?" I snapped at him, holding my ground. "I can sift the truth from a lie any day."

Chapter 8

My eyes slid to Bridgett, who'd raised her demon killer to rest it against Destiny's temple.

* * *

Cassie

"Turn it off or I kill her," Bridgett shouted at me. I saw Destiny through fiery tears before pulling the fire back. Everything went dark around me for a moment as all fire died, leaving only a bright moon overhead to light the battleground below.

"I love you, sissy," I whispered into the ensuing hush. She had to know I loved her before we died.

Bridgett didn't intend for us to live.

"I know," Destiny whispered back.

Bridgett turned the gun toward me, then. She intended to kill me first.

That was her biggest mistake, as it turned out.

Destiny burst into a larger form as Bridgett struggled to hold onto her and swing the gun around again.

It was already too late for that.

A fledgling ice demon can still freeze an unsuspecting water demon. I gaped as Bridgett's body froze, her gun halfway to Destiny's head.

The punch Destiny's ice demon delivered to Bridgett's frozen water demon would have made any older sister proud.

Bridgett's icy body burst into thousands of crystals that tinkled to the ground. The gun, now worthless, dropped on top of her crystals.

That's when I saw Daniel's ice demon appear. He grabbed Destiny and pulled her away from Ross, who was now attempting to strike a killing blow against her ice demon. I screamed.

Parke roared and leapt at Ross.

I burst into flames.

Ross and Jasper turned to face us as we raced toward them.

Parke and I—it didn't matter whether we died at that moment. Ross and Jasper died first, crushed and melted between rock and fire. The resulting boom shook the mountain and the fireball burned everything within a hundred feet.

Chapter 9

*P**arke*

"Did you see this one?" Mom held up the newspaper claiming that the devastation, which culminated in a huge, booming fireball at the foot of Mount Pilchuk, was attributed to a UFO crash.

"As long as it doesn't say Demon War Responsible, then I'm all for it," I shrugged.

"How's Cassie?"

"She's fine, just worn out. It helped when she realized she didn't hurt me at all; my shield held. Ross and Jasper died quickly between us. I told Cassie to go back to sleep when I got up," I said.

"Destiny's exhausted, too, poor baby. I took breakfast in, she ate and then went back to sleep."

"They've had a rough time of it," I said, accepting the cup of coffee Mom handed to me. "Cassie told me last night how they killed Dad. Do you want to hear this, or would you rather not know?"

"I want to know," Mom sounded determined.

"Ross positioned Geoffrey and Annabelle to take Lucas' third of the partnership after Lucas died. Lucas' family was coerced by Ross to sell to Geoffrey and Annabelle. Their assignment was to keep an eye on Dad and wait for the opportunity to take him down. They got that when they learned how much Dad loved to fish."

"How does Bridgett figure into this?" Mom asked.

"Ross approached her, too. Promised her she'd be the Chancellor's wife if she helped. At first, she took that to mean that she'd have me—something she'd always wanted. It didn't take much for a water demon to capsize Dad's boat."

"But he was a good swimmer," Mom pointed out.

"But nobody was taking Annabelle into consideration. She's a shapeshifter, Mom—just like Geoffrey. Know what sort of shapeshifter she might be?"

"No idea."

"She's a shark. I know they're rare, but that's what she is—Cassie figured it out. Dad was killed by Annabelle after Bridgett capsized the boat."

"And Geoffrey, the pig shapeshifter, waited onshore for both of them—with dry clothes and a car to drive them home," Cassie walked into the kitchen.

* * *

Cassie

"What happened to Geoffrey and Annabelle last night?" Kate glanced from Parke to me the moment I walked into the kitchen and made my announcement.

"One of the wolves got Geoffrey—he didn't want to be barbecued so he ran," I shrugged. "Annabelle, well, she didn't realize that a fire demon can burn normal water. I set her Olympic-sized swimming pool on fire last night while her shark was swimming in it.

Chapter 9

"I'm sorry, honey," I turned to Parke. "I wanted to fry her for you. Instead, she was boiled. You like bouillabaisse, by any chance?"

Parke laughed and pulled me onto his lap. "Merry Christmas, baby," he said and kissed me.

"Honey," I said when he pulled his mouth away.

"What?" Parke leaned back and offered a lazy smile.

"This is the best Christmas ever."

He kissed me again.

Part 2:

Alabama On My Mind

Chapter 10

Los Mochis, Mexico
January 2
Dalton King

"It'll be fine; we've hidden it well enough," I scolded Morton. We'd buried the sealed, metal box of cash on his beach property in Mexico before answering Ruudann's summons.

"You know the Chancellor's investigators will come for us; I'm surprised we haven't heard anything yet," Morton growled.

"That's why we're leaving. If Ruudann hadn't issued orders, I'd be on my way to Colombia."

"Too bad Ross wasn't strong enough to win the war; I hear his entire army was wiped out. That probably pissed Ruudann off plenty," Morton pointed out.

"Think the rumors are true? That the Chancellor found himself a fire demon?"

"There's only one fire demon he could find so fast—you know that."

"Ross fucked up when he let her get away," I snapped. "Who knew she'd finally change?"

"Ross was pissed about that, too—that she hadn't changed. She was his insurance against Ruudann, if they had a difference of opinion. Ruudann would have killed her himself, I think, if he found out she could change."

"Then he may get his opportunity, because that's what it looks like, now. Hope that doesn't bother you, since you're her dear old dad."

"You're her fucking grandfather. It doesn't bother you—it doesn't bother me, either. If Ruudann wants her dead, then she's dead. Come on, let's get out of here." Morton lifted his duffle and slung it over a shoulder. "I don't want those investigators breathing down my neck. I'm getting itchy about that, to be honest."

"Hmmph," I snorted. "Wait until Black Myth catches up with the Chancellor's bunch. They won't be so eager to hunt our asses after that."

"That's for damn sure."

* * *

Seattle, Washington

January 4

Cassie

"Sweetheart, look at it this way," Parke pleaded with me. "Two semesters, followed by an internship with the law firm and you'll be ready for the bar exam."

He was doing his best to convince me to return to Tuscaloosa, Alabama and the law school I'd left behind to get away from Ross Diablo.

"They say they'll take you back because you were such a good student. I can't even bribe anybody else to get you in until a year from now."

<h1 style="text-align:center">Chapter 10</h1>

"You tried to bribe people?" I gasped, horrified.

"No, but I offered a hefty donation," he muttered, turning away. I watched as he raked well-shaped fingers through thick, dark hair in frustration. Leaving Seattle and going back to Tuscaloosa would feel like a giant step backward to me. It would also separate us.

Parke had to stay in Seattle, not only to run his law firm, but to fill the positions left open when his erstwhile, evil partners, Annabelle Taylor and Geoffrey Gruber, died during the paranormal war. Everybody in the supernatural community was beginning to call it the Christmas war, but that only dealt with the date and not the cause.

Besides, Parke was new to the Chancellor's position for all things supernatural. He had to have a steady hand and a clear mind when dealing with all the problems that were bound to crop up. An uncomfortable and paranoid new wife wouldn't help him in the least.

It didn't matter that we were married for little more than two weeks. Parke had enough to worry about without me adding to his burden. It also didn't matter that spring semester would begin in a few days, or that I wasn't prepared to go back to law school.

What was I supposed to do—tell my new husband, who was a truth demon and the Chancellor, that I wanted to whine like a baby to stay with him?

Suck it up, Cassie King-Worth, I scolded myself. *He's paying for you to return to college to get your law degree. The least you can do is be grateful.*

"What's your answer?" Parke turned back to me.

"Uh, roll, tide," I said, my voice sounding weak.

"You'll be amazing," he pulled me to him and planted a kiss on my mouth.

I'll be away from you, I thought and wanted to cry. My little sister, Destiny, would get to stay in Seattle and go to school here.

I wanted to stay in Seattle, too.

"Baby, the new Prince of Alabama is a reasonable man and he's promised to watch over you. You won't be in danger anymore."

"Yeah." I pulled away from him. "Guess I ought to start studying so I can get back into my classes."

"Don't worry," Parke called after me as I walked away from him. "It'll be like you never missed a day of school."

* * *

"I can't believe you're leaving." Destiny sat cross-legged on my bed and watched me pack.

"Not my choice—not if I want to finish law school before I'm eligible for Medicare," I muttered.

"The only thing I miss is the Mellow Mushroom," Destiny sighed with longing. She'd named our favorite pizza place in Tuscaloosa. Aunt Shelbie would bring Destiny after school and meet me there once a week while I was in law school, so we could have a meal together.

"I miss the 'shroom, too," I said. "Just not enough to live in Alabama for another year." I didn't say that I missed Aunt Shelbie more. I wanted to curse the ground Ross Diablo died on, because he'd had her killed.

She'd died protecting Destiny and me—from him.

"Do you think Parke will go looking for Daddy? To do something about what he did?" Destiny picked at a loose thread on the quilt that covered the bed.

She'd skirted the truth—that if Parke found our father, he'd be brought up on charges serious enough to forfeit his life.

Daddy sold me to Ross Diablo, and likely turned his head when our mother was murdered years ago.

Sad, that one of your own could turn against you like that, and take money to make his life more comfortable on top of it.

Chapter 10

"I don't know, Sissy. He was in Mexico the last I heard, and they don't follow the rules so well down there."

"I'm really mad at him."

That makes two of us. I didn't say it aloud, but I wasn't sure what I'd do if I ever saw him again. He'd done nothing to protect us—as a father should.

Mom and Aunt Shelbie were the ones who looked out for us—until Mom disappeared one night years ago. After that, it was just Aunt Shelbie, making sure we were fed, clothed and cared for while Daddy drank and hung out with his friends.

Ross paid Daddy a ton of money for me when I turned twenty. I was supposed to be allowed to finish college, but my father disappeared, leaving me in Ross' clutches. After two years of law school, I hid Destiny with some of Shelbie's friends and ran away from Ross. He'd followed me, all while planning to unseat Parke as Chancellor.

Ross and his bunch were dead after the brief war on Christmas night, during the full moon when everything shifted, including the elemental demons and shape changers.

I thought I'd have time to get to know my new husband after that.

It wasn't to be.

I cursed Geoffrey and Annabelle, too, because they'd allied with Ross and his horde. They'd tried to kill all of us, so Ross could play Chancellor.

"Make sure Parke picks the right people to take Geoffrey and Annabelle's places," I told Destiny.

"Like he'd ask me," Destiny grinned. "You'd know better than I would. Kate says she's going to ask an old friend who's an ice demon to teach me three days a week, after school," she added.

"Then you're a lucky duck," I teased. "I didn't have anybody to help me."

"I know." Destiny's eyes dropped and she picked at the quilt again. "Louise says we're lucky that you have so much control."

She'd been discussing me with Parke's mother and sister. I sighed. Yes, they cared and meant well. It just made me uncomfortable, that they'd talked about me like that.

"I bet you'll miss this house," Destiny offered when her eyes met mine again. "Your dorm room before was too small."

"Parke says he's getting me an apartment close to campus, and a car." Those things were nice, but I wanted to stay with him. I didn't say that.

"Maybe I can come visit, then. We could go to the 'shroom."

"Sure. Any time," I said. "At least the bowl game and championship will be held in another state and I won't have to fight fans for a parking spot when I get there."

"You won't have to worry about clothes or paying your bills," Destiny pointed out. "Parke will take care of that."

"I'm looking forward to the day when I can do all that for myself," I said, closing the suitcase and zipping it shut. "I've done it myself for the past year."

"I know. But you'll be a lawyer, like Parke. And a millionaire."

I wasn't going to point it out, but my chances of being a millionaire were slim next to Parke's wealth. My little sister had a serious crush on my husband. He, Louise and Daniel had taken time off from busy schedules to play board and video games with her. It was nice to hear her giggling after one of Daniel's jokes or Parke and Louise's stories.

Kate, Parke's mother, invited me for tea or wine after dinner most nights, while she talked about Parke's father before his

Chapter 10

untimely death. Annabelle and Geoffrey had been the major players in his murder. I didn't miss either of them.

"Dinner's ready," Louise poked her head inside the bedroom door. "Parke just got home from the office, too."

"Cool," Destiny slid off the bed and grabbed my hand. "Let's eat."

* * *

Tuscaloosa, Alabama

Cassie

"Rent includes the furniture, washer, dryer and dishes," my new landlord showed me the apartment after my arrival in Tuscaloosa. The garage apartment stood behind a large, brick home, which wasn't far from UA. The landlord was also the homeowner; somehow, Parke had pulled strings to get such a nice place for me.

I imagined that the new Prince was also involved, somehow; he was a Supreme Court Judge for the state of Alabama and probably knew all sorts of well-placed people, human and otherwise.

"The furniture and other things are great, thank you," I said, pulling out my manners and dusting them off. My landlord, Talbert Cummings, didn't know (and didn't need to know) that I was already homesick for Seattle.

"You have the printout of the rules?" Talbert's brown eyes were sincere, as if he were putting me out, somehow, by mentioning the rules to begin with.

"I do. I promise I won't have much in the way of company; I intend to use all my free time studying, so quiet is always best," I smiled at him.

"You're married—that was a plus when we accepted your application," Talbert nodded.

"Yes. I tried to get into a school in Washington State, but there was a long waiting list. That's why I'm back—to finish up my law degree."

"Well, good luck. If you have questions or need anything, my cell number and my wife's are at the bottom of the printout."

"Thank you—it's good to know you'll be watching over me."

"Sure thing." Talbert lifted a hand and headed for the door. Once it was closed behind him and I heard his footsteps on the stairs outside my new apartment, I let the strap of my purse slide off my shoulder before I slumped onto a chair at the small kitchen table.

How was I going to get through this?

I missed Destiny, Parke and the others; already it had become a dull ache in my heart.

* * *

I'd already started reading my texts for Tax Law and Wills and Trusts, and still had two days before classes started. Therefore, I drove my new hybrid to the grocery store and spent part of my monthly grocery allowance to stock the apartment kitchen.

Yes, Parke had bought me a car. Yes, he'd given me an allowance—for food, gas and other necessities.

It was enough to feed a family of four for an entire year, and he'd paid my rent in advance.

I felt terrible about it.

A part of me understood that I was his wife; another part—a big part—wanted to be self-sufficient.

Telling Parke that was like talking to a stubborn rock.

No surprise, since he was a rock demon, in addition to being a truth demon. First and foremost, however, he was male and wasn't listening to a female for longer than it took to get the words past my lips.

He'd already made up his mind—about everything.

At times, a tiny voice said that he'd been anxious to get me out of the way so he could go about his business; ours was a marriage of convenience, after all. Sure, he'd said he loved me.

How many men had done that, just to get their way?

Stop thinking those thoughts; it will only make you crazy, I warned myself while lifting a whole chicken from the meat section and placing it in my basket. A baked chicken would get me through two or three days of dinners, if I made chicken and noodles on the third day.

* * *

Parke

Sending Cassie away was hard. Harder than I thought it would be. Yes, I saw the look on her face as she walked through security at the airport.

The look of abandonment.

I was responsible for that.

This way was best, though. If she weren't here, she wouldn't guess that I'd sent Daniel and two others to Mexico the same day, to look for her father.

He had a laundry list of crimes to answer for; the most important among them was the murder of Cassie's mother and then his selling Cassie to Ross Diablo.

There were laws in the demon world against those things, just as there were in the human world. The biggest difference in those laws was that if you were found guilty of those crimes in the demon world, you could pay with your life, depending on the Chancellor and his Council of Princes' decisions.

If I found that he'd had knowledge of Ross' treason and failed to report it; that would be another charge against his name. If he'd been complicit in that act of treason, well, Cassie didn't need those worries while going to school. Not if I could help it.

Morton King would be brought to judgment and if found guilty, sentenced appropriately for his crimes.

"You look like you're a million miles away." My new assistant, Pauline, set a Starbucks cup on my desk.

"Not a million," I lifted the cup and thanked her for the latte. "Maybe a few thousand. Look, if Daniel calls, put him right through, okay?"

"Sure thing." She smiled and swished out of my office.

I was having second thoughts on hiring her to replace Cassie as my assistant. Pauline wanted something, and she was the type who'd stand on somebody's head to reach it.

Daniel's call came ten minutes later, while I read through a case file. The court date was next week and I needed to refresh on the details.

"We found out where he was for the past year and a half," Daniel informed me. "But he cleared out less than a week ago, according to a neighbor."

"You think he heard what happened here and that it didn't go Ross' way?" I asked.

"That's what I think."

"Doesn't sound good for him, then," I said and paused for a moment. "Anybody know where he went?"

"No. Saw a realtor poking around, though. Said she'd been asking Mort to sell—somebody wants to buy his bungalow on the beach."

"I want that tied up if possible—if we end up seizing his assets, that bungalow should go to Cassie and Destiny."

"We can't tie anything up until we find the bastard," Daniel huffed. "He's still the legal owner—according to Mexican law."

Chapter 10

"Yeah. See if you can pick up his trail, then. Check for bank accounts and anything else. Hell, check the local bars and the cable company."

"Will do."

Daniel ended the call after that, leaving me more frustrated than before. Morton King wasn't just twiddling his thumbs for two years—you could bet on that.

Cassie said her father started drinking heavily after her mother's disappearance. While demons didn't, as a rule, become alcoholics—our systems burned through it too quickly—it wasn't out of the realm of possibilities.

I wondered, too, if Morton still had contacts in Alabama. Yes, Cassie would have been a good source for that information. She was also the last person I'd ask for it.

She needed to go back to school, get reacquainted with her friends, study hard and not worry about the fact that I intended to see her father face justice.

"Frank Hillman's on the phone," Pauline announced on the intercom. "Line four."

"Frank," I said when I lifted the handset.

"Just wanted to check in with you," Frank said. "Any word on a court date, yet?"

"No, but we could hear something any day. We've got everything ready to go. Fli-Bi-Net won't know what hit them."

"Good. I want to hit them until it really hurts," Frank replied. "They're undercutting my business with an ad campaign right now."

"Print or airtime?" I asked.

"Airtime. It's all over the TV. Saw it on the news last night."

"I'll get a copy and take a look. We may be able to file an injunction, since the software is involved in litigation."

"Whatever it takes. I can't believe how slimy they are."

"I'll see to it, and get back with you in the next few days," I promised.

"Thanks, Parke. You're just as reliable as your old man."

I didn't tell Frank that had it not been for Cassie, he wouldn't have a case. She'd kept it from being buried like Geoffrey wanted. Geoffrey had sold Frank out, because Fli-Bi-Net paid him under the table. I couldn't do anything about that, because it would give the firm a huge black eye. All I could do was show up and hammer Fli-Bi-Net in court until they gave up and paid Frank for the theft of his software plus related damages.

"Pauline," I hit the intercom button, "Get me a copy of the Fli-Bi-Net TV ad they've been running lately."

"Sure thing, Parke."

* * *

Cassie

"I never thought I'd see you again," Binita hugged me before taking the seat next to mine in Immigration Law. "What happened? Where did you go?"

"I got married," I held up my left hand so she could see the overly large diamond Parke had placed there.

Binita was an American-born daughter of Indian immigrants. Her parents were mostly traditional and she never ate beef, but she dressed in Western clothing most of the time.

"What's his name? You didn't even tell me you had a boyfriend," Binita examined my ring.

"His name is Parke. Parke Worth. He owns a law firm in Seattle. I've worked as a paralegal in his firm the past year, but he talked me into coming back to school to finish my degree."

No need to tell her I'd known Parke for barely six weeks and been married to him three of those weeks. "I'm glad he knows how smart you are," Binita said, letting go of my hand.

Chapter 10

"Like you don't study every waking minute?" I grinned at her.

"Want to get together to study two nights a week?" Binita asked.

"Sure. Library or my place? I actually have a decent apartment, now."

"Your place?" The dimple in her cheek showed. "We can cook dinner and discuss Immigration or Tax law."

"Sounds great."

My shoulders sagged in relief—I wasn't going to be alone at school; I had one friend, at least.

* * *

Parke

I was very surprised to hear from Blake Donovan; he hadn't even met Cassie yet.

Blake had served as a Supreme Court Justice for the State of Alabama for eleven years and was an ice demon.

He'd been the one to help get Cassie back into the University of Alabama School of Law, through Evan Haroldson, a water demon attorney in Birmingham. Evan was close friends with the Law School Dean. Once Blake contacted Evan, it was assured that Cassie would get back in.

"Blake, what can I do for you?" I asked while shuffling loose documents on my desk. They needed to be placed back in the file so I could take it home with me; a few things troubled me about the deposition from one of the witnesses.

"I understand your wife worked for your firm for a year or so, and did a good job," Blake said.

"She did," I replied, wondering what this had to do with anything.

"I have a friend in the Public Defender's office in Tuscaloosa, who could use an experienced intern two days a week. It'll get her extra credit for four hours' work on Tuesdays and Thursdays. Money's tight there at the county level, so an intern working for credit would be very welcome."

"I hear that," I agreed, attempting amiability. "Whom should I tell her to contact?"

"Cliff Young," Blake rattled off a phone number. "He's expecting her call."

"I'll pass along the message," I said, although I was seething inside. Usually, requests for favors came along later. This one was up front and didn't involve an infringement on my time.

Cassie, on the other hand, would have her study time cut down by the number of hours a county Public Defender could squeeze out of her. I considered telling the New Prince of Alabama that this was unacceptable. I'd asked for a favor to start with. It wasn't appropriate to start throwing my weight around as Chancellor, now.

Instead, I was left with the unsavory job of telling Cassie she didn't have a choice in the matter. Cursing wouldn't do any good. I did it anyway.

* * *

Cassie

I didn't get Parke's message until after the last class was over for the day. I listened while walking toward the commuter parking lot next to the law center. When mandatory internship with the county Public Defender sunk in, I stopped in my tracks.

I didn't want an internship. I wanted my spare time to study, instead of doing research and running errands for someone who wasn't bothering to ask me what I wanted. Somehow, I got the idea that Parke had pulled strings to get me back in school, and those strings were in the process of being pulled back.

By the time I'd listened to his message the third time, I was opening the door to my car and tossing my book bag onto the passenger seat. Yes, I was having a snit. No, I didn't care that I was having a snit in public.

Parke and I—we'd never had a fight. Not like the one I wanted to have with him over this. I felt like a puppet again; I'd merely changed puppet masters.

"Aunt Shelbie, help me stay calm," I breathed when I felt my body go hotter than it should.

My fire demon wanted out. It wanted to display its anger for the world to see. It took twenty minutes of breathing slowly in my car while the parking lot emptied around me to finally take control. After that, I drove to my apartment, calming my anger every time it threatened to resurface.

* * *

Parke

"How did she take it?"

I'd told my mother about the situation in Alabama, and the fact that I'd been forced to leave a message for Cassie because she'd been in class when I called.

Yes, I should have checked her schedule. I didn't. I worried that it was a subconscious and cowardly move on my part not to tell her in person.

"She responded with a text."

"What did she say?" Mom pulled a pan of rolls from the oven. Dinner was ready and I was supposed to collect Destiny from her room so we could eat.

"One word. Fine."

"Oh, dear."

"What? What's that supposed to mean?" I asked. Sometimes, I believed that women had a secret code that men would never learn. Cassie said fine. That meant okay—right?

"She's mad," Mom said. "You put those rolls on a plate. I'll go get Destiny. I really miss having Louise and Cassie in the house."

Without another word, Mom dropped her apron on the back of a barstool and walked out of the kitchen.

That meant one thing—she was mad, too. If Louise had been here, she'd be mad because Mom and Cassie were mad.

All the women ganging up on the one male in the house.

I figured if Destiny knew, she'd be just as mad as the rest of them.

A part of me—the small voice in the recesses of my mind—told me I deserved it. "Fuck," I muttered. At least it wasn't near the full moon. Something could get smashed if it were.

* * *

Cassie

At least it was too late to call the PD's office when I got home. If it hadn't been, my anger may have overflowed into our conversation.

Better to be as civil as possible, since I'd be working for them. My grade depended on it, now.

"Thanks, Parke," I hissed. Yes, he wasn't on my good list any longer. He could have done research for himself to discover the state of affairs. He could have said *not this time, she's too busy this semester*. He didn't.

Fuck.

With a capital F.

* * *

Parke

"I don't suppose you did any research on this," Mom dropped her tablet onto my lap after dinner. At least Destiny was doing homework in her room so she wouldn't hear.

"No," I said, lifting the tablet.

There it was—the first article, from the *New York Journal Record*, no less.

Alabama judges send poor to prison because they can't afford to pay fines for minor offenses.

"Dammit to hell," I snapped before throwing the tablet across the room and smashing it against the fireplace.

* * *

Cassie

By bedtime, instead of having my head filled with immigration law, I had a head filled with Alabama prison facts and statistics. At near two-hundred-percent capacity, it was a source of shame for the entire state.

Women's prisons had the taint of sexual abuse tacked onto the overcrowded conditions. Getting raped in prison was bad enough. Getting raped in jail because you couldn't afford a two-hundred-dollar fine for a traffic violation? That made my blood boil.

Just when you thought debtor's prisons were a thing belonging in a Dickens novel, the reality of the modern version came along to slap you in the face.

I was expected to go to work for the office whose hands were practically tied when it came to cases like this. Too many people were serving time when they should be sentenced to community service or something else to work off their fines.

Yes, I had to call the Public Defender's office in the morning and sound grateful for such a wonderful opportunity.

Fuck.

Fuck the broken judicial system in Alabama. Fuck the judges, politicians and anyone else who maintained that broken system. This was one of the reasons I'd run away from Alabama to begin with— all the way to Seattle. For me, Ross and what he believed tied directly into the Alabama laws and legal system. So much of it needed fixing; it was difficult to say where it could start—if anybody had a mind to fix it.

Chapter 11

C*assie*

"Yes, I'm the law student who'll intern for your office on Tuesday and Thursday mornings," I informed the clerk.

"We've been trying to get more law students for years," Rob Newbourne, the clerk for the PD's office, replied. "Glad to hear you're on board with us."

I wasn't on board with him or anybody else in Tuscaloosa County's judicial system. I didn't say that, though. "Thank you," I said, as politely as I could.

"When can you come in to fill out paperwork?" We were down to business already.

"I can do that today, or Thursday," I said, silently praying he'd say Thursday.

"Come this afternoon. The PD has some free time between two and three."

"All right. Thank you." I realized I was repeating the polite thank-yous, but didn't know what else to say. I wanted to say a huge *fuck off and leave me alone*, but that wouldn't do.

For the first time, I called Parke a nasty name in my mind. I hadn't heard back from him after I'd sent him the text. He probably thought everything was hunky-dory-okay in Cassie-land.

If he'd known me at all, he'd know that my response of *fine* was as far from fine as you could possibly be.

Three weeks of marriage.

Not enough time to get to know anybody.

* * *

"You know what will happen, don't you?" Binita shook her head as I explained my plight to her. We had dinner and study time at my place as planned, after I'd spent the afternoon filling out paperwork and shaking hands with the few employees at the Public Defender's office.

The Public Defender, Cliff Young, wasn't there; turns out he didn't think it important enough to meet with me after all. Rob Newbourne, the clerk, showed me around instead. I had a small cubicle to work in, a desktop computer, a filing cabinet and a stack of case files on the desk, ready for me to research.

I'd held back from sighing, because it wasn't polite.

"Yeah," I told Binita. "Hours of unpaid research for poor defendants. Fighting to keep people out of debtor's prison, because they're too poor to pay fines," I muttered, slamming open my Immigration Law book. "Which won't make one damn bit of difference, because that's how the Alabama judicial system operates. It won't matter that we're at nearly two-hundred percent capacity in the prisons we have," I added. "They'll go to jail, because they're poor."

"Or not white and poor." Binita said what I hadn't. I'd thought it often enough, though. "When do you start?"

"Thursday morning. I figure I'll be doing research for cases that are already decided in the court's mind," I sighed. I'd never intended

Chapter 11

to go into criminal law. In fact, I wanted to stay as far away from it as possible, especially in this state.

"Yeah," Binita agreed.

* * *

Parke

"He was in Juarez a few days ago," Daniel informed me. "No sign of him now, though."

"Is he nuts? Even if he is demon, nobody in their right mind stays in Juarez," I responded. "I'm a rock demon, and I wouldn't stay there."

"I'm concerned he may be headed for the States," Daniel said. "Or he may be misleading us, so he can disappear deeper into Mexico."

"There's that," I agreed. "You think he's that smart?"

"He kept off your dad's radar long enough," Daniel observed. "No big red flags to speak of."

"Well, Ross wasn't a reliable source when it came to reporting anything from Alabama, you know."

"Understood."

"I have something else," I said.

"What's that?"

"Know anybody who's good at hacking into computers? I don't have Geoffrey's or Annabelle's work e-mail passwords, and I think I need them. For professional reasons, you understand."

"Yeah. I may have somebody. I'll call and ask him to get in touch."

"Good. The earlier the better."

"No problem. I'll get back to hunting for Mort."

"Keep me posted."

"Always do."

Less than an hour later, I had a call from Dave Neville.

"I heard you needed to get into some files," he said after introducing himself and telling me he'd gotten a call from Daniel.

"I do. Two colleagues in the firm died in an unfortunate accident recently," I said. "I don't have access to their work e-mail accounts, and I need that to keep up with their case files."

"Sure. When?" Dave got right to business.

"Tomorrow morning?"

"Sounds good. I'll forward my rates to you."

"That will be fine."

* * *

Cassie

I made it through Wednesday's classes, although my trepidation mounted. I had an unpaid job to go to on Thursday morning. I wondered if the boss would bother to introduce himself then.

I hadn't asked about his caseload; he'd handle the biggest cases while portioning out the rest to his direct employees or those hapless, private attorneys selected by the county to represent indigent defendants.

While I'd worked in Parke's firm in Seattle, I'd seen the top side of court cases; those filing civil suits who could afford attorneys' fees. Here, it was the underbelly, with everything from murder one to petty crimes and the inability to pay fines.

"Everybody chips in for the coffee fund," Rob informed me after I arrived at eight sharp in the county courthouse, ready to begin my four-hour detention.

"How much is expected?" I asked, eyeing the stained coffee cup sitting on my desk. For a moment, I envisioned the previous intern who'd occupied that desk, holding that coffee cup while poring over endless case files.

He probably hadn't washed the cup once.

"Never mind, I'll skip coffee today," I sighed, handing a twenty from my purse to Rob.

"This will do for the first month," Rob grinned. "Bring your own cup—or cups, if you want."

"I will, don't worry," I said. The one on my desk belonged in the trash, in my opinion.

"Good. Cliff's out today; he has court this morning, and appointments this afternoon. You'll probably meet him next week. Get started on those files," he jerked his head toward the pile of folders on my desk. "Write a summary for each—which ones are defensible, which ones probably aren't."

Yes, I stared at him. Everybody was entitled to a defense. Rob sounded as though most of them wouldn't get much in the way of representation.

Fuck.

Fuck Parke for getting me into this mess. I'd have willingly waited to get into a school in Washington State.

Fuck, damn and runny effing crap.

* * *

I ended up spending seven hours at the PD's office instead of four, just to go through all the folders once, make as expert an assessment as possible, and then write up notes, saying that although the case looked hopeless, the defendant deserved a fair trial.

I'd done that seventeen times out of twenty-four. I also pulled up records in a handful of instances, which showed that others— who'd paid for their representation—had gotten off with either light sentences or community service or time served for the same crime.

The difference, of course, was money. Or race and money.

I wrote that down.

I figured I'd be called on the carpet, too, but by that time I was so mad I worried I'd burn down the PD's office.

I stopped by the local pharmacy to get ibuprofen on the way home—it would take a lot of it to get rid of the headache I had.

* * *

Parke

"Here's Annabelle's password," Dave handed a slip of paper to me. "I'm still working on Geoffrey's. His is harder to crack, for some reason."

"Stupid pig," I muttered.

"I heard almost the same thing from one of the secretaries in the office pool," Dave agreed. "She was getting coffee the same time I was," he added. "We struck up a conversation. Geoffrey may have come up."

"You were fishing for hints, weren't you?" My estimation of Dave went up a few points. Daniel was right about him.

"Yeah. The more you know, the better off you are at getting in," he shrugged. "The most inconsequential thing can often be the biggest help."

I unfolded the paper, which held Annabelle's password.

SharkTornado6377.

I wasn't surprised.

"Thanks for this," I waved the slip of paper. "Keep working on Geoffrey's and keep me informed."

"You bet." Dave grinned and walked out of my office.

* * *

Cassie

"How did it go at the PD's office?" Binita asked. She'd brought curried chicken with her that she'd made at home. I put a vegetable stir-fry together and we'd sat at my small dining table to eat and talk.

"That," I mumbled, dipping into the vegetables and dumping a spoonful on my plate. "I spent seven hours there, today. They may be so mad they cancel my internship before I go back next Tuesday."

Chapter 11

"What did you do?" Binita was suddenly interested.

"Rob, the clerk, asked me to make an assessment on twenty-four case files. I was supposed to weed out the hopeless cases from those who deserved a defense. Have you ever heard anything like that in your life? The law says everybody is entitled to a defense."

"So, what did you do?" she repeated her question.

"I wrote out my assessment, saying exactly that," I said. "And then did research on several cases, citing instances where other defendants who'd paid for their representation got off with time served or light sentences or community service."

"Uh-oh." Binita cut into her chicken, keeping her eyes on her plate for several seconds.

"Like I said, internship canceled," I said and speared a slice of zucchini.

"Was that your intention?"

"No. I was just so mad that he'd even insinuate that those people had hopeless cases," I muttered before stuffing the zucchini in my mouth and chewing. "You don't see the big, high profile cases going without proper representation. Look at the worst of the worst—mass murderers and such—they always have a big-name lawyer representing them, most likely for the notoriety and not the money. The rest of them—so many fall through the cracks."

"That's why I want to specialize in tax law," Binita said. "My father wants a lawyer in the family. My older brother is a doctor already. This way, I make my father happy and do something that makes me happy, too."

Staying in Seattle would have made me happy. That wasn't to be; Parke made sure of that. "At least you're not doing a forced march through the Public Defender's office," I grumbled and cut into my chicken.

* * *

"How was school?" I asked. Destiny called Saturday afternoon; she said that she'd been invited to a sleepover to watch movies, eat pizza and mostly not sleep.

"It's fine. Some of the kids are stuck up, but that happens everywhere."

"Wait until they get into the real world," I said. "Most people can't afford to keep their attitudes when they're faced with supporting themselves."

"Shelbie used to say the same thing," Destiny pointed out.

"Yeah. Shelbie taught us a lot," I agreed. Her death still caused my heart to hurt, but I didn't say that to Destiny.

"Have you been to the 'shroom?"

"You really want pizza, don't you?" I teased. "I hear you're getting some at the sleepover."

"Yeah, but it won't be 'shroom pizza."

"I know," I agreed. "No, I haven't been to the 'shroom yet. No time. Maybe I'll go tomorrow for dinner."

"Let me know how good it is," she begged.

"I will. Have fun at your sleepover. I'll be here, not having a sleepover and reading boring law books."

"Poor you," Destiny laughed.

"Yeah. Poor me."

* * *

Parke

"I'm in Matamoros," Daniel announced. "A bartender here says he remembers seeing Mort. Says he got drunk before wandering out of the bar. Local police, whom I had to bribe, by the way, say a murder occurred on the same night."

"Morton's dead?" I couldn't believe that.

"No, but he may be the prime suspect. The police don't know anything about Mort, but the method of the murder doesn't look

Chapter 11

good in my estimation. The victim was strangled, then locked in a freezer."

"You think he was strangled and frozen at the same time, then locked up in a freezer to hide the fact that he was frozen and strangled at the same time?" I leaned back in my study chair and watched the fire in the fireplace for a few seconds.

"That's exactly what I think. This was a restaurant freezer; the place was broken into the night before according to the employees I questioned, and they found the victim in their freezer shortly after."

"There's no reason to hide a victim in plain sight like that—if it were a normal murder, they'd just have dumped the body outside of town," I sighed. "Whether this was Mort or another ice demon we can't say for certain, but it's not looking good for Mort. Think the vic tried to rob him?"

"Possible. If Mort were drunk, the ice demon could have taken over the minute the victim attempted to rob him."

"Killing humans. Not smart," I said.

"At least the human police here have no clue and don't seem to care. Just another body, to them."

"No word on where Mort went after this probable murder?" I asked.

"None. Looks like the last person who recalls seeing him is dead. Matamoros is just a swim away from Brownsville, you know."

"Yeah. I'm familiar with the geography."

"If he were still ice demon, he could have floated across with little effort."

"Or let the Rio Bravo take him toward the gulf, and get out whenever he wanted or thought it safe enough."

"True. I'll widen the search area."

"Good."

* * *

Cassie

The Mellow Mushroom wasn't the same, sitting at a table by myself Sunday evening and eating a sausage and mushroom pizza. Shelbie was gone and Destiny may as well have been on the opposite side of the Earth.

Binita would be having dinner with her family; she always spent weekends at home. I still hadn't gotten a call from Parke—or even a text. An apology may have been accepted within a forty-eight-hour grace period.

That had long since passed.

I wondered what I should do. Shelbie could have given me advice—if she were still alive.

"Fuck you, Ross," I whispered. "I hope your rock demon is melting in hell, wherever that is." I'd forced myself not to drive to Shelbie's house in Birmingham—that would make me cry. As far as I knew, she had no family living and had never mentioned a will, so that meant her estate would be swallowed up by the State of Alabama.

Ross' place, on the other hand—I wouldn't mind seeing it razed. I figured he had somebody waiting to take it over, though. I hoped the new Prince of Alabama had already had a few words with whomever that might be.

Words to the effect of, *your deceased relative committed many crimes. Among those crimes was treason against the Chancellor. We'll be watching every step you make from here on out.*

Ross' antebellum mansion would probably be put on the market; many people would pay plenty to own it. I intended to stay away, in case my fire demon got the urge to burn it down.

Forcing my thoughts away from such morbid subjects, I opened a textbook to read. It wouldn't do to be unprepared for class, if I were called on by the professor.

Chapter 11

* * *

Tuesday morning, I forced myself out of bed at six. I'd paved the way for a drubbing and dismissal from the PD's office, after being brutally honest in my notes. It could be that Cliff Young wouldn't see me—Rob could act in his place, telling me not to come back.

No, I wouldn't be sorry not to go back, but I wasn't looking forward to explaining to Parke and the Law School Dean that I'd blatantly failed on my first day of an internship.

Parke. He still hadn't called. I was conveniently out of his sight and out of his mind. Perhaps he was having second thoughts on our marriage, too. A human divorce could be had easily.

A divorce in the elemental demon world couldn't be had for five, long years, unless abuse or other circumstances could be proven—and the Chancellor would have the last word on that.

Nice pants and a blouse. My hair pulled back and a minimum of makeup, in case I left the PD's office in tears. "Courage, fake and otherwise," I muttered to myself as I gazed at my image in the bathroom mirror.

The morning was in the foggy fifties in my part of Alabama. At least it wasn't raining as I trudged toward my car. I could be studying at the law library. Doing research on case law presented in my Immigration Law text so I'd be prepared for class on Wednesday.

Instead, I was headed toward a lynching—in a figurative way. *The last public execution took place in Kentucky in the thirties*, I reminded myself as I buckled in and started the car.

* * *

"Cliff wants to see you."

Rob didn't waste any time, appearing in my cubicle thirty seconds after I arrived. I hadn't even had time to pull off my jacket and settle it on the back of my chair.

"I'm sure he does," I sighed and followed Rob through the PD's office until we arrived at the closed door, which bore Cliff's name and title.

"She's here," Rob went in ahead of me. As I was behind Rob, I still hadn't seen Cliff, yet.

Until Rob moved out of the way and gestured for me to take a seat in front of Cliff's desk.

"Want to stay for this?" he asked Rob. Cliff Young didn't look as old as I imagined he would. Dark hair and a neatly trimmed beard framed a squarish, handsome face. Dark eyes bored into mine from the moment he could see me clearly.

I drew in a breath and didn't release it for several seconds.

Cliff Young was a werewolf.

Did he know about me? I wanted to panic as I sat in the indicated chair. Werewolves were notorious for sniffing out elementals.

Vampires, too, but this was daylight.

"I do want to stay," Rob said. His voice sounded almost gleeful.

Here it comes, I thought.

"Shut the door, Rob," Cliff Young's voice was low. Even. Commanding.

Rob shut the door, then took the guest chair next to mine.

"I read your notes," Cliff lifted one of the files I'd read.

I steeled myself for the news; I just wasn't sure how it would be delivered.

"Rob and I agree with you," Cliff said, shocking the hell out of me. "We've waited three years—since we first started here, in fact, to hear the truth from one of our interns."

"But," I couldn't force my voice above a whisper.

Chapter 11

"You thought you'd be dismissed immediately for speaking your mind, didn't you?" Cliff almost smiled. "None of our interns have had a spine—until now."

"We're trying to make things better, but we're understaffed, underfunded and held in check by an antiquated legal system," Rob grinned at me. "Not that you need to spread that around," he added.

"Yeah. I—uh—understand that very well," I said. I still hadn't recovered from the shock and felt dizzy as a result.

"To put your mind at ease," Cliff said, "I'm close friends with Blake Donovan and Evan Haroldson. They're the ones who helped get me into this position. They want things changed, too, but it's a slow process." Cliff's leather chair creaked as he leaned back in it. "In case you're wondering, I know what both are, as does Rob. He's a sprite, by the way."

My head jerked in Rob's direction. "What kind?" I whispered. Sprites didn't often interact with the human world.

"I could ask you the same thing," Rob was grinning again.

"You know about me?" I squeaked, turning back to Cliff.

"I know you're an elemental demon. Your husband didn't say what kind when he spoke with Blake, so I can't say what kind you are."

"Wow." My eyes dropped to the area rug that lay beneath my feet. It covered most of the utilitarian tile of Cliff's office.

"Will you tell us? You don't have to—you don't know us well enough to trust us, yet," Rob offered.

"I'll wait," I said, refusing to lift my eyes.

"That's fine," Cliff said. "I'm giving you seven of these cases back. Those are the ones the DA's office won't expect us to mount much of a defense on. Do your best and we'll hit them hard when the cases come to trial."

I lifted my eyes, then. "You can bet on it," I said.

* * *

I stayed six hours instead of four, and only left because my stomach was growling so loudly Rob commented on it.

I hadn't eaten breakfast; I'd felt too queasy. Two cups of coffee in one of Rob's (clean) cups hadn't settled well, either. Food was the best option.

At least I'd made a dent in two cases—the ones coming to trial first. I left the files and my notes with Rob so he could review my work, told him I'd see him on Thursday and walked out, wondering where the nearest fast-food restaurant was.

While I ate a burger in a tiny café not far from University Boulevard, I considered that Parke hadn't been brought up to speed on Cliff or Rob. He knew about Blake Donovan, since he'd approved Blake's election as the new Prince of Alabama. He probably knew about Evan Haroldson, too, but if he'd been told about Cliff, he'd have passed the information along to me.

Perhaps it was by design—Cliff asked for anonymity, perhaps, to see what kind of intern I'd be. *None of our interns have had a spine—until now*, he'd said.

That included his other current intern, who was human and worked on Wednesday and Friday afternoons. I realized I didn't even know his name, yet.

It didn't matter that things appeared to have come out right for me, as far as the internship went. I was still mad at Parke, because he hadn't called.

* * *

Parke

"How's your wife?" Pauline set a fresh cup of coffee on my desk. I blinked at her for a second or two before my brain engaged.

I wasn't used to that question.

Had never had a wife until four weeks ago.

Chapter 11

We'd been together only three of those weeks. I hadn't spoken to her in person since she'd left for Alabama.

No calls had come through Pauline—calls from Cassie, asking to speak with me—her husband.

She was still mad.

Pauline's eyes lit with interest when I hesitated to reply. I had no idea how Cassie was, other than pissed at me.

"She's fine," I said. "Thanks for the coffee."

I didn't like the devious smile that crossed Pauline's face.

I was her boss.

Her skirts had gotten shorter since she'd become my assistant.

I considered pointing her toward the office dress code, but held off for now. Pauline was human and I had no time for her. I hoped she figured that out for herself and soon. "I'm expecting a call from Daniel," I said, hinting that she should get back to her desk.

"I'll put him right through, Parke," Pauline purred and walked away.

"Jeezus," I muttered as the door closed behind her waggling ass.

My phone rang less than a minute later. "Daniel's on line two," Pauline said.

I lifted the handset without replying. "Daniel," I began, "What's up?"

"Big problems," he said. "Two murders, similar to the one in Matamoros."

"Where?"

"One in Corpus Christi, the other in McAllen. On the same night, at roughly the same time."

"Jeezus," I muttered for the second time in less than ten minutes.

* * *

"Mom, I have no idea," I tossed out a hand in frustration. Here I was, standing in my mother's kitchen while she finished pulling meatloaf from the oven, telling her my troubles regarding Morton King.

"You should tell Cassie you're having him tracked and investigated," Mom said, taking hot pads off her hands and slapping them on the counter.

"But," I began.

"You haven't talked to her, have you?"

"You said yourself she was mad at me. What am I supposed to do about that?"

"Call her and clear the air. Let her say what's on her mind. She was railroaded into that internship, and deserves to complain to somebody about it. That somebody should be her husband, don't you think?"

"But what if she gets upset that I've sent Daniel and two rock demon enforcers after her father?"

"You should have told her—and Destiny—before you sent Daniel. It's your duty to uphold the law, even when a family member is involved."

"He's the only family they have left," I sighed and turned away from my mother's accusing stare. "I'll probably end up ordering his execution."

"Oh, dear," Mom whispered behind me.

* * *

Cliff Young

Rob and I stood inside the greenhouse I'd built on my property three years earlier, when I'd first come to Tuscaloosa to take the Public Defender's job.

Chapter 11

Only Rob knew that I'd been asked by Blake Donovan to take the job. Blake, Evan Haroldson and I wanted to make changes in the judicial system, but there was some corruption to root out, first.

Rob was an earth sprite, and could do amazing things as long as he stood directly on the Earth itself. The greenhouse had a floor of grass and nothing else beneath it. Every time Rob met me here, my roses bloomed profusely for weeks afterward, no matter what season it was.

"I wish she'd told us what kind of elemental she is," Rob pursed his lips as he touched the stem of an orchid. I'd gotten the damn thing as a Christmas gift from an acquaintance and it was attempting suicide in my greenhouse.

With Rob's hands on it, it would be forced into a cheerful spate of bloom and growth.

"Even if she's a water demon, that could help us if we needed it," Rob said.

"I hesitate to tell her we're dealing with this much corruption," I pointed out. "Money is coming in, and that's what most of them are concerned about. It doesn't matter that the money to keep them in their elected office comes from gambling, drugs and who knows what else, or that the criminals are disguising themselves as a corporation operating privatized prisons, all of which they're busy pushing through the legislature. Not just in this state, but across the country."

"From their slick representation, it all looks good—reduce the overcrowding conditions in state prisons, all while turning a profit and gaining access to the best criminal minds the country has to offer." Rob never minced words. He and I—we'd been working together for nearly twenty years. I'd saved his life; he was determined to repay the debt.

"If the politicians weren't so busy taking money to fatten their coffers, they might wonder where Corvina Corrections came from to begin with."

"True. We have to find the one behind Corvina Corrections, first, before we get too crazy about pointing fingers."

"Or the ones," Rob shook his head. "I was hoping Ross Diablo was the one. I wasn't sad to hear he died."

"His relatives died with him, I checked," I agreed. "You know our new girl was engaged to Ross? Ran away from him, too, before he could get his hands on her. Smart move on her part."

"How did you find that out?"

"Blake. No idea where he got it, but says it's gospel."

"Interesting," Rob removed his hands from the orchid. Already it looked perky and willing to grow in its new pot. "If we find the bastards behind all this, we may need Cassie's help to take them down."

"I hope she's not the squeamish type, then," I growled.

"You need to tell her she may be involved in extracurricular activities—before they happen," Rob advised.

Chapter 12

Cassie

"So, did they send you packing?" Binita asked. We were having chicken tacos for dinner; it was something easy to make while discussing classes and case law.

"No." I dumped a tablespoon of chicken taco meat in a shell before adding lettuce, cheese and tomato. "Things turned out to be better than I thought. They didn't yell and actually gave me seven cases to research so we can mount a decent defense."

"Outstanding," Binita crunched into a taco. "Will you sit with the attorney on the case?"

"We didn't discuss that," I said.

"I hope they allow it—wouldn't it be cool to sit at the table and pass notes to the attorney? You could make a big difference in the case."

"I hope I make a big difference anyway, whether I'm at the trial or not," I said. "In some cases, I just hope the judge listens to reason and doesn't push the maximum sentence onto a couple of the defendants. There are extenuating circumstances."

"Good luck with that," Binita took another bite.

"Yeah."

* * *

Wednesday, I was called on in class. It made me more than grateful that Binita and I had discussed the reading material and associated cases the night before. At least the professor appeared satisfied with my answers; any preparation was better than standing up in class and admitting you weren't prepared.

It felt like a small victory, at least, when I made my way to the apartment. I considered calling Parke, too, since I hadn't heard from him. Unless there was a trial date, he'd be at the office since Seattle was two hours earlier.

No, I hadn't expected a woman to answer the phone, or for her to sound as disinterested as she did.

"He's out," she said. I didn't recognize her voice.

"Will you tell him I called, then?"

"Of course."

She hung up before I could say anything else, which left me fuming. I'd never handled his calls like that. Trust him to hire somebody who could be Annabelle's twin sister—that's how she'd sounded over the phone.

Well, I hadn't talked to Kate lately. I dialed her number next.

"Cassie," Kate sounded happy to hear from me.

"Is Parke in court today?" I asked.

"I don't think so. Why?"

"I just called his office. His new assistant said he was out."

"He could have gone for a cup of coffee," Kate said.

"True. I asked her to tell him I called, but she hung up before I could leave a message."

"That doesn't sound professional. I'll ask him about it when he gets home."

Chapter 12

"Thanks. How's Destiny?"

"She's doing well. Today is one of her training days—Bea says she's learning rapidly and already has a tight leash on her ice demon."

"Great. That's so cool. So to speak."

"She's enjoying her lessons, and she found new friends at the private school she's attending."

"She told me about the sleepover."

"I don't think they slept more than five minutes," Kate chuckled. "Stayed up to watch movies and had cold pizza for breakfast."

"Good times," I agreed. Cold pizza for breakfast had been a staple in my first two years of law school. "Well, I should go—I got called on in class today. I was barely prepared, and I've been reading everything I could get my hands on since I got here."

"At least you were able to answer—that's wonderful," Kate said. "I knew you'd get right back into it; you're so focused when you work."

"Yeah." I didn't say it, but Parke was so focused on everything else that he'd forgotten about me. Hadn't called or written, other than the text telling me I had an internship to go to that I hadn't chosen for myself.

If Cliff and Rob hadn't turned out to be allies, in a way, I'd be complaining my head off to Kate, because I needed somebody to listen who'd fully understand. Even then, I couldn't unload about Parke—he was her son.

"Look, I really have to go—wish I could come home to one of your meals at least one day a week."

"Perhaps during spring break?" Kate asked.

"Yeah. That sounds good. Bye, Kate. It was really nice talking to you."

I ended the call and felt like crying. Not once did Kate say that Parke missed me or even thought about me.

That was the way things worked with me; I was used until I wasn't needed, then shunted aside. I knew about several of Ross' women while we were supposedly engaged. Some of them had been human. A handful were not.

Was that how it would be with Parke, too?

I'd never asked about former girlfriends while he worked in D.C. At the time, I felt it would be prying. Now, I wished I knew something about his life before. As it was, I didn't know any private investigators, and certainly none in the D.C. area.

"You're fucked no matter what, Cassie King," I informed myself as I opened the fridge to find something for dinner. "And not in the traditional sense, either."

* * *

Things were subdued when I walked into the county courthouse on Thursday, heading for the PD's office.

Something had happened, that was a given. I just didn't know what. "The boss wants to see you in his office," Rob said.

For the second time, I followed Rob straight back to Cliff's office, passing an attorney and someone from the Sheriff's Department in the hall on the way.

Questions bubbled in my confused brain, but I didn't want to look or sound stupid, so I kept my mouth shut.

Rob and I took the same chairs we had last time, after Rob closed the door behind us.

"Bad news, I'm afraid," Cliff said right away. "A District Judge in Birmingham was shot and killed early this morning. Everybody's on edge—there was another shooting attempt with a judge in Mobile."

Chapter 12

"You think the two are connected?" I asked. Yes, I was attempting to make sense out of new (and troubling) information. "Who?" I added another question to the first one before Cliff could answer.

"Two judges who don't want privatization of our prison system," Rob said. "Or didn't, at least in one case. The other has a bodyguard from the local Sheriff's Department, now."

"I didn't realize people were still kicking that idea around," I chewed my lower lip for a moment.

"It never went away," Cliff said. "They say they can house prisoners cheaper than the state."

"I know some states are already on board with privatization," I said.

"There are problems," Rob offered. "Nobody is connecting the dots on this, yet; still too early in the investigation and they don't have many leads on the shooters involved. I want both of you to drive to Birmingham with me this morning, so we can talk to a few people and poke around."

"But Birmingham is out of our jurisdiction," I pointed out before snapping my mouth shut. Nobody knew that better than the Tuscaloosa County Public Defender. "You knew him—the judge who died," I sighed and rubbed my forehead.

"Yes. Worked with him for several years when I was in the Jefferson County PD's office. Had dinner with him and his wife too many times to count." Cliff's dark eyes didn't indicate his pain, but it came through in his voice.

"Somebody shot him when he opened the door to take the dog out this morning," Rob said when Cliff fell silent. "That means they've been watching him—for a while."

Something else I hadn't considered occurred to me, then.

Cliff was a werewolf. Perhaps he could scent the killer. I jerked my head in his direction and blinked at him for several seconds.

"The light just came on for our intern," Cliff lifted his suitcoat from his chair and slipped into it. "We'll be gone most of the day. You can study in the car," he informed me and shouldered his way past Rob and me.

I was grateful I'd charged my phone and tablet before coming to work; I'd need both if I were to get any work done while riding in the back of a car.

* * *

Birmingham is roughly sixty miles from Tuscaloosa—not a long drive but I managed to get some reading done for class the following day. "This is it," Cliff slowed down while driving through an affluent neighborhood in Birmingham.

Lifting my head to gaze out the window, I saw the house—with yellow crime scene tape still flapping in the January breeze. Two Birmingham police officers stood guard at the perimeter. Cliff was stopped—he showed his credentials and was waved through; the officer recognized him.

After parking the car, Cliff led us toward the back door, where another police officer stood. We were allowed inside—the judge's wife sat at a breakfast nook table, a pile of tissues near her elbow and still sniffling as she spoke with two detectives.

"Laura, I came as soon as I could," Cliff took one of her hands and patted it.

"Oh, my God, Cliff, please tell me this is all a dream," Laura Wembley broke into fresh tears.

Cliff took a chair next to hers and pulled her against him. "I'm so sorry," he mumbled as she wept on his shoulder. "So, so, sorry."

"Come with me," Rob whispered and steered me away from the kitchen. In moments, we were through the back door again.

"She's upset," Rob waved at the officer guarding the door. "We just need to step outside for a minute or two. Come with me," Rob hissed under his breath and pulled me toward a corner of the fenced backyard.

"What?" I hissed back at him.

"I need to take my shoes off, and I don't want anybody else to see that," he whispered. "You have to block me from view while I put my feet on the ground. Hold onto my hand, so it'll look like I'm comforting you."

I blinked. Rob was an earth sprite. He had to connect with the ground beneath his feet for whatever he intended to do. As requested, I held his hand and stood between him and the officer at the back door, while Rob slipped out of his Loafers.

He wasn't wearing socks.

I wanted to ask what he was doing, or how it would help, but didn't. I was supposed to be upset, after all. I ducked my head and watched as Rob's toes dug into the grass beneath them.

Maybe he would tell me later.

Maybe he wouldn't.

Sprites were notoriously close-mouthed about their talent and abilities. If I could bet on the situation, though, I'd bet that Cliff would know soon enough.

After ten minutes, during which Rob kept his eyes on his feet and I hugged myself with one arm in the cool morning air in Birmingham, Rob let my other hand drop, slid his feet into his Loafers and lifted his eyes to mine.

I almost gasped. His eyes were so pale a blue they were nearly white. I suppose he knew what my expression meant; he pulled a pair of Wayfarers out of a pocket and slipped them on.

"We'll go back to the car. I'll text Cliff when we get there," he muttered and pulled me toward the back gate.

He and I waited in the car another half-hour before Cliff opened the driver's side door and slid gracefully onto the leather seat. "They're taking her to her brother's house—he lives just outside town," Cliff sighed as he started the car. "What did you find out?"

"Shooter climbed a tree two houses over," Rob said. "I can show you."

"Let me call Detective James, first," Cliff said, steering the car away from the curb. "I'll put him onto this, and there'll be a proper trail of evidence after that."

My breath stopped for several seconds. Rob was more than talented, if he could get that sort of information just by digging his toes into the ground.

"It doesn't work if the shooting was done from a section of concrete," Rob said, answering my unasked question. "We're fortunate the perp climbed a tree. I was hoping that was the case, since initial evidence says Judge Wembley was shot from a high angle."

* * *

Detective Kent James met us at a coffee shop half a mile away from Judge Wembley's home. I watched in fascination as Rob drew a map of the area surrounding the judge's house and indicated the tree the shooter climbed to kill the judge.

"I'll handle this," Detective James said, stuffing the drawing in a pocket. "Wish you could be there with us to help sniff this out, but it could be questioned later."

Like Cliff, Kent James was a werewolf. That meant he knew everybody at our small table was a supernatural. Before, I'd hidden away from everybody—for a reason.

Ross had werewolf friends.

Shady, werewolf friends.

Chapter 12

I'd wanted to stay away from anybody who could be linked in any way to him. I hoped sincerely that Kent James wasn't on Ross' payroll, because I suspected that Ross had plenty of people on his payroll.

People who'd look the other way when he broke human (and other) laws. How else could Ross have escaped the notice of the Chancellor for so long? He and Jasper Bridges, the former Prince of Alabama, too. They'd conspired to take the Chancellor's position. What the now-deceased Prince hadn't known, however, was that Ross wanted the Chancellor's position for himself.

He'd intended to kill Jasper, once the Christmas war was won.

They'd both lost and were dead as a result. Parke was still in charge and his rock demon was still angry enough about the attempted coup to crush anyone who thought to follow in Ross' footsteps.

That's why we hadn't made love after the war; he said his demon was still processing everything and he didn't want to let it out until it had time to consider everything and calm down.

I'd been disappointed, but I'd slept in the adjoining bedroom of Parke's suite. He hadn't even wanted the human version of sex and that only made things worse, from my perspective.

"There's something else," Detective James drummed his fingers on the polished wood table.

"What's that?"

"Diablo's house was broken into yesterday. No sign of anything taken, but since there wasn't anybody there to say whether something was stolen, we can't say for sure."

"Who reported the break-in?" Cliff asked while I held my breath and attempted to behave normally.

"A neighbor driving by on his way into town," Kent shrugged. "I was on my way there when you called. Headed that way when we're done here."

"I'd like to go with you, if you don't mind," Cliff said.

No, I begged silently. I never wanted to set foot in Ross' house again.

"No problem. Blake asked me to check on it—as a personal favor—and report anything we find to him. I can put somebody else on this," he patted the pocket that held Rob's drawing. "It'll be a good thing—to separate me from conveniently finding the tree," he added.

* * *

Kent James took ten minutes to make a phone call to a colleague about the tree on the edge of a neighbor's property, then asked us to ride in his unmarked car to Ross' mansion.

I worked to keep myself from hyperventilating in the back seat while he and Cliff talked in the front.

"Something wrong?" Rob lifted an eyebrow at me when I twisted my fingers together.

"N-no," I stuttered before pulling my tablet from my purse and pretending to read. My insides felt so shaky they could have been made of gelatin. I needed a friend. Someone to confide in. I needed Parke more right then than I'd ever needed him before.

Terrible memories threatened.

Memories of Ross handing me to some of his—what almost happened that night terrified me, still.

No, they hadn't raped me.

They wanted to.

Ross decided to teach me a lesson after I'd had the temerity to disagree with him. He'd watched while they'd torn my clothing away

Chapter 12

and I screamed. That was the last time I'd been to his mansion, less than a year and a half before.

Yes, I was grateful he was dead.

More than grateful. Shortly after, I'd asked Aunt Shelbie for help getting Destiny away and then ran for my life from Alabama.

Parke didn't know anything about this.

I wasn't about to tell him now. I'd left a message for him—with his assistant and with his mother.

He hadn't bothered to call back.

"We're here," Rob tapped my arm. I jumped and stifled a shriek.

* * *

Cliff Young

"She doesn't want to go in," Rob whispered. Cassie hung back while Kent unlocked the front door of Ross Diablo's antebellum mansion.

"You think something happened to her here?" I asked, keeping my voice soft.

"I do. I don't know whether to force the issue or let her stay outside."

"Bring her in. We should tell her we know about the forced engagement."

"All right, but don't say I didn't warn you," Rob said.

* * *

Cassie

Rob came to get me when I hung back. I wanted to refuse to go inside, but forced my feet to take the steps. I kept reminding myself that the house was empty and Ross was dead as I walked reluctantly through the front door.

Everything looked the same; the expansive, marble-tiled foyer and twin staircases greeted me as I walked inside. So many women would have agreed to marry Ross just from a peek inside his home.

They'd have fallen at his feet if they'd caught a whiff of his offshore bank accounts. I knew what he was the moment I'd been shoved in front of him when I was fourteen. I'm sure a down payment had changed hands between him and my father shortly after.

One year later, my mother was missing. A part of me understood she was dead, but I didn't say it—Destiny wanted to believe she was alive, so I left her with that illusion.

She knows now, I reminded myself.

"Everything looks like it belongs where it is—no dust rings or anything, to show something's missing," Kent said, breaking the silence. On the left side, the grandfather clock ticked.

I remembered that clock and the distinctive, clicking noise it made.

Panic rose and almost closed my throat. "Somebody's been here," I choked out before the floor burst open with a roar at our feet, flinging shards of tile everywhere. My vision was blurred by splintered wooden beams and debris at first; I was knocked backward and halfway through the front door when the rock demon emerged from the hidden cellar beneath the house, bellowing his fury at our presence.

Two werewolves—Kent and Cliff in werewolf form, were covered in marble dust as they growled and backed away from an angry rock demon.

Where was Rob?

I blinked—it felt as if it took forever to blink once and then twice—Rob lay on the antique wood floor halfway inside the right front parlor. He was unconscious, or at least I hoped he was unconscious.

He could be dead, a small voice informed me.

The rock demon swung a massive arm, sweeping one of the werewolves out of his path and into what remained of the wall to the left. The other werewolf leapt at him, only to be batted aside like a Ping-Pong ball hit by a baseball bat.

"No," I shouted, scrambling to my feet as the rock demon crunched across what was left of the floor, heading toward the first werewolf, who was struggling to his feet.

The rock demon turned toward me, huffed out a huge, deafening breath that blew dust everywhere, determined I wasn't a threat to him and went after the werewolf again. It wasn't until I'd leapt across the chasm the rock demon created in the floor that I realized I was on fire.

Rocky had his back turned to me and was reaching for the wolf again when I landed on his back, my prelim skipped over in favor of my full, fire demon.

He roared loud enough to shake half the ceiling down on us, which caught fire the moment it touched any part of me.

"Get them out," I shouted to the half-dazed werewolf. To my ears, it sounded as if I were roaring as loudly as the rock demon, who was now screaming beneath my weight and my fire.

I didn't have time to determine what happened after that—the rock demon went into survival mode and leapt as high as his melting legs could take him, only to turn and fall backward in mid-leap, so his weight would land on top of mine.

By that time, the front half of Ross' mansion was engulfed by a thundering, insatiable fire.

The rock demon and I fell past the ground level of the mansion, into the hole he'd created when he burst through the floor. We landed hard on the stone floor beneath, but I wasn't the one whose breath was knocked out of me—the rock demon was melting fast. I had to stick to him as well as I could to destroy enough of him that he'd die.

I can't say why I wanted to destroy him—something in my brain insisted on it. My fire demon wouldn't be satisfied until he was dead, so I held on, like a burr caught in a cow's tail.

He rolled across the wide cellar, my flames lighting the depths of it eerily while he struggled to loosen me from his body. His roar had weakened, though, when he rolled again after hitting a far wall and switching directions.

I hadn't known this cellar was here.

Ross certainly had.

The rock demon and I crashed into shelf after shelf, while boxes, jars and whatever else had been piled upon them fell in a deafening heap of destruction and flying sparks, before burning around us. Yes, I should have been concerned that we were destroying evidence, but my goal hadn't been met as yet.

This one had attacked us.

He may have killed Rob, too. I had no idea as to the status of the werewolves. All I knew was that this one wasn't getting away— not if I had anything to say about it. The rock demon practiced his version of stop, drop and roll as we took another trip across the cellar, crashing into more shelves as we went.

These shelves held wine bottles.

How did I know that?

The bloom of flame and subsequent explosions were almost earsplitting afterward. The rock demon made one more attempt to dislodge me as we came to rest against another wall; this time he strained to elbow me off his back.

His body was turning into a river of molten rock beneath me, and still I held on.

Chapter 12

Fire knows fire, the words flitted through my brain. *Fire melts rock.*

I heard sirens in the distance and there was nothing left of my adversary before my fire demon rose from the cellar floor and climbed out of Ross' burning mansion. Turning humanoid and shivering in my nakedness, I walked toward the car where an injured Rob, Kent and Cliff waited.

Chapter 13

*C*assie

I huddled in the back of Kent's vehicle, wrapped in Cliff's suit jacket while he, Kent and Rob talked to police and the fire department. I had no idea what tale they were telling and didn't care.

I wondered briefly if Parke would come bail me out if I were taken to jail for burning Ross' mansion to the ground.

Yes, I'd wanted to do that very thing, but never intended to make my fantasy a reality. I had no idea, too, whom I'd destroyed after he'd attacked all of us. Yes, the shock of it was setting in, and I trembled inside Cliff's jacket.

All my clothes had burned away the moment I became fire demon. It was something else to explain to the police and fire department, I'm sure—that yes, my clothes had been burned off me. No, I had absolutely no burns on my body to be treated.

"Thank goodness that's over," Rob settled himself on the seat beside me. He held one arm against his chest as if it pained him.

"Is it broken?" I asked. My voice quavered on the question.

"You're going into shock," Rob said. "Let me see if I can speed things up outside." He opened the door and was gone again.

"Sorry," Cliff slid onto the front passenger seat while Rob took his seat again right behind Cliff. "Kent will be here in a few. Hang on, all right? Damn, if you hadn't come with us, we'd all be smashed flat and buried somewhere."

"H-how do you know that?" The trembling in my voice was now worse.

"Because that, dear intern, was Ross' brother, Ray."

"H-he h-has a br-other?"

"Missing for many years, because he committed murder and skipped town," Cliff said. "After a while, Ross reported him dead."

"Yo-your arm is broken, isn't it?" I accused Rob, who hadn't answered my question—he'd allowed Cliff to talk.

"Baby doll, it would have been a hell of a lot worse if you hadn't jumped Ray when you did," Rob turned away to stare out the window. Kent had returned and the vehicle was now in motion, taking us back to Birmingham.

"B-but you need help," I hissed at him.

"As do you. Kent's taking us to a healer now."

"Cassie, how did you know someone was there?" Cliff asked. "At Ross' house?"

"Th-the gra-andfather clock," I ducked my head and hugged myself tighter. "It h-has t-to be w-wound once a w-week. R-ross h-has b-been dead f-for s-several."

I hated to admit that I knew anything about Ross—before or after his death. I certainly hadn't known he had a brother.

"We know about the forced engagement," Cliff said, turning back in his seat. "Stop worrying about that shit. You were a hero today. You saved all of us."

Chapter 13

"L-like th-that'll m-make a d-difference in class t-tomorrow," I muttered.

"Yeah. Sorry about that," Cliff sighed.

* * *

Parke

"Blake Donovan is on line one," Pauline informed me.

"What the fuck does he want now?" I mumbled before lifting the handset. "Parke Worth, here, your honor," I answered.

"There's been an incident here," Blake said right away. "Your wife was suffering from shock afterward, so she's been sedated."

"What the hell?" I was on my feet in an instant, upset and blazingly angry at the same time.

"Ray Diablo, Ross' brother, attacked her, two werewolves and an earth sprite at Ross' old place. She took him down, but she and the others needed medical care afterward. Ross' mansion is pretty much a total loss, but that's understandable, under the circumstances."

"What the bloody hell happened?" I demanded. Donovan might be an Alabama Supreme Court Justice, but right then, I was the Chancellor of all things paranormal, which included his broad, bench-sitting ass.

"I asked Cliff, her boss, and his clerk, who's an earth sprite, to go with one of our werewolf detectives out to Ross' place. It was broken into two days ago," he snapped. "Your wife had come to Birmingham with those two, to look into the District Judge's murder early this morning. She was with them when they went to Ross' place. Ross' brother, who was listed as dead fifteen years ago, attacked all of them. Your wife took him down before he could kill her and the others."

"There was a District Judge murdered?"

"Early this morning, just before dawn. I'm surprised you haven't heard."

"I've been tied up in court today," I mumbled an excuse. "Where's Cassie? Is she safe?"

"As safe as we can keep her for the moment; she'll miss class tomorrow, at the healer's insistence. I'll keep you posted on her condition," Donovan said and hung up.

That's when I remembered that Mom said Cassie had called, and that she'd also left a message with Pauline, which I'd never received.

"Pauline, can you come in here for a moment?" I tapped the intercom and asked as evenly as I could. Yes, I was pissed, and somebody was about to go down for it.

"Yes, Parke?" Pauline was dressed in a see-through blouse today, making sure that I could see the black, lacy bra she wore beneath it.

"Sit down," I indicated one of my guest chairs.

She sat, crossing her legs as seductively as she could.

"Comfortable?" I asked.

"Yes, Parke."

"Good. You're fired for not telling me my wife called. Clear out your things and leave before I call security."

* * *

Dalton King

"Our mole was fired in Seattle," I informed Morton. "I don't have anybody else lined up to apply for that position, so we'll have to have his movements tracked from outside."

"That bitch," Morton growled. "I knew she'd try to get in bed with him. I told you it was a mistake."

"How was I to know he wouldn't want sex with her? The opportunity was too good if he did—she could get us inside information instead of waiting on phone calls from Daniel Frank to find out where he is. He has a shield nobody can see through, so we have to have reliable information from another source, unless we want to end up dead."

"And now that source is gone. You should have told her not to do her usual thing—this isn't one of those cases where we want to destroy somebody's reputation. This was for information to keep us alive."

"Look, it's done. At least he and Cassie are separated, now."

"We don't have an army or the resources that Ross did. We can't make a frontal assault against the Chancellor. We have to be more devious than that."

"Have you heard from Ray?" I asked.

"Not since two days ago. He was supposed to get into Ross' house, get what we needed and then get the hell out. No word on any of that."

"Call me if you hear from him. We need that information, and soon."

* * *

Parke

I was in the middle of reserving a seat on a plane headed for Birmingham when Dave walked into my office.

He looked pale. A flash drive was set on the corner of my desk, after which he backed away as if it burned him to touch it.

"What the hell is that?" I asked, nodding toward the flash drive.

"Something I didn't want to see, and something you probably need to know," he said. "I'll send an invoice for my work, and I hope you never need my services again."

"Look, today isn't a good day to play twenty questions. Tell me what this means," I demanded.

"It involves Fli-Bi-Net—and the software they stole," Dave sighed. "I'm afraid they'll show up at my door and arrest me, now."

"Who will arrest you?"

"The feds," he said and turned to go.

"Fucking hell," I breathed as I watched him disappear down the hall leading to my office. At least Cassie was unconscious and wouldn't know I was ignoring her to look at information contained on a flash drive.

* * *

Cassie

"Cassie, wake up. You're having a bad dream."

Rob's voice.

Swimming through thick unconsciousness to open my eyes was hard. Once that difficult task was accomplished, I had to blink several times to bring Rob's face into focus.

"Broken." I frowned at the sling on his arm.

"It's not broken now—just really sore," he frowned back at me. It took several seconds for me to realize he was doing it to tease me.

"Where are we?" I asked. I couldn't recall where Kent had driven us, or how I'd ended up in a bed.

"Between Birmingham and Tuscaloosa. New Quinlan."

"Never heard of it." I turned my head to stare at the ceiling.

"Because it's not an official place," he said. "A few supernaturals live here. One of them is a very talented healer."

"Awesome."

"The last person who said awesome to me was fired from the office two days later."

"Fire me. Please," I turned back to him.

"Not a chance, and you can say awesome whenever you want. I'd be a sprite sandwich if you hadn't saved our asses."

"How come you're not all groggy?" I asked, doing my best not to slur the words.

"Because I only had a broken arm. You had a meltdown. So to speak."

"Funny. What about Cliff? And Kent?"

"Both fine, although Kent may have a few patches of fur missing from his wolf come the full moon."

"My fault?"

"No. Mine, actually. He came back in to pull my ass out of your fire."

"Sorry." I covered my face with a shaky hand. "What time is it?"

"After eleven. You're not going to class tomorrow—the healer says so."

"But," I attempted to argue.

"His honor, Judge Donovan, also insists. He says that nobody will give you grief over it, either. He knows Evan, who knows the Dean. You'll be fine."

"Binita," I whispered in alarm. I just remembered that she and I had a study date.

"Her call came through. Cliff told her you'd been injured in an automobile accident and was under observation at a Birmingham facility. He told her she could see you Friday, when you came home. You can call her yourself if you want."

"It's too late to call tonight," I sighed. "Tell Cliff thanks for covering for me. I'll call her tomorrow, when classes are over," I mumbled.

"Good. That's taken care of. Are you hungry? Want something to eat?"

"I am hungry, I think," I said.

"I'll find something for you," he grinned and rose from his bedside chair. "Cliff is back in Tuscaloosa, so he can go to work tomorrow. We'll straggle in later."

"Straggle. Probably a good word for how I look," I closed my eyes.

"You're fine. Stop worrying about nonsense," Rob said and walked out of the room.

* * *

Parke

Cassie's phone rang five times before the call was answered. A male voice said hello.

"Where's Cassie?" I demanded.

"She's asleep again. I assume this is her husband, the Chancellor?"

"Who the hell are you?" I demanded.

"Robin Newbourne, earth sprite," he replied. "You've been ignoring your wife, Chancellor. It upsets her."

"How the fuck do you know that?" I almost shouted.

"When I stand upon the Earth, I know a great many things. Especially if I reach out to touch the one in question. She thinks you don't want her. If you don't want her, at least have the courtesy of saying so. It's causing her a great deal of pain and anxiety."

"Fuck," I breathed. "Look, when will she be awake? I'd be on my way there if an emergency hadn't cropped up here."

"Right. I'll be sure to tell her you called and said that."

"I'll call her in the morning," I said. "Without fail."

"I'll tell her that, too. Make sure it doesn't turn into a lie, Chancellor."

* * *

Cassie

Chapter 13

I saw the healer for the first time after Rob brought clothes for me in the morning. He then pulled me from the bedroom where I'd slept and into a kitchen down the hall.

"Yes, I'm a half-demon," she said, indicating two chairs at the small table. "The other half, as you can probably guess, is were-leopard. Georgina Small," she held out her hand.

"You're one of the rare ones," I whispered, staring longer than was necessary at the dark, spotted patterns that covered her skin.

"Some people don't see it that way," she hmmphed and set a plate of bacon on the table. "Some think I'm a mutant."

"I don't think that. Thank you for your help," I said.

"I hear you're a fire demon. Also rare," Georgina smiled for the first time. "How do you like your eggs?"

"Scrambled sounds great," I replied, realizing I was hungry.

"Mine, too," Rob said. "Need help?"

"You sit right there," Georgina pointed a finger at Rob. "I'll do breakfast since you're banged up. I'll take barbecue sometime, when you pay me back."

"You're on," Rob grinned and helped himself to bacon.

"Georgina, I can pay, too," I said.

"You've paid enough," Georgina said while cracking eggs into a bowl. "You saved Kent, Rob and Cliff. That's more than enough. Call me Gina," she added. "All my friends do."

* * *

Parke

I had someone from the secretary pool sitting at my assistant's desk when I walked in. "Mr. Worth, I'm Jonathan Wrigley," he held out a hand.

"Jonathan?" I asked. "How long have you worked here?"

"A year and a half," he said. He'd stood to greet me when I walked in, and I shook hands with him. Nearly as tall as I am, Jon had a thin build and light-brown hair.

"Are you efficient?" I asked.

"As efficient as possible," he replied. His handshake was firm enough, although he expected to be sent back to the pool the second I found a female to sit in my assistant's chair. He was also telling the truth about his efficiency.

"Ever been written up while employed here?"

"No, sir."

"Good. Get Frank Hillman on the phone and make sure I'm not disturbed while I'm talking to him," I said.

"Of course, Mr. Worth."

"You married?" I nodded at the ring he wore.

"Yes. My husband works as an administrator for a nursing facility."

"May I call you Jon?" I asked.

"Most people do." He smiled for the first time since we'd met.

"Great. Jon, I'm going to hire you temporarily as my personal assistant. If I find your work satisfactory, you'll have a permanent position, if you want it."

"I so want to hug you right now, but that would be awkward," Jon grinned. "Is there anything I can do for you, other than seeing you're not disturbed?"

"If my wife calls, let me know. She's the only thing I want to be disturbed about. Wait, that didn't come out the way I wanted," I winced.

"I know what you meant," Jon waved off my gaffe. "If she calls, I'll let you know."

"Thanks. Welcome to the assistant's position. If you bring me a coffee, I'll toss in a bonus for your first paycheck."

Chapter 13

"Coffee coming right up," he said and took off toward the break room.

* * *

Cassie

"Your husband called after you went back to bed last night," Rob told me as we climbed into a borrowed car to drive home. "He said to tell you he called and that he'd be here if something important hadn't cropped up. I didn't want to tell you in front of Gina, in case it upset you."

"It's fine. At least he called." I huddled into the jacket Rob found for me. I had no idea where the clothes I wore came from and was afraid to ask. They fit well enough and were nice; I just wasn't sure whether I should offer to pay for them or wash them and hand them back to whoever loaned them to me.

"Are you going to call your husband back?"

"I don't know." It made me uncomfortable that Parke found something else more important than his wife.

You've been married for about a month, I reminded myself.

"You should probably call him back."

"I'll call him back." I twisted my fingers together. What was I supposed to say to Parke? That I'd gone into shock after killing Ross' brother—the one I didn't know about? Did he know Ross had a brother? Why wasn't I told?

"Look, I didn't mean to make you uncomfortable," Rob said. "Just—call him when you get a minute, all right?"

It took half an hour to get back to the courthouse in Tuscaloosa, another fifteen minutes to drive my car back to my apartment.

By that time, I wanted nothing more than to huddle on my bed, wrap myself in blankets and hope all my troubles would stop troubling me.

My troubles concerning Parke wouldn't go away until I called him and straightened things out. I dialed his office number while sitting at the kitchen table and listened while it rang three times.

"Parke Worth's office, Jonathan speaking."

I knew that voice. He and I had started working at Gruber, Taylor and Worth the same week. Parke would have to change the name of the firm, now that Gruber and Taylor were both dead. "Jon?" I said, sounding surprised at the familiar voice on the other end of the call.

"Cassie?"

"Yeah, uh, Parke tried to call me last night. I'm calling him back." I wanted to ask why he'd answered the phone instead of Pauline, but I didn't.

"He said to let him know immediately if you called. Hold on, I'll let him know. He's talking to Frank Hillman on another line."

"How's that case coming along?" I asked.

"Can't say, just started working for Mr. Worth this morning. Hang on, he wants to talk to you."

"Oh. Okay."

* * *

Parke

While Frank Hillman was still trying to digest what I'd told him, Jon informed me that Cassie was on the phone. "Frank, I need to get this call," I told him.

"That's fine—go ahead," Frank said. "I need to think about all this anyway."

"I'll call you back later," I said and hung up before picking up Cassie's call.

"Baby, are you all right?" I said.

"Parke?" Her voice trembled.

"Baby, I'd be there if I could. What happened?" I asked.

"Did you know Ross had a brother?" she sniffled.

"No, sweetheart. I didn't know that. Where is he now?"

"He's uh, he's dead. I had to kill him. He was trying to kill Rob and Cliff. And Kent."

I wanted to curse. I didn't. Cassie was crying already and I wasn't fucking there to do anything about it.

"Who are Kent and Cliff?" I asked.

"Cliff is the Public Defender. You know—where I intern?"

"All right. Who is Kent?"

"He's uh, a werewolf detective in Birmingham. Cliff is werewolf, too. Somebody broke into Ross' old place. We were already in Birmingham, because Cliff knew the judge who was killed. We ended up at Ross' house. Ray—that's his brother's name, was in the cellar. He broke through the floor into the foyer. He was a rock demon. I had to kill him, because he tried to kill the others." She stifled a sob; I gripped the handset harder.

"Baby, you did what you had to do to protect yourself and the ones you were with. If Ray had good intentions, he'd never have done that. He'd have introduced himself, like a civilized supernatural."

"I know." Another sob.

"I'm sorry I didn't call you back. Or call to begin with. I should have," I said. That's when she started sobbing continuously and set the phone down. Seconds later, the call ended. That's when I cursed.

* * *

Cassie

My face was a mess when I finally stopped crying. I'd hung up on Parke because I couldn't talk any more—all I could do was sob. A chasm had opened between us and it wasn't completely due to the number of states and miles between.

He'd shut me out, as if I were someone he dated for a few weeks and then dropped. Nice words after the events in Birmingham hadn't helped very much. It only made me realize what I missed and what he felt obligated to say.

Stop this and start studying; class starts at nine in the morning, I reminded myself. It did. There wasn't a soul to talk to about any of this, either. Binita was a friend, but I wasn't prepared to burden her with my problems. Parke was my husband, and I didn't have a shoulder familiar enough in Alabama to cry on.

* * *

Cliff Young

"Kent and two others went back to the house last night to sniff around," I told Rob. We were in a coffee shop down the street from the courthouse. I didn't want to talk about this sort of thing inside the courthouse, in case someone was listening.

"Find anything?" Rob asked, lifting his latte and saluting me with it. His arm was healed completely and probably didn't have a bruise to show for it.

"Everything was burned or melted. Some of it may have been on the arcane side, if you know what I mean." I sipped my own coffee and watched Rob's eyes narrow as he considered my words.

"What the hell would Ross be doing with any of that?" Rob said after several moments went by. "He was an elemental demon. No power to do anything with that sort of thing."

"Ross knew a lot of people," I pointed out.

"Who, then? We have eyes on just about anybody who could cause damage with that stuff."

"But we didn't know Ray was still alive, did we?" I said.

"There's that," Rob agreed and nursed his latte. "We have a caseload, need I remind you? We can't go haring after every unusual mystery in the state, let alone the country."

"We may have to bring the Chancellor in on this, and it won't sit well with him."

"What's there to lose?" Rob asked. "Either he thinks we're nuts and there isn't another Mystic War brewing, or there is another Mystic War brewing and we're seeing the beginnings of it now. Why else would Ross want Cassie under his thumb, unless it was to protect his ass and further his cause with *Shakkor Agdah,* more commonly known as Black Myth?"

"A lot of paranormals aren't going to believe it, if it's true," I said.

"Hmmph. They weren't there during the Dark Ages, or during any of the plague pandemics," Rob muttered. "There are a few who recognize that the plague spread too fast for rats and fleas to be responsible for all of it. They'll never guess that it had help from *Shakkor Agdah*—especially the airborne part of it."

"That's depressing," I said, pointing a finger at Rob. "Stop depressing me. We almost died yesterday. Give more bad news a week, at least."

"I merely want to add this," Rob said. "I lived through that. Stood with my Prince who is now King, to bring them down before they destroyed all humans. That's what they wanted, you know—Earth for paranormals only. Humans were cattle or fodder to them—take your pick."

"I've read the history the wolves keep," I said. "And you're still depressing me. I thought all *Shakkor Agdah* were killed by the late nineteenth century."

"A few could have escaped," Rob muttered before finishing off his coffee and setting the paper cup down with a muffled thump. "It wouldn't be difficult for them to hide within small tribes in out-of-the-way places. I spoke with my King last night. He says the same."

"Have you had contact with the fire sprites and the air sprites?"

"We haven't gathered to discuss it, no, but the Kings and Queen are of a mind on this. It may not be only disease, this time, as you surely realize. This time, it could be disease and war, brought on by fomented hate, unrest and then focused annihilation. Once humankind is out of the way, *Shakkor Agdah* will seek to rule the rest of us."

"Well, now I'm really depressed. Thanks."

"Anytime."

"We have to talk to the Chancellor, don't we? How do you suggest we approach him?"

"His wife works for us, remember?"

* * *

Cassie

Binita was almost breathless in her concern for me. I should have quizzed Rob on what, exactly, Cliff told her. She thought I'd been at death's door, the way she fussed over me before class started Friday morning.

"I'm fine, I was just shaken up. They say I was going into shock after it was over, so they wanted to watch me for a few hours. Really, I'm fine," I gazed into Binita's dark eyes as sincerely as I could.

"You look pale," Binita announced.

Our professor walked in, hushing the crowd of law students around us. Binita turned away and focused on him. I was grateful.

* * *

"Kate, I'm fine. Really. Just—emotional, that's all. I didn't feel this way Christmas night after all that happened," I stumbled through my conversation with Parke's mother. She'd called the minute I'd made it home after classes that afternoon.

"Because you had people with you, sharing that experience and supporting you," Kate's assessment was more than shrewd. "This time, you were forced to act on your own and it was a shock, in addition to leaving you to feel as if you'd been abandoned."

"I really can't talk about it without crying," I admitted. "I was scared, but the three I was with would have died if I didn't do something." I wiped tears away. At least I wasn't sobbing, like I'd done with Parke.

"I know, dear. You did the right thing. The Prince of Alabama has already spoken with the detective—his name is Kevin?"

"Kent," I said.

"Yes. That's it. Blake got a clear enough account from the detective, so there'll be no need to ask you questions about the incident. You've been cleared, as have the others, and Ray Diablo is now listed as irrevocably dead."

"Do you think Ray was trying to take over Ross' empire? All of Ross' allies are dead, aren't they? I thought he brought everybody to Seattle for the war," My voice quavered.

"I don't know. I think he merely wanted whatever he could steal from Ross' house before disappearing again," Kate speculated. "I think Ross had plenty of valuables inside the house, and Ray has been missing and on the run for a very long time."

"How do you know that?" I asked.

"I read the report Blake forwarded to Parke. It's protocol to send a copy to the Chancellor, to eliminate wrongdoing and maintain the records."

A part of me wanted to read the report. Another part wanted to be as far away from the details as I could get. I let my shoulders sag. There was so much I didn't know about elemental etiquette and protocol that it embarrassed me.

Yes, Ross and Daddy hadn't given me appropriate information regarding the rules and laws, because they were too busy breaking them. I'd have known they were running an illegal operation if anyone had bothered to tell me what the actual laws were.

Everything I knew came from Aunt Shelbie, and I think she was too afraid to tell me some of those things. People could have died—well, people had died, Shelbie among them.

"Cassie?" Kate's voice broke into my thoughts.

"Sorry, I'm still here," I spoke into the phone.

"Do you want me to talk to Destiny?" she asked.

"About this? No way," I said. "She has enough to worry about. This could bring back bad memories, too. She hardly talks about how Ross treated her after he kidnapped her in California."

"I know. We'll wait, then, until she's had some time. It's crazy, isn't it, how last Christmas seems a lifetime ago, instead of a few weeks?"

"Yeah."

"Don't let this trouble you. You should concentrate on your studies instead of this," Kate said. "Louise called earlier—she says her classes and internship are going very well."

"That's great," I said. Louise, Parke's younger sister, was studying veterinary medicine in Oregon. She would be an amazing vet; she was attending her last semester of school and scheduled to graduate in June.

I, on the other hand, had two excruciating semesters left, after which I had no idea which way to go. Louise already had a job lined up; I would go back to Seattle to deal with a husband who'd become a stranger, almost, from the moment I boarded a plane to return to Alabama.

I'd already whined to Kate once because he hadn't called me back. I'd called him the last time, after Rob insisted.

Parke hadn't tried to call me back after I became so upset I couldn't talk any more. I had studying to catch up on over the weekend; I almost wished I could work on the files sitting on my intern's desk at the PD's office, just to take my mind off my personal agonies.

* * *

Dalton King

"I got a call from Claude Ullery this morning," I told Morton over the phone. "He says Ray left a package at his office for us. He also says there's a rumor going around that Ray's dead. Whether he is or not may be irrelevant; Ross' house was burned to the ground on the same day Ray left the package with Claude."

"You think he found what we wanted?" Mort asked.

"I sure as hell hope so. We don't get it, a few people will be mighty pissed."

"That means one of us will have to go back to Alabama, or stay in one place long enough to have it mailed."

"I'll go back; nobody will recognize me, son," I said. "Besides, I want to see Ross' place for myself. See what kind of damage was done and if anything can be salvaged. You know Ross had a lot of stuff our friends might be interested in."

"I understand that," Mort agreed. "But what if whoever killed Ray comes looking for you?"

"I'm not sure Ray's dead. Remember, he disappeared before—successfully, I might add. I think he found our package, left it where we could get it and then torched the place himself, just to get away again. He sure doesn't want the new Chancellor chasing his ass."

"Yeah. It would take somebody tough to kill Ray, now that you mention it. It sounds like him, too, to get rid of the rest of it and skip town."

"Just like I said," I agreed. "Are you supervising that shipment coming in tomorrow?"

"Yeah. Good thing they got the Panama Canal widened when they did, huh? You can hide more stuff on the supertankers than those older class ships."

"That's for damn sure. Plus, if half of it comes in as parts and certain people are open to bribes, you're home free."

Chapter 14

Cassie

"Huh?" I blinked at Rob, who stood outside my apartment door. He held large, takeout bags in both hands. Behind him stood Cliff and Gina. Gina wore a loose, black sweater with the hood up, to hide her spots from humans.

Her eyes glowed like a cat's within the depths of the hood, which she'd pulled forward as far as it would go.

It was Saturday evening, I'd been studying all day and recently realized that I'd skipped lunch and was now hungry.

"We brought dinner," Rob held up the bags. "Hope you like barbecue."

"I love barbecue," I stuttered as Rob shouldered his way past me. I remembered my manners and stepped aside so Gina and Cliff could follow Rob. I shut the door behind them, too, and locked it.

"Gina said she wanted to check on you and I owed her barbecue, so here we are," Rob said. He and Gina were now occupied with setting containers from the bags on my small table.

It smelled heavenly—like the best barbecue ever.

"Beef, pork, turkey and hot links," Rob grinned. "Got anything to drink?"

"Uh, wine?" I asked, recalling that I'd bought two bottles and shoved them into the bottom of the fridge so I could have a glass or two now and then. I missed my glasses of wine with Kate in the evenings, and that had precipitated the purchase.

"Good enough," Rob shrugged. I pulled the bottles of my favorite white from the fridge and set them on the table.

"This is a good choice," Rob lifted a bottle to study the label, "although a red would have gone better with the meal."

"Parke's mother stocked it—I liked it so I bought it," I said. I was no wine aficionado; before I met Parke, I seldom drank anything other than water, tea or soda.

"What is he?" Rob asked, searching my gadget drawer for a corkscrew.

"Huh?"

"What sort of elemental," Gina grinned. At least she'd removed the hooded sweater once she was inside the house. Her spots covered the sides of her face and neck, then disappeared below the collar of her button-down oxford.

"You don't know?" I blinked at her. I thought everybody knew. At least the rock demon part; that had been present at the Christmas war.

"I'm not sure when the Chancellor last visited Alabama," Cliff said. "I'm talking about Parke's father," he added.

"Oh. Wow. I thought everybody knew, because he scares the bejeezus out of some people," I said.

"Sit and eat," Rob said, grabbing wineglasses from the cabinet and pouring wine for all of us. "Tell us about your husband, too," he chuckled. "Why does he scare the bejeezus out of people?"

"Because he's a truth demon," I sighed and studied the barbecued beef on my plate before lifting a plastic fork.

Everything went quiet as I stuffed a forkful of barbecue in my mouth. My eyes went from one to the other around the table while I chewed uncomfortably. They were watching me intently as I swallowed.

"Well, that *would* scare the bejeezus out of most people," Rob sighed and lifted his glass. He emptied half of it before setting it down. I watched as he placed sliced pork on his plate and added barbecue sauce, his mouth set in a grim line. "What else is he? Truth demons usually have another form, just like the others."

"Rock." I blew out a sigh. "He and I—we killed Ross between us during the Christmas war. I burned down half a mountain, too, while we were at it." I pushed barbecue around my plate; my appetite had fled.

"Understandable," Cliff interjected. "Look, I can see this upsets you," he said. "Let's eat and we'll talk about that stuff later. Where are you going on the full moon? It's next week," he added.

"I don't know. I never changed before—well, before Christmas," I confessed. "I always kept it under control. I guess that'll change now, huh?"

"That's mind-boggling, that you could force yourself not to change," Gina breathed.

"It kept Ross away from me," I whispered. "He wanted to use me—that part of me."

"That's not frightening," Rob said, sounding indignant. "If you'd fought on his side during the—what did you call it—the Christmas war, how do you think it would have turned out?"

"I don't know."

I did know. Ross had enough of an army that Parke could have fallen. I'd come from behind Ross' army, killing or knocking everyone out of my way (including a few water demons), to reach Ross, who'd held Destiny captive.

I'd been running toward Parke, too, to fight beside him.

He'd said he loved me.

Was it to keep me at his side, because he needed the fire demon, too?

I felt used.

Cheated.

Foolish.

I wasn't a truth demon, like Parke. I didn't know that he hadn't spoken the truth to me. I was poor, stupid, Cassie King-Worth, who'd fallen for a line and a handsome face.

"I didn't ask that question to cause trouble," Rob said.

"I heard there weren't any more fire demons," Cliff said quietly when I didn't respond to Rob's words.

"Surely that's wrong," my eyes locked with his.

"Maybe you should ask your husband," Cliff said and cut into his barbecued hotlink. "A lot of them were killed or so I hear, in the last century or two."

"How?" I asked.

"I don't know. Records don't show that."

"Then how can you be sure they're dead? Ray Diablo sure wasn't, but the records showed he was."

"Jasper Bridges, the Prince of Alabama at the time, recorded Ray's death, after Ross reported it," Rob said. "In the case of the fire demons, humanoid bodies were actually found and catalogued before burial."

"That sounds so comforting. Were the murderers ever found?"

"There were ah, wet spots around several of the bodies."

"Water demons. Great. Were they brought to justice?"

"The ah, amount of water suggests that both demons died."

Chapter 14

"Seriously? They had a death wish after accomplishing a murder? That sounds weirdly stupid. Maybe insane."

"Stranger things have happened," Rob shrugged.

"Such as?" I turned my gaze on him.

"Too much to go into," he wriggled away from the question.

"You brought it up," I waved my fork between him and Cliff. "Gina, what do you think? Which side of the family is your demon side?"

"My mother's and she was a water demon."

"Well, that's not awkward or anything," I glared at Rob, who frowned and turned away from my look.

"She was killed by an ice demon," Gina continued. "Frozen and then broken. You don't come back after that."

"That's—sorry. Sorry for your loss." I tossed my plastic fork onto my plate and stood. I had absolutely no appetite, now.

"That's really not what we came here to discuss," Cliff admitted. "Sit down. Please. We want to present a theory to your husband, and we need your help to do it."

"What theory?" I didn't sit, choosing to stare at Cliff until the werewolf felt uncomfortable.

"The theory that *Shakkor Agdah* has returned," Cliff breathed and turned his head away.

* * *

"*Shakkor Agdah* means Black Myth, as closely as you can translate it, and it isn't tied to their skin color, which could be any color," Parke added. "It refers to their arcane practices, none of which were reportedly good or fair. They're mostly a fairy tale, Cassie."

"Rob says they're not a fairy tale," I said. Yes, Parke and I were having another conversation.

Yes, I'd called him.

Again.

At least I wasn't crying this time. "Rob knows this how?" Parke demanded.

"I don't know. He wouldn't tell me."

"You have to see this from my perspective," Parke said, as if he were practicing his utmost patience with me. "Unless I have solid proof, there's nothing I'm willing to do. This could serve to spook every Prince and Princess, merely because two paranormals think the world is about to end."

He had a point, and I felt like a fool.

Again.

"All right. If proof crops up, I'll be sure to let you know." I hung up on him.

Again.

* * *

Sunday I studied. At least I ate lunch while reading, then crunched into an apple for an afternoon snack. I planned to have dinner at the 'shroom, just like I had the week before. I also needed to scope out places where it would be safe to turn on the full moon the following Saturday.

Monday went without a hitch; Tuesday rolled around and I was on time for my four-hour stint as an intern, which turned into nine hours, doing research and digging through prior decisions to help our cases.

"Figured out where you're going Saturday night?" Rob pulled a chair beside my desk and sat on it after the rest of the office cleared out.

"No. Got any places that won't burn like loose hay in a barn fire if I show up?" I asked, making notes on a legal pad before closing the text and looking up at him. "Parke thinks I'm an idiot and that you and Cliff are alarmists who will spook the whole country, at the very least," I added.

"I figured he'd say that," Rob raked fingers through his hair.

"You wanted me to be your errand girl, so I'd be the one he yelled at," I accused. I slammed the bottom drawer of the desk harder than I'd intended after pulling my purse out of it.

"He yelled at you?"

"Practically. Mostly he made me feel like a gullible fool. It wasn't a nice feeling," I snapped.

"No wonder you didn't come see Cliff or me when you came in today."

"Right. How's the investigation into the judge's death coming along?" I steered Rob away from the current subject, much like a tugboat steering a barge through rough current.

"They found footprints beneath the tree, and scraped places where the shooter's boots scrubbed bark to climb up, but that's about it so far."

"What kind of gun was used?" I pulled keys from my purse.

"Rifle. Semiautomatic. Probably with a powerful scope, to shoot from that distance."

"Nice," I grumped my sarcastic response.

"Yeah. Cliff says there's a huge hole in the back of the head."

"Ugh. Why did you tell me that?" I whined. My imagination offered a picture of it, which was neither pleasant nor planted in the shortest of short-term memory.

"You're squeamish?"

"When it comes to humans. They're fragile."

"True. That's not what I came here to tell you. There's a dry creek bed on Cliff's property, if you're interested. No rain predicted between now and Saturday, so it could be an option."

"Where and what time should I arrive before things get—hairy?"

"I'll give you the address on Thursday. Cliff says to be there around four, before the yips set in with him."

"Yips. Right."

"You haven't heard him yip. I have."

"You sound so serious."

"I am serious. Like a heart attack."

"I don't know whether to laugh or be concerned," I pulled the purse strap over my shoulder and stood.

"Either would be appropriate. Perhaps both. You choose. I'll walk you out. I have to lock up anyway."

"What happens with Gina? On a full moon?" I asked as I walked toward the door.

"She hates for people to know."

"Then I'll shut up. Maybe I'll stop at Guppy's for a burger on the way home."

"Guppy's is good." Rob shooed me through the door before turning to lock it behind him.

* * *

Parke

"I don't know, Daniel," I said. "It looks like they're filling her head with crap, and because I'm not there to quash it, she believes it."

"Go back to the part about Ray Diablo showing up and Cassie having to kill him," Daniel said.

"I've asked for more information and images of the burned property, but Blake hasn't sent them, yet. I have no idea if he believes this crap, too."

"Did you quiz Cassie on what happened, exactly? I'm interested in this."

"I was waiting on the images before I asked questions, and you know I can't keep her on the phone long, in case she starts asking questions about what's going on. I can't tell her a thing about tracking her father. She was already upset when she was forced to take care of Ray. This could make things a lot worse, and I'd prefer to do this without her knowledge."

Daniel didn't say anything for several seconds. I thought the call had dropped when he finally spoke. "You know, my dad always said to be careful around rumors of *Shakkor Agdah*. As if they were listening whenever their name was called."

"Oh, please. Not you, too," I muttered.

"Listen, bro, I don't think this is something to fool around with."

"You think we should investigate?"

"We? Send somebody else to investigate. I want no part of Black Myth." He'd given their common name—I knew that much, at least.

Daniel's words forced me to scramble for a reply. I had no idea he was afraid of anything. "I don't have anybody to send, and wouldn't know where to start anyway."

"Start with that burned-down mansion outside Birmingham," Daniel snapped. "If they're rising again, you can bet Ross was in it up to his eyebrows."

Daniel actually believed in Shakkor Agdah. I had no idea why or how he'd become so superstitious; the whole thing sounded like a crock to me. Before Daniel's reluctance to investigate what he believed in, I was ready to dismiss the entire thing as complete nonsense.

Making a mental note to ask my mother about it, I told Daniel to keep me updated on his pursuit of Morton King and ended the call. I had an appointment with Frank Hillman in the morning, and we would discuss an amendment to the lawsuit, asking for more money.

That's what you did, after all, when you discovered that your stolen software was being used for a government contract worth billions.

* * *

Cliff Young

"They're already building the facilities; that's how confident they are," I slid a folder of photographs across the table to Blake Donovan, Prince of Alabama.

"I had no idea they would move on this so quickly," Blake opened the folder to study the top photograph. "I know they bought plenty of unoccupied ground, but to start building so fast? That's foolish."

"I think they intend to buy their way into privatization this year," I said. "There's more information at the back of the folder—they're doing the same thing all across the South and into the Midwest. Some of those states are already on board, but they're building more. I think they intend to move all prisoners into their facilities before this is over. While their cost of housing a prisoner sounds reasonable at today's prices, wait until they have all of them and the state prisons are shut down. They'll raise their rates and we won't have a ready place to take all those felons back."

"I see they're already digging deep holes—figure that's for solitary?" He pointed to a large, concrete-lined square at least fifteen feet deep, lying two hundred yards away from the prison wall construction.

"Or storage, or storm shelters," I shook my head. "Who knows or cares what the deep holes are for? The prison walls are already halfway up in the State of Alabama, while proposed legislation isn't out of committee yet. In my estimation, that bill, when it hits the senate floor, won't contain provisions for health care or psychiatric treatment. Those things will be extra, if they ever determine it's necessary."

"You know how some people feel about that," Blake set aside the first photograph to look at the second. "Cells look to be narrower."

"Yeah. I know how some people see that," I agreed. "For them, they see a prisoner getting free health care. A part of me understands that. Another part understands how horrible it would be to allow a prisoner to die, when they're in there for their inability to pay a fine."

"The entire prison system is broken, and the legislative system is broken, too. Nobody can agree on anything, anymore."

"I know. Look, I'll leave those copies with you," I said, rising to stretch. I'd had a long day in court, followed by a drive to Birmingham to meet with Blake at a restaurant. I had another long day in court tomorrow.

Time to go home and sleep.

"Did you hear anything from Cassie? Has she spoken with the Chancellor, yet about—you know?"

"I haven't heard anything. When I do, I'll let you know."

"Thanks for this," Blake shut the folder and tapped it with an index finger. "I'll do some digging into this—metaphorically speaking."

"I'd appreciate hearing what you find, if anything," I said and shrugged into my suitcoat. "What do you think they'll do with those massive buildings, if the legislation isn't passed?"

"They're not planning to open malls. Not with this stuff," Blake lifted the folder. "They're serious, and as you said, may pay their way into it."

"My question is this," I mused. "Where's all that money coming from?"

"Good question. Let's find out, shall we?" Blake offered a grim smile. I nodded to him and made my way out of the restaurant.

* * *

Parke

"It started out as gaming software—for friendly drones to hit enemy drones in the game," Frank gripped the arms of the chair where he sat. I'd offered him coffee when he came in; he'd refused. "We designed it to be proactive—in a way that could project which way the target would move, just to make it easier for the player to hit it. I never realized that if left on its own, the program would solve the movements without help. With only slight adjustments, you can allow the program to shoot the drones on its own, without human interaction."

"What if they're not just targeting drones after a while?" I asked.

Frank grimaced. "I worry about that, too," he admitted. "We haven't done anything with the software since we hired this firm to sue Fli-Bi-Net. I never thought it would take this long to get anything going."

"It's going now," I sighed. If Geoffrey had still been alive, I might have killed him myself over that. He knew all along about the government contract and that Fli-Bi-Net stood to make a mountain of money off it. Instead, Geoffrey took ten million under the table, with the promise of much more if he let the lawsuit die. All that had been implied or written in plain English in his e-mail correspondence with Fli-Bi-Net. "Do you think you could have adapted the software, like Fli-Bi-Net has done?" I asked.

"Hmmph," Frank almost chuckled. "We could have done a better job of it," he said. "They're struggling with the original design, because they had flawed intel. We have the original design. While

Fli-Bi-Net's accuracy rate is around eighty-one percent, ours would be ninety-eight percent."

"You've already tweaked it, haven't you?"

"All I had to do was imagine what could be done according to the written descriptions exchanged in the e-mails between the government and Fli-Bi-Net," Frank huffed. "We're working on a prototype drone, now. As for the government contract, I figure they handed all that to Geoffrey, since he's the one hired by Fli-Bi-Net."

"I know what you're thinking," I held up a hand. "Geoffrey should never have been involved in that; it was a conflict of interest. Geoffrey's death precludes disciplinary action and a court case against him," I added. "I'd appreciate it if you didn't sue the firm over it, too."

"You've been straight with me so far—just like your father. Geoffrey did this. Why should you pay for what Geoffrey Gruber hid from everybody?"

"I'm glad you see it that way," I said. "I don't intend to ask for a fee in this case—after court and filing fees are paid, you'll owe me nothing. Any proceeds will be yours."

"We'll see," Frank said. "Have you gotten a reply from the government, yet?"

"Nothing so far, but you understand how slowly they move at times."

"I know that for sure," Frank agreed.

* * *

Cassie

Guppy's was crowded when I arrived, so I waited in the vestibule with several others to get a table. The restaurant served great, handmade burgers, fried chicken and a few other Southern specialties. Definitely worth waiting for and since I'd found a parking place, didn't want to leave until I'd eaten.

After fifteen minutes, my name was called and I followed a waitress to a small table near the restrooms. If you were alone, you didn't get the best table in the restaurant.

Get used to it, I reminded myself, took the offered seat and accepted the menu. A glass of water was set in front of me while I studied the burger section—I could have anything from a barbecue burger with bacon to one covered in avocado slices.

After deciding on the plain cheeseburger, I closed my menu to give the waitress a signal that I was ready to order.

Halfway across the restaurant, I saw someone I recognized. No, it wasn't someone I liked, either. Ross' half-human attorney, Claude Ullery, sat alone at a table, a thick manila envelope at his elbow. He drank beer from a glass and had apparently been waiting for someone to join him.

That someone showed up two minutes later.

Claude's guest reminded me of my father. I knew it wasn't him, but it sent a shiver through me anyway.

What would you do if it had been your father? The thought pricked my brain and wouldn't leave.

I knew what I'd like to do—slap him several times and demand to know what happened to my mother. He had to know. He hadn't been surprised in the least when she didn't come home.

Destiny and I had been devastated.

Morton King just drank more.

There'd never been a service or any memorial. Those things cost money, and Daddy was on the stingy side. Aunt Shelbie got us through our grief, although Destiny still held hope that Mom would come back the whole time we lived in Alabama.

That hope was now gone and we'd never know what happened to our mother. I watched Claude as he pushed the envelope toward his guest, who gripped it in hands that, in my mind, resembled my father's. He then rose and left the restaurant without ordering a drink or anything else.

In a hurry to get out, perhaps?

You're imagining things, I scolded myself. *Like Parke accused you of doing.* If Shelbie were alive, I'd talk to her about *Shakkor Agdah*. Maybe she'd heard of them. I sure hadn't.

I'd told Parke that, too—that it was information I'd gotten from a werewolf and an earth sprite. Parke had scoffed and practically called me delusional.

Perhaps I was. Since I'd run away from Alabama, I'd been afraid. Afraid Ross would find me. Afraid he'd kill me, once he did find me. Afraid he'd kill Destiny. Afraid of coming back to Alabama by myself, where so many bad memories waited.

Parke didn't understand any of that. He wasn't afraid, so I shouldn't be, either. If I could find a paranormal shrink, maybe I should make an appointment.

I'd have to trust him or her, first, I recalled, before I told them anything about my life. I was married to the Chancellor, after all, and blackmail was always waiting around every corner and in every alleyway.

Parke would call me delusional again if I so much as mentioned that. Perhaps he'd led a sheltered life until last Christmas, but nothing about my life had been sheltered since my mother disappeared.

Calling Parke to relay my fears was the last thing I could or would do, now. Sure, I could tell him that Ross' lawyer just passed a heavy envelope to someone who looked enough like my father to be related in some way.

People looked like other people—it happened all the time. My fears were likely playing mind tricks, showing me things it was terrified of seeing. After all, Ross' brother had appeared from nowhere and tried to kill three others and me.

Perhaps I would be imagining all my enemies in a slight resemblance to other people. "Ready to order?" The waitress was back.

"Yes. I'd like a regular cheeseburger with onion rings to go, please," I said, handing her the menu.

I'd decided not to stay. I couldn't sit there, watching Claude drink and not remember painful things. I'd eat at my apartment, which held some form of safety for me.

* * *

Parke

I hadn't taken time to open mail, so I did that before going home for the day. Too much of it was plain junk, some of it important, and lastly, a manila envelope from a law firm in Birmingham, addressed to Cassie in care of my firm.

"What's this about?" I mumbled while slitting it open with one of my dad's old letter openers. The opener had been a favorite of his—with a painted, rainbow trout on the handle. I'd taken it to use before sending his other things home to Mom.

A letter from the law firm lay atop a copy of a will, belonging to Shelbie A. Foster. For a moment, I was surprised, before realizing I shouldn't be.

Shelbie Foster, whom Cassie and Destiny had called Aunt Shelbie, had left her entire estate to Cassie and Destiny King.

Ms. King, it is our understanding that you are now married and living in Seattle. You are named as the executor in Ms. Foster's estate. We have forwarded all appropriate information, and request that you contact us at your earliest convenience so we may hand house keys and banking information to you personally. Ms. Foster was very fond of you and Destiny, and mentioned you often.

The will left the house and half the bank account to Cassie, with the other half of the money going to Destiny, who was a minor, still. I figured Shelbie knew that Cassie would do whatever was needed to meet Destiny's needs; therefore, she'd left the bulk of the estate to her.

It wasn't a huge amount of money—less than fifty thousand, but the house was worth several times that. I wondered if Cassie would keep it or sell it. I doubted Shelbie had died there or someone would have surely said something. Cassie would have to go to the law firm herself to get the keys and other items held for her, in addition to getting the probate started.

Cassie should clear out the house and decide to sell or keep it afterward. I wrote a note on my calendar to call her the following evening, shoved the contents of the envelope into a file and left it in my top drawer.

My cell phone rang as I closed the car door to drive home. Daniel was calling. "Another murder," Daniel didn't waste any time telling me the important news. "This time in Houston."

"He's actually heading back into the States? That's foolish of him," I growled. "I'll get the Prince of Texas on the phone when I get home and have him help track Morton. I'm sure Texas doesn't want a rogue ice demon running loose and murdering its citizens. It could expose us, so close to the full moon."

"I was hoping you'd say that," Daniel acknowledged. "It's all we can do to halfway keep up with the bastard. I still haven't figured out how things happened in Corpus Christi and McAllen on the same night."

"Coincidence, maybe?" I suggested.

"I didn't have time to go to McAllen, so there's no way to tell how similar the murders were. Could be a copycat, but it feels too early for that sort of thing. This hasn't made national news, you know."

"Yes, I do know. Where are you now?" I thought to ask.

"Port Lavaca, on the way to Houston. I figure he's staying close to the gulf so he'll have easy access to water come the full moon."

"True. Look, keep me posted if you see or hear anything, all right? I'm concerned that he knows we're on his trail and now he's getting desperate. Have there been any reports of stolen vehicles associated with the victims?"

"Stolen vehicles, yes. Associated with the victims? No."

"Close by, then?"

"Yes."

"You think he's killing and then stealing, so the theft will get shuffled aside in favor of the murder investigation?"

"Could be."

* * *

Morton King

The human lay on the freezer floor, where I'd left him after going through his pockets and taking his wallet.

He hadn't had much cash, and that's what I wanted. Cash to keep going. I'd been forced to leave the bulk of what I had in Mexico, buried in a safe place. My father said to leave it there and take what was needed along the way.

I cursed the human, who'd had less than fifty dollars on him. The restaurant's alarm system was sounding, too, so I had very little time. I could hear the sounds of police coming through the small café, searching for me.

It would take them less than a minute to reach the freezer, and I had no time to waste.

I'd already stashed my clothes, the victim's wallet and other items in the stolen car I'd parked three blocks away. I felt the cold of frozen boxes of meat at my back and leaned into it, as if it were a lover's arms.

My father, Dalton, had taught me this trick.

"They won't search a thin glaze of ice," he'd said. "Spread yourself out over something already frozen. Humans won't think twice about it."

They didn't. I'd been inside most of the freezers, watching as bodies were examined and evidence was collected. I wanted to laugh at the ineptitude of humans as they scurried this way and that before leaving.

They'd lock up, too, but there was always a way out—from the inside.

Chapter 15

Cassie

I stayed up late studying, because I couldn't get the images of Claude Ullery and the man who'd met him at Guppy's out of my head. Lack of sleep meant my first class Wednesday morning was filled with covered yawns and wishes for more coffee.

That guaranteed I'd be called on to answer the professor's question. He blinked when I not only answered the question, but cited appropriate case law to support the answer.

I hadn't had enough sleep because I'd studied the very thing I was asked about. My brain was tired, not dead.

"Ms. Worth, please see me after class," the professor said before class was over. That's how I ended up walking along the hall with my Immigration Law professor when I wanted nothing more than to grab a cup of coffee from somewhere before I had to show up for my next class.

"I thought perhaps you'd had a late night doing other things," Professor Sanders admitted as I hefted my book bag over a shoulder while keeping up with his longer strides.

"I couldn't sleep, so I studied," I told him truthfully.

"I can see that—now," he nodded. "Come with me; I'll get you a cup of coffee from the faculty lounge so you won't be yawning in your next class," he grinned.

"I never expected to see a smile on your face," I blurted without thinking. "You're always so serious during class."

"We have to be inhuman while we're teaching," he chuckled. "The human comes out once class is over. Don't spread that around; I have a reputation, you know."

"I'll uh, keep that to myself. Wouldn't want you to be ridiculed and made a target of spitballs," I replied.

"Spitballs. And we call ourselves civilized humans," he laughed.

I got my cup of coffee, with cream and sugar, before Professor Sanders sent me on my way. I figured Binita would want to know why I'd been asked to stay behind; I intended to show her the empty coffee cup as evidence.

* * *

Cliff Young

"That was a fiasco," I dropped my briefcase on Rob's desk and frowned at him.

"How much time did he get?" Rob dropped his eyes.

"Thirty years," I replied. "He should have gotten ten."

"One more to clutter up the system for twenty years too many," Rob said. "I have Cassie's research if you'd like to look at it. One of those cases comes up next week. Ben is handling it, but you know how he hates somebody telling him what to do or how to handle anything."

Chapter 15

"If he weren't appointed by the judge, I'd have assigned this to someone else," I said. "We have to live with it; I'll call him in and discuss it after I see what Cassie found. You haven't heard from her, have you? On what the Chancellor said?"

"He, ah, dismissed it," Rob admitted. "He told her he wanted proof."

"Well, we have no proof. No substantial proof, anyway. Only a half-heard conversation reported by a now convicted felon who said it during an interview with his attorney, who happened to be the Public Defender," I breathed a sigh. "Client-attorney privilege, and not something to report in a human court to begin with. The Chancellor will recognize it as the hearsay it is."

"Which makes it impossible to give to anyone else," Rob agreed. "The judge ordered the records sealed, since a minor was involved. The Sheriff would love any excuse to get rid of both of us, so we have to be careful."

"This is so fucked up," I said.

"Maybe it wouldn't be so bad—if we lost our jobs," Rob mused. "That would give us plenty of time to investigate on our own."

"What—let Sheriff Yee-Haw Haney have his way? I don't like that idea," I huffed. "Besides, how do we explain to the public that we don't need the money we're earning from the PD's office? I can imagine Haney looking into the matter and concluding that we took bribes, when both of us have been alive long enough to build up considerable wealth? If they discover we have bank accounts under different names to hide our longevity, well, you know what they'll think."

"Yes. I do know. This really is fucked up."

"I hope the Chancellor will change his mind and send someone to investigate, at the very least. Keep your head down for now and keep working. That's all we can do."

* * *

Cassie

"He thinks I'm delusional," I informed Cliff and Rob at lunch on Thursday. Since Cliff asked me what, specifically, Parke had said during our conversation, I'd waited to discuss it when we were away from the courthouse. Lunch was a good cover for that.

"So he wasn't even curious?" Cliff asked.

"He called them a fairy tale."

Rob hmmphed and looked away.

"Now I'm seeing things in every shadow," I admitted.

"What things?" Cliff was suddenly interested, and Rob turned his eyes toward me.

"It's nothing. I just saw Ross' attorney, Claude Ullery at Guppy's Tuesday night."

"That's not seeing things. That bastard gets around well enough," Cliff said.

"But the person who showed up to take a package from Claude looked similar to my father. That's seeing things," I said. "I know it wasn't my father," I held up a hand to stop Rob from saying anything. He pursed his lips for a moment, as if he were holding back corked-up air. "Too many things were different between that guy and my father," I said, watching while Rob released his pent-up breath. "It just gave me the willies," I added. "Now I'm worried that I'm losing it."

"Every law student thinks they're losing it—at one time or another," Cliff soothed. "It's a lot of work."

Chapter 15

"Yes, but does that include hallucinations?" I was beginning to feel sorry for myself, and recalled that I was expected to straighten my spine and suck it up.

"I don't remember other interns having hallucinations, but they've never had your particular background," Rob observed.

"Well, it's unnerving," I mumbled.

"Did Claude see you?" Cliff asked.

"No. I made sure he didn't—Guppy's was crowded that night. Seeing him brings back memories of Ross," I stifled a shudder.

"I hate it when Claude is on the other side of a case," Cliff said. "His scent permeates the entire courtroom. The humans don't smell it, but I do."

"Do you see him often?"

"Once or twice a year," Cliff shrugged. "My nose is clogged up for at least two weeks afterward."

"So he's a health hazard?" I asked, attempting to lighten my mood.

"To me," Cliff grinned. "Nobody else is affected like a werewolf would be. Want to sit with me the next time he's on a case?"

"No," I shivered. I must have looked pitiful for a few seconds; Cliff chuckled and patted my shoulder.

"Where am I supposed to go Saturday night?" I asked, getting away from the subject of Claude Ullery.

"Come out to my place; the dry ravine is a quarter mile behind the house and clear of brush and weeds. It's deep enough that you shouldn't be noticed," Cliff said. "The only time it has water in it is if the big pond overflows, and that's usually in the spring. Normal water shouldn't have an effect, anyway."

"Yeah." I'd already seen that much for myself—it's how I'd boiled Annabelle's shark on Christmas night. Shark shifters were rare; she'd built an Olympic size pool at her home outside Seattle, just so her shark could change there if she didn't want to wander into the bay on a full moon.

She'd been instrumental in killing Parke's father, so I'd exacted revenge on Parke and his family's behalf.

I wouldn't have second thoughts about doing it again; Annabelle had aligned herself with Ross, and had killed and betrayed for him. Everyone in the paranormal community was better off with them gone.

"If you'll meet Rob and me at the house two hours before sundown, I'll have pizza delivered," Cliff said. "What kind do you like?"

* * *

I worked two more hours after lunch, handed my research to Rob and drove back to my apartment. I wanted homemade chili for dinner and time to study while it cooked.

"That smells good," Talbert, my landlord, had come by to check on me. I'd opened the door, letting out the amazing smell of cooking chili.

"It's my aunt's recipe for homemade chili," I said, moving aside in case he wanted to come in.

"I don't need to come in. Just wanted to check in with you, to make sure everything is fine. You're so quiet, I hardly know there's anybody here," he grinned.

"Usually a friend comes for dinner and studying, but tonight she had other plans, so I decided to cook chili," I said. "Thanks for dropping by."

"No trouble. Remember, if anything breaks down or you need help, just let me know."

"I will."

Chapter 15

I watched him go down the steps and walk toward the house before closing the door completely. For a moment, I wondered if Parke were paying him to check on me. After all, I'd never had such a solicitous landlord.

That's when my cell phone range.

"Speak of the devil," I muttered before answering Parke's call.

"Cassie, Shelbie Foster's will was mailed to you in care of the law firm here," Parke said. "She left everything to you and Destiny."

"Oh. I hadn't expected that." Shelbie never said she had a will. I paused to let it sink in.

"The house and half the money goes to you, the other half of the money goes to Destiny. You're named as executor, so you'll have to call the law firm and make an appointment with them."

"I'd like to see a copy of the will, first," I said, realizing I felt numb all over.

"I had Jon scan it. You should have it in your e-mail already."

"Oh. All right. Thank you."

"You sound as though you don't feel good. What's wrong?"

I wanted to say *everything*. I didn't. "Just a long day, and a lot of reading and studying to do," I said. "Thinking about the full moon on Saturday."

"Ah. That makes sense. You've never gone out, have you?"

"No, but I have a place to go," I said.

"Is it safe?"

"It should be."

"Look, I'm sorry I was short with you the other day," Parke said. "Too many things going on with the Hillman case."

"Yeah."

"I wish you were here to help me with it."

"But I'm not."

"Right. If you need help with the will, or have questions, call me back."

"All right."

"Make an appointment with the attorney soon; the house probably should be checked. If it doesn't have a security alarm, have one put in. That's your property, Cassie, and you can decide later whether to keep or sell it."

"Okay."

* * *

Parke

What was wrong with her? Or with me, for that matter? We spoke as if we were near-strangers. *Married for too short a period before splitting up again*, I reminded myself. I spent the next ten minutes looking to see when her spring break was. I'd buy her a plane ticket, bring her home for a week and we'd get reacquainted.

"Jon, make a reservation for my wife to fly from Birmingham to Seattle on March twelfth," I said through the intercom. "The earlier the flight, the better."

"You got it," Jon replied.

I was beginning to appreciate Jon's efficiency. He was almost as good as Cassie at reading my mind, too. He'd already arranged to have Pauline's last check mailed to her so she wouldn't be coming back in to pick it up.

I was grateful for that. It was bad enough that I'd seen her twice since firing her—both times at the Starbucks where I got my coffee. I think she did it on purpose; Jon said that he'd heard from someone in the secretary pool that she'd already found a job with another law firm.

I hoped her new boss didn't have a wife; Pauline was probably prepared to take him and hang him up in her spider's web. The thought made me shudder.

Chapter 15

* * *

Cassie

"Can you come in Saturday morning?"

I spoke with Aunt Shelbie's attorney before class Friday morning. I'd hoped to talk with his secretary or assistant. Instead, he answered the phone.

"Around nine?" I asked.

"That sounds fine. Just a few things to go over, I'll have you sign the papers to get the probate started and hand the house keys and the bank information over to you. The car was missing from the garage and never found, although she was discovered by the side of the road west of Birmingham," he said.

"Oh." I'd never been told the details, just that Shelbie had been murdered.

"You didn't know that, did you? I have a copy of the police report, if you'd like to read it."

"Yes, please. Where is she now—was there—a service?"

"She'd made arrangements with a local funeral home; they took care of everything. She's buried in a small cemetery outside town. I have that information, too."

I wanted to cry for Shelbie again. I hadn't been there to say good-bye. The whole thing was too tragic and I resolved to place flowers on her grave soon. "I'll be there at nine tomorrow," I promised. "I have to let you go and get to class."

"I'll see you in the morning, then."

* * *

"What's this?" I accepted a final, large envelope from Reynolds Finn, Aunt Shelbie's attorney on Saturday morning, after signing the papers to start the probate process.

"The guest book and related items—from Shelbie's funeral," Reynolds answered. He was in his sixties, with graying hair and a kind smile. He offered tissues after I'd sniffled a few times when he handed keys and banking information to me.

"People came?" I blinked at him stupidly.

"Several," he said. "I was there—I knew her for twenty years, at least."

"Thank you," I sniffled again. "I wasn't able to come," I added, recognizing how lame that excuse sounded.

"That happens sometimes," he said. "Nothing to worry about. If you need help with anything, my card and information are in the envelope with the checkbook and bank information."

"Thank you. I can't tell you how much I appreciate this. Shelbie trusted you, and that means a lot to my sister and me."

"You should consider going by the house while you're in Birmingham," he suggested when I stood to leave. "I imagine her refrigerator should be cleared out and things like that."

"I know. It will be hard, but I intend to do it," I said.

* * *

Reynolds was right about clearing out the fridge. I'd stopped by the grocery that Shelbie always went to and bought garbage bags and cleaning supplies. The fridge wasn't in horrible shape, but I cried when I dumped the leftover stew; I'm sure she meant to have it for a meal before she died.

The trash that hadn't been emptied caused the kitchen to smell, so I took it to the cart, put a new bag in the can and set about clearing up anything else that needed to be done.

I kept an eye on the clock, too, so I'd leave in time to get to Cliff's place at the right time. I recalled what Rob said about Cliff getting the yips before turning on a full moon.

Once the fridge and kitchen were clean and smelling better than they did when I arrived, I sorted through home security companies

Chapter 15

and made a list to call on Monday. I certainly didn't want anyone breaking in; that would be frightening.

After locking everything up and making a mental promise to come back soon, I left Shelbie's house behind and drove toward Cliff's place, outside Tuscaloosa.

* * *

Cliff Young

"Pizza's on the way; Harve is picking it up," I said, ending the call and turning to Rob.

"Good. You think Cassie will freak when she finds out you're the Packmaster, among other things, and that she'll be eating pizza with fourteen werewolves?"

"She hasn't freaked yet, plus she's a fire demon. What can one of us do to that?"

"She's still vulnerable while she's humanoid," Rob pointed out. "She did change really fast when she took Ray down, though."

"Noticed that, did you?"

"While I was being tossed across the room like a Ping-Pong ball," Rob snorted. "Her quick change means we're alive to talk about it now."

"I hear a car," I said, turning away from Rob and heading for the front door. "It's Cassie," I said. "She's parking beside your truck."

"Easier to get out," Rob agreed, going to the window to watch as Cassie locked her car door. "The rest of you will be out until dawn, since tomorrow's Sunday."

"It's not often we can do that, you know," I pointed out. "Harve just turned in. We get first dibs on the pizza."

* * *

Cassie

183

Cliff had a huge ranch house on three hundred acres of land. To the east stood a thick stand of trees that stretched for half a mile, and probably extended onto a neighbor's property.

"It helps if your neighbor is a werewolf, too," Cliff said as I gazed at the trees through his kitchen window. "We hunt both properties on a full moon. Are you sure you don't want more pizza?"

"I'm good," I held up a hand. I didn't want to admit to him that I had butterflies about turning by myself on a full moon. A part of me wanted to hide in Cliff's guest bathroom and call Parke. Another part was upset with him.

Yes, he'd be turning, too. I hoped he'd made arrangements for Destiny, since her first official turn had been Christmas night, just as mine had been.

"You'll be expending energy, remember? You were starved after the last incident," Rob reminded me.

"I know. I can always eat afterward."

"Don't forget to put your clothes where you can find 'em," Harve, the werewolf who'd brought the pizza and was Cliff's second for the pack, informed me.

"You're right. I'll find a good place," I agreed.

While I was in the kitchen with Rob, Cliff and Harve, thirteen more werewolves laughed and joked in Cliff's media room while polishing off twenty boxes of pizza. The tales were true; werewolves could eat a lot.

"The best place is straight behind the house about a quarter of a mile," Cliff said. "We'll be going out in half an hour; moonrise is coming."

I blinked at him. Rob was right; Cliff was getting the yips. Half his words were growled, half yipped.

"I think I'll head out now," I said, pulling a small flashlight from my purse and stuffing it in my pocket. Aunt Shelbie always said to take a flashlight. I was following her instructions, in case the dark overwhelmed me when I turned back.

"Good idea," Rob inclined his head. "Ready?"

"Yeah." I squared my shoulders and stalked toward the back door.

* * *

Parke

I wasn't thinking about the time change when I called Cassie on her cell phone. After six rings, it went to voicemail.

"Baby, I hope things go well for you tonight," I said. Yes, it hit me that she'd be turning by herself. I should have been there, and considered that I should have bought a plane ticket to fly out the night before.

Too late, now. Mom and her friend Bea were taking Destiny into the mountains, not far from where I'd be, in case they needed help.

My conscience nagged me that Cassie could need help, too. I sighed and shoved it aside. We'd leave in an hour to reach our turning spots. I had no idea how my rock demon would react to Cassie's absence.

* * *

Cassie

The moon lifted above the trees while I sat on the bank of Cliff's ravine, wondering why the urge hadn't hit me as it was likely hitting the werewolves. To the east, where the trees were, I heard a howl.

They'd gone through the change and were greeting the moon before the hunt. Rob—I'd forgotten to ask what his plans were. I'd never heard of sprites, pixies or anything like them changing for any reason, although some revered the solstices and held celebrations or rituals.

"Maybe Rob sticks his toes in the dirt to figure out where the wolves are," I shrugged. I took a mental inventory of how I was feeling—still nothing. Had suppressing my fire demon for years out of fear caused this?

I didn't have another fire demon to ask or mentor me in any way. There had to be others—perhaps in foreign countries. I didn't know about them; they didn't know about me.

I should have brought a book to study, perhaps, or even something to read for pleasure. My cell phone was still tucked in my purse, which Cliff had stuck in a half-empty drawer in his kitchen. He'd left the back door unlocked, too, so I could get in and retrieve it when I was done.

He and the others planned to stay out most of the night.

Was there any reason to force the fire demon out, when I wasn't feeling it? Perhaps that was a question for Kate. I could call her tomorrow and ask if anyone else had experienced this.

I worried that I wasn't normal in any sense.

* * *

Robin Newbourne

The last time I'd had my toes buried in dirt and grass, Cassie had watched my feet in fascination. It made me smile as I stood in Cliff's greenhouse, doing exactly the same. This way, I'd know where the wolves were at all times, as long as they stayed within a three-mile radius and didn't take off down a paved road or sidewalk.

Cliff was important in the werewolf community and not only in the Southern states. He watched everything closely, and had been a better source of information than the previous Prince of Alabama ever dreamed of being.

It will start in the Southern United States, the King's seer—my eldest brother—declared two solstices ago.

Chapter 15

He'd predicted a rising of *Shakkor Agdah*. While one seer could be dismissed, air and fire had similar foretellings. Seldom did the Kings and Queen meet. They met shortly after those dire predictions.

I'd kept watch with Cliff afterward. He and I suspected that Ross could be involved in something that would bring harm to all of us, but it turned out to be a bid for the Chancellorship.

At least that's what we'd thought at the time.

Cliff and the pack were now turning away from the edges of Harve's property, looking for deer or something else to hunt. They'd double back onto Cliff's farm, running through his portion of the forested areas.

Cassie, though—I didn't feel her.

Anywhere.

That troubled me. I'd had my hand on her the last time, but hadn't tried to find her this way since then. Surely I'd feel her, if she were there. I cast my psychic touch through the soil and toward the ravine.

Still nothing. The wolves were still running strong—southwestward, this time. Turning away from that strong vibration, I went looking for Cassie again. If she were barefoot, I should be able to detect her.

The surge of wrongness went through me like a knife and almost made me fall while gasping for breath.

Whatever had arrived was now directly in the path of running wolves.

* * *

Cliff Young

They appeared from nothing. I might have missed them if it hadn't been for the humans they'd brought with them. Their scent and the sight of them had me veering away from that small crowd. I recognized the smell of one of the humans as I scrambled to turn away.

Sheriff Haney.

He'd found powerful friends. I didn't have time then to determine whether he knew what he'd allied himself with. A dark cloak tossed a glowing orb at the pack while I scrambled to steer them away from danger.

I turned and ran toward the invaders when the orb's explosion rocked the ground beneath my paws.

* * *

Cassie

Yes, I'd heard Parke speak to me, mind-to-mind. This message, however, wasn't as clear as Parke's had been. It also came from Rob, which terrified me—mostly because he was terrified.

Something was very, very wrong. Cliff and his wolves were in danger. Rob knew exactly where they were, which meant I knew exactly where they were. Without wasting time to puzzle out the how or why of it, I was running toward the trouble instead of away from it.

A part of me knew that Rob was doing something to get there, too, but my fire demon, which had burst into being almost from the moment I began to run, only cared about what was happening to Cliff and his pack.

In seconds, my much taller, burning self could hear the sounds of wolves fighting for their lives. It only took a moment or two longer to see that several humans had arrived, but they held back, allowing what had come with them to kill wolves.

Dark clothing was all I saw at first, as those dark-cloaked beings tossed exploding orbs at the wolves. Most of the wolves got out of the way, but one or two were flung high into the moonlit night following an explosion.

Chapter 15

Surely the authorities would hear that much racket?

It didn't matter. One of those wolves didn't get up.

The line of six humans screamed when my fire demon bowled through them, intent on reaching the dark-clothed minions who continued to toss exploding orbs. At least a dozen had come, several of which were now pulling long, black swords from beneath cloaks. When I hit the first one, the howl that came from his throat caught me off-guard.

He sounded as if the hounds of hell inhabited his cloak instead of a humanoid of some kind.

I headed for the next one, disregarding the keening that had stopped short with an explosion of fiery sparks.

Behind me, gunshots rang out. I wanted to laugh—bullets would melt before they reached anything important on a flaming fire demon. Two of the dark cloaks thought to attack me together.

They burned together.

More shots rang out behind me, before screams sounded.

Human screams of pain. I hoped the werewolves had gotten to those men; I suspected they'd brought the dark cloaks with them, to kill werewolves. More screams and shouts came as I chased after the last four dark cloaks; they ran from me. Perhaps if I'd been human, I'd have let them go in favor of checking werewolf injured.

My fire demon had their images in its brain and wasn't willing to let any of them live. For a few moments, it looked as if they'd outrun me.

Until I tucked into myself and became a rolling ball of demon fire.

Whatever they were, they burned easily enough when I rolled over them. Once they were dead, I stopped, stood upright and roared my victory to anyone listening.

Chapter 16

Cassie

"Here." Cliff set a large mug of soup in my hands. Rob—whom I almost didn't recognize, stood nearby in Cliff's kitchen.

The earth sprite was dressed like a warrior from a fantasy novel, with a gold helmet and a long sword in a scabbard that hung from a belt at his waist. Tight-fitting breeches were topped with an elaborately embroidered coat over a silk shirt.

I watched as Rob removed the helmet and set it on the kitchen counter, then raked fingers through his hair, which had flattened and bore streaks of sweat.

At least Cliff was still alive, although he was covered in cuts and bruises. He hadn't bothered to button the shirt he'd thrown on while he tended wounded and sent others for help.

Three of his pack didn't make it. One of those was Harve. If I hadn't already killed the ones responsible for Harve's death, I'd have gone after them again.

"What about the humans who were there?" I asked. At least my voice was mostly steady when I spoke.

"Their deaths will be attributed to more mundane causes by tomorrow," Cliff barked. "Eat your soup. If you want a sandwich, we can do that, too."

"This is fine. I'm sorry about the ones who didn't make it."

"Me, too. If you and Rob hadn't come, we'd all be dead."

"Is this how you dress at home?" I turned to Rob.

"My dear fire demon, this is how I dress when I do battle," Rob offered a weary grin. "Or when I stand at court with the King."

"Nice." I nodded at him and drank some of my soup.

"I should go; we have an elaborate vehicle crash to arrange," Cliff muttered and stalked out of the kitchen. I pulled the borrowed blanket closer about me and watched him go; his shoulders were tight as he made his way through the house, until he turned a corner and was out of my sight.

"This is awful," I sighed, shaking my head.

"It is awful. The Prince of Alabama will call the Chancellor in the morning, to tell him that we have his proof—two dead *Shakkor Agdah* for him to examine at his leisure. Those are the ones I killed," Rob held up a hand before I could say anything. "The ones you killed are nothing but ash."

"What were those things they were throwing?" I asked. "What about the humans who were with them?"

"Those orbs are spelled. The entire pack would be dead if I hadn't placed a muting charm against dark magic on Cliff's property two years ago. If they'd been unhindered, things would be so much worse, now."

"You must be talented to do something like that," I breathed.

"I am old and talented enough," Rob said, pulling a chair away from the breakfast table and sitting beside me. "The humans are dead—Cliff and I took care of them. They imagined they'd be watching while we died. Perhaps they also imagined that they'd shoot already dying wolves, to hurry the process. They imagined wrongly."

"I hope your King appreciates you. I sure do," I mumbled before drinking more of my soup. "It didn't matter that those people were shooting at me while I'm on fire, but it would matter to the wolves."

"It would matter to you while you're humanoid," Rob pointed out. "While it is more difficult to kill an elemental demon in their common form, it is not impossible, if enough bullets are used."

"That's a fun fact," I breathed and slurped soup.

"I think all the wolves would be dead if things had gone differently," Rob leaned back in his chair with a sigh. "I wonder how long Virgil Haney knew that Cliff was werewolf?"

"I hope he brought everybody he'd told with him tonight," I countered. "We don't need more vigilantes shooting innocent werewolves. Or spreading tales to others."

"I agree. My concern is this; where did he meet with *Shakkor Agdah*, or had they insinuated themselves into his mind long ago?"

"They can do that?"

"With some humans, yes. The weak-minded, or those prone to evil are easy targets."

"That's not good news."

"As you say." Rob dipped his head in a half-nod.

"Do you want some coffee? I think I need it," I said. Rising, I made sure my blanket didn't fall as I walked toward Cliff's kitchen counter and the coffeepot beside the sink.

"I will take coffee. This will be a long night, dear fire demon."

* * *

Cliff Young

I was on my way back to the house; staging an inferno of a car crash to explain deaths of paranormals is never easy. Having that same accident account for the lives of homicidal humans is much worse.

That's why I didn't turn my cell phone on again until I drove past the gate onto my property. I had a voicemail from Evan Haroldson. Evan was a good friend of Blake Donovan's, an attorney who helped Blake in the duties assigned to the Prince's position. Had he and Blake heard about the fuck-up on my property already?

I called him back the minute I parked the truck in the front yard. He answered almost immediately. "Blake's dead," Evan informed me. "A rock demon and an ice demon killed him last night."

Fucking, bloody hell.

* * *

Parke

The call came from Evan Haroldson. Blake Donovan, Prince of Alabama for less than a month, was dead. Killed by a rock demon and an ice demon who'd attacked on the full moon. Evan, who'd been with Blake, tried to fight off their attackers but was injured.

Evan called me from the hospital, where they'd kept him after setting broken bones. The attack had taken Blake and Evan by surprise, targeting Blake first and shattering his ice demon easily. Evan's water demon fought back, but water has little to use against a rock demon and nothing to combat an ice demon.

Evan's water had scattered when the ice demon came for him; it was the only defense he had. He'd pulled together and became humanoid—the rock demon batted him away easily in that form.

Becoming full water demon again, Evan went after the rock demon a second time while struggling to stay away from the ice demon. That's when the mysterious, black-cloaked men appeared, tossing out glowing orbs that exploded around Evan, sending him sailing and breaking humanoid bones when he was forced to change again.

Evan crawled half a mile in humanoid form to get to his clothing and cell phone. He was picked up by paramedics there and transported to the hospital.

Someone he trusted was guarding the door to his hospital room while he spoke to me on the phone.

"Cliff Young's place was attacked by black cloaks, too, last night," Evan sighed. "He lost three wolves. It could have been worse—he says the sprite and your wife took care of what attacked them. Blake's attackers disappeared when they thought I was dead, too; they didn't wait around to see whether I survived the explosions."

"So Blake was their real target." I said what I knew while my brain scrambled to digest the information thrown at it in a single conversation.

"Looks that way. Blake and Cliff, actually. Cliff's black cloaks brought humans along. One of those humans was the county sheriff, who hated Cliff. All dead, now. That's been covered; it's already on the local news that a three-car pileup is responsible. Cliff has two bodies for you to examine—black cloaks the sprite killed. I think you need to see them."

I felt like a fool. Cassie had approached me about *Shakkor Agdah*. I'd scoffed at the notion, telling her they were a fairy tale.

To most, they were. Most people understood that the last had died out long ago.

Except they obviously hadn't, if these were real *Shakkor Agdah*. "I'll be on the next plane to Alabama," I sighed. "What is the news reporting about Blake's disappearance?"

"They're blaming it on the recent killing and attempted killing of two other judges—the rumor is that somebody has an axe to grind with judges. They don't have a body and won't find one—sunlight melted and evaporated what was left of Blake."

"I understand. Look, get back in bed and rest up. I'll be there as soon as I can," I told him and ended the call.

"What happened?" Destiny walked into my study, her eyes wide and her face pale. I had no idea how much of the conversation she'd overheard.

"The Prince of Alabama is dead," I sighed before dropping my face in both hands. "Cassie tried to tell me something was wrong. I didn't listen." I dropped my hands to look at Destiny again. She was so young. Already, she'd been forced into adulthood when Ross kidnapped her. Her ice demon had fought back in the Christmas war, killing the water demon who'd held her and intended to kill her.

"Are you going to see Cassie?" Destiny wiped a tear away with the heel of a hand.

"Yes. I have to talk to her and the werewolf she's interning for. Somebody tried to kill him last night. Probably about the same time the Prince died."

"Is Cassie okay?"

"I think so, baby doll. Stop worrying about it, all right? I'll call Daniel, too. See if he can meet me in Birmingham."

Destiny came to me and put her arms around my neck. "Don't cry, sweetheart," I hugged her for several seconds. "I'll make sure Cassie is safe."

"Parke?" Mom walked in, then. "I heard Blake Donovan is missing on the news just now."

"He's dead," I sighed and let Destiny go. "We have big problems. I need to get on a plane to Alabama as soon as I can book a flight."

Chapter 16

* * *

Cassie

Rob handled the caffeine better than I did. I felt as if I hadn't slept in a week, and was too wound up by several cups of coffee and the previous night's events to even doze off. Cliff—I had no idea how he was still standing. Gina arrived around lunchtime and tended to his injuries.

The rest of his pack had already gone home—to sleep, I hoped. At least I was dressed—sort of—in a pair of fleece shorts (clean, thankfully) and a t-shirt belonging to Cliff that he'd found at the bottom of a drawer. The draw-string on the shorts was tied as tight as I could make it, or they'd have dropped to my ankles.

Rob and I put sandwiches together for lunch; Cliff ate and talked on the phone at the same time—to Harve's human wife, who was almost inconsolable, and to the other two wolves' families, who now had deaths to mourn and private ceremonies to hold on Cliff's property, away from human eyes.

They'd died as wolves—they wouldn't turn back for a traditional, human service. I was cleaning Cliff's kitchen when my cell phone rang.

No, I hadn't considered calling Parke. So many things had happened, and I wasn't prepared to discuss them with anyone who'd inspect every centimeter of my story in a calculating and detached manner.

Rob, Cliff and I—we'd lived through it, so there was little need for us to discuss it. Parke's name showed on my cell phone. He was calling now. Wanting to talk, I'm sure, about the death of the Prince of Alabama and the night's other events.

I thought about letting it go to voicemail.

"You should answer that," Rob said, peering over my shoulder to see who the caller might be.

"Yeah. Hello?" My voice didn't sound friendly when I answered.

"Cassie? Thank goodness," Parke said. "Are you all right? Did you get hurt? I'm at SeaTac, waiting on a flight. I'll leave here in twenty, and be in Birmingham at six. Tell me you're all right, sweetheart."

"I'm okay." I didn't sound okay. I was blubbering all over my borrowed t-shirt.

"Sweetheart, they're calling my flight. I'll be there in a few hours. I'll call you when I hit the ground in Birmingham."

"Okay," I stuttered.

"I love you," Parke whispered before the call ended.

"You're not going home," Rob put his hand over mine as I reached for my purse. "You're staying here. They knew where we'd be last night. They may know where you're staying, too. We have a better chance at survival if we're together. Your human landlords won't stand a chance against what attacked us last night. Don't place them in danger, Cassie. The Chancellor can meet us here."

He was right. I hadn't even considered that I'd place Talbert and his wife in danger, merely by renting their garage apartment. What was I supposed to do about all of this? "Here," Rob pulled the box of tissues off the table and handed them to me. "It'll be fine," he soothed, pulling me against him while I wiped my eyes. "We'll figure this out."

* * *

Parke

The connecting flight in Houston got away late; I landed in Birmingham at six-thirty, half an hour later than planned. I called Cassie while the plane taxied to the gate.

"I'm still at Cliff's place," she informed me. "Rob thinks my landlord may be targeted if I go back to the apartment."

I hadn't thought about that. At least not yet. She'd been forced to kill twice since she'd been here, which was less than three weeks. I'd thought Alabama safe enough, once Ross and his bunch were eliminated.

How wrong I was. "Daniel's flying in from Shreveport; he'll be here in an hour," I said. "I'll wait for him, rent a car and come find you."

"All right." She rattled off an address; I made a note on my phone.

"Have you had any sleep? You sound dead tired," I pointed out.

"I haven't been able to sleep. Cliff has the two dismembered bodies in his barn; I'm afraid to go look, it all gives me the shivers."

"Then don't. Daniel and I will take a look when we get there," I said. At that moment, I wished I could send her back to Seattle, where Mom and Destiny were. I couldn't. Whether I wanted it or not, Cassie was the best defense anybody in Alabama had so far. "I'll let you know when we're on the road," I said. "See you soon, sweetheart." I ended the call and pocketed my phone.

I'd be a fool if I didn't connect the murderous ice demon to Morton King, who'd found a murderous rock demon, and together they'd killed Blake Donovan. All this had happened quickly after Ray Diablo's death, which led me to believe that Mort had known Ray was alive and digging around in Ross' house for who knew what. He'd also learned that Ray was dead, unless I was mistaken in my guesses.

Daniel agreed; I'd talked to him about it while I waited on the delayed flight out of Houston. It isn't easy to find a private place for a conversation in an airport; I was grateful for a member's lounge available during the layover.

Daniel also reported another murder in Shreveport the night before. We came to the conclusion that there were two ice demons, perhaps working together to confuse us and the authorities.

I figured there was plenty more to learn from Cassie and those she worked for; I merely waited for the opportunity to speak face to face about it.

Daniel was bringing his two rock demon enforcers with him; I made a mental note to find more enforcers to put on the payroll. It looked as if we would need them and soon.

How had things gone so badly so fast? Had my head been too buried in the sand to realize that my father's murder was only the opening volley of what looked to be an extended war? Somehow, I'd managed to toss Cassie right in the middle of it, too. How could anyone guess that Alabama would be ground zero when *Shakkor Agdah* reappeared?

Yes, Dad told me about them when I was sixteen, after my rock demon manifested the first time. He'd believed the cloaked ones exterminated long ago—like many did. I'd already begun to worry about where they'd reappeared—and how.

My cell phone rang; it was Daniel. His flight was on the ground. "I'll meet you in baggage claim," I said and strode in that direction.

* * *

Cassie

"We have four in the van—Daniel and two enforcers," Parke said. "Is there enough room for all of us, or do we need hotel rooms?"

Cliff could hear a mouse cough from two houses away. Of course he heard what Parke said. "We have enough room," he nodded.

Chapter 16

"Cliff says there's enough room. I called the landlord earlier and told him I was spending the weekend in Birmingham."

"Good idea—he won't be able to give your location away," Parke agreed. "We'll be there in half an hour, I think—we just got on the highway."

"All right, be careful," I said. I didn't tell him I'd seen people die the night before. The idea of him being on the road scared me witless. At this point, I had no idea who wanted us dead or how they'd gotten information on any of us.

"We will. Don't worry, sweetheart. We're coming."

"Sounds like he's willing to listen to us now," Cliff drawled after I ended the call.

Gina, who'd decided to stay the night, frowned at Cliff. "Stop being a werewolf for five minutes, all right? Cassie's having a hard enough time as it is."

"Yeah," Cliff looked apologetic for a moment. "Sorry. I know you're not used to bodies or hearing about covered up murders."

"No." I hugged myself and shivered. Demons that died on a full moon reverted to their elements if killed in demon form. That's what I'd seen the night of the Christmas war. Dead werewolves and shifters had already been carted away by the time I came back to myself that night.

"Kent's on the way," Gina said, coming to me and giving me a hug. "He and I," she hesitated and pulled away.

"I know. I figured that out when I met you the first time," I gave her a weak smile.

"Thanks for saving the furball over there," she pointed at Cliff. "Again."

"Not a problem. I'm used to him by now," I shrugged. "Rob, too, although he sort of saved himself, last night. At least he's dressed more comfortably, now."

"That helmet doesn't do a thing for his hair," Gina grinned.

"I've had a bath," Rob pretended to be upset.

"You smell so much better, too," Gina went to him and pinched his cheek. He laughed. It was a nice sound; one I hadn't heard since the evening before. Everything that happened since then ensured that nobody felt like laughing.

When I'd showered earlier, I'd used more hot water than I usually did, waiting for the steam and moist air to purge my fear and revulsion away. I'd killed three times, now. Every time, it was to save someone else.

I should be happy with that. I was satisfied with other people who'd done the same. It wasn't so easy when it came to yourself and the realization that barely two months earlier, I'd never dreamed of doing anything like this.

"Sit down; I'll find something to drink," Gina was back and leading me toward a chair in Cliff's media room. The television was on but muted; we were watching for any news updates on Blake Donovan's disappearance.

If anybody found anything, it would be a human's way of explaining the impossible. Blake's ice had melted into the ground hours ago. The state Supreme Court would have to find another to replace him.

I worried that it wouldn't be anyone who agreed with Blake's policies. He and two others were often the voices of reason for the cases heard at the state level.

"They'll put a puppet in Blake's place on the court, won't they?" I asked as I sat on one of Cliff's recliners.

"It's early to start worrying about that," Cliff hedged.

I didn't need a truth demon to understand that he worried about the same thing.

Chapter 16

"Lights coming up the drive," Kent walked in and went straight to Gina to give her a kiss.

"I hope it's Parke," I muttered.

"That makes two of us," Cliff said and headed for the front door.

* * *

Parke

Two werewolves met us at the front door.

"Cliff Young," the taller of the two held out a hand. "Pack Alpha for the Tuscaloosa pack, or what's left of it."

"I'm sorry for your loss," I said. "I'm Parke Worth, Chancellor. This is Daniel Frank, ice demon and my Chief Investigator; these two are rock demons, Lance and Lyle Thorne, Enforcers for the Chancellor."

"Thank you for coming," Cliff said. "This is Kent James, detective for Birmingham PD," he introduced the other werewolf. "If you'll follow me, we were just about to have a drink. Cassie's not doing very well," he added quietly. "Killing twice in as many weeks is hitting her hard."

"Lead the way," I said. It was time for me to act like a husband. It was time, too, to come clean about the investigation into Cassie's father. We needed all our cards on the table if we were to deal with what could be coming.

* * *

Cassie

Rob waited until I'd drank the huge dollop of Scotch he'd poured into a short glass. He'd taken the glass from my hand the moment Parke strode into the room behind Cliff. I gripped the arms of Cliff's recliner to stand.

I felt shaky. Wobbly. I hadn't slept since Friday night and it was now Sunday evening. I wasn't even standing when Parke pulled me up and into his arms. *Baby, I've missed you*, his mind invaded mine.

Few demons had that talent. Parke had it in full force. I almost fell when he kissed me; if he hadn't held me up, I would have.

"She hasn't slept," Rob, the traitor, announced.

Parke kissed me again before lifting me in his arms. "Show me her bedroom. Now."

* * *

Parke

It took nearly an hour and something herbal from the healer to get Cassie to sleep. The others waited patiently while this happened; if they hadn't, I intended to let them know just who had saved their asses the evening before.

It was Cassie.

She looked exhausted, pale and worried when I found her in Cliff's media room, and almost fell when I kissed her.

Yes, I should have been listening to her when she'd called me about *Shakkor Agdah*. I resolved not to make that mistake again. "You need to see the bodies," Daniel said when I walked into the kitchen after leaving Cassie asleep on the bed.

"You don't think somebody's playing at fooling us, do you?" I could see it easily in his face; Daniel was worried.

"No, boss. Come see for yourself."

"We'll be here, standing guard," Kent pointed to himself and Gina, the half-demon, half were-leopard. She hadn't spoken much, but her gaze followed me. Perhaps she wanted to let me have it for neglecting Cassie.

She was right to feel that way.

I followed Cliff, Rob and Daniel to Cliff's barn a hundred yards away; Lyle and Lance stayed in the house with Kent and Gina. Both had a cell phone; they'd warn us if anything unfriendly paid a visit.

Both bodies lay beneath a tarp inside a horse stall; Cliff tossed the tarp aside so I could see for myself. Both heads had been severed—neatly, I might add. "Is that—normal?" I asked after studying the bodies for several moments.

"For their kind, yes," Rob said. Both had pale skin, as if they abhorred the sun. Tattoos covered much of their faces and chests; black pants, boots and cloaks covered the rest of their bodies. Their exposed skin was covered in lumps, too, as if they'd been infected with boils.

"It's poison," Rob informed me when I asked. "If anyone thinks to cut them with anything other than a spelled sword, they'll die shortly after."

"What keeps them from dying from it? The poison they're carrying?" I shook my head at Rob's explanation.

"Dark spells," Rob replied.

"How do you know all this?" I turned toward him.

"Because I fought them the last time they started a war."

"Cassie will have to burn their bodies—we don't need any part of these where someone can get their human or humanoid hands on them," Cliff said. "Her fire is hot enough to destroy them quickly— and the poisons they carry."

"Tomorrow, then," I nodded. "When she's rested."

"Tomorrow she has classes," Rob pointed out. "It will have to be early, and it's hardly fair to ask her not to gag over this before going to school."

"This just keeps getting worse," I said. "We need a meeting with everybody, Cassie included, to sort this out. I suggest finding another place to stay," I pointed my words at Cliff. "They know where this place is, and you've lost wolves because of it."

"Virgil Haney knew where this place was," Cliff sounded angry. "He led them straight to us. Rob's spells and charms would have befuddled them without direct information."

"I suggest keeping Cassie at home tomorrow, then," Daniel suggested. "We have to discuss this with everyone involved, and then find a new place for all of them to stay."

"We may run out of excuses to keep her out of class," Cliff frowned. "She's already stayed home once, after she killed Ray Diablo and then went into shock."

"Missing class isn't the best option, but we don't have another at this point," I said. "She'll stay here and dispose of these bodies; we'll talk this out and decide where to put everybody after that."

* * *

Cassie

"Sweetheart, breakfast is ready." I jumped at the voice so close to my ear, waking from a troubled dream that had me searching for something I couldn't find.

"Baby?" Parke's arms were around me as I struggled to breathe, I'd been so frightened.

"Parke?" My eyes must have been as wild as my breathing as I gripped his shirt in both hands; concern shone in his eyes, which mirrored mine.

"Hey, I didn't mean to scare you." His arms wrapped around me, pulling me into a sitting position without letting me go. Fingers then stroked my hair while he spoke softly to calm my terror.

"Daniel and Lance went to get clothes for you earlier. I called your landlord this morning to tell him you'd be gone for a while and they'd be by to pick up a few things. I just don't want anyone finding

Chapter 16

you so easily, or putting the landlord in danger because you're renting his apartment."

"You think so?" I pulled away from him, although I still felt shaky.

"It's nothing to worry about for now—just a precaution." Parke's dark eyes studied my face for a moment. He'd never say it, but he was worried.

As he should be.

I'm sure he'd seen the bodies of the two dark-cloaks Rob killed. That could mean another paranormal war had been dumped in his lap, when he wasn't expecting anything of the sort.

"I can't stay here," I said, wanting more than anything to bury myself in his arms again and hope he could make things right for all of us. That would be delusional on my part. Parke would need help if there were more dark-cloaks coming.

"We're going to discuss everything—right after breakfast," Parke pulled me against his chest again. "Some things may not be easy for you to hear, but we may have to pull everyone together for this. That means telling everything we know that could be connected."

"Okay." I settled my forehead between his neck and shoulder. He'd showered and smelled like heaven. I probably didn't smell quite so fresh. "Do I have time for a shower before breakfast?"

"I think so. Your suitcase is in the bathroom already. If you need something, let me know." He pulled away, taking his warmth with him.

"I thought you abandoned me," I admitted while sliding off the bed.

"I know. I'm an idiot. There's a reason, but it's not really a good one," he confessed. "You'll hear it in the meeting."

* * *

"Rob and I have the day off," Cliff explained when I sat at his kitchen table to eat. It was nearly ten; Parke allowed me to sleep in until he'd wakened me less than an hour earlier.

"Several people took the day off—after hearing Virgil Haney died in an accident," Rob said. "The only difference is that they're upset. Cliff and I aren't, since the bastard tried to kill us."

"Then I stand in solidarity with you and Cliff," I bit into a slice of bacon.

"Good. It's part of your job description; you have to stand in solidarity with us. If you don't, we'll make you drink from a stained coffee cup for the rest of your internship."

"That coffee cup makes me want to gag," I pointed a finger at Rob. "I've been trying to find a good time to toss it in the trash, but you keep walking by my desk every time I think about it."

"I saw you brought your own last week," Rob grinned. "I can put a spell on it to make it look stained, too."

"You wouldn't," I made a face at him.

"No. But it's fun to think about."

"Right." I stabbed scrambled eggs with my fork and chewed them more forcefully than necessary while still making a face at Rob. He laughed. I almost choked when I laughed, too.

"Well, I lost that bet," Cliff handed twenty dollars to Rob.

"I told him I could make you laugh," Rob grinned. "He said you were too upset."

"Right," I turned to Cliff and made the same face. He chuckled. Rob handed me the twenty. I stuffed it in a pocket of my jeans and went back to eating.

Chapter 17

assie

"I think we're dealing with two rogue ice demons, plus the rock demon. One of those ice demons is Cassie's father, Morton King," Parke looked guilty as he made that announcement. "We don't know who the others ice demon is, but somehow, they've all managed to stay a step ahead of Daniel and that's unusual. It's almost like they can predict his movements. They've split up at least twice that we know of, to commit similar murders and confuse us. We believe Morton is here, now, or somewhere close."

"Cassie said she saw someone who reminded her of her father at Guppy's one night. He met with Ross Diablo's attorney, Claude Ullery."

"Are you sure it wasn't your father?" Daniel asked me. He'd gone still the moment Rob mentioned Ross' attorney.

Daniel knew Claude's name.

"It wasn't him," I confirmed. "But it made me feel weird, like I should recognize him or something."

"Paranormal?" Parke asked. "You have a good sense of these things, Cassie. Tell the truth."

Oh, no. Parke was laying his truth demon on me. He didn't have to; it upset me, somehow, that he'd thought it necessary.

"He could have been. I got so shaky when I saw him that I wasn't even thinking of that. His hands looked like Daddy's, and something about his face and expressions did, too. It wasn't Daddy, Parke. I'd know if it were."

"Claude will know," Daniel said quietly.

"And if we approach Claude, it could alert anybody who doesn't already know we're in town," Parke reminded him. "We'll table that, unless there's no other option."

"What happened during this meeting?" Parke asked, turning back to me.

"Not much. Claude was already there at a table when I walked in. He didn't see me; I saw him first and made sure to stay out of his sight. That's when the other man walked in. They only talked for a minute or two. Claude handed him a legal-size manila envelope. It had something thick in the middle, and odd-shaped, maybe. It wasn't just papers," I added.

"I can work on getting security video," Daniel offered.

"I think that's a good idea," Cliff said. "If you need local help, I may be able to do that for you."

"Where is Guppy's?" Daniel asked, pulling out his cell phone. I gave him the location—it wasn't far from the courthouse, actually.

"We have to assume that Ray Diablo may have been in this, too," Rob pointed out. "His appearance is too close to these other events to be anything besides suspicious. His death may have been a catalyst, too, for the murder of Blake Donovan and the attempt to kill Cliff."

Chapter 17

"Do you think the first judge's death was ordered to misdirect the authorities?" Daniel asked Cliff. "They're connecting Blake's disappearance to that murder and the attempt on the second judge's life."

"It may be," Cliff said. "But if that's the case, the district judge was killed before Cassie killed Ray. I think Blake's death was planned all along; they just didn't want anybody picking up paranormal scent around any of it. If you link a human shooter to the first death and a second attempt, when a State Supreme Court Justice disappears afterward, everything points to foul play again—with the same perpetrator."

"It's to our advantage that they're looking for a human," Rob said. "We don't need even the rumor of paranormal involvement. We don't need witch, vampire or werewolf hunts in this day and age—weapons are much more sophisticated than the last time those things happened."

"They'll never find Blake's body, that's a given," Daniel shrugged. Daniel was an ice demon like Blake; he'd know that as well as anyone.

"You said that somebody was predicting your movements," I pursed my lips as I frowned at Parke. I had no immediate plans to forgive him for bringing out the truth demon to question me. "Do you think somebody may have been watching—or listening—in Seattle? Whenever you made phone calls on your landline in the office or something?"

Parke blinked at me for several seconds before his eyes widened.

"Daniel, get somebody on the phone in Seattle," he barked. "Have my office swept for bugs." He cursed, then, and the name Pauline may have been mentioned.

Daniel understood that somebody needed to hunt Pauline, too, to ask questions. If she knew what Parke was, she could screw him and Daniel with that information. If she were connected to my father in some way, I was just as screwed.

She knew where my apartment was.

She likely had my cell-phone number and several others that she shouldn't have. Parke and Cliff were right to believe Talbert and his wife could be in danger. My breathing went ragged then, and my hands shook. I'd never met Pauline; she'd come to work for Parke just before I left to return to Alabama.

"Jeezus," I muttered and rubbed my forehead to stave off a tension headache. Daniel stalked out of the room, Lance right behind him. Lyle stayed to guard Parke. All of us needed to get the hell away from where we were; Pauline knew where my internship was; she could have the means to track all of us.

"We need another place and fast," Parke snapped. His mind had likely traveled the same road mine had, and reached a similar conclusion. The war we'd only recently been made aware of was poised to take all of us down before we could begin to fight back.

* * *

"This will do for now." Parke looked around Aunt Shelbie's house. It held three bedrooms and was furnished in what Shelbie always called "old South," with things she'd inherited from her mother and grandmother.

I remembered polishing the furniture when I was young to earn money to buy treats and Saturday movie tickets. When I was older, I carefully vacuumed the handmade rugs for additional money.

When Destiny began to spend more time with Shelbie than with our father after Mom disappeared, it became our home until I went to college. I hated Daddy for what he'd done to all of us; he and Ross were responsible for so much evil.

Chapter 17

"I hope they're not watching the place," I shivered as my gaze fell on Shelbie's antique piano. I'd never learned to play; Destiny was taking lessons when she and I ran away.

Shelbie stayed behind to defend us as best she could. That brave act took her life. "Do you think she knew that they'd kill her?" I asked aloud. "When she arranged to get Destiny and me away?"

"I can't say, sweetheart. I never met her," Parke replied. "This furniture must be worth quite a bit—it's old and in excellent shape."

"It's not for sale," I sighed, staring down at the handmade Persian rug I'd cleaned so carefully for Shelbie.

"No sign of anyone nearby," Daniel walked in, followed by Lance and Lyle, the rock demons. "The werewolf and sprite have a house two blocks over, in case they're needed. The sprite was digging his toes into the backyard when we left."

"That's how he connects to everything around him," I said.

"He said the same thing," Daniel held up a hand. "And then he lectured me about knowing what's coming through his perimeter spells."

"Is it bad that we're separated?" I asked Parke. "I feel— insecure, with them being somewhere else."

"We're looking for a larger place, but that could take time—we need a fortress and we're very short on those, right now."

"Too bad I burned down Ross' mansion," I sighed and tossed up a hand in resignation. "He had an army camped there, most of the time."

"The army we killed on Pilchuck," Daniel reminded me.

"She's right, though," Parke looked thoughtful for a moment. "A house like that would be perfect, with some land around it."

"Good luck finding one," Daniel pointed out.

"Let me see if there are strings to pull," Parke countered.

"What am I supposed to do about school?" I asked. A part of me wanted to go back to class. Another part realized I could be putting all my classmates in jeopardy by showing up.

"Baby, I'm thinking about that now," Parke said, holding up a hand to keep me from saying more. I realized that as Chancellor, he likely had a multitude of problems and tasks whirling in his brain. I hoped he knew that law school was a low priority in all that. If the enemy found and killed us, it would be moot anyway.

My cell phone rang as I considered what to do about dinner; we couldn't just go to a local restaurant—could we?

"Rob?" I answered the call.

"We may have located a place to go," he said. "That will house all of us with more room if needed. It's a mansion built twenty years ago in the antebellum style, but with upgrades and better security. I hope the Chancellor can get his hands on half of twelve million quick or we won't get it."

"Twelve million?" I drew in a breath at the cost.

"Cliff and I are willing to pay half of the twelve million price tag. As long as we don't destroy the property, we can resell it later."

"Does he have something?" Parke was now standing beside me.

"Here," I handed the phone to him. "Rob says we need to pay half—that's six million."

"That's not a problem," Parke told Rob after putting the phone to his ear. "Will it work? Can you do your thing there?" He listened for a moment. "Good. I can have a cashier's check by tomorrow. Is it furnished? No problem—we can buy beds and equip the kitchen."

That told me the other furniture was included in the house. For twelve million, it should cook our meals for us, as far as I was concerned.

"We need possession when we hand over the check. Paperwork can be completed later," Parke said before listening to Rob again.

"Yes, I can pull in more security. Of course I'll take any help I can get."

"Where is it?" I thought to ask.

"It's on the east bank of Lake Tuscaloosa," Parke covered the phone to answer. "It has plenty of wooded area around it, a private boathouse and a six-car garage."

"Well, it has to have a boathouse," I mumbled sarcastically when Parke went back to his conversation with Rob.

Daniel covered a snicker; Lance grinned and shook his head.

"We can put water demons in the boathouse," Parke's forehead wrinkled in a frown. He'd heard me. I raked a hand through my hair and walked away from him to peer through the blinds of Shelbie's front window.

* * *

Parke

I watched as Cassie's blue eyes darkened with concern at my stern words; she turned away from me while raking fingers through her silky, dark hair. Damn, she was beautiful. She barely considered that; I sighed as she walked away from me to peer through the blinds covering a tall window at the front of the house.

"We can meet with the seller tonight," Rob's voice sounded in my ear. Already, the sprite was proving to be an invaluable member of the small army I was gathering.

"Make it a private meeting in an out-of-the-way location," I instructed. "We don't want to be seen or heard if at all possible. Dinner would be nice, too, but also in a not-so-well-known location."

"I can arrange it," Rob said and ended the call.

"Cassie?" I strode toward her, holding out her phone. She turned toward me. She still looked pale, in my estimation. Perhaps it was due to her turning earlier, to burn the bodies in Cliff's barn.

Somehow, the sprite placed a shield around the rest of the barn so it wouldn't burn with the bodies. I'd waited nearby with Cassie's robe; she'd left it with me and walked naked toward the bodies on the concrete floor; Rob, Cliff, Daniel and I watched as she'd skipped her prelim completely to become full fire demon. She'd then scoured the floor of the two *Shakkor Agdah* that had stained it with their blood.

Only scorch marks remained when Cassie was done. She'd turned back to humanoid after that; I'd watched her shoulders slump as she surveyed her work. I went to my prelim to carry her robe forward and place it around her; being half rock demon at the time gave me some protection against the heat the floor still held.

"Baby," I said when Cassie took her phone and refused to look at me, "We need to talk."

* * *

Morton King

The motel Dad chose was on the west side of Tuscaloosa, not far from Coker. It wasn't the best available and I considered telling him that.

He had the *MythStone*, or said he did. Ross' attorney, the half-demon Claude Ullery, had gotten it from Ray shortly before Ray disappeared. Dad hadn't opened the envelope; I wondered what had possessed Ray to place such a dangerous thing inside an envelope. A steel box would have been more to my liking.

My cell phone rang; Pauline's number showed on the screen. She'd managed to bug the Chancellor's office; we were still getting information from her on his calls with others.

"Pauline, what do you have?" I barked at her.

"Pauline doesn't have anything anymore," a cold voice informed me. "The FBI would appreciate everything you have to say on the subject, Mr. King."

Chapter 17

My cell phone was smashed to bits before I got my prelim under control. *What the fucking hell did Pauline do to draw the attention of the fucking FBI?*

* * *

Seattle

Kate Worth

"Ma'am, I'm Special Agent Trey Rivers with the FBI," the man introduced himself. He was a paranormal, I understood that almost immediately. Vampire, unless I missed my guess. He'd come to the house and was escorted in, once the night guards saw his badge.

"What can I do for you, Mr. Rivers?" I asked.

"I'd prefer to speak with Parke Worth, your son. I understand he's out of town?"

"That's right. I won't reveal his location until I know he's not in danger," I said.

"He isn't in danger from us," Agent Rivers said. "It's his involvement in a case that we need to speak with him about—in regard to national security, you understand."

"I see," I said. "Have you tried his number?"

"Yes, but he isn't answering."

"He's in a meeting, then," I said. "Where he is."

"We know he's in Alabama," Agent Rivers said. "Really, you have nothing to worry about from us; it's just imperative that we speak to him. We've learned that his office was bugged and private information may have been gathered by less than well-meaning individuals."

"What?" I breathed. That was a shocking revelation and one that would certainly upset Parke.

"Grammie Kate, what's going on?" Destiny walked into the kitchen.

"Sweetie, it's nothing," I waved off her apprehension. "This gentleman needs to talk to Parke."

"It's nothing to be concerned about," Agent Rivers offered Destiny a smile. I gave him points for that; he was attempting to make her comfortable, when most vampires would continue to scowl or keep a noncommittal expression in place.

"Here's my card," Agent Rivers handed a card to me. "I'd appreciate it if you'd tell him to call—if you hear from him. It's very important."

"I will," I said. If it involved national security, I'd call Cassie to see if she'd answer, then have her interrupt Parke if it were possible to do so.

"If there are problems or you don't feel safe, call me," Agent Rivers added before turning to leave.

My breath caught. Did he know something about the things Parke was investigating? I couldn't ask; those were questions Parke needed to answer. I nodded my assent and walked him to the door.

* * *

Cassie

"Kate?" I was surprised that she'd called. I left the table at the tiny restaurant outside Birmingham to answer; Parke, Cliff and Rob were still talking to the attorney representing the seller. They were making arrangements to bring cashier's checks the following morning, so we could take possession of the property by nightfall.

The sale wouldn't be official until all paperwork was done, but this was a cash sale and some things could be worked around.

"I really need to speak with Parke, and I know he's in the middle of something or his phone wouldn't be turned off," Kate said.

"It may be another half hour," I said.

"I know. Tell him this is extremely important and I have to talk to him the minute he's free."

"I'll make sure he calls," I said. "Is there something I can do in the meantime?"

"No, we're safe enough, I think."

Her words frightened me. "Are the guards not there to watch the house?" I asked.

"They're here. I'm just concerned about Parke—and you. The uh, FBI dropped by earlier. Parke's office was bugged, did you know that?"

"He just heard recently that it was possible," I hedged. "Do we know for sure?"

"The FBI Agent says it was. I think he was vampire, Cassie. That means there may be paranormal involvement. They have a paranormal division, it's just that most people don't know about it. The Chancellor seldom hears anything from them, unless there's something they can't handle."

"And we're hearing from them now. He didn't say anything as to what this is about?"

"No. It's scaring me and I have my hands full, keeping this from Destiny."

"I'll make sure he calls the second this meeting is over," I promised. "Call me again if you need help with Destiny."

"It should be fine. She's just curious."

Kate and I didn't discuss the obvious; that it had been a stranger at the door who'd taken Destiny and killed those she'd been with in California. She'd been tied up, blindfolded, gagged and carried to Ross shortly after.

Destiny had nightmares about those things. A stranger at Kate's door probably terrified her, even if he were a well-meaning public servant-slash-vampire.

Kate and I said good-bye; I headed back to the table. The seller's attorney stood just before I reached my seat. Parke and the others stood, too. Parke shook hands with the man; I breathed a relieved sigh. Parke could call his mother back in the next few minutes.

I placed a hand on Parke's arm before he could sit again. "Your mother has an emergency," I said, holding my phone out.

"What is it?" Parke asked, taking the phone and tapping in his mother's number.

"Ask her—she knows more than I do."

* * *

Parke

"Mom? What's going on?" I asked immediately.

"I have a name and phone number of an FBI Special Agent," Mom said. "He came by tonight, said your office has been bugged and that sensitive information may have gone where it shouldn't."

I went still. Pauline was at the bottom of this. I wondered if the FBI knew about her. "Give me the information," I said. "I'll call him now." Jerking my phone from a pocket, I tapped the information into it that Mom read from the agent's card.

"Mom, don't worry, all right," I said. "I'll call him and get back to you. Make sure the guards are doing their jobs; I think this has more to do with human things rather than other things."

"I hope so, although that's bad enough," she said.

"Yeah. I know. I'll call you back."

"Agent Rivers." He answered on the first ring.

"Agent Rivers, this is Parke Worth."

"Mr. Worth, a government agency I can't name at the moment needs a private meeting with you concerning the software Frank Hillman's company created, which was then stolen by Fli-Bi-Net Enterprises."

"You know it was stolen?" I struggled to keep the surprise from my voice.

Chapter 17

"We do, now. We also know that your client has improved on the original design, and those improvements are needed by the agency."

"The unnamed one?" I asked, forcing myself to remain calm. "What about the lawsuit?" I asked.

"I believe the lawsuit can be settled out of court, in a manner of speaking. Let me bring you up to speed on what we know."

"Please," I said.

"Pauline Higgs is a spy—for less than savory characters. One of those characters is your wife's father, although I understand they are estranged. Pauline was carefully placed in your firm by the same ones who backed Geoffrey Gruber. You may not realize this, Mr. Worth, but Fli-Bi-Net is in business with Morton King and his allies."

"Allies?"

"Something is stirring, Mr. Worth. I'm sure your mother reported that I was likely a vampire. She is correct. While the ancient ones of my race are generally content to sit back and watch the world fight with itself, what is growing now is a pestilence upon all, including the vampires. Some are more than old enough to recall the Black Death. Those old ones are now concerned."

"And they want the Chancellor to do something about it?"

"Some of them are willing to help, Chancellor. It is not a light burden, I hope you realize."

"I know." He didn't need to remind me of their history at this point. How his race had been hunted after their discovery, when they'd offered to help a Chancellor centuries in the past.

It had taken a concentrated effort and the limiting of the making of vampires to quell the fears and convince the masses that vampires and werewolves were nothing but a myth.

"When and where can we meet?" I asked, feeling weary.

"I can come to you, if you'd like."

"Fine." I gave him the address of the house we'd just bought. "If all goes well, we should be there tomorrow night."

"This place—is large enough to accommodate a small army, I hope."

"A small army, yes."

"Good. I'll see you tomorrow evening, Chancellor."

* * *

"How did this happen?" I raked fingers through my hair for perhaps the tenth time as I paced. Daniel watched me from a chair in the corner of Shelbie's living room, his eyes hooded.

"I believe it probably sneaked up on everybody the last time, too," Daniel said softly.

"Do you think Ross and his horde wanted the Chancellor's office so it would be easier for a takeover?"

"In my opinion, yes."

"How could I be so blind?" I muttered.

"Parke, you were mourning your father. Like the rest of your family. That has a tendency to shut out rumors of external difficulties."

"Have you talked to Louise?"

"Yes. I sent two guards, too. Discreet ones, of course. We don't need more kidnappings."

"What about Destiny?"

"I hope she's safe enough. We can always arrange for homeschooling until this is over."

"She's making friends at her school. I don't want to destroy that," I said. "I've already destroyed Cassie's return to school. There's no way we can let her go back. They'll know where to find her easily enough."

"I agree. It will place students and faculty in danger if she goes back, in addition to announcing to the world what she is if she is forced to defend them."

"I know. So far, everything she's done as fire demon has been hidden well enough. Send her to a public place and that anonymity could be destroyed in a hurry."

"And it could panic humans, which is to be avoided at all costs."

"I hope that agent is in contact with the CDC, in case we have another outbreak."

"We'll discuss that with him tomorrow. Go to bed. It's late."

"I still have to tell Cassie why I can't go to bed with her."

"A male's fertility period is nothing to trifle with, Parke. In other circumstances, I'd say get her pregnant—as soon as you can. This isn't the time, and until your fertility period is over, you really shouldn't sleep with her."

"Trust fate to intervene like this—now, of all times," I growled.

"This is how half-demons are made—when a male, unaware that he is fertile, makes a human female pregnant. It isn't fair to the children that they are cheated by both races."

"Three months," I blinked unhappily at Daniel. "Three months, and Cassie's wondering whether I want her or not. That's bullshit," I snapped. I wanted to destroy the house, I was so angry.

"You're lucky it didn't happen until you changed Christmas night," Daniel observed. "It could have happened before and you'd have a child on the way. That would take Cassie out of the ranks, and let's face it, we need her."

"I hate this. I really, fucking hate this." Why was it the male demons who controlled the births of their children? Humans were the exact opposite. My other concern was this; after a male demon's fertility period, which generally lasted three months, it could be years before he became fertile again.

Cassie could leave me after our first five-year period was up, and we'd never have a child together.

Yes, I wanted that. I also didn't want to destroy her chance at the career of her choice and an equal partnership in the firm. How was I going to explain this to her? I'd tried earlier, but Cliff had called to discuss the property before I could get Cassie alone to do so.

"I'll go find her," I mumbled and stalked out of the room.

* * *

Cassie

"Baby?" Parke knocked on the bedroom door. I'd left it half-open, hoping he'd show up eventually.

"Parke?" I'd been reading a textbook while waiting for him.

"I have to tell you something," he said. "What I wanted to tell you earlier, when Cliff called me back."

"Oh." I wasn't sure what to make of the fact that his hair looked as if a mowing machine had been run through it rather than his fingers, or that there was a concerned frown on his lips.

He walked toward the bed and sat on the edge of it. "Come here," he patted the sheet-covered mattress beside him. I set my book down and scooted over until I was leaning against him. He buried his nose in my hair for a moment before kissing the top of my head and leaning away to lock eyes with mine.

"I should have told you after Christmas. I didn't. I don't even know if anybody has explained the demon birds and bees to you properly."

"Huh?" I blinked at him in alarm.

"I'm in a fertile period," he sighed and turned his head away.

Chapter 17

I went still. For elemental demons, the males had fertility periods instead of the females. They tended to last a few months and then not reappear again for years. It kept the demon population under control. It wasn't dependent on the female, like it was for humans.

"Oh, no," I mumbled and covered my face with both hands. Parke had a shot at getting a child. Our circumstances ruined it completely. We couldn't even have sex with a condom, because demon seed—well, it had a way of getting through just about anything to fertilize a waiting egg.

"Parke, I'm so sorry," I breathed after dropping my hands.

"I know. I thought we'd have plenty of time to have fun. Turns out, for the next three months at least, that won't be true. We don't need to be parents during a crisis. We have the race itself to consider. I know you thought I didn't want you, or was just ignoring you. That wasn't the case. Plus, I was worried about what you'd think if I had to order your father's death."

"Parke, look at me," I said. He turned dark, tormented eyes in my direction. "I would order his death myself," I said. "Just for his involvement with Ross and for what he did to Destiny and me."

"It looks like he's involved in other things, too, and some of it may be worse," Parke said.

"Like what?"

"Like he's involved with Fli-Bi-Net. The government knows they stole from Hillman. The agent I talked with didn't go into detail, but Fli-Bi-Net may be involved in this paranormal war in some way."

"You're joking?" I breathed.

"We'll find out more tomorrow night, I hope," Parke said. "I'm officially putting you back on the firm's payroll—as my personal assistant in the field. I can't wait to hear what Fli-Bi-Net and your father have been up to."

Chapter 18

*C*assie

I was watching the noon news the following day while having a sandwich with Parke and Daniel. A small California town was getting flooded by heavy rainfall. Most residents left after the flood warnings went out, but several decided to stay and tough it out.

A reporter, draped in a hooded poncho, interviewed one of the remaining residents while I munched on ham and cheese.

"Crazy," Parke nodded at the small television screen sitting on the kitchen counter. "Half the town washed away already and that guy wants to stay."

"They stay during tornadoes, volcanoes and every other kind of natural disaster, and then wonder what happened when they're placed in dire straits and the authorities have to pull them out, or worse still, they die." I set the rest of my sandwich back on my plate with a sigh.

After our talk the evening before, Parke had slept on the living-room sofa. I didn't like that at all.

I needed my head on his shoulder and his arms around me. He'd said he loved me the night before, and gave me a quick peck before leaving me alone in Shelbie's bed. I considered that I should be in class, too, but Parke had already started the withdrawal process at school, so I wouldn't be penalized when I tried to get back in sometime later.

For now, none of us knew how much later that could be. I'd sent a text message to Binita, telling her I had a family emergency and had to withdraw from classes. I hoped she'd accept that excuse and wouldn't try to call me back.

I didn't want her in more danger than she already was, if my suspicions were correct.

Daddy, what have you done? I asked silently. *Did Mom find out your hands were this dirty? Is that why she's dead? How does Fli-Bi-Net fit into all this? I never considered you a technophile, or anything other than Ross' patsy.*

I still considered Ross the catalyst in all this, but what if I were wrong? What if he and Daddy were partners? What if Daddy left town, in case Ross' attempt to claim the Chancellor's seat didn't go as planned?

"I'm driving myself crazy," I admitted aloud, startling Lance, who'd walked into the kitchen to get something to drink.

"I think that's going around," Daniel said, his voice dry. "I'm still wondering why Alabama is ground zero for this. You'd think they'd pick a bigger, more important venue to unleash Armageddon."

"You got me there," I said. "I don't have a clue, either."

"Mail." Lyle walked in, waving a handful of envelopes he'd pulled from Shelbie's mailbox. It looked as if the Post Office didn't know that Shelbie was gone, yet. He handed it to me before I could ask for it.

"Her PO Box is up for renewal," I waved the card. "I guess I'll have to go check it before closing that out."

"We can do that this afternoon, if you want," Parke said.

"Not without me," Daniel held up a hand.

"Wouldn't have it any other way," Parke agreed.

* * *

"There's a package notice," I said, going through the pile of mail that had stacked up in Aunt Shelbie's mailbox.

"I'll get it," Daniel held out a hand.

"Awesome," I said, handing him the card before sifting through the rest of the mail. "It's probably the lotion she always ordered online."

"Most of these are junk, with a few bills," Parke said, looking over my shoulder. Daniel was back in less than five minutes. "We need to do this in the car," Daniel's voice was curt.

"Huh?" I looked up from the stack of mail. He held a carefully wrapped, four-slice toaster-sized box in his hand, with *Fragile* stickers pasted on it. "This is addressed to you," Daniel lowered his voice. "In care of your aunt, and sent by your aunt."

"Let's go." Parke pulled me toward the glass doors of the Post Office before I could mumble a reply. He wouldn't allow me to open it on the way back to Shelbie's house, either. I'd seen the postmark; the package was mailed just before Shelbie died.

What was so important that she'd mailed it to me? She could have given it to her attorney. Had she known she was about to die? If she'd had time to mail the package, she'd had time to carry it to her lawyer's office.

"Careful," Parke said as I cut through three layers of tape to open the box on the kitchen table.

I held my breath—and my retort—for several seconds before continuing with my task. Pulling back the flaps after setting Shelbie's kitchen knife on the table, I stared at the small, white envelope with my name carefully written on it, which lay atop a folded pile of documents and a large manila envelope. The manila envelope looked suspiciously like the one Claude had passed to the stranger who resembled Daddy.

"Letter first," Parke breathed.

My hands shook as I lifted the flap and pulled out a single sheet.

Cassie, Shelbie wrote, *I don't have much time. They're coming for me, and not just because I helped you and Destiny get away. I took something from Ross that he needs to continue with his plans.*

I didn't know until recently what he was doing, but I know now. He has made friends with something terrible, baby girl. Those friends want to eliminate everything human, but only after they destroy any paranormal who stands against them.

I know you probably haven't heard of Shakkor Agdah *before, and I should have told you. I thought they were gone for good after the last paranormal war. I was wrong. I hope you're the one reading this letter instead of Ross; if he gets it, then the world is already his.*

I'll close with this; your mother always said the fire demons were instrumental in winning the last war. There may only be a few of them left. Don't let them take you. You are more important than you think.

One more thing; when you were born, I bought shares for you from a small computer company that was only beginning to make its way in the world. Those shares have split several times since then. I give them to you now. I'd have done it sooner, but Ross came into the picture and I didn't want the money going to him.

Guard what I stole from Ross with your life, and never let Shakkor Agdah *get near it. They want it badly and learned that Ross had acquired it from somewhere. That object is likely the reason they*

Chapter 18

made any sort of deal with him. It certainly wasn't his manners or stellar personality that drew them into his orbit.

I love you. Destiny, too.

Aunt Shelbie.

Parke held me while I wept.

* * *

Parke

Daniel sent for the werewolf and the sprite. I wanted them there when the object was pulled from the envelope. I hoped the sprite would know what it was if the rest of us didn't.

Once Cassie calmed down after reading her aunt's letter, she opened the stock documents. As Shelbie said, she'd purchased stock in what was now the most popular technology company in the world.

A five-thousand-dollar initial investment was now worth more than eight million. I agreed with Shelbie—Ross Diablo would have taken the money if she'd given the stock certificates to Cassie.

"How did she take this from Ross?" Cassie blinked at me. At least tears no longer clung to her lashes, although her eyes still bore the pain of reading Shelbie's last words to her.

"Sweetheart, long ago, according to my father, water demons were the most cunning spies. Water is everywhere. What better way to disguise yourself to get in almost anywhere?"

"This envelope looks a lot like the one Claude gave to that man," she said.

I went still for a moment. "You're sure?" I asked.

"Yeah. I saw it, Parke. Shape is similar, size similar, I swear."

"I believe you," I held up a hand—Cassie looked as if she would start crying again, and I didn't want to upset her with my skepticism. Daniel said we should question Claude. I was beginning to think he was right.

Something else bothered me, too. Why hadn't *Shakkor Agdah* come out in greater force against us already? Why hadn't they stood with Ross in the Christmas war? Something unusual was going on, and I had no clue how to answer any of my questions.

Or where to start.

"Are you packed, baby?" I asked Cassie. So far, at least, things were moving smoothly on the new quarters. I was becoming claustrophobic and paranoid inside Shelbie's old house.

"I'm packed, but I want to go through some of Shelbie's things—her jewelry and stuff. Destiny and I want those things because Shelbie loved them."

"Then go look through them now. I'll let you know when Rob and Cliff get here."

* * *

Cassie

Shelbie, what did you do? How did you do it? I asked silently as I opened the top drawer in her jewelry chest. *Why did you know to do it?* I added.

Had she overheard something, or seen something, to lead her to believe Ross had something *Shakkor Agdah* wanted?

Too many objects from too many scenes in popular films invaded my mind. Those were foolish imaginings. It could be something as inane as a spoon, used to feed the first baby *Shakkor Agdah*, for all I knew.

"It's not the right size for a spoon," I reminded myself as I lifted Shelbie's favorite diamond earrings from the drawer. They were small diamond drops; I'd seen her wear them to funerals and other functions, when she had to dress for the occasion.

A jade necklace lay in the drawer, with matching studs, and a bracelet Destiny and I had bought for Shelbie's last birthday. She'd worn it almost constantly after we'd given it to her. She hadn't died with it on, however.

"I'll take the whole chest," I mumbled, shutting the drawer. "Parke can complain if he wants to; I can't do this right now."

"They're here," Parke poked his head in Shelbie's closet to inform me.

"I'm taking the chest with me," I said. "I can't go through all her things right now. It's too painful."

"I know. Mom waited nine months before she set foot in Dad's closet," he said, reaching for my hand. "Let's see what's in that envelope for now. We'll take the chest with us when we leave."

Rob and Cliff waited in the kitchen when Parke and I walked in; Daniel, Lance and Lyle had gathered, too, in case the envelope's contents were dangerous.

I had a feeling Shelbie would have said that in her letter if it were true—after all, she'd placed it in the box after stealing it from Ross. Nevertheless, I watched as Rob covered his hands in blue investigator's gloves and lifted the gummed flap of the envelope, much like a surgeon might if he were about to perform a transplant.

The object was stone of some sort—marble, maybe, almost black with veins of gold and silver. Carved in the form of a pyramid, it fit easily in Rob's palm and gleamed beneath the light in Shelby's kitchen. It had one flaw—the pyramid's top had been broken off. Carved, minute writings covered every side, including the bottom.

"What the hell is that?" Parke asked.

"It's a dedication, I think," Rob said, lifting the pyramid to examine one side. "This side is written in ancient Greek. This side," he turned the thing around, "is written in Latin. The third side, here," he turned it again, "is in Coptic Egyptian."

"What about the bottom?" I asked.

Rob turned the pyramid upside down. "I don't recognize this one."

"Is this *Shakkor Agdah's* version of the Rosetta Stone?" Parke asked.

"I don't think so," Rob replied, studying the side written in Latin. "This side doesn't say the same thing as the Greek side."

"Great. Three sides in three languages that say different things, and no way in hell to figure out what the bottom says," Daniel sighed.

"Like I said, it looks like a dedication—to three different people—at least in the languages that I can decipher. The top part in each case is broken off, and who knows where that is," Rob grumbled.

"Does it list names?" Parke asked.

"No, that's the part that's broken off. Each one starts with a description, as near as I can tell," he said, holding up the pyramid. "Each description is different, so it's not the same person."

"So we have a dedication to possibly four people, the fourth in a language we don't recognize. Is there somebody who might recognize it?" I asked.

"I can ask scholars from earth, fire and air to take a look," Rob said, naming three sprite races. "They'll be the final authority on the exact wording in each of these cases anyway. They can determine age, too, I think."

"What the hell does *Shakkor Agdah* want with that?" Lance asked. "It looks useless to me."

"A memento, perhaps?" Cliff suggested.

"That's all it could be," Lance snorted. "Otherwise, it's just a hunk of rock."

"It has pretty veins of gold and silver," I pointed out. "I think they chose that piece of marble because of the nice lines and swirls in it."

"So *Shakkor Agdah* has an artistic side—provided they made the thing to start with," Daniel frowned. "Remember, they're responsible for the Black Death, or so the sprite says."

"I was there," Rob said quietly, placing the pyramid on the table and shaking his head. "When they do their worst this time, what will stop them? They have access to sophisticated weapons, not just biological ones."

"I say we put it back in the box and make sure nobody knows we have it until the scholars examine it," Parke held up a hand. He was acting as the Chancellor and making a decision on the matter.

"I will send a message to my King," Rob said, bowing to the Chancellor.

* * *

"We should have thought about supplies," I said, going through empty kitchen cabinets in the new house. I could have brought what wasn't perishable from Shelbie's house at least.

I hadn't thought about that until now. She'd had staples—sugar, flour, coffee—that sort of thing, plus a coffeepot and pots and pans.

"I can have Daniel and Lance clear out her kitchen for you tomorrow," Parke placed a hand on the back of my neck and massaged it gently. *I want to take you to bed, I just can't*, his mental sending made me sigh with longing.

"I know," I whispered and hugged myself. Park's hand left my skin, making me shiver. I wanted that warmth—that reassurance.

Why did this happen now, when we needed each other?

"I managed to get the utilities in my name and the alarm system reactivated with a few phone calls," Parke said and walked away to look out the kitchen window. Less than fifty yards away was the boathouse and the lake beyond that. Sunset was almost upon us, so you could barely see the water.

"What about dinner tonight?" I asked.

"Lyle is picking up pizza and a few necessities," Parke said. "Stop worrying; we can take care of ourselves if we're forced to," he turned a wry smile in my direction.

"What about the FBI Agent?" I asked.

"He won't call until sundown; I figure we'll know something in the next hour or so." Parke's cell phone rang before he could say anything else. I wasn't close enough to see who it was, but it looked as if Parke recognized the name and number on his cell before answering with a curt "Yeah?"

Parke's right hand raked through his hair, indicating his aggravation and stress after only a few seconds listening to the one on the other end. "I don't know what to do about that," Parke admitted. "How many? Have they managed to stop it before it went farther downstream?"

"Fuck," Parke mumbled after listening for a few more seconds. "Yes, I'll do research. I've never heard of this happening before."

Several more seconds passed before Parke said, "I'll do what I can, but it won't bring anybody back." He ended the call shortly after that.

"Trouble," his dark eyes met mine. I watched his mouth curl into an angry, frustrated frown. "That was the Prince of California. He says a water demon was killed by poison and their water was somehow poured into the floodwaters going through Tyree, California. The people who decided to stay all died this morning, after coming in contact with the contaminated water."

"How?" I whispered. "How is that possible? I didn't think any of us were susceptible to poisons."

"I've never seen a poison that could take one of us down, sweetheart," he walked toward me and took my face in his hands. "I think an ice demon killed the water demon, and a poison was added to the melting water after the fact. I believe Prince Alfred is jumping the gun on the facts. Like I told him, I'll have to do research to see whether something like that has ever been reported."

"This is crazy," I let my forehead sink onto Parke's shoulder. "How many died?"

"Seventeen," his chest rumbled with his answer. "Seventeen humans, who should have been relatively safe. Alfred is waiting to hear the human announcement of what sort of poison was used."

"There are so many kinds of poison that can kill them," I said, wrapping my arms around his waist and burrowing against him. "They're so fragile at times."

"I know."

"We have supplies," Cliff and Rob walked in, filled grocery bags gripped in strong fingers. The clunk of canned goods onto granite countertops interrupted my hug with Parke.

Rob winked at me when I stepped away. "Want to help put this stuff away? There's more in the van outside," he grinned.

"I didn't know you had a van," I said, frowning at Rob. It was no use trying to tell him we'd just gotten bad news; he and Cliff had gone out of their way to stock the kitchen for us. That deserved a big thank you, in my opinion.

"Just bought it before heading for the store. Don't need anybody looking for existing vehicles, do we?"

"I guess not," I said while digging into the first grocery bag.

"We bought it under an alternate identity, so they'll have a hard time tracking us down," Cliff said. "Fridge stuff in these two," he pointed out two bags he'd just set on the counter.

"At least we have a fridge," I said and moved toward the built-in behemoth that had come with the property. We wouldn't have beds until they were delivered in two days. Sofas, rugs and other furniture would have to provide sleeping surfaces until that happened.

I set two gallons of milk and three dozen eggs into the fridge while Parke followed Cliff and Rob back to the van to unload more groceries. I wondered about Agent Rivers and where he would stay, if he stayed to investigate.

I wondered, too, whether Daniel and Parke had a plan for digging into what had happened here already, in addition to the new problem cropping up in California.

"We have room, I think there's a large storm shelter in the garage," I heard Parke say as he hefted two bags of groceries onto the counter with one hand. His cell was held between shoulder and ear as he set two more bags beside the first two.

He was talking to the vampire agent—that much was clear. Parke was offering him a place to stay with us. I'd never been that close to a vampire before and wondered what it would be like.

He'll only be awake during night hours, I reminded myself. Vampires never drank from an elemental demon—our blood wouldn't provide sustenance for them. Human blood was best; vampires were once human, after all.

"He'll be here in forty-five," Parke said after ending the call and tucking his cell phone in a pocket.

"Are we still having pizza for dinner?" I asked, unloading a bag filled with spaghetti and jars of sauce.

"Pizza sounds good, actually," Cliff said. "Who's getting it?"

"Lyle," Parke said. "Should be here any time."

* * *

Trey Rivers

The drive from Birmingham to the address the Chancellor gave me wasn't a long one. I had information on the California poisonings, too, that I needed to give him. I realized the Prince of California had probably believed initial evidence, when nothing could be further from the truth.

Yes, a water demon died. That water demon was there at the request of my superior, in an attempt to keep the stubborn humans who remained in Tyree from drowning in the waters of their own hubris.

That water demon died trying to protect them. He was the first to fall; the humans died afterward. Yes, his water joined the other, but it was merely a by-product of the entire, grisly murders, in my estimation.

I had information on a murder in Houston; a vampire colleague had gone in after the fact and smelled ice demon. Likely, the ice demon in question had disguised himself easily enough inside a walk-in freezer and gotten away afterward, when nobody was looking.

A name my division hadn't seen in years had also cropped up; someone said they'd caught a glimpse of Dalton King.

Dalton's name gave everybody the shivers, and for good reason. It wasn't often you heard of an elemental turning into a serial killer. Dalton King was the poster boy for that small cult.

Dalton had been dead for half a century. Now there was a reported sighting. Morton King, Cassandra's father, could be following in his own father's footsteps. I had photographs of Dalton to show Cassie, so she could tell me how much Dalton resembled her father. If someone had mistaken Morton for Dalton, I needed to report that to my boss.

"Records are kept by each race as to how old its members are," Leondras Christopher, my direct supervisor, told me when I first started working in his division. "The other races are generally unaware as to how old the vampires or werewolves are. Sprites, elemental demons and others are most secretive about their ages. While some of those races are immortal like the vampires are, they can be killed or may give up their lives if they choose to do so."

The report on Dalton King's death was particularly nasty; his ice demon was crushed by a rock demon, bent on revenge for one of Dalton's murders. We'd closed his file after that, content to let the crime of that particular demon's annihilation go.

I almost missed the turnoff for the addition where the Chancellor's new quarters were located. I'd have to pay better attention than that, or I could lead an enemy straight to him. At least no vehicles followed me in; I breathed a sigh once I determined that much.

I'd been too caught up in my thoughts. Leondras would be more than disappointed. He'd ask if I were slipping.

"I'm not slipping," I whispered. "I am engaged, as I should be."

* * *

Cassie

"I drove by Claude Ullery's office on the way in," Lyle reported while everyone else searched through half a dozen pizza boxes for their favorite.

"See anything?" Daniel set three pieces of pepperoni and sausage on a paper plate before grabbing a napkin.

"His car was out front, so he was there," Lyle shrugged. "Two more cars besides his—but there are two other attorneys in his office."

"Doesn't sound like business is booming, then," Parke observed.

"We can get into his financials," Daniel suggested.

"Do it. I'd be interested to know whether he's gotten a large infusion of cash, recently."

"I want to know about his partners," I said before I thought. "Who they are, are they half-demons or humans, and how and when they became partners."

"Good idea. Get that information, too." Parke bit into a slice of pizza.

Rob went still and drew in an audible breath. "My King arrives," his eyes were wide as he turned toward me.

"What?" Parke set down his slice of pizza and wiped his hands.

"Come," Rob pulled me toward the back door. "We must greet him when he arrives."

The front doorbell rang as Rob and I reached the back door.

"I have to get that," Parke said behind me. Rob waved him off, flung the back door open and gripping my hand in his, towed me toward the grass behind the house.

At the front door, Parke was likely greeting the vampire FBI agent. At the back door, Rob and I were waiting for the earth sprite King.

The gibbous moon shining overhead lent sufficient light to cast weak shadows as Rob slipped out of his shoes before moving forward again. "Bow," Rob hissed as a rift split the yard.

I bowed as he did, keeping my eyes on the ground splitting before us. Why was the Earth King coming? I imagined that the pyramid Aunt Shelbie stole would be handed off to scholars to examine.

My breath caught when grass and ground fountained upward before us, as if a giant earthworm had erupted from the backyard.

This was no earthworm.

There was light, which I didn't expect. Two sprites, dressed in battle gear much like Rob's at the full moon, stepped out of the abyss first, followed by *their King.*

* * *

Parke

"Trey Rivers," he held out his hand. I shook with the vampire agent while my mind was occupied elsewhere.

Of all those in the kitchen, Rob had grabbed Cassie's hand and pulled her toward the backyard. He wanted her to meet his sprite King first.

Why was that?

"I'm very interested in what you have to say about Pauline, Fli-Bi-Net and anyone else involved in this mess," I said, inviting the vampire into the house. "At the moment, however, we should go to the backyard, where the earth sprite King is arriving."

"What?"

"It's very seldom that you will ever surprise a vampire," my father always said. This vampire was surprised.

"Follow me," I beckoned. The vampire followed as I headed for the kitchen and the back door there. "We just found out he was arriving two minutes ago," I explained as we walked through the expansive house.

Why had Rob not expected his King's visit? I attempted to puzzle that out in my head.

Light blasted through the open back door the moment we reached the kitchen. Trey, vampire that he was, narrowed his eyes in response. Vampires weren't used to such bright light, and, I admit, I almost lifted an arm to block some of the light myself.

That would be rude.

<h1 align="center">Chapter 18</h1>

I kept my hands at my sides, as did Trey. Lance, Cliff and Lyle followed us out of the house in time to see Cassie and Rob bowing to the sprite King, who emerged from a cleft in the backyard.

I wasn't about to ask whether the sprinkler system had been damaged with the arrival. I'd worry about that later.

"Bow," I hissed at the others gathering about me. Yes, I'd learned paranormal etiquette from my father.

I'd never had to use it until now. I dipped my head; the Chancellor wasn't required to bow to a King, only acknowledge him.

"Ah, my dear," the King went straight to Cassie first, breaking protocol by not coming to me instead. I blinked after lifting my head; the King, dressed in rich leather and velvet, lifted Cassie from her bow. "I must thank you," he said, his voice smooth and accented as he spoke in English. "For saving my General."

Chapter 19

assie

King Averill of the earth sprites sat at the kitchen table, eating pizza and drinking hard cider as if he were used to doing it every day.

Three scholars he'd brought with him also sat at the table, eating pizza, drinking hard cider and examining the pyramid as if they were used to doing that every day.

The King's guards stood by the back door, watching the King and the scholars carefully while they tended to business.

Who knew that Rob was the King's General? I sure didn't. I was learning that Rob's position was sort of important in the earth sprite realm.

Rob must have guessed what I was thinking—he and I leaned against the kitchen counter, side-by-side, watching the sprite scholars as they mumbled to each other in their own language while looking at the small pyramid.

"See," Rob whispered, bumping his shoulder against mine, "We're not just a soft drink."

I slapped a hand over my mouth in an attempt to mute the laugh; the gesture was mostly unsuccessful. The King turned toward us and offered a brilliant smile. My cheeks heated, but I smiled back at him.

Earlier, after excusing himself, Parke had taken Daniel and the vampire agent to another room to discuss business. A part of me wanted to know what that entailed. Another part wanted to watch the King and the scholars, hoping they'd tell us something eventually regarding the object they held.

"We believe the words are inconsequential to the object itself," one scholar lifted his eyes to King Averill. "We also believe that the names, which are broken off at the point," he tapped the rough, uneven surface where the pyramid was damaged, "may be more important than the rest. As for the language on the bottom, it is no language that has ever been written on Earth."

The scholar's light-blue eyes rested unblinking, on the King's face. Wispy, pale hair surrounded his face and lifted whenever a breeze blew into the kitchen through the still-open back door.

I wondered why Rob insisted that it stay open, but didn't question his judgement. He was General to the King and the expert in these matters. If the King wanted the door open, then the door would remain open.

At least the outside temperature wasn't unbearably chilly.

"We have no idea why *Shakkor Agdah* would want this," another scholar spoke. "However, it is an ancient object, and may be important in a way we cannot guess. It would be prudent, therefore, to keep it away from them." His hair and eyes were acorn-brown, in contrast to the first scholar's. The third hadn't bothered to speak in English the entire time. His hair was the orange-gold of an evening sunset.

I wondered at the apparent age differences in the three.

The brown-haired scholar was also stating the obvious, in my opinion. Aunt Shelbie died for that thing. I had no plans to hand it to those who may have played a role in her murder.

* * *

Parke

"Pauline is dead."

Trey's news did and didn't shock me. She was human. She knew about paranormals. She'd been questioned by vampire agents to learn what she knew. "How, then?" I couldn't help asking.

"Not like you think, I'll wager," Trey responded. His dark eyes watched me carefully—was he searching for signs of squeamishness?

He won't find it, I reminded myself.

"Compulsion was placed and she was released. The following day, her body was found in a Dumpster outside a restaurant. Her friends were likely satisfied that she was no longer useful to them."

Compulsion. Vampires, even the weakest among them, had it in some measure. It meant nothing to demons and sprites; we weren't affected by it. Humans and half demons almost always were.

They'd gotten what they wanted from Pauline, probably told her to forget that she'd been questioned, in addition to instructing her to forget everything she'd heard while listening to the bug placed in my office, and then sent on her way.

"Efficient," I nodded respectfully to the vampire. "What about the bug in my office?"

"It has been removed. No need to worry," he held up a hand, "It was removed after hours, with none the wiser. We placed one of ours with your cleaning service, for one night."

"Good. Thank you," I sighed. It concerned me that everyone in the office could be alarmed that my office was bugged. I felt foolish that I'd never suspected Pauline of such duplicity.

I was a fucking truth demon. I should have asked hard questions. I'd have bet money that Cassie would have noticed something right away. While she didn't have my resources to get to the root of a problem, she had a talent for knowing when something felt off.

She'd nailed Geoffrey and Annabelle quickly enough. "Do you know whether Pauline was connected to Geoffrey Gruber and Annabelle Taylor?" I had to know.

"Yes. She said as much. She said you were involved in their deaths."

"As the Chancellor, in a war and after they attacked mine first," I said. "They killed my father."

"Yes, we suspected it after we questioned Pauline. Have no fear, Chancellor. Humans will never know what happened that night—not from us."

"Thank you. I greatly appreciate the cooperation of the vampires," I nodded to Trey. "Tell me about Fli-Bi-Net and their involvement."

"We are still attempting to unravel that connection," Trey admitted. "We have moved to protect Frank Hillman, however. We contacted him last week, to discuss terms for his software. As you know, we can't tip our hand with Fli-Bi-Net, as they are still under investigation. It should appear that the legal matter is proceeding as normal. If and when we learn what we want, we will apply pressure for them to settle this lawsuit out of court. They are guilty of piracy; we have proof of it."

"What about Morton King?" I asked. "How is he involved with all this?"

"We know he was fed information by Pauline. She didn't know why he asked for that information; she merely supplied it. As for his connections to Fli-Bi-Net, we only have that information on our end.

Pauline wasn't being compensated enough to realize she was involved in industrial espionage."

"What sort of weapon is Fli-Bi-Net building—for their government contract?" I asked. After all, if they were now working with Frank Hillman, he was probably working the same contract from a separate angle.

"Assassin drones," Trey said, as if that were an everyday occurrence. "The proper software produced by Hillman's company would guarantee at least a ninety-eight-point-four percent kill rate."

"Because it will predict a target's movements," I guessed.

"Yes. The software is a work of genius. Too bad Fli-Bi-Net is managing to fuck it up. Their best accuracy rate is fifteen points less and not likely to improve from that. At least from the schematics our experts have seen and analyzed."

"I'm still not sure how Morton King and Fli-Bi-Net could be connected. *Shakkor Agdah* I could understand; I can imagine they'd love drones that could kill anybody they wanted, without expending power or energy to do it," I said.

"Have you discussed that with any of your colleagues?" Trey asked.

"Not yet. It's a theory I've come up with since we spoke the first time. It concerns me greatly, because werewolves are vulnerable, as are shapeshifters and several other paranormal races. I don't want to get ahead of myself, though, and panic the entire community based on a supposition."

"The Council has already asked their experts to work out the worst-case scenarios if such a theory proved correct," Trey replied.

"So the vamps got there before I did." That troubled me, for some reason.

"We had information you were not privy to, Chancellor. We did not wish to bring this to your attention, for the very reason you have not alarmed the paranormal community. It could prove false, although the likelihood of that is becoming less with the appearance of Black Myth and their assassination of the Prince of Alabama."

"How did you know about that? I haven't made the announcement," I pointed out.

"The Prince has shapeshifters in his employ. They know. That information has traveled beyond the borders of this state, almost from the moment it happened," Trey said. "My kind are always listening."

"That's more than I was doing," I admitted reluctantly. "That has changed in recent days."

"As you say." Trey was an interesting mix; I understood that he was centuries old; upon occasion, his speech became more formal. I imagined he preferred it and only used modern patterns and vernacular when forced to do so.

"You said you had information on the California flood poisonings?" I asked, breaking away from my wandering thoughts.

"Yes. The Prince has only partial information. The murdered water demon worked for my department. He was there to protect lives. He was killed by an ice demon, and poison was added to his water when it melted. Hence the mistaken belief that a water demon was poisoned and consequently caused the deaths of humans."

I cursed. I wasn't quiet when I did it, either. Trey watched with hooded eyes while I had my fit of anger; I imagined he wanted to have a fit, too, but his training as a vampire prevented it.

Unless I missed my guess, the water demon in question had been a friend.

"I'm sorry," I stopped after a while and rubbed my forehead. "I'll update the Prince of California. You have a death to mourn. Anything I can do to make this loss more bearable, let me know."

Chapter 19

"I thank you for that," Trey stood and nodded respectfully. "I must speak with your wife, first. Someone reported a sighting of Dalton King, Morton's father. He was reported as deceased half a century ago. I merely need to show her a photograph of Dalton King, to see how well he resembles her father. We suspect that the sighting was of Morton and not Dalton."

"That's insane," I said. "Where was the sighting?"

"In Houston."

"That's where one of the murders took place—wait, you know all about that, don't you?"

"Yes. We can table that discussion for later; I suspect your investigator should join that conversation."

"He should, and the enforcers who were with him. They saw most of the murder scenes firsthand."

"Then they have the advantage; I have only seen photographs. It troubles me, too, that *Shakkor Agdah* made an appearance on the full moon and has not been seen, since."

"My wife and the sprite did a full squad of them in," I pointed out, my words dry. "Daniel has photographs of the last two bodies we examined before they were destroyed."

"The ones the sprite killed?"

"Yes. He says it requires a vampire's claws or a spelled blade to kill them by beheading."

"That is what my contact with the Council says as well. He tells me the only spelled blades are produced and wielded by sprites. I know of no other magical paranormals capable of producing the necessary spells."

"I can't think of other paranormals who can appear from a manufactured hole in my backyard, either," I said.

Trey hid a smile; he found it funny, which I'd intended. "I will show my photograph to your wife, and would like to see those your investigator has of the *dark cloaks*."

"Deal," I said. "Follow me; I hope the scholars know something about that pyramid by now."

"Pyramid?"

"Come to the kitchen and see for yourself. Otherwise, it's a long story," I said.

* * *

Cassie

I was glad vampires didn't eat pizza; every box was empty by the time Parke walked into the kitchen with the vampire FBI agent. Introductions were made; Trey Rivers was very respectful to Averill.

"Trey has a photograph of Dalton King, your father's father," Parke said. "Someone reported a sighting of Dalton in the Houston area; he wants to know if Dalton resembles your father well enough that they mistook Mort for Dalton."

"All right," I said. "I've never seen pictures of my grandfather, so this will be something new," I added.

Trey pulled a photograph from a jacket pocket and handed it to me. I couldn't speak at first, when I saw the image. When I got my breath back, I almost didn't want to speak.

"Parke," I turned worried eyes on him, "This is the man I saw with Claude Ullery."

* * *

Parke

"It may not be Dalton," Daniel said.

"And yet it may," I countered. "Cassie sounded pretty sure of it."

"She's never seen him before? I find that odd," Daniel argued.

"I don't find it odd at all—Dalton was hunted as a serial killer," Trey said. "When he was reported dead, many in the paranormal community breathed happy sighs and went about their business."

"That's two we know of who were reported dead and conveniently came back to life," I said.

"Who else?" Trey asked. We hadn't discussed Ray Diablo, yet.

"Ray Diablo," I grimaced. "He attacked Rob, Cliff and Cassie. Cassie was forced to take him down."

"Your wife has been busy of late," Trey observed.

"I realize that," I said. "How was I to know this would become ground zero for what looks to be another war?"

"Where was Ray killed?" Trey asked.

"Ross' mansion. It's a burned-out ruin, now. Cassie swears that Claude Ullery passed a package similar to the one her aunt sent to her. If she is correct, then that envelope could have a pyramid in it, too."

"I will send photographs of the pyramid you have to my Council contact, but it is likely they have no more idea of what it is than the sprite King's scholars," Trey said. "The mystery of it, and the fact that there could be two that *Shakkor Agdah* may or may not seek, troubles me."

"It troubles me that we haven't seen any of them since the full moon," Daniel said. "Are they gathering again, to strike again? I worry that they know where we are and could show up at any moment."

"Rob has placed a perimeter shield about the property," I said. "Only someone who knows us and knows where we are can lead *Shakkor Agdah* in, like they did on Cliff's property."

"Why did the sprite King not take the pyramid with him?" Daniel asked.

"He saw no reason to, and perhaps has no desire to lead *Shakkor Agdah* to his own door," I said.

"How will we know they want the thing?" Daniel continued his questioning.

"No idea. They didn't announce their purpose, other than trying to kill us when they showed up during the full moon," Cliff strode in and took a seat in the media room where Trey, Daniel and I had settled for our meeting. "Nobody said anything about a pyramid; they were too busy attacking my pack."

"We need to talk to Claude," Daniel reiterated.

"Tomorrow," I agreed. "Take Cliff or one of the others with you; he can't stand against both of you anyway."

"You'll need compulsion, I think," Trey said. "We will visit him after dark."

* * *

Cassie

"You're waiting for Trey to rise before questioning Claude?" Parke had made the announcement shortly after he raided the fridge to make himself a sandwich. He'd only gotten one piece of pizza before Trey arrived. The sprite King and his entourage had eaten the rest.

I didn't tell Rob that his pizza-loving King had destroyed all my myths about them living organically and only eating vegan or something.

"We should probably consider asking for nominations for a new Prince of Alabama," Rob said while handing a loaf of wheat bread to Parke. Parke stilled for a moment to consider the suggestion, then nodded and set two pieces of bread on a plate.

"Tomorrow," he agreed. "I'll send a message. We need a short turnaround on this, since we could use someone in that seat as of yesterday."

Chapter 19

Parke's calendar was filling up; I knew he had to have a long conversation with the Prince of California about the flood and poisoning deaths. I still hadn't been caught up on that story.

Finding a suitable Prince for Alabama, after the last one had been murdered, could prove difficult. "Want chips?" I asked, going toward the cabinet that held several varieties. It was easy to tell that men had done the shopping; there was a multitude of items for quick meals, while fresh meat hadn't been on the list at all.

"Cliff and I may have a suggestion," Rob said. "We'll let you know when we see your e-mail."

"Tomorrow," Parke repeated. "I'll fit it in. I'll take chips," he said when I held up a bag.

* * *

When someone knocked on the bedroom door later, I thought it was Parke. It wasn't—it was Rob.

"Blankets on the floor, not the most comfortable bed," Rob made a face at my makeshift pallet.

"The beds should be here tomorrow; Parke doesn't want delivery people out here, so Lance and Lyle are renting a moving truck to bring mattress sets and headboards," I said. "What's up?"

"My King asked me to give you this," he held out a small box. It was made of wood and delicately carved.

"What's this?" I asked, taking the box from Rob's hand.

"It's a gift of gratitude. Not many receive them," he said.

"For what?" I asked.

"For saving me twice. And Cliff twice."

"I don't recall saving you a second time," I pointed out while staring at the box in my hands.

"I couldn't have stood against all the dark cloaks sent against us; you trimmed the numbers down to something I could manage."

"I would have done it anyway; there's no need for a gift," I said.

"Open it," he nodded toward the box. I lifted the lid carefully; the box felt so fragile in my hands.

Inside, on a scrap of red velvet, lay a necklace. I blinked; the chain was gold, its pendant a tiny, golden acorn. It looked like filigree; it had been so carefully made. "This is beautiful," I breathed, touching it reverently.

"It will survive your fire, if there is need when you wear it," Rob said. "This means we hold you in the highest regard."

"Really?" I blinked at Rob in confusion. "Everything gets destroyed when I turn."

"Not this. Wear it as a token of our esteem."

"I will." Lifting the necklace from its bed of velvet, I settled it around my neck. The tiny acorn lay over my heart and moved with my breath.

"It looks good," Rob grinned.

"Thank you. Thank your King, too. This is such a thoughtful gift."

"I'll let him know. He loves pizza, by the way. Doesn't get it often, as you can guess."

"Why is that?" I asked. If he were King, surely he could get whatever he wanted to eat.

"His master cook says it isn't real food," Rob grinned. "Averill learned long ago not to argue with the cook."

"Because you won't get decent meals?" I guessed.

"Something like that."

"You're his General?"

"I am, and have been for centuries."

"Wow." I touched the acorn again. "I feel as if I should be more respectful, somehow."

Chapter 19

"After a while, bowing and scraping, as humans put it, becomes an annoyance. I like it better when I'm treated as an equal. I laugh more and enjoy my life when that happens."

"I'm grateful for you and Cliff," I admitted. "When I first had that internship forced on me, I was pissed. I didn't think anybody was looking out for the people who couldn't afford lawyers."

"And that meant the poorest of the poor, more than anything," Rob nodded. "Yes, many of them are guilty. By the law of the land, they are still entitled to representation, and not just a sham performance in a courtroom before a judge and jury who may have already made up their minds."

"Yeah. I thought that, too, what with the prison system and the overcrowding in Alabama," I agreed. "Which I still don't understand. Everybody knows it's overcrowded, and they're still putting people in jail for nonpayment of fines."

"I can see this upsets you. Shall we talk of other things? Discussing a troubling subject before bed causes sleepless nights."

Rob was right—if I dwelled too long on this, it would only mean little sleep and a sluggish morning. "All right, what kind of pizza is Averill's favorite?" I changed subjects.

"He loves the ones with thick crusts and meat piled high. He looks for any reason to visit Chicago," Rob chuckled. "Now, with that, I will say good-night," he turned toward the door. "Pleasant dreams."

* * *

Zedarius

Why am I waking? It was my first coherent thought after staring at the stone ceiling above me for who knew how long.

The stone slab beneath me was uncomfortable, too; I'd only just realized it. *Why had I chosen this place to fall asleep?* My mind struggled to make sense of that. I also searched for a name to call the place where I lay.

Crypt. Mausoleum. Those words in many languages filtered into my brain.

Brain. Yes, I had one. I was beginning to recall that it was stuffed with information, some of which I never wanted to know again.

They are waking, my brain informed me.

"I am still tired," I croaked, my voice as dry as the dust that lay upon me. I hadn't moved for centuries; I understood that.

Never intended to wake or move again, I reminded myself. *Rest in Peace*. I laughed a humorless laugh. That was my intention—to rest in peace. Would it do to curse my fate?

None could be left to hear me.

When I sat up, a waterfall of dust from centuries of non-movement slid off me. I coughed as some of it entered my lungs.

I hadn't breathed in all that time. The stench of stale air offended me. With a scraping noise that pained my ears, I turned on my stone perch to set my feet upon the floor. There was a way out of here; I merely had to remember where it was.

* * *

Parke

I decided to send the e-mail to the Alabama Paranormal Society while having breakfast in the kitchen. Cassie sat nearby, eating quietly while I worked on my tablet. I had two fears regarding the e-mail; one, that I'd get too many nominations and would be forced to weed out the unsuitable; two, that I wouldn't get any nominations, after what happened to Blake Donovan.

To me, it looked as if Blake had a huge target painted on his back from the beginning. For whatever reason, *Shakkor Agdah* waited for the full moon to murder him and attempt to murder Cliff and Rob.

It was too early to contact Prince Alfred in California. Daniel was doing research on the back patio, searching Claude's financial records and such in preparation for the questioning later.

I was glad Trey wanted to go with Daniel; a vampire was a good ally to have at your back. Rock demons were good; a vampire combined with rock demons was much better.

Especially if Dalton King were still alive.

I'd spent several hours the previous evening going into my father's records on Dalton King. He'd killed human and paranormal; robbery was sometimes a motive. Not always, though. Dalton had a volatile temper. In one of my father's notes, he'd written that Dalton was probably dealing with mental illness of some sort.

It mattered not to me; Dalton was dead (again) if we ever crossed paths with him. I'd completed and signed his death warrant after doing my research; every Prince in the United States received a copy in an e-mail, along with the offer of a reward for Dalton's death.

I toyed with the idea of placing a reward for Morton's death, too, but held back; I wanted to talk to him first. Too many questions concerning Ross Diablo needed answers, and I had no doubts, now, that Morton held those answers.

The murder of Delyn King, Cassie's mother, was also a topic for discussion. I wanted Cassie to have some kind of closure on that front.

Mostly what I wanted to know was this; where the hell was *Shakkor Agdah* based, and how many of them were there? *How* were they connected to Morton King, Ross Diablo and Fli-Bi-Net?

Why were they connected to those things? There had to be an advantage to them somehow or they wouldn't consider any sort of alliance.

When would they strike again? Were they involved in the water demon murder in California? I still hadn't heard what type of poison was used.

Last time, they'd used a terrible plague to destroy hundreds of millions. This time, there were so many more humans inhabiting the Earth, and so many new ways to commit genocide. I doubted they'd allow all their genocidal plans to rest on a single method of destruction.

Trey said the vamps had records of the Black Death and *Shakkor Agdah's* involvement in that plague. He claimed that they'd interviewed a handful of *Shakkor Agdah* before beheading them.

I wanted to see those records for myself. Determine the truth in them, if there was any. In all my research into my father's records, nobody claimed to have questioned any member of *Shakkor Agdah.*

The other thing that troubled me was this; I felt as if the air had been sucked away from the Earth; as if it were waiting for a definitive shoe to drop, revealing *Shakkor Agdah's* plans.

A part of me wanted to put that off as long as possible.

Another part of me wanted the waiting to be over.

I had no idea which of those options we'd end up dealing with.

* * *

Cassie

Since Parke was buried in work, I poured him a fresh cup of coffee, put his empty breakfast plate in the dishwasher, wiped off counters and then went looking for something else to do.

Bedding would come with beds and mattresses; new sheets would have to be washed before being placed on beds. I hoped Lyle and Lance knew what they were doing and bought mattress pads, too.

Cliff and Rob had gone back to the PD's Office to turn in official resignations. They intended to use paid leave to cover their final two weeks' notice.

As an intern, I wasn't required to do anything; Rob would handle that part for me. With my cell phone in a sweater pocket, I walked out the back door, past the covered patio where Daniel worked while drinking coffee and wandered toward the boathouse.

The section of ground Averill split for his arrival had disappeared as if he'd never been. I wondered at that. I'd never asked Rob about what power he and his kind held; I'm sure he didn't like talking about it. It could place them in danger with someone searching for vulnerabilities.

My cell phone rang. Lifting it from my pocket, I saw Rob's number displayed.

"Rob?" I answered.

"Cassie, the courthouse is on fire and Cliff and I are trapped in my office," Rob coughed.

Chapter 20

*C*assie

"Daniel," I screeched, running toward the house while holding my cell phone aloft. "We have to get to the courthouse. It's on fire and Rob and Cliff are trapped inside."

Before I could reach the patio, the ground between us erupted. Three earth sprites boiled from the split.

"Come, there is no time to waste," one sprite shouted. Daniel, who'd risen and strode toward me, was pulled into the cleft with barely a struggle by one of the sprites. The other two each grabbed one of my arms and pulled me in, too.

What occurred in the following thirty seconds I will never describe properly. Everything was so dark, I felt as if I were riding a roller coaster through mud while veering around rocks and other obstacles.

Somewhere behind us, Parke could be clueless as to what was happening.

How was the Courthouse on fire? Most of it was built of brick and concrete, so it had to be an interior fire.

Didn't it?

You'll have to go through the floor to reach them, filtered into my mind. Well, it wasn't only Parke who could send messages mentally. *We will wait below with the ice demon; they may be burned and have need of his cold,* the voice added.

I hadn't thought about that. What I was thinking about was that I had to control the external fire. Shelbie said there were myths and legends of other fire demons doing exactly that, but I had no clue where to start, if such a thing were even possible.

What I could do was burn through the floor or floors, and create an opening to get through in order to rescue Cliff and Rob. My main worry was harming them further when I burst through the floor beneath their feet to perform the rescue.

Robin is above us, here, the voice came again. *We will retreat into our temporary tunnel while you move upward and create an opening for their escape.*

I hoped they knew to shield themselves from my fire, especially Daniel, who could be harmed greatly if he weren't prepared.

We are far enough back, the voice replied, as if he'd heard my thoughts.

Yes, there were many things I should have considered before becoming fifteen feet of fire demon and bursting through the basement level of the courthouse.

I didn't have time to think of any of them. Pulling myself through the first hole quickly, I burned my way through the ground floor of the building before going through another floor to reach Rob's small office.

All around me, the courthouse burned. If it were flammable in any part of it, it was on fire. Pops and explosions sounded as things labeled with *Do not puncture or incinerate* warnings, burst open

Chapter 20

with ear-popping jolts. Somewhere, a window shattered, showering glass and sparks onto a screaming crowd below.

Fire knows fire, I reminded myself as I forced my way into Rob's office through the hole I'd created in his floor. At least he and Cliff knew to move the desk out of the way, or I'd have burned right through it, too.

"I can't hold this shield much longer," Rob shouted. I was forced to read his lips; the noise of the fire throughout the PD's Office was deafening.

"Go," I shouted back, flames spouting from my mouth as I spoke.

This wasn't the time for modesty or embarrassment; Rob lifted Cliff in his arms and leapt down the hole I'd created.

I moved toward the hole to follow, only then realizing that if I followed them as I was, I'd be taking the fire with me. With Rob's shield gone, the walls of his office exploded inward. If I didn't keep my fire going—if I became humanoid again to drop down the hole— I'd likely be killed.

Not by fire; I'd be killed by falling debris instead, when the roof caved in and brought the heavy brick structure down with it.

I'd have to go out another way and that, in any human's mind, would present an improbability that couldn't be explained by human means.

Unless—there were trees on the perimeter outside. Making the decision swiftly, I ran, burning through walls to reach windows that hadn't yet been blown outward.

* * *

Parke

"The courthouse is on fire," Lance announced when he and Lyle arrived with beds and mattress sets.

"What?" I looked up from my laptop; I'd been so engrossed in my work I'd shut everything else out for a while. "Cliff and Rob were supposed to go there," I mumbled.

"It's all over the news," Lyle said, clicking the remote for the small television on the nearby kitchen counter.

"Call Cliff. Now," I snapped, standing abruptly. The enemy had already attempted to kill him once. Were they trying a second time?

"There's no need." Rob, his clothes smelling like smoke and burning, walked into the kitchen followed by Cliff, Daniel and three more earth sprites. "The problem is Cassie. We had to leave her inside the courthouse, and it's about to collapse on itself."

I cursed everyone in the room while watching the courthouse crumble into burning debris on live television.

* * *

Charles de Gaulle Airport, Paris
Zedarius

While I'd slept, humans had learned to fly. It took a great deal of work to clothe myself properly and provide identification sufficient enough to get myself onto a flying tube with wings on a deeply troubled world.

While waiting for my flight, I watched the many screens depicting news from many countries. One in particular drew my attention.

A building in a state named Alabama was on fire; I watched it collapse, standing beside humans who found the sight entertaining in some way. It made me sigh instead. Lifting my airline ticket from a pocket, I began to walk toward the airline check-in; I would have to change my flight from Seattle in the state of Washington to Birmingham, in the state of Alabama.

* * *

Cassie

Chapter 20

I clung to the tree trunk, naked except for the necklace Rob gave me, feeling cold and abandoned while pressed against rough bark.

If anyone had thought to look, I'd be visible enough; it was winter and the tree was as naked as I was.

The idea of flinging myself through a window as a fireball was a sound one; I'd changed from fire demon to humanoid when I'd almost reached the tree I'd aimed for. Hitting the trunk and sliding down several feet of it before reaching a sturdy limb had taken a toll on bare skin, however.

As a result, my thighs, breasts and face were on fire from bark burn.

Without a cell phone, I couldn't call anyone. Rob, Cliff and Daniel had left me to fend for myself; that much was obvious. Half an hour had passed and nobody arrived to pull me from the tree and haul me home.

* * *

"There's a woman in that tree," a small, curious child stood at the base of the trunk and pointed upward at me.

"Oh, my goodness," his mother arrived and stared upward, just as her child was doing.

"I'm sorry, I got blasted from the courthouse and landed in this tree," I said, hugging rough bark harder to hide important bits that children shouldn't see.

"Over here," the woman turned and screamed. "We need paramedics, now."

What followed was perhaps a bizarre, waking nightmare as I was pulled from the tree by firefighters in a bucket, covered by a firefighter's coat and hauled to the ground before being loaded into the back of an ambulance and transported to the hospital.

Still, there was no sign of Parke or anyone else who might care about what was happening.

Fluorescent lights in the ER bathed my scraped and gouged body while a nurse and an intern took stock of my wounds and cleaned debris away.

It hurt.

"You're lucky you were blown out of the building before the fire got to you," the intern mused as he pulled a twig from beneath a breast.

"Didn't do much for my clothes," I mumbled.

"The blast must have ripped them from your body. You're lucky to be in one piece—for the most part," the nurse said, filling a gouged spot with cold betadine from a squirt bottle.

"Do you work at the courthouse?" the intern asked.

"As an intern," I said. "In the Public Defender's Office." I watched as the intern gave the nurse a meaningful glance before tending my wounds again. "Actually, I was there, picking up my stuff; I had to withdraw from law school, and the internship went with it. I was only there to get my personal stuff when everything happened."

Since I had no idea how the fire started, I didn't want to trap myself in erroneous details.

"What do you remember?" the intern asked.

"Right now, all I can remember is getting blasted through a window and waking up in that tree."

"Sounds about right—the bomb went off in the PD's Office, or so I hear."

"Great. Any idea who did this?"

"None yet, although the Public Defender says the list may be a long one."

Chapter 20

Perfect. Cliff had time to do a press conference and no time to devote to handling a colleague who'd saved his ass from the fire to begin with.

Two hours had passed and there was still no word from Parke, Daniel or anyone else. I'd been abandoned for real, as far as I could tell.

That's how I came to wear scrubs and someone's donated athletic shoes to walk out of the hospital, after promising to bring an insurance card by later. Three nurses offered to pay for a cab to take me home; I was grateful for the twenty-dollar donation. Without it, I'd have to walk fifteen miles to get to the new house.

* * *

"Just let me out here," I said, as the cab drew up at a house half a mile from the new one. I'd walk the rest of the way. It wouldn't do to lead anybody straight to the house if they chose to follow me for any reason.

The cab driver didn't need to recall my exact address, either. I paid him and watched him drive out of sight before starting my pain-filled trek toward the house.

My muscles had plenty of time to begin their aching on the drive home; I limped toward the house, cursing everybody in it while I walked. It was cold, too, and the borrowed scrubs did nothing to eliminate the wind that whipped around me.

* * *

Parke

"She'll call," Daniel said for perhaps the fiftieth time as I paced in the media room. That's when I heard the security chime; someone had used their code to shut off the alarm, which meant the front door had opened and closed.

I almost ran toward the front door, Daniel right behind me. Skidding to a stop, I took in the sight of Cassie, who looked as if she'd been in a fight.

Skin from her face had been scrubbed raw; I had no idea how that had happened. Taped gauze on her left temple indicated a more severe wound. She moved stiffly in my direction.

When she skirted around me to go past, I reached out an arm to stop her. I should have spoken, first. Explained things, perhaps. Anything would have been better than what did happen.

Cassie drew back a fist and punched me in the mouth, knocking me to the floor before stumbling past me toward her bedroom.

* * *

Cliff

The Chancellor held a bag of frozen pizza bites against a swollen lip when Rob and I made our way into the kitchen. We'd finally shaken the last of the reporters, who wanted to know immediately who was responsible for the courthouse bombing and subsequent fire.

It hadn't gone past any of us that the bomb was planted in the PD's office. Three people were dead because of it.

"Where's Cassie?" Rob asked, before moving forward and pulling the defrosting bag of pizza bites away from Parke's wound.

"She's in her room. I fucked this up," Daniel walked in and answered Rob's question.

"Fucked up how?" I asked.

"After we saw her fireball fly through that window on television, I told Parke she'd call and let us know where she was so we could go get her."

"And that was wrong in how many ways?" Rob was angry in less than a second. "We told you to go to the courthouse—that she would find a way out."

Chapter 20

"I told Parke she'd call, so we wouldn't waste time looking," Daniel sighed and lowered his gaze. "She ended up at the hospital after landing naked in a tree and getting half her skin scrubbed off by rough bark."

"Fucking, brain-blasting, ass-reaming hell," Rob exploded. "What in the name of the First Tree were you thinking?"

"Cassie do that?" I indicated Parke's swollen lip.

"Yeah," Parke mumbled.

"Good." I stalked toward the back door, opened it to go onto the patio and slammed it behind me.

* * *

"Stop worrying about it," Rob set one of two cups of coffee he held on the patio table so I could reach it easily. "The last thing we said to them before we drove back to the courthouse to do damage control was 'go find Cassie.'"

"Is she in pain?" I turned to Rob and asked.

"Probably, but she's not opening the door to anybody right now."

"Human painkillers won't have much of an effect," I sighed.

"It was genius, what she did to get out of the building," Rob grimaced before sipping from the coffee cup in his hand. "If they'd only gone to look for her, they could have gotten her away, brought her here and handled the wounds well enough. As it is, she was forced to go to the hospital and lie about it to humans, all while waiting for somebody to show up."

"She'll call," I tossed up a hand in disbelief while mimicking Daniel's words. "They had no idea what shape she was in, and she was supposed to blithely walk across the courthouse lawn naked and ask to borrow somebody's cell phone?"

"I'm glad you see things my way," Cassie limped onto the patio. She was wrapped in a blanket as if she were freezing. "I want a divorce," she said. "You're a lawyer. Tell me what I need to do."

* * *

Cassie

"This is my fault," Daniel said for the fourth time. "I advised Parke. It was my decision."

"He's the Chancellor," I snarled. "He can make up his own fucking mind. He decided that not coming for me was a good idea. This whole marriage thing happened too fast and now I'm regretting it."

"Is that how you really feel?" Parke's mouth was tight as he asked the question.

"It's how I feel now. You couldn't wait to shove me out your door and send me back to Alabama. You don't have time to be bothered with a wife, do you, Parke? I was just a way to win the Christmas war. Ross wanted me for the same fucking reason; to tip the scales in his favor. Well, I'm tired of being used. If we can't divorce, I want an annulment."

"You don't have grounds for," Daniel began before turning to Parke, who refused to look at me. "Oh," he amended and shut up.

"As Chancellor, I'll grant an annulment on one condition," Parke lifted his eyes to lock with mine.

"What's that?" I demanded.

"That you allow me to court you in three months. I warn you, others will come, and some of their reasons won't be as honorable as mine. Daniel, I need the room," he said.

Daniel hesitated. Yes, he was used to advising the Chancellor. He'd been Parke's father's Investigator before he worked for Parke. He wasn't used to being questioned, I could tell.

Chapter 20

If Louise, Parke's sister, had any sense, she'd run from him if he made an amorous move in her direction. I knew she was in love with him, but he held back because she was rock demon while he was ice.

I kept those words behind my teeth while Daniel left the room, anger in every muscle as he moved stiffly toward the door.

"I fucked this up, sweetheart," Parke said, rubbing his forehead. "I've never been married before."

"And you felt it was all right to make all my decisions for me, without asking me beforehand, or explaining anything. Today was the last straw. I was terrified, Parke, and waiting for you to come. You didn't. I had to borrow money from nurses at the hospital to get a cab. I walked the last half mile by myself because I didn't want the cab driver to know where I really live. So far, it hasn't done me much good to have a husband, has it?"

"No."

"I have the stock Aunt Shelbie left me. I can find another place to live," I said and began walking toward the door.

"You can stay here. We already have separate bedrooms. I'm sorry I made that decision on my own, too. I deeply regret it now."

I didn't reply, I walked out of the media room as quickly as my stiff joints would allow. It was a hollow victory I'd won; I cared about Parke, but he'd done nothing to convince me to remain married to him.

* * *

Cliff

The Chancellor had taken over the media room for his temporary office; Rob and I owned half the house, so I took the game room for my office. Rob and I could share; I suspected the Chancellor was holed up in his while thinking about having a drink or three.

A part of me felt bad that I'd advised Cassie on the annulment; it was a viable alternative to spending five years with a demon spouse who hadn't performed his duties as a husband.

I figured the Chancellor wanted to beat me into a pulp because I'd advised her, but honestly, Rob could have told her the same thing.

Daniel Frank could go screw himself into a wooden plank, too, for advising Parke the way he did. Fire demons were so rare nowadays they almost didn't exist. Cassie was young, too, and hadn't had a decent training period for her demon. The Chancellor should have attended to that.

He hadn't.

I wasn't looking forward to living in a house where most of its inhabitants weren't speaking to one another. Cassie moved stiffly, which indicated she needed help. Parke hadn't offered to do anything for her.

Rob, on the other hand, had put in a call to Gina, who was scheduled to arrive after sundown.

* * *

Cassie

"Gina's here," Rob said, opening my bedroom door after knocking. Gina stood on tiptoe to peer over his shoulder at me. I winced when I moved to sit up on the bed; I'd spent most of the afternoon huddled under a blanket, hoping the pain would subside.

By this time, my pajamas were stuck to half the scrapes and I didn't have the courage to pull the two apart.

Rob stayed while Gina worked; I thought about sending him away but didn't have the strength to argue with him. If he hadn't seen worse in his lifetime, then he shouldn't be a General to the King.

The tears fell when Gina began pulling away fabric that was stuck to my wounds. Part of the prescription the intern had given me was for an antibiotic ointment for the worst scrapes; nobody had offered to pick it up for me, so I'd done without.

"I hear you punched out the Chancellor," Gina said while pulling more fabric away. My body felt as if it were on fire again, but not in any good way. I wiped my eyes as Gina worked and didn't answer.

* * *

Robin Newbourne

"She had a prescription for an ointment; I imagine she'd have told us that if we'd asked," I said, setting two small slips of paper onto the kitchen table in front of Parke. "Her clothes stuck to the wounds. Gina had to rip them off. It was pretty bloody after that."

"Look, I don't know how many times I can say I fucked up," Parke mumbled. "I fucked up. Now she wants nothing to do with me. Can I be left in peace for a few minutes?"

"If that's what you want," I said and turned to walk away.

He'd had no business marrying her so quickly in the first place. That was his first fuck up, in my opinion. Averill told me the Chancellor wasn't ready to be a husband. My King was correct.

* * *

Parke

"If you think I'll take your side in this, you are wrong," Mom dressed me down over the phone. "When did your marriage become a committee consisting of you and an unmarried male friend? You and Daniel made a stupid decision, when Cassie's life could have been in terrible danger. What if *Shakkor Agdah* came for her while she was in that tree?"

I went cold and shivered. She was right; I hadn't considered that sort of danger. "Have you signed the annulment yet?" Mom demanded, waking me from my darkening thoughts.

"No, I wanted to talk to you, first, but I already promised," I fumbled.

"Then take it back. Now. Get down on your knees if you have to. If you don't think that's the right woman for you, then you are more wrong than I've ever seen you be wrong. Apologize. Beg her to take you back. Find a demon hollow and show her you belong together."

"Mom, I'm fertile right now," I said.

"What would be the worst thing to happen, if that's the case?" She demanded. "It's not easy to get pregnant, even if the male is fertile. Your father and I tried for years before you came along. It's why demons don't overpopulate the planet, you know."

"But she's got scrapes and bruises," I began.

"Which will heal fast if she goes to prelim. Problem solved."

"Fuck," I breathed, rubbing my forehead with my free hand.

"Parke, do you love her?"

"I do, it's just that there are so many things in the way," I attempted to wriggle away from Mom's accusing tone.

"Good. Go tell her, and follow that up with showing her that you love her. This is the worst honeymoon story I've ever heard."

My head snapped up at that. Cassie wasn't getting any kind of a honeymoon. I'd just shoved her in the directions I wanted her to go and left it like that.

"Has she handed your ring back?" Mom persisted.

"No, I don't have it," I began.

"Then she's giving you room to make this right. Go make it right, Parke, or I swear I won't cook for you for a year."

"I'm on it," I said and ended the call. By the time I was out of my temporary office, I'd broken into a trot.

* * *

Cassie

I felt much better the following morning—physically, anyway. With Gina's help, my wounds were more than half-healed. Parke hadn't come to the kitchen for coffee while I was there eating breakfast; Daniel slunk in and out as if he were guilty.

In my opinion, he was more than guilty. He and Parke both. Rob finally pulled me away from my spot at the kitchen table, where I'd sat while sipping coffee and steeping myself in moroseness.

I stood in Cliff's makeshift office in the empty game room. Cliff stood by the window, framed by the light filtering through plantation blinds, to survey the room and decide where he wanted his desk to go.

"It won't matter where you put your desk if you get a non-glare computer monitor," I pointed out.

"That's true," Rob agreed. "You could set it here," he indicated a space perpendicular to the windows, where Cliff could see the door and the view through the windows by a turn of the head.

"File cabinets here," I pointed to the wall adjacent to the door. "What else do you want in your office?"

"Sofa opposite the desk?" Cliff moved away from the window and went to stand against the designated wall.

"Sure," I shrugged. "Leather, maybe? That would look good."

"I need a spot where I can bring in the rest of my Pack, if necessary," Cliff said. "We can meet in here if we have to."

That's when Parke blew into Cliff's domain like a tropical storm. Rob started to say something but I never heard his words; Parke's mouth was on mine before I could move a hand to stop him.

The next thing I knew, Parke was kissing me while carrying me toward the back door. The moment he stepped onto the grass of the backyard, he went to prelim. *Turn Cassie*, his mental voice begged. *I want to love you until we're exhausted.*

If my mind said no, it wasn't loud enough to make a difference. My body was speaking to Parke's, turning to prelim in his arms. He grunted in satisfaction. Who needs a ready-made demon hollow if a rock and fire demon roll on the backyard enough times to create their own?

If some of the grass caught fire when flames licked from my prelim's skin during my first orgasm, I didn't really care. Park's rock demon prelim rolled over the small fires and put them out while he laughed.

* * *

Robin Newbourne

"I may have been mistaken," I sighed and placed a cup of coffee at Cliff's elbow.

"About what? Oh, they're starting up again."

"About that. Who knew he'd come to his senses?" I asked, lifting my own cup and drinking. I'd added half a cup of Scotch to my coffee; I needed it, what with the sound of demon sex going on in the backyard.

"I hope they don't intend to make that hollow a permanent one," Cliff muttered and drank his coffee.

One of my eyebrows rose before I could stop it; Cassie's prelim was screaming Parke's name. A nonspecific deity's name may have been added to the mix, too. "When's the last time you had sex?" I asked.

"Not for a while. Why? You asking?"

"Hell no, I just wondered."

"Got more of that Scotch?"

"Yes."

"Good," Cliff held out his cup. "Pour until I say stop."

* * *

Cassie

Chapter 20

"I love you," Parke breathed against a nipple before emphasizing his words with a firm nip.

I was exhausted. He'd been right before—he'd loved both of us into exhaustion. There we were, too tired and sated to move, while in full view of anybody who thought to look through a window inside the house.

Like our first time, too, we'd made enough noise for everybody to hear if they hadn't looked.

"Should we be embarrassed?" I mumbled, my voice weak and soft.

"Fuck no, I'm not embarrassed. I'm happy," Parke breathed against my neck before placing a kiss there. "Please say you won't leave me. I love you too much. It will destroy me."

He should have said that in the beginning, but that was before we'd almost set the backyard on fire. I was willing to give him slack—this time.

"How about probation?" I traced the ridge above his right eye—it was where an eyebrow would be if he were humanoid. In his prelim, it very much resembled the rock he could become.

"I'll settle for probation, if we can sleep together every night."

Also something he should have said in the beginning.

"Then we'll do that," I sighed and closed my eyes. Sometime, while I drifted in and out of sleep, Parke carried me into the house and put me to bed. For the moment, I was happy.

Chapter 21

*P**arke*

"I don't have good news, I'm afraid," Prince Alfred informed me. I was showered, dressed and back in my office when he called.

"What news is that?" I asked, mentally preparing myself for whatever he was about to say.

"The poison has turned into a disease, like a time-released drug," Alfred informed me. "A hospital downriver from Tyree is filling up with patients. They don't know what to make of it—it's not any plague they've ever seen. The CDC has quarantined the place until they can identify and treat it, but I'm concerned people will die before that happens."

"Not good. Have you seen any signs of *Shakkor Agdah*?"

"None, but that means nothing if they can do this from the shadows. Remember, there were no human records of their involvement before; only those records the vampires, sprites and demons kept."

"True. I have a vampire here, and he says something similar. I'll ask if there's a way to see his Council's records on the matter."

"Chancellor, I believe that when *Shakkor Agdah* comes into the light, it will be far too late—for any of us."

"Then we have to hunt them," I said. I already had a good place to start, too; Claude Ullery. "Call back if the situation worsens. In the meantime, put your best investigators and trackers on this. See if they left a trail."

"I will. Thank you, Chancellor."

I shouted for Daniel the moment Alfred ended the call.

* * *

Cliff

Kent was on his way with Gina; it was a rare day off for him; I'd asked him to bring two more wolves from the Birmingham Pack, too, so we could sniff around Claude Ullery's house while he was at work.

I'd heard the Chancellor bellowing for Daniel Frank; he and the investigator would go to Claude's office. That presented the perfect opportunity for anyone with a decent nose to trace comings and goings at the Ullery home while he was occupied elsewhere.

They'd made a late appointment with Claude on some trumped up legal case; pretending to hire the asshole was as good a ruse as any. It also gave them time to get the vampire up and ready to go.

A part of me wished to see Ullery squirm under compulsion, but knew my time would be better spent at his home.

If Claude had demon visitors, my wolves and I would know it by scent. Rob offered to stay at the house, watching out for Cassie and Gina and preparing dinner. He'd also called the previous owner to find out who did their yard work; until demon sex had occurred in the backyard earlier, the lawn had been perfect.

I laughed when Rob said he wasn't touching that grass for any amount of money; half of it was burned, the other half ripped out and flung in every direction. The dirt beneath was flattened into a bowl-shape, like any demon hollow would be after several uses.

Rob didn't have much experience with lawn sprinklers, either, and those would need work before they were turned on for the summer.

"Their guy is coming by tomorrow," Rob walked past me as I pulled on a jacket. "They told me he'd lived in their boathouse before they sold the place, because he was their handyman, too. They gave him a big thumbs-up, and said he worked cheap, since they provided housing."

"Trustworthy?" I asked, stuffing truck keys in my jacket pocket.

"One hundred percent, according to them."

"Good. Work it out," I waved a hand. "We have demons to hunt."

* * *

Parke

Three werewolves and the healer drove up just as Trey, Daniel and I were ready to leave for our appointment. Cliff walked out of the house, leaving the door open for Gina to go inside.

"Grand Master," one of the new werewolves dipped his head to Cliff.

I went still.

No wonder *Shakkor Agdah* was so interested in killing him. Things were starting to clear up on that front. It was something I probably should have known or guessed. We'd have a talk when I got back, I decided.

It was never a good idea to piss off the Grand Master. Daniel whistled low after Cliff and his wolves loaded into his truck and drove away. "Never saw that coming," he mumbled and shook his head.

"I knew it," Trey offered. "I thought you did, too."

"Come on or we'll be late," I snapped. I was Chancellor, dammit. People needed to stop keeping secrets around me.

* * *

Cliff

Claude's porch light was on. No surprise, it was dark outside. I'd parked two blocks away, in front of a house that was being renovated. A roll-off Dumpster was in the driveway, providing partial cover for the three wolves that spilled out of my truck.

They'd turned to wolf on the drive to Claude's house, to leave their clothing inside the truck. It wouldn't do to be caught naked if we were stopped on the way back; it was werewolf 101 not to be seen in human form without clothing.

Hastily shucking shoes, shirt and jeans, I opened the door before making the change. Truck keys were on the floor in front of the driver's seat, ready for a hasty exit if needed.

My wolf closed the door with his muzzle once I slipped off the seat and onto the street.

* * *

Parke

Claude's receptionist was working late, too. "Have a seat, he's on the phone," she smiled at us when we checked in. I used the time to send Jon a text at my office; he was keeping me abreast of my caseload and I was beginning to trust him to get necessary paperwork done and filed with the court clerk.

He also had a knack for soothing clients; I'd spoken to two on the phone earlier in the day, after he'd calmed their fears concerning their cases.

I hadn't told Cassie, yet, but I needed to fly back to Seattle in two days for a court appearance.

"He'll see you now," the receptionist, a middle-aged woman with hair such an unnatural color it looked as if it had clawed its way out of a bottle to attack her head, led us toward Claude's office.

"Hello," Claude's greeting was as false as his smile. "Claude Ullery," he shook with Daniel, first, as Daniel had gone ahead of me to provide protection.

"Dan Githens," Dan supplied the alias we'd given on the phone.

Trey held out his hand next. "Trey Githens," he said. "You will tell us everything we ask, and you will forget we were ever here afterward."

* * *

Cliff

Kent crossed into the yard first, slipping from shadow to shadow to hide his presence from Claude's neighbors. Claude lived on two acres of ground, but reported sightings of four large wolves or giant dogs in the neighborhood could bring the local police.

We didn't want that. I wanted to sniff around, learn what I could and then beat a path back to the truck. I didn't trust Claude for a second; his smell alone could make any werewolf gag.

It was my decision to divide the yard into quarters and assign those quarters to my posse. I took the quarter closest to the front door; the others spread out silently, heading for their own area.

Claude's walkway curved from the driveway to the front door; decorative shrubs and dead or dormant flowers filled flowerbeds lining the walk.

I supposed I should feel grateful that it was winter and the plant was dry and withered; instead of making me ill, it made me sneeze.

And sneeze again.

Aconitum Lycoctonum—wolfsbane. Claude had planted wolfsbane around his house, preventing exactly what I intended to do; sniff around his house for clues. In the distance, I heard Kent begin to sneeze, and then the other two.

We needed to get out fast; the neighbors could be calling the police already. With a nasal-clogged yip, I let the others know to get the hell away.

When three sets of paws hit the driveway and scrabbled toward the street, I turned and ran after them. Claude shouldn't have been smart enough to plant wolfsbane.

Dalton and Morton King, however, would likely know exactly what to plant and where to plant it. Forced to breathe through my mouth, I raced as swiftly and silently as I could toward the truck, determined to get my people away before all hell broke loose.

* * *

Parke

"Recognize this man? Word has it you passed a package to him recently in a local restaurant," Trey held Dalton King's photograph in Claude's face.

"S-Steve Killborn," Claude hissed.

An alias, Trey's voice whispered in my mind. It was rare for vampires to mindspeak; it only made me blink as I registered the words.

"Who gave you the package to deliver to Steve?" Trey almost hissed the name.

"Ray—uh, Ross' brother," Claude was sweating. At least he knew Ray, who hadn't bothered with an alias. It didn't matter, Ray was dead and of no use to us.

"What was in that package?" Trey demanded.

"I don't know. I was told not to open it or I could die."

"But it was all right to carry it around in an envelope?"

"Ray said it was safe that way," Claude whined. "I didn't handle it much."

"How much were you paid for the delivery?"

"Wasn't paid," Claude's voice betrayed disappointment. "Favor owed to Ross," he babbled.

"For what, exactly?"

"Hiding bodies." Claude shrank away from Trey as the vampire hissed in his face.

I turned to blink at Daniel, who was just as stunned as I was.

"A list of names, please," Trey pulled a legal pad and pen toward Claude. "Start writing. Who did you kill and where are they now?"

"I don't know where they are," Claude's hand shook as he began to write. "Ross disposed of them."

"Bloody, fucking hell," I breathed. The questioning had taken a turn I didn't like, and we still had nothing new on Dalton and Morton King.

* * *

Cassie

Cliff, Kent and two other werewolves in human form walked into the house, all breathing through their mouths, their faces looking as if someone had punched them multiple times.

They were puffy and purplish, especially around the nose and eyes. "Wolfsbane," Gina cursed the word and went to Kent, first. "Ice," she snapped at Rob and me. "Wrap it in towels. We have to get the swelling down before it spreads."

While Rob and I handed towels filled with ice to werewolves to hold against their faces, Gina dug through her cloth bag of medicines until she found what she wanted.

"Benadryl?" I stared skeptically at the box of human antihistamine in her hand.

"It works, but it has to be in larger doses," she said, working to pop the pills out of the plastic and foil packets.

I worked on a second packet while she did the first. "Six each, to start," she slammed pills in front of Kent while Rob served him a glass of water. He was gasping for breath by that time; I was beginning to be afraid.

More pills were handed to the others who took them quickly, between rasping breaths. No wonder they called it wolfsbane; even when the plant was dead it had a terrible effect.

"I have no idea why they couldn't smell it until they were right on top of it," Gina muttered, placing the ice pack against Kent's face after he swallowed the pills.

"It could be spelled to do that," Rob said, setting Kent's empty glass in the sink.

"By whom?" Gina lifted her head. Flashing eyes betrayed her anger; not at Rob, but at the idea that someone could casually kill a werewolf by muting the scent of wolfsbane until it was too late.

"Who are we currently fighting that can cast spells?" Rob lifted an eyebrow.

"*Shakkor Agdah*," Gina muttered and went back to tending Kent.

"You okay?" I lifted Cliff's ice pack away from his eyes and nose.

"Hope so," he croaked. I could tell he wanted to say more, but his condition prevented it.

"Cover up," I tipped the pack over his face again. Like Cliff, I wanted to curse Claude Ullery. If this had been springtime and those plants in bloom, Cliff and the others would be dead already.

* * *

Parke

Chapter 21

"Cliff and the others tripped over wolfsbane before they could smell it," Cassie informed me. "Claude was worried the werewolves would come. If the plants weren't dead, we'd have dead werewolves. They all had severe allergic reactions anyway; that's why Cliff can't talk right now."

"Could this night get any worse?" I raked fingers through my hair.

"What happened?" Cassie asked, concern in her voice.

"I'm fine," I reassured her. "It's just that Claude is being booked into the county jail—on multiple murder charges. He's been killing and paying Ross to hide the bodies—in exchange for favors, now and then."

"What kind of favors?"

"Like taking a package from Ray and handing it to your grandfather."

"Oh."

I realized I shouldn't have said grandfather; I should have said Dalton King, so Cassie could have some separation from the criminal elements in her family.

"Did he, uh, say what was in the package?"

"Ray told him it was dangerous; he couldn't pass it off to Dalton fast enough. Claude doesn't have any qualms about other people being in danger—he only worries about himself, apparently."

"Yeah. Hence the wolfsbane planted on his property. It makes me wonder how his gardener got around that stuff—it's toxic to humans, too."

"He may do the yard work himself—as a half-demon he'd be immune."

"Well, that makes sense, unless he has a half-demon gardener."

"True. I'll have to research that."

"How long will you be out?" she asked.

"No idea. There's a long list of victims—sixteen, or so Claude says. Trey did us a favor—he ordered Claude to report that Ross was his last victim—it sort of ties everything up, since Claude reportedly hid the body in Ross' basement recently and burned the house down."

"You didn't," Cassie breathed.

"It was convenient, and points the blame in a logical direction. Claude and Ross have a disagreement; Claude kills Ross, hides the body until a convenient time and then destroys all evidence with a fire."

"Yeah. I just hope nobody looks too closely at that story."

"Trey was very thorough. He's done this before."

"Awesome." I could tell she was being sarcastic.

"We're paranormals, baby. Hiding what we are is second nature. Lies are told every day in the interest of the greater good."

"That's great, until something like *Shakkor Agdah* shows up and starts whittling away at the human population," she snapped.

"I know you're upset," I said, attempting to deflect her anger. "We'll talk when I get home, okay?"

"Sure."

* * *

Cassie

"How many murders?" Rob set a cup of tea at my elbow.

"Claude confessed to sixteen. Trey added Ross as the seventeenth victim, so that mystery would be cleared up."

"I can understand his reasoning, although I wouldn't have muddied the waters like that."

"Me, either," I confessed. "Thanks for the tea," I lifted the cup and drank.

"Gina says the wolves are doing better—Cliff is actually breathing through his nose, although he sounds like a foghorn."

Chapter 21

"Thank goodness," I sighed and let my forehead drop onto the kitchen table.

* * *

Tuscaloosa, Alabama

Zedarius

Humans and others ran out of the building housing the jail, many of them screaming as a second explosion sent a plume of sparks boiling into the night sky.

The first one out, although few could have seen it, was a vampire carrying two others. Yes, I knew where the explosion originated. Humans and one half-demon were dead as a result.

Had I been Black Myth, I would have killed the half-demon, too. He held a tenuous link to their doings, although he failed to realize it.

The human deaths disturbed me. The objective could have been achieved in a less spectacular fashion, and the other deaths prevented. Soon, it would be time to delve into Black Myth's leadership.

That could wait; other things had to be accomplished first.

* * *

Cassie

"You're home earlier than I expected," I said, but pulled back at the dark look Parke sent in my direction.

Angry wouldn't begin to describe what he was. He was ready to turn to rock demon and tear the house apart around him.

Daniel wasn't in a better mood, it's just that he'd be less destructive than Parke if he turned to ice demon.

Trey, the vampire agent, was the only one who hid his feelings. "What happened?" I asked him, hoping for a reasonable answer rather than a barked order to be quiet.

"Claude exploded," Trey said.

"What?" People didn't just explode, did they?

"*Shakkor Agdah*, no doubt," Parke's explanation was tight-lipped. "All those people poisoned in California are dead—I got the text from Prince Alfred while I was at the county jail. It's no longer the jail—it was still exploding and burning when Trey hauled us out of there."

My breath caught. Humans had likely died there, too. Not all of them had a vampire to carry them away faster than the eye could follow.

"It'll be on the news," Daniel nodded toward the small television on the kitchen counter.

I really didn't want to see it; it gave me the shivers. First the courthouse, now the jail. Somebody wanted Cliff and Rob dead at the courthouse. That same somebody, in all likelihood, had killed Claude Ullery and who knew how many humans at the same time?

"Did you get anything useful from Claude, other than he was a serial killer?" I asked. My lips were numb and I stumbled over the term *serial killer*.

"Not a lot," Daniel confessed. "Too stupid for the enemy to hand much information to him," he added.

"He could have killed four wolves tonight," Gina walked into the kitchen to fill a towel with fresh ice.

"We get that," Parke held up a hand. "If the police weren't swarming over his place like flies on a carcass right now, I'd go check it out myself."

"It wouldn't surprise me if that isn't booby-trapped, too," I announced.

"Kent got a call from Birmingham PD," Cliff shuffled into the kitchen, his face still puffy and dark, his voice barely above a weak croak. "Ullery's house blew up ten minutes after the police walked

Chapter 21

into it. Three officers are dead; two others are wounded and at the hospital."

"Bloody, fucking hell," Parke exploded.

* * *

Parke

"They can't find the source of the explosions, but that's no surprise," Daniel handed his report to me the following morning. He hadn't slept much, either, so he'd decided to use the time to write a report for the Chancellor's files.

He'd been watching television too; it wasn't just the Birmingham news stations that picked up the happenings in Tuscaloosa; a national news program in Atlanta was now on the scene, speculating about everything.

Trey had supplied the list of Claude's victims to his department at the FBI; at least they had that information to report, although the fact that Claude himself had exploded first, bringing the jail down around him, wasn't reported.

Probably because he'd been searched for weapons and other contraband before being booked.

"I need to be here, and I need to be in California," I said. "I need to be in Seattle in two days. Can things get more fucked up than this?" I asked Daniel.

"I'm not one to tempt fate by saying no," he said.

"You're right. They can be worse. Please don't get worse," I held up a hand.

"Want me to book a flight to California?"

"Yes. For both of us, plus Lance. Lyle can stay here with the others for now."

"Do you plan to leave a temp in the Prince's slot?"

"I'd like to do that; I'll see if there are any responses to my e-mails before making that decision. Get the latest flight out of Birmingham you can," I said.

"Will do."

"The gardener-slash-handyman is here," Rob poked his head inside the door before Daniel turned to leave.

"Fine. Take him to the kitchen; I'll be there in a minute."

* * *

Cassie

I couldn't determine his age, although his hair was still dark, if a bit shaggy. He held out a resume and a letter of reference the previous owners had written for him. Part of me felt embarrassed that his first job was to repair the lawn where Parke and I had damaged it.

"This looks good," Rob read the letter quickly. "Are you still interested in living in the boathouse as part of your pay?"

"Yes," he nodded. "It's a comfortable place, everything in the kitchen works; fridge could be updated, though."

"We'll look into replacing it," Rob said, handing the resume and letter to me.

"William Z. Berry? Do you prefer William or something else?" I asked after reading the name listed on the resume.

"Will," he shrugged.

"What's the Z for?" I asked. You didn't see many people with a middle name starting with Z. Or a first name, for that matter.

"Zedarius," he smiled. "My father insisted."

Parke arrived then; I handed the papers to him. "Everything looks good; I see you haven't had a raise in two years," Parke said after leafing through Will's information. "I'll give you a ten percent increase."

"Thank you," Will sounded surprised. "I'm just grateful I can have my job back."

"If you need tools or supplies, let Cassie know. Someone will make arrangements."

"Thank you. I'll bring my things later; I see there's a spot on the lawn that needs repairs," Will said.

"Yes. It would be great if you'd fix that first," Rob's words were dry.

"Welcome home," Parke held out his hand and shook with Will. "We appreciate the effort you've put into the lawn in the past; it's in perfect condition."

"Except for the mess we left in the backyard," I muttered.

* * *

Parke

Cliff sat inside my makeshift office, his eyes hooded. I suspected he was behind this campaign and had no idea what to do about it.

I had six nominations for Prince of Alabama.

Every nomination was the same.

"That's a pretty deep frown," Cliff said. At least I could understand him clearly, now; the facial swelling had gone down dramatically.

"You know this isn't possible," I handed him six printed copies of the e-mails I'd received.

"I don't know why not."

"The Chancellor cannot be married to any Prince or Princess. I can show you the exact passage in the paranormal laws," I said. "It's to prevent one state from having an unfair advantage over another."

"But," Cliff raised a hand, "a couple of days ago, she asked for an annulment. What if that were to go through? For the greater good, you understand. Those who nominated her know she killed Ray and saved Rob and me—twice. After Blake died so quickly, they want someone in that position who may not be so easy to kill."

"One of these nominations is from Rob," I snarled, holding up the proper e-mail as if it offended me.

Actually, I did find it offensive.

"She has the favor of the earth sprite King, because she saved his General. Twice." Cliff was unmoved by my anger. "If she gains this position, he is willing to provide extra protection. As am I."

"I don't like this. I almost fucked up our marriage once already. I'm not willing to tempt fate," I said.

"Explain it to her. Tell her this is temporary, until another can be found. I will sing and dance at a proper wedding between you afterward, I promise."

"Are you saying our wedding wasn't a proper one?" My anger rose.

"I'm saying you barely knew each other, it was rushed and she may not have been wholly conscious at the time."

He was right; Cassie had been on heavy pain medication, following a car accident. I'd pushed her onto a plane and forced the wedding to go through in Las Vegas. She was right in part, too, that I'd done it to keep Ross away from her. The fact that she'd been a pivotal piece in turning the Christmas war in my favor was just an unexpected plus.

How Cliff came by this information I had no idea—wait. Rob had told me himself that if he touched her, he could tell all sorts of things.

Fuck. I rubbed my forehead. "Go get her," I mumbled. "The decision will be hers."

* * *

Cassie

Chapter 21

Cliff came to find me, after he'd found Rob somewhere and asked him to come to Parke's office.

"What's this about?" I asked as I was hustled toward the media room where Parke's temporary office lay.

"He'll tell you," Cliff said.

Already I could see that Cliff wanted to hide something from me as long as possible. Something I might not like, by the look of things.

Parke's face looked haggard as I was settled onto a chair in front of his desk. Cliff and Rob drew up chairs, too. I felt as if I'd been delivered to a firing squad, for some reason.

"I—we need to discuss the fact that I'm flying to California tonight to see about the poison released there," Parke began. He hadn't told me he was leaving, but I'd suspected after listening to Daniel make flight reservations on the phone earlier.

"Okay," I said. "I know you have to go, you're the Chancellor and that's your job."

"That's true. I also have a case coming up in Seattle, so I have to fly from California to Seattle to deal with that."

"I know you have work to do, outside of dealing with the Chancellor's duties," I said. "I'm not that needy—at least I hope I'm not."

"You're not—it troubles me that you suffer in silence until it's time to punch me in the mouth," Parke grimaced.

"That was a fine punch," Rob stifled a snicker.

Parke held up a hand; Rob went silent immediately. "That's not what this is really about," Parke continued. "Alabama needs a Prince. I've had six valid responses to my request for nominations. All six are for the same person."

"Well, unless that person is unsuitable, it makes this easy, doesn't it?" I asked. *Why did they need me for this?* I wondered. They could have done it without me.

"You're the person they nominated, Cassie, and I'm convinced they're right."

Chapter 22

*C*assie

"It's temporary," Rob repeated. "When we find someone suitable, you can hand it over and marry Parke again."

The annulment papers had been signed shortly before Parke, Trey, Daniel and Lance left for the airport. They were somewhere in the air between Alabama and California by now.

I felt cold and abandoned as a result. I'd handed Parke his ring back; I had no right to it after the papers were signed. I wondered if he'd file for a human divorce, too, while he was at it.

"I'm sort of mad at you. And Cliff," I hissed between clenched teeth.

"We know. I'm sorry about the annulment, but not sorry you're the Princess of Alabama."

"I don't even know what I'm supposed to be doing," I flung out a hand.

Rob chuckled. "Don't worry, Cliff and I can get your through this," he said. "Mostly it's listening to complaints, making decisions that appear wise and nodding and smiling at paranormal events."

"Until *Shakkor Agdah* shows up," I said.

"True."

"If you don't think they're behind Claude and his house exploding, then I have news for you," I snapped.

"I figure they are," Rob agreed. "I figure they didn't want Claude to spill certain things, if you get my drift. Those murders he confessed to—I think they were a smoke screen. Oh, he committed them, all right, but you see those confessions kept the vampire busy asking all the related questions, while ignoring the ones he should have asked."

"What are you talking about?" I turned in my chair to stare at Rob.

"The vampire knows that Dalton and Morton King have ties to *Shakkor Agdah*. He also knows that those two have ties to a company called Fli-Bi-Net. Now, that cannot be a coincidence. Perhaps Claude knew of that connection, too, and confessed to his murders to steer away from that subject?"

"That makes sense, I guess, but it still feels like a reach."

"It does and doesn't," Rob said. "If I could have placed hands on the half-demon while digging my toes into the soil," he sighed and leaned back in his chair. We'd chosen the covered patio at the back of the house to hold our conversation; I'd gone there in a snit after Parke left. Rob found me a few minutes later and began his attempt to defend his and Cliff's decision in the matter.

"Well, it's a little late for toes in the soil," I huffed. "You know something is going on—the poisonings in California are probably the tip of the iceberg."

"Or in Dalton and Morton King's case, the tip of the ice demon-berg."

"Please don't say those names to me. It's bad enough that my name reverts to King after the annulment."

"Oh. I didn't realize you had difficulty with that." Rob looked mortified for almost half a second.

"My father killed my mother, I think. Probably had a hand in killing Aunt Shelbie, too. I loved Mom and Aunt Shelbie. I can't recall when I last felt anything for him, other than loathing."

"We can have your name changed legally," Rob suggested. "Or look at it this way—your human marriage is still intact—Parke can't change that without going through the legal system. Keep the Worth name if you want."

"Right, because everybody knows who I am already, and a name change will make them conveniently forget."

"It's deeds, not words—or names—that make us who we are." Will, the gardener-slash-handyman set a pile of PVC pipe on the patio. "Just getting ready to fix the sprinkler system in the morning," he nodded at Rob and me.

I frowned at him; how much had he heard?

"Why would you want to change your name?" he asked. The tension went out of my shoulders then; he'd only heard the last part about changing my name, and missed the part about my father murdering my mother and Aunt Shelbie.

"It was just a thought," Rob replied smoothly. "Do you need anything before we go back inside?"

"Nah, I'm fine," Will shook his head. "Just wanted a quick start in the morning, that's all."

"Thank you for fixing things for us," I said. "We really appreciate it."

A nod was all I got from him; he was busy separating lengths of pipe.

* * *

Parke

I held a cup of coffee in my hand as we walked through the house. Prince Alfred had gotten us inside; it was quarantined, according to the papers slapped on the door and all the windows outside.

Trey was still asleep somewhere; he didn't tell me where he was going the night before after we'd landed.

"You think this is *Shakkor Agdah's* hiding place?" I asked.

"Neighbors say four men moved in right after the flooding started, and then disappeared during the night after the flooding reached its peak. Clothing left behind holds traces of the poison—or disease—they can't make up their minds what it is."

"Too early, I guess," I mumbled.

"That's what they're saying. I understand little of it, other than it kills quickly, no matter what they do."

The small town we visited was upstream from Tyree, where all the victims lived. These had likely killed the water demon, infected his water and sent it downstream to claim whoever touched it.

"Does it have a shelf life, or will we see more victims farther downstream?" Daniel asked.

"They're trying to determine that now, while telling everybody to keep away from connected rivers and streams. I'm not sure even boiling the water will be safe at this point." Prince Alfred was grimmer than I'd ever seen him; he didn't like that his state had been targeted like this.

"Have we seen dead animals?" Lance thought to ask.

Chapter 22

"None reported," Alfred hunched his shoulders. "If we find these," he swept out a hand to encompass the interior of the small house, "what should we do with them?"

"I've seen them die by fire and beheading recently," I said, "but if it isn't a vampire doing the beheading, the weapon has to be a spelled weapon, according to the earth sprite General."

"I'm a rock demon," Alfred sputtered. "Why the hell would I have spelled weapons?"

"No reason at all," I attempted to calm his anger. "We've not dealt with this in our lifetime. We'll find a way to handle it, don't worry."

I could tell he was skeptical of my words.

Hell, *I* was skeptical of my words.

I'd spoken truth, though, to the fact that we hadn't seen this before. We needed solutions and we needed them fast. I had no doubt that *Shakkor Agdah* was celebrating this victory somewhere, even as they plotted their next move.

* * *

Dalton King

Morton waited in the car outside the restaurant. I was inside, having a second cup of coffee and waiting for our contact to arrive.

I blinked as he approached my booth; the fool had worn his uniform. My hands flexed as I considered killing him and finding another victim to bribe. I'd done this six times already; the others knew to come dressed in street clothes.

"Want coffee?" I gritted through clenched teeth.

"I wouldn't mind," he said.

I was forced to sit with the fool for half an hour, while he drank coffee and talked about his hunting dogs. I was glad to hand the packages to him and get out after leaving money for the bill on the table.

* * *

Cassie

I got a text from Parke around eleven the following morning. *Found a house where Shakkor Agdah probably stayed*, he informed me. *Upstream from Tyree. No sign of them now. Be safe, baby.*

First, I was surprised that he'd texted me. Second, that he sounded as if he still cared. *You be careful, too.* I replied.

He'd let me go too easily, in my opinion. Anybody who loved someone would fight to keep them. Screw being Princess of Alabama. I didn't feel like a princess. I felt like a woman who'd been abandoned by her husband—for the second or third time.

"Having second thoughts?" Cliff came to stand beside me, a cup of coffee in his hands. I stood at the windows in Parke's makeshift office—well, it was my office, now. Outside, Will was repairing the sprinkler system.

"Somebody who can turn furry probably shouldn't stand so close to somebody who can become a fireball in a matter of seconds," I pointed out. "Especially when they're angry."

"If you burn the King of the Werewolves to a crisp, I can't imagine that my furry brethren would be pleased," he said before sipping his coffee.

"I don't know another fire demon," I pointed out. "I've never met one. At least you have furry brethren."

"Rob and I can fill in for fire demon friends—until you find some." I watched the corner of Cliff's mouth curl upward as he took another sip of coffee.

"I didn't say I was looking for fire demon friends," I pointed out. "Just that I'd never met another one."

"I know you feel abandoned," Cliff lowered his cup.

"Oh, we're being serious now?" I glared at him.

"It wasn't our intention to break up a marriage. When it looked as if it would break on its own, we stood aside. It's too important that you take this position, Cassie. The enemy will have to think twice about a full, frontal assault against you."

"Cliff, I have no idea what I'm doing. I have zero experience. Rob glossed over that last night. I can't imagine that either of you want to hold my hand constantly so I won't fuck this up in every way possible."

"Cassie, I'd hug you if you weren't so mad at me," Cliff said. "This can be temporary, remember? Rob and I made that promise to Parke, and you don't tell lies to the Chancellor."

"There can be a huge difference between temporary in human situations and temporary in paranormal circumstances."

"I know. I just feel a war is coming, and we need our best to fight back."

"I'm not one of our best," I pointed out. "I feel like a fool—an inexperienced fool—most of the time. The whole time I was trying to kill Ray, all I could do was hold onto him while he rolled around in Ross' cellar. I had absolutely no control—until he melted."

"How else would you kill a rock demon?" Cliff went back to his coffee.

"I'm thinking of a name for you right now," I said, turning my gaze to the yard again. "It isn't a nice one, either."

"What name would that be?"

"Dickhead, since you asked so politely."

Cliff snorted a laugh into his coffee cup.

* * *

"We ah, have a meeting scheduled, Princess," Rob announced when I walked into the kitchen in search of lunch.

"What?" I stopped halfway between the door and the fridge to stare at him.

"The air sprite Queen and the fire sprite King are requesting an audience. I set up a dinner meeting. Averill is coming, too, so three sprite royals will be present."

"No," I wiped a hand down my face. "Say it's a joke. Please."

"It's not a joke," Gina, who stood at the sink loading dishes into the dishwasher, turned toward me. "We have to figure out what to do about dinner."

"Pizza has been requested, Princess," Rob gave a mock bow. I wanted to slap my forehead.

"Stop bowing—even if you're teasing," I hissed at him. It was bad enough that we were serving pizza to sprite royalty. Bowing was so far over the top I wanted to scream.

"Of course, Princess," Rob curtsied.

"I want to hit you," I growled before closing the distance between the fridge and me and flinging the door open. Rob snickered behind me while I jerked sliced ham and mustard from the fridge and headed for the counter to make a sandwich.

* * *

Parke

"Anything important that I need to see right away?" I walked past Jon's cubicle toward my office as I spoke.

"It's on your desk," Jon said. "I put everything together in order of priority," he added. "Want coffee?"

"Yes, please."

"You got it." Jon rose and sprinted toward the break room.

Prince Alfred hadn't been pleased when I'd boarded the plane in California. If I didn't have the bloody court appearance scheduled the following day, I'd have stayed to keep him calm. I worried that he would do something rash to expose us if things weren't handled properly.

Trey and Daniel stayed behind to do what they could to keep Alfred happy and track *Shakkor Agdah* with some of Alfred's people.

Like Alfred, I worried that more deaths would come soon; it was only a matter of where and when.

"I'm at the office, Mom," I spoke into my cell phone. "How's everything there?"

"We're fine," Mom replied. "I haven't told Destiny about the annulment." Mom said the word as if it made her ill.

"Let me tell her, all right? I hope I can explain this well enough that she'll understand."

"She's a fledgling ice demon, going through puberty. Good luck with that," Mom voiced her opinion.

"Yeah. Great. Look, I have a pile of stuff to take care of. I'll be home late."

"All right. Let me know when you head this way."

"I will. Thanks, Mom."

"Don't thank me," she said. "I'm still planning to yell at you about this."

"Yeah. I know."

* * *

Cassie

Some of Averill's people arrived before he did. They took over the formal dining room, which we hadn't used, yet. When they were finished, the table was set with fine linens, delicate china, polished silver and crystal glasses for wine and water.

"All this for pizza?" I hissed at Rob, who stood in the wide doorway, surveying the results with arms crossed over his chest.

"It's expected," he shrugged.

"Right. It's outrageous, in my opinion."

"Get used to it, Princess," Rob grinned. I wanted to smack him. "Wear something nice but casual," he added.

"Urrgh," I growled and stomped away. I could hear him laughing all the way to my bedroom.

* * *

Queen De-Leah of the air sprites and King Keiran of the fire sprites sat across from one another; King Averill sat at the end of the table while I sat at the head, opposite him. Rob, Cliff and a few others took their places along the table in-between.

"I am most pleased to have a fire demon Princess in charge of Alabama," De-Leah smiled before lifting a wedge of pizza to her lips and biting into it.

Damn—these people really liked their pizza.

"Thank you," I nodded respectfully to De-Leah.

"I hear you helped win the Christmas war in Seattle," King Keiran said next.

"I was certainly there," I said, hoping not to trap myself with my own words. I had no idea who'd told him anything about the Christmas war and wasn't prepared to get into a debate regarding the veracity of what he'd heard.

"Many in the paranormal community are pleased to hear of Ross' death—and that of the Prince he served," De-Leah observed.

I was one of those people. I still wanted to curse the ground Ross died on, but didn't say it. I'm sure my audience knew I'd been engaged to the asshole, albeit unwillingly. They appeared to know everything else.

It made me wonder what their communications network consisted of, and if it were spoken mind-to-mind or whether they depended upon more mundane means for the sharing of information.

Those were questions for Rob when this was over. "Excellent pizza, better than last time," Averill lifted a wedge and smiled at me.

This time, at my insistence, we'd ordered from the Mellow Mushroom. Shredded and grated parmesan in small, crystal bowls with silver spoons for dipping were scattered throughout the table, so anyone could reach either. Pepper flakes in crystal shakers sat beside the small bowls.

I'd never eaten pizza at such an elegantly appointed table in my life.

Rob had chosen the wine; I didn't know what to get. Until I met Parke, I'd had limited experience with alcoholic beverages.

I was learning—slowly.

As for other things—I had the idea that I couldn't afford to learn those slowly. Cliff and Rob both believed a war was coming; a war much bigger than the Christmas war. I still didn't know much about *Shakkor Agdah* and needed information.

"I need information on *Shakkor Agdah*," I blurted before I could stop myself.

One of Rob's eyebrows was lifted so high it almost disappeared into his hairline. Averill beamed at me; De-Leah blinked at my abruptness.

"Gets right to the point," Keiran said. "I find that refreshing."

* * *

By the time our guests had left, I'd been gifted with earrings from De-Leah and a bracelet from Keiran; trinkets for the new Princess of Alabama. The earrings were opals, with all the colors the sky could turn in them. The bracelet was rubies the color of fire.

Keiran's race, the fire sprites, could only form fire. They couldn't *be* fire, like I could. Rob told me afterward that the fire sprites often revered fire demons, since they could handle the same element.

I was promised information on *Shakkor Agdah*, translated into English. I had no idea when it would arrive; Rob merely shrugged when I asked him about it.

The vampires had records, too, but I worried the information from them would go straight to Parke and I'd have to ask him for it. I also worried that the vamps didn't want anybody else reading their records; therefore, they could be withheld.

There'd been no information—no new sightings or murders—attributed to my father and grandfather. I didn't think of them as actually related; their actions were so far removed from anything I would do.

I suppose it was ironic that I was now Princess of Alabama instead of Jasper Bridges, the Prince Ross and my father had supported in the past. Either way, I suspected my estranged relatives had something planned, probably at *Shakkor Agdah's* command.

With a sigh, I folded the jeans I'd worn at dinner and set them on the high chest beside the bathroom door, next to the pyramid Aunt Shelbie sent me. It made me wonder if Claude passed the same thing to my grandfather, or if it were actually another artifact.

What did it matter? We didn't know what this artifact really was, or why Shelbie thought it was important. Regardless, the broken-topped object sat upon the chest, teasing me with questions about its origin and purpose on most nights.

I thought about Parke, too, although I knew I was torturing myself. Yes, part of me understood. A bigger part of me didn't. Mostly I felt like a fraud. Princess of Alabama. What a full-blown, fucked-up joke.

* * *

Zedarius

One of the pyramids was in the house a few yards away. One was now in the hands of the enemy. A third—I could only assume it had been destroyed, somehow. I couldn't feel it, so that was my conclusion.

Chapter 22

The one in the house was damaged; perhaps someone had attempted to destroy it as well. Nevertheless, it still held power.

The one in enemy hands?

Whole and pulsing.

That meant only one of the original four was still buried where it should be. Someone had found the others.

They should have left all of them alone, hidden and buried where they were. To use a human phrase, they were playing with fire and expecting not to get burned.

Fools.

The one nearby lay quiet, as if it were content to be where it was. I was satisfied with that. Yes, I knew it was damaged. As yet, it hadn't acted to correct that damage. If things changed with it, however, I could be forced to deal with that.

I worried that I would have to deal with a great many things.

* * *

Parke

After the hearing, I headed back to the office to work on what I hadn't touched the day before. I had resumes sitting on my desk, too, for those who wanted Geoffrey and Annabelle's spots.

A partner's position required a buy-in. I couldn't believe how many wanted to waive that requirement. I held out three from the stack; they'd make good associates, with a potential for a partner's position in a few years. I'd discuss that with them when I had time.

Time. I had no idea when I'd have time. Yes, we were in a lull. I merely waited for *Shakkor Agdah* to make their move. I hoped we'd have what it took to stand our ground against them and this new, poisonous disease they'd developed.

* * *

Ruudann

I was named after a god. It was written in the language of my ancestors, although few could read the words any longer. I could make out names and places; little else. We had translations, and those translations had been translated, to keep up with the planet's turnings.

We knew—my followers and I, that the artifacts held our immortality. One was destroyed already, loosening the grip on our power to create spells.

One I held in my compound; it had been delivered by my demon slaves. They knew not that they were slaves; they thought they were cooperating for a piece of the new planet we intended to create.

Once our abilities were unlocked completely.

I held off destroying the artifact in my possession. I had to be sure of my followers before bestowing that level of power upon them indiscriminately. Those I deemed unworthy would die. Then I would destroy the small pyramid.

After that, the third and fourth artifacts must be found, so we will have our full power and immortality again. It was promised in the ancient texts. I intended to bring about that reality.

The stage was set; all I had to do was give the word for the play to begin.

* * *

Cassie

"Will, would you like to have lunch with us? We have more than enough chili to go around."

Yes, I'd made a pot of chili—enough for an army, by the look of things. I'd sent Cliff and Lyle to the grocery store with an actual list so decent meals could be cooked.

Chapter 22

Will looked up from his work, his eyes squinting in noon sunlight. A baseball cap, with the visor turned toward the back, was doing him no good whatsoever at the moment.

"I am hungry," he admitted, his words evenly spaced, as if he'd only noticed that he was hungry when I mentioned it.

"There's plenty, and cornbread or crackers to go with it, your choice," I said. Gina made cornbread, saying she preferred it to crackers.

"Thank you. I'll wash up and be right in."

* * *

"This is good," Will pointed the cracker he held toward his bowl of chili. "I like the added beans and cheese, too."

We'd made chili beans, too; you could add them to your chili or not, because some people didn't want them. To me, it wasn't chili if it didn't have beans and shredded cheese.

"Averill would love this," Rob said, having a second bowl.

"Let me guess—his cook doesn't make chili, either," I said. We carefully skirted the fact that Averill was King of the earth sprites; for all Will knew, he could be Rob's friend who was wealthy enough to have his own cook.

"As I said, healthy and natural, all the way," Rob smirked.

Will didn't seem to notice the spots visible on Gina's neck; I was ready to tell him it was a tattoo. He didn't ask and appreciated the meal. He offered to help with the dishes and clearing away, too, but I told him he had enough to do.

He grinned at me before walking out the door; I realized then that I hadn't seen him smile until then.

"Nice guy. Well spoken," Gina said while rinsing bowls in the sink.

"Not what I expected," I said. "Although I really didn't know what to expect, I guess. I thought he'd be in a T-shirt and overalls all the time. Younger than I thought, too."

"Yeah. Well put together."

"If you two will stop ogling the help," Rob interrupted our conversation by laying the cornbread pan on the counter between us.

"Why? Jealous?" Gina teased. "It's obvious he gets plenty of exercise."

"Hmmph," Rob lifted his nose in the air and stalked out of the kitchen. Gina smothered a laugh.

* * *

Parke

"We found a trail, but it ended at the border," Daniel informed me. He'd called just before I left the office to go home for the night.

"How did they cross—car, or on foot?"

"Private plane. Rented it, according to the records we found. Six of them. When the plane wasn't returned, the company reported it as stolen. Transponder stopped working after they crossed into Mexico."

"So they probably landed and destroyed the plane," I guessed.

"That's what we think. Alfred and I questioned the man who rented the plane; he says they were all dressed alike, in jeans and black hooded sweatshirts."

"Were the hoods down, at least?"

"Yes, when their pilot signed papers. We've looked up his license—it's stolen, from a pilot who died in a crash two years ago."

"Of course," I said. "Do we have images?"

"Yes, but they're blurry. Hard to make out features. We checked the camera; it worked fine while we were there."

"You think they were able to manipulate that, somehow?"

"It's the only conclusion I have at the moment."

"Right. Do you think it will do any good to try to track them in Mexico?"

"Not if that's what they're expecting. Not with only two or three of us. An ambush could be in our future."

"True. What do you suggest, then?"

"Giving the information we have to the Border Patrol, for a start. Trey suggested that. He says he has a scent from two of them, so he'd recognize that, at least. He's talked with people from his department, too. Sounds like they're getting worried. I don't like it when the Paranormal Division of the FBI gets worried," Daniel said.

"Anything new from the CDC?"

"They're still working on this, but I can tell they're worried, too. Trey heard from his boss that two people working in the lab were so scared of whatever this poison-disease thing is that they quit rather than deal with it."

"But somebody is still working on it?" I asked.

"Yes. The government moved more people in to do research. So far, no progress."

For now, this was reported as an isolated incident, so the people weren't panicked. That could change in an instant if the scenario were duplicated elsewhere. I had no doubt it would be duplicated elsewhere; it was merely a matter of where.

"What are we going to do?" I whispered. I hadn't meant for Daniel to hear that. He did anyway.

"Keep working at it," he advised. "You know I don't like anything to do with Black Myth, but we're involved, now. I'm determined to see it through. It's all new to us, but they've probably been planning this for a very long time."

"Right under our noses, no doubt," I snorted. "I feel like a fool."

"Right there with you, bro," Daniel acknowledged. "Right there with you."

316

Chapter 23

C*assie*

Will joined us for dinner when Gina invited him, and it was decided that he'd eat with us if we were at the house.

It curtailed conversations regarding what we were and things we were dealing with, but he needed a meal, just like the rest of us. Gina and I worried that Will was living off sandwiches and canned soup.

"This is really good," Will said, cutting another bite off his smothered pork chops.

"We made it in the slow cooker," Gina grinned at him. "Easy."

We made small talk after that, enjoying the meal and company until Cliff's cell phone rang.

"It's Kent," he said and rose from the table to take the call elsewhere. He was back in less than two minutes.

"Your aunt's house burned down," Cliff's dark eyes looked worried. "We need to go. I have no idea whether anything's salvageable."

I sat, stunned and unmoving, as I stared at Cliff.

"I'll come and help," Will stood and carried his plate to the sink.

"Yeah. Me, too," Gina agreed.

"It's cold out; get a jacket," Rob instructed.

"Yeah." I moved as if I were only learning to do so. I felt disjointed.

Awkward.

Unsure.

"We'll sort this out," Rob took my arm and led me from the kitchen.

On the hour drive to Birmingham, I found it difficult and painful to breathe. Everything that belonged to Shelbie, except for her jewelry chest, was likely ash. I wanted to cry and couldn't. So many people were around me, and tears were something I wished to release in private.

Cliff drove; Will, Gina and I huddled together in the back seat of his truck. Rob, sitting up front with Cliff, turned to check on me from time to time. I was grateful for the warm jacket he'd pulled from my closet and forced me to wear; even in a warm truck with people snugged next to me, I felt cold.

A single firetruck was parked on the street in front of the house when we arrived. I steeled myself when the door was opened and Will extended his hand to help me from the truck.

The scent of burning lay all around us as I walked across the ash-strewn lawn. Shelbie's home was little more than a pile of burnt wreckage. Had we forgotten to turn something off? A thousand causes for the fire raced through my brain, without any of them standing out.

"We believe it was arson," a firefighter approached us. His jacket had Capt. Knight printed on it.

"Huh?" I blinked at him in confusion.

Chapter 23

"We're pretty sure it was set," he said. "Fire started in the back bedroom and moved forward. Probably an accelerant tossed through a window, but we're still investigating."

"This is the owner," Cliff said, producing ID and showing it to the captain. "She recently inherited the house, and has been in Tuscaloosa with me all day."

"No worries," the captain waved away Cliff's concern that I might become a person of interest. "A neighbor saw two men in the area shortly before the fire was reported. That's who we're looking for."

Two men. "Do you have a description?" Cliff asked.

"Just a sketchy one—it was after sundown, with only streetlamps to light the area. It wasn't easy to see detail. You can ask for a police report, if you want."

"We will."

* * *

Dalton King

"How the hell are we going to tell them that the windows and windshield fogged over in the car—for half an hour?" Morton hissed.

He and I had cleaned repeatedly, working to get the foggy moisture off the windows. We'd even removed our shirts to wipe glass and turned the heat on high to clear it up. Nothing had worked.

When the windows finally cleared, the scene down the street hadn't changed, allowing us to breathe a relieved sigh. Our associates wanted to flush someone out. Morton and I had a good idea who it was. It didn't matter; the effort failed. When the firetruck moved away in the early-morning hours, we waited ten more minutes before we left to make our report.

* * *

Cassie

"We'll notify the insurance company tomorrow," Cliff said. "They'll do their own investigation, and that could take a while. Just be patient; it'll all work out."

We sat in a twenty-four-hour diner on the outskirts of Birmingham, having coffee and dessert. Well, the others were having dessert. Kent met us there and he and Gina sat together to share a piece of apple pie a la mode.

"I know that part will be fine," I croaked. Those were the first words I'd spoken since we'd left the burned ruin of Shelbie's house behind.

"We associate objects with the people who've left us behind," Will said. "This is like losing your aunt again, isn't it?"

"Yes. Cliff, do you think the same ones are responsible for bombing the courthouse?"

"I hadn't considered that, but it's a possibility." I watched his face; he was considering it and didn't like the conclusions he was drawing. "Let me pull the police reports on that, and I'll compare the two," he said.

"Thank you." I already had two people in mind who could be responsible, and I didn't like that at all.

They weren't only targeting Cliff and Rob.

I was on their list, too.

It made sense; they'd likely killed my mother. Why would a daughter or granddaughter make any difference?

My question was this; what did they have to gain? Mom probably knew too much. Shelbie became a target the moment she helped get Destiny and me away from Alabama. I—what did I know? I'd only recently learned Dalton King was alive. I knew nothing about him, other than the information Trey had given Parke.

"I have murderers in my family," I whispered and covered my face with both hands.

Chapter 23

* * *

Cliff

If Rob hadn't done it, I would have. The sprite had both arms around Cassie as she wept. If I'd had any concerns about Will hearing what he had, they were somewhat dispelled when he reached over and patted Cassie's arm.

It was clear he was already loyal to her; she and Gina treated him as an equal, nothing less. I figured he appreciated that.

As it was, if I could have gotten my hands on the culprits who'd burned down Shelbie's house, I'd kill both before they had time to become ice demon.

Yes, I considered that Cassie was right; her father and grandfather were probably behind all this. They weren't above murdering anyone, family included, if the rumors were true.

The Chancellor said Morton was responsible for killing Cassie's mother. I could believe that easily enough.

Those two had left a string of unsolved murders behind them, between Texas and Alabama. Perhaps *Shakkor Agdah* pulled their strings, but not in every case, I figured. A gun would get you money; you didn't have to kill to rob someone.

Dalton and Morton appeared to take pleasure in the killings. They'd gotten away with it, too; they weren't on human radar anywhere.

My cell phone pinged; the screen said I had an e-mail from the Chancellor. I'd answer it later—we had enough to deal with at the moment.

* * *

Cassie

"Want something to help you sleep?" Gina asked.

She'd followed me to my bedroom, where I sat at the foot of the bed, wondering what to do next.

"I really don't," I said. "But thanks for the offer."

I was grateful to Rob for letting me cry on his shoulder. The tears had come anyway, as much as I'd tried to hold them back.

Cliff explained to the concerned waitress that my aunt's house had burned down. She was sympathetic; we'd left her a big tip when we paid the bill.

"All right, but knock on my door if you change your mind," Gina said and left the bedroom, closing the door behind her.

"Yeah." I said to myself. I was at loose ends. I'd had decaf at the restaurant, just so it wouldn't keep me awake. I was awake anyway.

This—all this—was like physical blows, coming one right after another. What would they do next? How would they hit me again? I found myself in fear of that blow.

Perhaps that's what they wanted—to make me afraid.

"That's my battle, to not be afraid," I told myself sternly.

As if that would cure my fear instantly. I had a long road ahead of me; I knew that as I rose, pulled back the comforter and slid into bed, wrapping myself in covers to stop the shivering.

* * *

Cliff

I read the Chancellor's e-mail twice. They'd managed to track the *Shakkor Agdah* responsible for the California deaths to Mexico, where plane wreckage had recently been discovered.

Nobody knew where they'd gone after that; the plane was rented in San Diego. The wreckage was discovered two hundred miles south of the Mexico border. No bodies were found with the plane—they'd gotten away, somehow.

When I wrote my reply, I included information on Shelbie's house and the fact that two men had been seen in the area before the fire was reported. I also told him that we suspected Dalton and

Morton King. I promised copies of police reports, too, as soon as I was able to procure them.

Officially, I was still on the Tuscaloosa PD's payroll until my two-week notice was up. That carried a small amount of clout—enough to get police reports, anyway.

Tonight, Cassie had been overwhelmed. I left that out of my e-mail. We would handle that, whatever it took.

* * *

Cassie

"Feel better?" Will sat at the kitchen table, having breakfast with Lyle, Gina, Cliff and Rob when I shuffled into the kitchen.

If no sleep and a worried night constituted feeling better, then sure, I felt better. "I'm fine," I lied and went to get a cup of coffee.

"Sounds just like the lie it is," Will sipped his coffee.

"It's easier than telling the truth," I thumped a coffee mug onto the counter and poured from the carafe.

"Sounds about right," Rob grunted. "Sit down and eat." He patted the chair beside his. A platter of bacon and scrambled eggs waited; I realized I was hungry.

"Thanks for breakfast, Gina," I nodded to her.

"Will helped cook," she offered a smile.

"Then thank you, too," I nodded at Will.

"Not a problem," he said, biting into a strip of bacon and chewing.

"We need to go back to the store," Gina said, lifting her empty plate and heading toward the sink.

"I want to go," I said. I intended to force myself not to hide in the house. If they wanted me dead, we'd see about that.

"I'll drive you in my truck," Will offered.

I turned to Rob, who shrugged. They might be looking for Cliff's vehicle; Will's was sturdy enough to get us to the grocery store and back.

"Is there enough room for Lyle?" Cliff asked.

"The back seat's small, but yes," Will agreed.

"I'll ride in the back," I said.

"Me, too—we can fit," Gina added.

"Good. That's settled. Make sure nothing blows out of the truck bed on the way back; I don't want toilet paper rolling down the road," Cliff grinned. "When you get back," he directed his words to me, "We'll deal with a few things that have shown up for you to take care of."

Princess work. My shoulders drooped.

"Sure," I said, determined not to let it upset me.

"What are you waiting for?" Rob asked. "Shoo. Go." He gestured with a hand, dismissing all of us.

"I always get suspicious when he's that happy to get rid of me," Gina said.

"He probably wants to look at dirty pictures on the Internet while we're gone," I whispered loudly. Gina laughed as we walked out of the kitchen.

* * *

Zedarius

At least we had cash to spend; the werewolf had seen to that. A wise move, to keep those bent on destruction from tracking them in that way.

The grocery store parking lot was mostly empty when I parked and followed the rock demon and his charges into the store.

Yes, I'd placed a ward around the truck; that was easy enough to do. I'd know it if unfriendly feet approached. The two women

Lyle and I guarded—I was beginning to understand how important they were.

Half-demon shifters were unusual enough; a fire demon female—there were no others like her.

I'd checked.

Shakkor Agdah knew what they were doing; they'd managed to kill many fire demons in the past two centuries. Two other fire demons remained; both males and living in other countries. I hoped that would be enough in the coming days.

I worried that the fire demon race would become extinct. That went against everything I'd worked for in the past. It was bad enough that humans caused the extinction of animal species; this would be so much worse.

"Get it if you want it," I stood behind Cassie as she studied the donuts displayed behind clear plastic.

"What about you?" she asked, turning bright blue eyes in my direction.

"I'd take one," I said.

"I'll get a dozen—the others may want one, too."

"You do that." I grinned at her; I couldn't help myself. If something as simple as a donut would make her happy, I was certainly in favor of it.

* * *

Cassie

"This is so good," Gina bit into her donut on the drive home. Lyle was having a donut, too, with a small container of milk he'd pulled from the dairy section. I held the box on my lap so it wouldn't get crushed in the tightly packed batch of sacks in the back of Will's truck.

Nobody wanted their donut frosting stuck to a box top.

I was saving mine to have with a cup of coffee. Maybe it would make Princess duty easier to deal with when I got home.

* * *

"Four requests for private audiences; three duplicate submissions for arbitration. The arbitration duplicates were originally submitted to Blake Donovan." Cliff handed a sheaf of papers to me when I took a seat at my desk. "I suggest hiring someone to cook and clean; there's a budget attached to your office, you know, with allowances for such."

"What about the private audiences?" I waved those requests after I segregated them from the others. I didn't want private audiences.

"The werewolves call it a butt-sniffing," Cliff said. Laughter shown in his eyes, although it didn't travel to his mouth.

"They want to see how tough I am?" I squeaked.

"In a manner of speaking. Private audiences don't mean completely private. Rob and I can be with you, and present evidence of how tough you are. The last thing on your agenda is a request—from me."

"What is it?" I asked.

"That you ask the Chancellor to make the announcement to all that *Shakkor Agdah* has reappeared. I think we should prepare ourselves now."

"Yeah." I lowered my head and stared at the papers in my hand; they'd grown unimportant against more terrible things.

"And we need to send out notices that Dalton and Morton King are in Black Myth's Camp."

"Yeah." I let out a slow breath, attempting to keep my heart rate from skyrocketing. What would the paranormal community in Alabama—and across the country—think when they learned I was related to the schmucks?

Chapter 23

"I say keep your married name—it's your prerogative," Cliff said. "The papers are signed, showing you and Parke are no longer married. That should be enough for anybody. You're Cassie Worth."

"Right. Until they start digging."

"Stop worrying about it. Tell them you're just as anxious to capture or kill those two as anyone. Tell the naysayers that they killed your mother and your aunt. That should be enough to prove your determination."

"Sure." I rubbed my forehead before looking up at Cliff. "How is this going to work?" I moaned.

"It'll work, don't worry. You have the trust of the sprite Kings and Queen. You bear their gifts. You have the trust of the Grand Master and the Chancellor. That should be enough."

"I wish I could be as confident as you," I told him.

"It'll come," Cliff grinned. "Stop worrying, send a message to the Chancellor, tell the private meeting folks that you'll get back to them when you're finished sorting out the duties and work left behind by the former Prince, and tell the arbitration people that we'll schedule dates soon."

"Who is going to keep track of all this?" I asked.

"Rob is excellent at it," Cliff said. "He's just waiting for you to ask him."

"He really wants to?" I blinked at Cliff. I couldn't keep the confusion out of my voice.

"He liked working at the courthouse, too," Cliff said. "He enjoys putting things—and people—in order."

"I can see that," I agreed. "I'll ask him after dinner."

"Good. He'll handle the paperwork you have on your desk," a corner of Cliff's mouth curled upward. "I think he'll be happy to deal with it."

"Good."

"I have eyes on Claude's property—in case anybody comes sniffing around the rubble," Cliff added. "Don't worry," he held up a hand when I started to say something, "They're far enough away that the wolfsbane won't affect them."

"You think Dalton and Morton may show up, don't you?" I asked.

"It's possible," he lifted a shoulder in a half-shrug. "Better to cover all the bases, or all the known bases, anyway."

"True. Have there been any more murders?" I asked casually while pretending to straighten the papers on my desk.

"None using their MO," Cliff said. "It makes sense, though, because they're probably lying low at this point."

"Right."

"One more thing," Cliff said.

"What's that?"

"Rob and I—have access to half a dozen demon killers."

I froze. Demon killers. The rifles too heavy for anyone except a supernatural to carry. Rifles so deadly, they could kill a demon. Ordinary bullets wouldn't do it, if the demon were in their alternate form.

"Can we, ah, table that unless they're needed?" I whispered.

"Yes. I just wanted you to know, in case they're needed to take Dalton and Morton down."

"Do you think they have some, too?" I did and didn't want to know the answer. Those two were murderous enough. We didn't need this kind of threat.

"We have to assume the worst," Cliff replied.

He was right—we had to assume the worst, because they were capable of it.

"We need to find them," I said, rising from my chair. "I need my donut now."

Chapter 23

* * *

Parke

For the tenth time, I wished that Pauline wasn't dead. I wanted to question her. Ask her how she contacted her employers with information. For the tenth time, I castigated myself for not delving deeper into her secrets while she worked for me.

Cassie would have known right away that something was wrong, I reminded myself. She'd known about Geoffrey and Annabelle easily enough. I was a truth demon. I didn't have the sixth sense that Cassie appeared to possess.

I felt guilty (again) for dismissing her concern about *Shakkor Agdah* when she first reported Cliff and Rob's fears to me. She'd felt it warranted my attention and I'd ignored it.

Destiny was right—I wasn't a good husband. I'd waited to tell her about my apparent split with Cassie until the day before; she hadn't been happy about the dissolved marriage. I attempted to explain that we couldn't be married if Cassie were the Princess of Alabama.

"A good husband would change the law," Destiny had informed me, her thin arms crossed over her chest in obvious anger. "If he's the Chancellor."

She'd zinged me twice—about being a bad husband and a poor Chancellor, too. Leave it to a twelve-year-old to say the truth nobody else was willing to tell.

"You're right, Dess," I whispered. "I've fucked this up for sure."

Time to get your act together and start behaving like the Chancellor, I told myself. Cassie's e-mail caused my tablet to ding. I opened it right away.

We should tell the royalty that Shakkor Agdah is active again, she wrote. *So they won't be blindsided if something happens in their principality.*

She was right. I had a feeling Cliff had urged her to write the message. He was right, too.

Tell them Dalton and Morton have likely allied with SA she added.

"On it, baby," I breathed and pulled my cell phone into my hand.

* * *

Cassie

"What did you say to him? We've had six calls already," Rob said, holding up his cell phone.

"I just told him he should make the announcement," I replied.

"He got it done in a hurry, then," Rob scrolled through messages on his phone. Evidently, the message had come to Cliff, first, as he was Grand Master of the werewolves. He'd sent it out to all his Packmasters immediately.

The message also went to all the demon royalty and the sprite races.

"At least they're on notice, now, and have Morton and Dalton's images out," Cliff stalked into the room like a caged wolf.

"I'm concerned they may discover we've put out the word," I said.

"I'm not—those fuckers know we know about them, now," Cliff growled. "They know we'll be watching for them. All of us."

"I'm concerned for the humans," I pointed a finger at Cliff. "They were the targets last time, or so I hear. It was humans who died in California, remember?"

"And one water demon," Cliff pointed out.

"True. But that was done by an ice demon, not *Shakkor Agdah*."

"Also true."

"My question is this; was the ice demon Dalton or Morton, or someone else?" I asked.

"Good question. I suppose it could have been done by one of those two; they can get on a plane just like anyone else."

"Or rent one, maybe?" I asked. "The *Shakkor Agdah* we saw had tattoos and poison boils all over them. Nobody said anything about the person renting the plane looking anything but ordinary."

"Perhaps a spell?" Rob suggested.

"Maybe," Cliff nodded.

"Or spells and an ice demon, who helped them with the rental after he killed the water demon in California."

"All the camera images were blurry," Rob acknowledged. "There could have been more than initially reported, and there certainly could have been an ice demon with them."

"And nobody knows where they went after wrecking the plane in Mexico," Cliff said.

"So we know there has to be at least six *Shakkor Agdah* involved in that. Who knows how many more there are?"

"They've had centuries to build up their numbers," Rob observed. "It was a dream to think they were all dead after the last paranormal war."

"Too bad for us," Cliff said.

"Wait—these aren't humans who've gone bad?" I asked. I admit, that hadn't crossed my mind before. What I'd killed had certainly looked human—except for the boils and strange tattoos on their skin.

"Separate race," Cliff said. "Smell different from humans; I can vouch for that. Ask the vamps, too; they sure as hell know because of scent."

"They can perform minor spells, according to the records," Rob said. "Enough to confound humans or get them killed. They hate the humans, too, for reasons known only to *Shakkor Agdah*."

"Averill will send the records soon; I have communicated with him recently," Rob promised. "The scholars are still working on the translations."

"Thank you." I didn't say that I felt afraid to read those records. The Black Death was a form of genocide, if what Cliff and Rob said were true. *Shakkor Agdah* had almost accomplished their goal in the past.

It was my guess that only the paranormal community, working together, had prevented complete annihilation.

How were we going to defeat them this time?

"So far, they've only struck in an isolated incident," Cliff reminded me. Perhaps he'd seen the worry on my face, or scented fear about me.

It didn't matter—he was right. I worried about the hammer dropping, as Aunt Shelbie used to say.

* * *

Zedarius

My head jerked up when I felt the first death. Not by *Shakkor Agdah*, but by their puppet ice demons.

Four deaths, in swift succession. All of them with connections to Cassie.

I'd stopped thinking of her in terms of fire demon only. She bore a name and I used it. These deaths would grieve her greatly.

They were attempting to stop her.

Weaken her.

Convince her to give up the fight.

I hissed my anger into the wind.

* * *

Chapter 23

Cassie

Rob and I were going over our replies to the requests I'd been handed earlier when Cliff strode into my office.

"Bad news," he said. He wore an expression of fury, and struggled to keep it from his voice.

"What is it?" I was on my feet immediately.

"Four people are dead," Cliff hissed. "All frozen to death, with no human explanation as to how that might occur."

Chapter 24

*C*assie

Of the four deaths, Binita's was the one that made me want to cry forever. The law professor who'd been kind to me and my former landlords were among the dead.

All had connections to me.

"They're attempting to weaken you," Rob handed a cup of coffee to me. I sat in the kitchen, shivering and staring at the digital clock on the microwave. Time had slowed to a stop, I think, while I went numb.

"Weaken? Hell, they want to render her useless," Cliff snapped and stalked out of the kitchen.

He was right—at the moment, I was useless. I couldn't move, I was so dazed.

They like killing, I reminded myself. A part of me wept and silently begged that the deaths had been swift.

Binita had been sentenced to death because she knew me.

That kept playing through my mind continuously, like a loop of film running through an outdated projector, the same scenes appearing over and over.

"You can't take the blame for this," Rob raked fingers through his hair, making it uncharacteristically untidy. "If *Shakkor Agdah* has their way, we'll all die eventually. Without you it may be sooner, rather than later."

"It came sooner for Binita."

"I know," his voice became gentle. "Don't let them win the war in the first volley, Princess."

"Will you notify Parke—the Chancellor, on my behalf?" My eyes and face felt swollen.

Frozen.

It was difficult to speak the words through numbed lips.

"Yes. Cliff has likely done it already, but I will send official notice from the Princess of Alabama."

"Thank you." I whispered. He turned to go. "Rob," I said before he left the kitchen.

"What do you need, Cassie?" He turned concerned eyes in my direction.

"Tell Parke that I think it's time the human population had images of Dalton and Morton to look at. Tell him to ask Trey to put that forward to his superiors. Humans need to know to stay away from those two."

"I'll make the suggestion on your behalf."

"Thank you."

* * *

Zedarius

Gina told me the news the following morning at breakfast. I already knew, but listened anyway. She carefully avoided mention of paranormal involvement, choosing to say four people that Cassie knew had perished.

My superior died the last time *Shakkor Agdah* went to war. He'd waited too long to wade into the fight and too many had fallen because of it. I understood Cassie's grief all too well.

They thought to cripple her at a critical time.

I worried that they would succeed in their goal.

"How is she?" I asked, meaning Cassie.

"As well as can be expected," Gina's shoulders slumped.

"Too many blows," I said, sipping coffee.

"Yes. Too close together," she agreed.

"You'll let me know if there's anything I can do?" I placed power in my words.

"I will."

"Good." Better that she didn't know that the attacks would come soon. Today would be a sunny day in February. Let them enjoy as much of it as they could.

* * *

Parke

"We've already sent out the bulletins," a voice on the phone informed me.

Trey had done his part the night before; his superiors understood the urgency and the necessity of alerting the human population.

Dalton and Morton King's images would be splashed on news programs across the country, as persons of interest in four Alabama deaths.

One of those deaths meant much to Cassie; Binita Singh, the closest friend she'd had in law school.

I'd stayed home for the day. Daniel, Trey and Lance had flown in from California the night before; I'd asked Trey for help shortly after his arrival.

He was now sleeping in a shuttered and closed-off bedroom in the house; the rest of us were up and around. Word had gone out about Dalton and Morton, early enough to hit all the morning news programs.

Humans had awakened to the news of four deaths in Alabama, with associated photographs of the two suspects.

"Problem," Daniel strode through the door of my home office, a tablet in his hand.

"What's this?" I asked as he propped the device on my desk so I could watch a video.

"This just came through the news networks," Daniel said. "This happened in Mobile."

I hit the arrow to play the video and watched as the recording from a Mobile Police station played.

The image wasn't the best, but sound was included.

A man, dressed in a prison guard's uniform, rushed in and demanded to see the Captain.

The desk sergeant informed him that the Captain was out.

"I want to make a report," the guard shouted.

"You'll have to calm down," the sergeant replied.

"I saw him," the guard insisted. He was fidgeting and nervous, as if he couldn't stay still for a moment.

"Saw who?" the sergeant demanded.

"Him. On the news, M-M-Mo," the man clutched his chest and fell to his knees.

The desk sergeant went to the guard when he slumped to the floor. "He's not breathing," the sergeant shouted. "Call the paramedics."

The journalist appeared onscreen, then, announcing that the prison guard was pronounced dead at the scene from an apparent heart attack.

"Who do you think he might have meant?" Daniel looked grim as I stopped the video.

"He saw Morton, looks like, and *Shakkor Agdah* stopped him before he could do anything about it."

"Get on a plane to Alabama," I snapped. "Take Lance with you. I'll ask the Prince of Washington to provide guards while you're gone."

"What about Trey?" Daniel asked.

"I'm hoping he has a dozen vampire friends he can call when he gets to Alabama later tonight," I said. "The manhunt starts now."

* * *

Cassie

"The Chancellor is sending Daniel and Lance to Mobile after that prison guard died," Cliff informed me.

I sat listlessly at my desk. I was supposed to approve the replies Rob and I put together the night before, but I was only seeing paper and no words. Yes, I'd been shown the guard's death. All of us were sure he'd been trying to say Morton's name before he died.

Morton.

My father.

Murderer.

Had he killed Binita himself, or allowed my equally as murderous grandfather to do it?

"He also says that the vampire will follow on a night flight. He expects us to put a team together to assist Daniel."

"Who do we have?" I allowed my right hand to slide off the desk and onto my lap. I clenched my fist there, trying to force feeling into it.

"I have a short list prepared, with their type and abilities," Cliff set another paper in front of me.

Two were rock demons. Two were werewolf. Another two—vampire. "Rob says that the sprites will send one from each race—trackers," Cliff added.

"Good," I allowed a sigh to escape. Trackers of any kind would surely be helpful.

"We need the word from you—to kill Dalton, Morton or any *Shakkor Agdah* they find."

"The word is given," I said without hesitation.

* * *

Dalton King

"It's hilarious," Morton said.

"It's inconvenient," I snapped back. "Where do you think you'll get barbecue, if the restaurant you like recognizes you and calls the police?"

"Human police," Morton snorted.

"Right behind the human police could be the paranormal kind," I reminded him. "Not so easy to kill if they know what they're looking for. I say it's time to tell our allies that we're bowing out of the picture and going back to Mexico. For a while, anyway."

"They know where the house is, remember?" Morton's sullenness was evident in his tone. "We can't get to the hidden money if they're watching the property."

"Get another house. I'm sure we can put money together on the way."

"We'll have to go farther south. I hear Ecuador is a good place to go."

"I don't give a fuck where it is, I say we head in that direction and let our contacts know when we're halfway there."

"Whatever you say, Dad."

Chapter 24

"I hate it when you call me that."

"It's why I said it, *Dad*."

* * *

Cassie

My mood swung from depression to anger most of the day. I didn't turn on the news after a while; all the local channels could talk about were the deaths and the suspects.

I'd never met Binita's parents. I wanted to weep for them, just as I did for Binita. A part of me wanted to confess my involvement to them. Another part cringed from the accusations that would come.

All of it involved what I was and what was waging war against me—my own family and their allies. That meant I could never approach anyone who'd suffered losses because of me.

It could make them targets, too.

* * *

Cliff

"I expect them to attack us at any time," Rob said. "Now that they've managed to hit her like this."

"We don't have a clue how they'll do it," I snarled. Yes, I'd been thinking the same thing and my temper was short because of it. We'd sent those we'd chosen toward Mobile; they'd be joining Daniel and Lance to begin their investigation.

The guard was a place to start; I'm sure his family was being questioned at length. It may have been cruel to plan a second questioning of grieving relatives, but it had to be done.

Where had the guard seen Morton? Had he made contact in some way?

A thousand questions crowded my brain and my response was to snap at Rob. "Sorry," I held up a hand. "I didn't mean that."

"Those two have to know they're hunted, now, and not just by humans," Rob waved off my apology.

"You're right. What do you suppose they will do about that?"

"It's my guess they're cowards, at their core," Rob said. "They're fine killing humans. We can't attribute any paranormal deaths to them, though, outside of Cassie's mother and perhaps her aunt. Nothing recent, anyway, unless they managed to kill the water demon in California. I have the idea it wasn't them doing that job."

"So, what does this mean?" I asked.

"I think they'll do what Morton did the first time, and head for the border."

"The Chancellor knows where that house is," I began.

"No, Morton found a way the last time. There's nothing to prevent him from acquiring another property—by legal or illegal means."

"You're telling me we could be seeing more deaths on their way to the border?"

"Yes. If we managed to spook them, they may be hightailing it out of the state now."

"Leaving *Shakkor Agdah* and their plans behind, whatever those are."

"Yes."

"Should we discuss this with Cassie?"

"I'd like to wait, but as Princess, we really ought to tell her what we think."

"Trial by fire," Rob said, "and I'm aware of the pun."

* * *

Cassie

"So we're waiting to hear about more murders on the way to Mexico?" I asked.

"Morton did it before," Cliff pointed out.

"Yeah. Maybe he was worried somebody would turn him in after Mom disappeared."

"Perhaps your aunt?" Rob suggested.

"I don't know. Shelbie never said anything about that, although we both sort of knew."

"My concern is that Ross and his bunch may have had dealings with *Shakkor Agdah* back then," Cliff said. "And the Prince may have been involved, too, although I suspect he was in it for the money and whatever power he could gain from it."

"You knew him?" I turned to Cliff. Cliff looked grim, Rob snorted.

"I take it you both did," I said, my voice dry.

"We kept away from him as much as we could," Cliff explained. "Relations between the demons and werewolves were rather strained at the time."

"The sprite kingdoms withdrew from contact," Rob said. "I came to support Cliff, should the need arise."

"Are you talking an uprising?" My eyes widened as I gazed from Rob to Cliff and back again.

"In a manner of speaking," Cliff hedged. "Nobody liked Jasper."

"That name gives me the shivers," I said. I worried that Shelbie's access to the Chancellor was through Jasper Bridges, Prince of Alabama and secret ally of Ross Diablo, back when Mom disappeared.

Her concern, if she'd voiced it, would never have reached Parke's father, who was Chancellor at the time.

It's the way things worked—you went through channels. The Chancellor was inundated enough with concerns from the royalty regarding their subjects. Shelbie's voice wouldn't have been heard, in all likelihood.

"Then I hope you relay this information to Daniel," I said, coming to a decision. "I'm concerned about sending all our investigators toward the border, though."

"I'll let him know to split his forces if he has to travel out of state to follow their trail," Rob agreed.

* * *

Parke

"Where do you believe you'll be the most effective?" I asked. Daniel had called, telling me that Dalton and Morton could be headed toward the border, after they learned they'd been associated with the Alabama murders.

"I'd prefer to track them," Daniel said. "Lance and a few others can continue their search here. I'll take the earth sprite tracker, another rock demon and a werewolf with me."

"Do it, then," I gave my permission. "Let me know if you pick up their trail. Tell Lance the same. If I have to get on a plane to come down there myself, I will."

"Will do." Daniel ended the call.

I had no idea what shape Cassie was in, but she'd issued orders through Rob, who'd signed on as her personal assistant. At least she wasn't completely closed off from everything, although the deaths had to be a terrible blow to her.

I understood that she felt responsible.

She hadn't committed the murders and was blameless under the law. They were attempting to attack her any way they could—through emotions and self-blame.

It was despicable and the act of cowards.

Baby, I tapped on my cell phone, *stop blaming yourself. They'd attack whoever was in the royal chair in your place, if you'd refused. This is the act of cowards, nothing more. Love you.*

I hit send before I could erase the message.

Chapter 24

That's when the text from Daniel came through. *Suspicious murder reported in Pascagoula*, he sent. *Motive: robbery of victim carrying cash receipts to bank from business. Thawing body of vic found in marsh water near a bridge.*

* * *

Cassie

"It looks like they may have murdered the assistant manager from a Pascagoula grocery and gas station," Cliff said, handing his tablet to me. "The body was pulled from marsh water, north of the I-90 Bridge. It was thawing after being frozen."

"They just can't stop themselves, can they?" I frowned at Cliff.

"Doesn't look like it. Rumor is they got away with around five thousand, cash. That will get them to the border."

"What are they driving?" I asked.

"Good question. Nobody saw anything when the victim was attacked earlier. His car is still where he left it—in the bank parking lot."

"You think they were staking out the bank or the business?"

"Could be either one. Both near the highway."

"Fuck."

"Exactly what I was thinking, Princess."

* * *

Dinner was chicken and dumplings—Gina was a master at making it, because it woke up my appetite. Will nodded his approval and kept eating. Cliff got a text, read it, then handed his phone to me.

There'd been another murder—this one in New Orleans. They really were heading toward the border and killing indiscriminately along the way.

My cell phone dinged; I'd gotten a text. I handed Cliff's phone back and looked at my own.

Daniel has reported sighting; matches descriptions of DK and MK. Louisiana State Police on trail. Trey's department warning them to stay back until Feds can step in. Daniel trying to get there first.

I handed my phone to Cliff, who read the message, let Rob read it, then passed it back to me.

Tell him to be careful, I texted back. *They're evil.*

Understood, appeared on my phone.

I was still miffed with Daniel for giving Parke rotten advice, but as we were now separated, I suppose it no longer mattered. I released a pent-up breath and pocketed the phone.

Will had continued eating throughout and didn't question anything. I was grateful.

* * *

Ruudann

"Let them go. They will distract the enemy," I responded to Vaalenn's question concerning the fleeing ice demons. "We will collect them later, when their flight is no longer beneficial to our plan. We have others to depend on, should there be need."

Vaalenn's smile was lovely to see. Her skin was flawless, her face free of the poison sacs. She'd said it was her strategy. She'd placed extra sacs on other parts of her body. Vaalenn could release that poison if an enemy touched any part of her torso.

It made me smile that she was so canny. She would appeal to any human and many paranormals with her beauty.

She was the spider; her body was the web they would never leave alive.

* * *

Dalton King

They were on our trail and had been since we'd killed the convenience store manager in the bank parking lot.

Chapter 24

We needed more money; I'd expected more cash than what the fucking human carried. People used too many credit cards these days.

It didn't matter; we had friends in New Orleans. We'd lose our tail there.

* * *

Cassie

"Go to bed; you can't help them—the Chancellor's team will deal with this," Gina said.

"I just want to make sure our guys shoot first and ask questions later, when those two are both dead," I whispered. Was it wrong to say that about members of your family?

"Kent says the trail is cold in Mobile—that guard didn't talk to anybody about the sighting, and it's too late to ask him questions."

"I feel like we're missing something," I said. "Something important. As if we've been looking in the wrong direction all along."

"I know, but what can we do about it? My gran says that sometimes we have to be hit over the head with something before we notice," Gina grinned.

"Yeah, but what if we're hit so hard we don't wake up again?" I was Princess of Alabama, and this was so far out of my league it was frightening.

Had *Shakkor Agdah* waited for this? For an untried Chancellor? Why hadn't Ross waited to go to war with them? Was he so confident that he could win the Christmas war that he struck first?

I was untried, too. They would see me as an easy target, with my inexperience. That made me more than grateful that Rob and Cliff stood with me.

It did nothing to ease my fears.

"Stop fretting and go to bed," Gina ordered. "You can't function if you don't get some sleep. By the way, I'll take the job as chief cook and bottle washer, but we need to find somebody to clean. I have a couple of suggestions. We can talk about that in the morning."

"All right. We really do need somebody to clean and do laundry," I agreed. "I can't keep up with all of it."

"Great. We can send them to get groceries, too," Gina said.

"Fine. I'm going to bed," I yawned. "See you at breakfast."

"Sounds good, Princess."

"Please don't Princess me," I waved a hand and walked toward the doorway. "I feel enough like a fraud already."

* * *

Ruudann

The tiny cameras worked perfectly. I watched the live feed as the box was opened by a bribed prison guard. He expressed his surprise just before the first of three tiny drones fired at him, their poison darts piercing his eyes and blinding him instantly. His death was assured, once the prisoners escaped their cells.

Trucks driven by my subjects were already on their way, prepared to take the select few we'd chosen. The others—their fate was already sealed.

* * *

Parke

"They're in New Orleans somewhere." Daniel called when he and his crew reached that city.

"Trey said his people are aware," I responded. "We may have to hold back and let them handle this for a while. Unless they kill again."

"They'd be fools to do it," Daniel grumbled. I could tell he was frustrated that he and his team had lost sight of Dalton and Morton.

Chapter 24

Daniel was focused on taking them down and didn't like to admit defeat, especially when he'd gotten as close as he had.

"What about the car they were driving?" I asked.

"Abandoned at a service station outside town. My guess is somebody picked them up, but the station in question didn't have surveillance cameras on that part of the parking lot. Nobody saw anything."

"So they have friends in the city," I surmised.

"Looks that way."

"What do you want to do now?" I asked. "Go back to Alabama, or stay in New Orleans and keep looking for those two."

"You know I want to stay here."

"Then stay there. See if the sprite tracker can do anything at all to help find them."

"He's working on it. He says they have to stand on open ground for him to get a vibe," Daniel explained.

"Understood. Keep me posted." I ended the call and forced my body to relax. I'd been tense since learning that Dalton and Morton managed to disappear in New Orleans.

* * *

Ruudann

After the sixth bribed guard died at a sixth prison, I considered the effort and careful planning worthwhile. It had taken years to perfect this, and all of it was going smoothly—frighteningly so. This made up my losses and for the ineptitude of two ice demons to bring about the deaths of the werewolf king and his earth sprite follower.

A seventh guard died while I considered those things.

As for this plan, I imagined the panic that would come of it— and the increased panic when the country learned what we had in store for it. It made me laugh with joy.

* * *

Cassie

Cassie, wake. Those words jolted my brain like an electric charge. It wasn't Parke's voice, or Rob's or any other I might expect.

Will.

Will, telling me to wake. I was still groggy enough to consider that I could be dreaming.

Cassie. Wake. Now.

It wasn't a dream. "Huh?" I spoke foolishly aloud.

There are too many of them, Will spoke again. *We must do what we can.*

Chapter 25

*C*liff   He hadn't spoken only to me. I joined a frightened Cassie and a very worried Rob in the kitchen.

All of us had dressed hastily, without concern as to what we'd flung on our backs. Will walked through the back door.

He hadn't bothered to open it. He merely walked *through* it.

"No need to fear," he held up a hand. "Your ancestors would have called me a wizard. Or a sorcerer. Maybe a dozen other things," he said. "We have no time. *Shakkor Agdah* has released the prisoners from fifteen prisons inside the state. Other prisons in other states are experiencing the same. Alabama is perhaps hardest hit. We must do what we can, although it will be a pittance, when all is said and done."

"We can call the state police," Cliff pulled his cell from a pocket.

"You will sentence them to death. Every prisoner on the loose is infected with Black Myth's new poison. They will infect other humans, who will not know to protect themselves."

"Fuck me," Rob cursed. "This will require paranormals only," he added.

"Yes. I suspected something on a grand scale, but this surpasses my worst fears," Will said. "Come. We have work to do."

* * *

Parke

The voice that woke me from a deep sleep commanded me to attend to business as the Chancellor.

What the hell? Who is this? I demanded.

Will—the gardener in Alabama, he replied. *Every state prison in Alabama has been breached, the prisoners infected by Black Myth's poison and the escapees are heading toward the population centers. We will attempt to stop what we can.*

Prisons in other states are facing the same. Oklahoma. Arizona. Colorado. New York. Notify your people. Unprotected humans attempting to apprehend these will also be infected.

Why should I believe you? I snapped. *I have no idea whether to believe any of this.*

Then I will allow you to see through my eyes and speak with those who are with me.

I blinked.

I'd been transported mentally to a wooded area. Cassie, Rob and Cliff stood before me. "Cassie?" My voice came through the one I inhabited.

"We've only found a few," Cassie said, pointing to the leaf-strewn ground behind her. "They're scattering," panic made her voice higher.

Three men, dressed in prison garb, lay on the ground. "They're already showing signs of the poison," Rob stated flatly.

My host's legs carried me toward the dead men. Red and black veins showed on their faces. It was exactly how Prince Alfred described the humans infected in California—shortly before they died.

They have a short span of time to infect others before they die, Will's voice spoke in my mind again. *We are too slow at this; these escapees number in the many thousands.*

How long? I asked.

Days, at best. Adverse conditions will hasten their demise. They can still infect after their deaths, however, so humans without protection cannot touch.

That meant checking for a pulse would infect anyone thinking to help or looking for signs of life. First responders would be extremely vulnerable.

This had disaster written all over it.

I'll get with Trey's department, I sent, before recalling that Will probably didn't know anything about it.

I do know, he replied. *I merely can't be in two places at once.*

* * *

"This is Director Logan." I'd finally reached Trey's superior, after raising a near-fit with two other people who'd answered the phone.

"We have a disaster on our hands," I said. "It involves Black Myth and the poison they've developed."

"The same as that in California?"

"Yes. And if you'll check, there have been massive prison escapes in five states. It's my understanding that all the escapees have been infected, and will also infect anyone who touches them."

* * *

Cassie

Daylight found us exhausted at the kitchen table. We'd killed perhaps eight hundred out of thousands of escapees in Alabama alone.

News of massive prison breaks were on every television channel. People were warned to lock themselves inside their homes and stay home from work unless they were first responders or medical personnel. Photographs provided by the CDC from the California poisonings were splashed across screens everywhere, so they'd know what signs of the poison disease to look for.

Parke's last text indicated that vampires could be effective against the escapees, but they could only work at night. It would take time for the Vampire Council to coordinate the search.

As for the rest of us paranormals, he'd already called for those able to travel immediately to go to the affected states and join with the royalty there. Assignments would be handed out upon arrival.

Surrounding states were all on alert; Cliff, looking wearier than the night of the full moon after fighting off *Shakkor Agdah*, had called for werewolves to pick up the scent of escapees who'd headed for hills, wooded areas and forests.

Will, though, looked weary and grim. Anger still flashed in his eyes, as if he were furious that this had sneaked up on him.

He'd said he hadn't expected Black Myth's attack to be so widespread.

People were already beginning to panic. Grocery stores were running out of supplies in the affected states. They were hunkering down for a storm that could prove deadlier than any that had come before.

Parke had sent Daniel in our direction. I had the idea that he didn't appreciate that his hunt for my relatives had been called off. The others from Mobile were scheduled to arrive at any time.

I wanted to sleep.

I wanted to drink enough coffee to stay awake and do what I could.

All the escapees we'd killed the night before; I'd burned the bodies so they couldn't infect anyone else. They were nothing but ash, now.

It shocked me how effective Rob and Cliff were at killing.

Will only had to raise his hand and send a bolt of energy in a prisoner's direction. It hit them directly in the forehead, killing them instantly.

Surely, that was a better death than dying slowly of the poison in their system.

"How did they do it?" I asked aloud, startling everyone at the breakfast table. "How did they infect so many so fast?"

"I suggest searching the prisons involved," Will said. "Others are coming, and are taking up the hunt for escapees. We will rest a few hours and resume our work."

* * *

Parke

"People are already calling it the apocalypse," Mom said, setting a sandwich in front of me. "The infected haven't had time to get here yet, but there are reports coming in from all over about stolen vehicles, homes broken into, guns taken, murders and robberies everywhere, and everybody screaming and running if they think somebody's infected."

"Half of those rumors are probably not true," I said and bit into the sandwich. I had reports coming in, too. Royalty reported that the werewolves were having some success at tracking prisoners—until they got into a stolen vehicle somewhere.

"Around six hundred killed after sunrise," I mumbled around a mouthful of food.

"They're saying more than fifty thousand escaped, Parke. Six hundred is a drop in the bucket. Do we have any guarantee that more prisons won't see mass escapes tonight—or tomorrow night?"

"They're looking," I said after swallowing. "Trouble is, they don't know what they're looking for."

"Has anybody searched the empty prisons?"

"I've got Daniel and his crew headed that way. We have to clear it through the human authorities. Director Logan is working on that."

"They need to work faster," Mom grumped and walked out of the kitchen.

"I hear that," I said and lifted the sandwich for another bite.

* * *

Cassie

"What the fuck do they think they're doing?" I said. I wanted to scream. A father, incarcerated for attempted murder, had snatched his three small children after killing their mother. It was obvious he wasn't aware that he'd signed their death warrants, too.

Other reports were coming in by the fistful. A prostitute infected. Good Samaritans infected. Doors closed in neighbors' faces on suspicion only. Sales of weapons skyrocketing. Crazed politicians saying that the five affected states should be carpet-bombed.

I wasn't looking forward to the deaths of innocents, because somebody believed them infected.

"I used to watch zombie movies and laugh, because that sort of thing was impossible," Gina said beside me.

"These aren't zombies," I said. "These are thinking, mobile humans with a terrible disease."

"Yeah. I know. Some of them probably don't even know that, yet. They have three to five days to live, at most. They'll drop wherever they are, and it's more than dangerous to pick up their bodies afterward."

"At least everybody knows it's dangerous," I said, turning to look out the kitchen window. Will had removed every sign that Parke and I'd had sex on the grass in the backyard.

Those were happier days.

Who knew that the end times could come so swiftly?

"The CDC has been approved for emergency funding to search for a vaccine," Rob walked into the kitchen carrying an empty coffee cup. "It could take years, according to their director."

"Yeah. Every human on Earth could be dead by then."

"They're shutting down international flights to the affected states. It won't be long before they're all canceled," Cliff walked into the kitchen, turning off his cell phone with a familiar click as he did so.

"What about the borders?" I asked.

"Canada may cut us off soon—the border in New York is already being watched closely. Mexico is still open except for the Arizona border, but who knows how long that will last? Daniel and his crew are looking through one of the empty prisons. Actually, it wasn't completely empty—they found six inmates who hadn't gone out with the others. Don't appear to be infected, either. The State Police and State Bureau of Investigations are still trying to figure that out. Feds are on the way to ask questions."

"We need those interviews," I said.

"We're trying," Cliff said. "Give me some time, okay?"

"We must concentrate on finding the leaders of *Shakkor Agdah*," Will walked through the back door again.

"Will, that's unnerving," I said.

"My apologies, lady demon," he dipped his head. "It is merely more convenient and less time consuming."

"You think our time will be better spent doing that than tracking escapees?" Cliff asked.

"Yes. This may not be the full extent of their plan. It is already bad enough, don't you agree?"

"That's comforting to hear," Rob mumbled. "Averill, De-Leah and Keiran are sending out some of ours tonight," he added. "Those able to proficiently wield a blade."

"I'll let the vamps and my wolves know," Cliff hauled out his cell phone again. "So they won't be working against each other."

"Averill is attempting to contact some of the larger shifters, but they don't have appointed leaders or a strong track record of joining in," Rob said as Cliff walked out to speak on his phone. "He's targeting those who have human mates."

"Averill should attempt to contact the water sprites," Will said flatly.

Rob stiffened.

That wasn't a good sign.

* * *

Gina knew more about it than I suspected. "Water and earth have had a feud going for as long as anybody can remember," she told me.

We sat on my bed so she could tell me privately what had upset Rob so much. "Fire and air took Averill's part in this, which angered Queen Re-Anne. She hasn't cooperated or agreed to meet with any of them since then."

"How long has this been going on?" I asked. "Did Parke's father know?"

"Three hundred years, and he probably did know."

"I'm not sure Parke has had time to go through all his father's records and notes," I confessed.

"He hasn't been in office long, and much of that time was taken up in the Christmas war with Ross and Jasper," she defended Parke.

That was true, but she hadn't considered the year Parke had dithered between his father's death and his acceptance of the

Chancellor's position. Plenty of time to acquaint himself with his father's records and personal journals. He hadn't done that.

His decision to wait was *coming home to roost*, as Aunt Shelbie used to say.

No, I wasn't placing blame on him; he'd had trauma in his life and he'd dealt with that grief the only way he'd known how—by returning to his life and work at a law firm in the nation's capital.

It had taken him a year to come to grips with all of it.

In hindsight, that year could cost all of us.

"I've never heard of an actual wizard before," I said. "And one just shows up in our backyard, so to speak?" I said what had been racing through my mind since Will woke us all in the early hours after midnight.

"My grandmother tells tales that some had foresight, but she also says that they died out centuries ago."

"Well, that would be a convenient explanation, and I hope it's the right one," I replied.

"You don't trust him? Look at what he did last night," Gina pointed out. "If he hadn't told us, we'd be in big trouble today."

"It's not that," I waved off her concern. "I just find it too convenient, if you know what I mean."

"Maybe you should talk to him, then," she suggested. "To clear the air."

"There's not much time to talk, when we've got infected escapees to deal with."

"I worry that *Shakkor Agdah* may not be finished with us," Gina whispered, as if she were hiding her fears from a listening world.

"As long as they're alive, they won't be finished with us," I said and rose from my spot on the bed. "They attacked us. Will is right—

we have to find out where their leaders are holed up and take them out."

* * *

"Take a look at this," Cliff handed his tablet to me when I walked into my office.

"What's this?" I asked as he hit the arrow to play the video.

"Trucks—two of them, driving past a service station not far from one of the state prisons," Cliff explained.

"Those are military-type trucks," I said, recognizing the cloth-covered backs on both.

"That road is the only one coming in or going out of the prison area, which connects to a highway. The service station owner put extra cameras up, in case it was robbed by escaping inmates. We got these images from him. The time stamp indicates those trucks moved out shortly after midnight."

"But who or what would they be carrying?" I asked. The whole thing confused me.

"We know already that a handful of inmates weren't infected. Some of those were still cowering in their cells, even with the doors open so they could leave."

"You think there were some who weren't targeted on purpose?" I blinked at Cliff.

"The guards are all dead. We have no idea whether any prisoners escaped by vehicle as opposed to being on foot. Those trucks are built to transport soldiers. These may have transported prisoners last night."

"But who would they carry away?"

"At this point, nobody knows. You can bet they have an ulterior motive, though, if *Shakkor Agdah* stooped to saving humans."

"Did you send this to Parke?"

"Yes. He's coordinating with the FBI's Paranormal Division to look for other sightings of those trucks."

"When will sundown come?" I asked. "How many vamps can join the hunt?"

"I don't have numbers, yet, and won't until nightfall, when they answer the Council's summons. The werewolves are limited in their hunting areas, too. They have to stay in rural or forested areas during daylight."

"It sucks to be hidden, doesn't it?" I frowned at Cliff.

"At times, yes. Most of the time, it's for the best. We don't need humans hunting us present day."

"This is the worst," I said.

"It'll be a while before we can clean up the mess," Cliff agreed.

* * *

Zedarius

I walked through an empty prison silently. One floor up, I could hear humans searching through cells, looking for clues.

They didn't know of my arrival; I could walk through distance as easily as walking through Cassie's back door. It's how I'd transported them the night before, although they were too stunned to take notice.

Short distances were of no consequence. Crossing oceans was a different matter. That's why I'd used conventional means to fly from Europe to the United States.

Those searching cells above me would likely find nothing of value to help their investigation. All were dressed in protective suits as they traveled from one cell to another, with no idea what to search for.

I looked for something small. Mobile. It was the only way Black Myth could distribute the disease so rapidly. My worry was that it might have destroyed itself when it was done.

The prison kitchen was my chosen destination. Pots, pans, dishes, equipment—all clean and waiting to be used for a breakfast that never occurred, lay all about me. Stainless steel tables for food preparation lined walls.

At the far end, racks with piles of folded kitchen towels stood; with posters outlining safe food handling procedures hanging on the wall beside them. I closed my eyes. If something new were here that hadn't been until the night before, I would find it.

My senses reached out for the smallest of clues.

* * *

Parke

"So far we haven't found anything," Daniel reported.

"We're tracking two trucks that left one of the Alabama prisons last night," I said. "We may be dealing with the abduction of certain prisoners for something other than infecting humans."

"That's not good news," Daniel said after taking a moment to let the information sink in. "Is someone looking through the inmate lists to see what their specialties were?"

"It's in Director Logan's hands; I hope he's looking into that," I replied. "He's certainly looking for trucks seen near other prisons last night."

"*Shakkor Agdah* holds humans in contempt," Daniel pointed out the obvious. "If they took any of them away, it was for another purpose, you can bet on that."

"You're right," I said. "So you found no clues at the prison?"

"We've gone through two and nothing turned up. I'm about to head north, to a third. It's slow going, I'm afraid."

"I'd say ask for help from the Prince, but it's the Princess and she's stretched to the limit."

"I still have my team with me; the earth sprite tracker is out on the grounds and he's coordinating with Cliff as to the directions the prisoners took and how many went that way. During daylight, the wolves can only track them on open ground or forested areas, you know that."

"I do. When night falls, I hope the Council sends out vamps in a large enough force to do some good."

"Where will they leave the bodies? Has that been coordinated? They can't just bury them all—there are too many."

"That information is supposed to be passed on," I said. "To appropriate authorities, with no questions asked."

"I heard some states are sending out police helicopters," Daniel broached another subject.

"I know. Werewolves have been warned in those areas," I said. "The troopers have been told not to shoot at wolves or dogs. I hope they follow those orders." I felt the knot of pain forming in my brain; this had been nothing but a headache from the get-go. I worried we'd be so focused on hunting prisoners that *Shakkor Agdah* would escape our notice and continue their attack.

We should have been actively hunting them sooner, I realized.

* * *

Cassie

"This is what I found."

Will set a small, stainless-steel pot on the breakfast table. Inside lay what looked to be the remains of a toy.

Rob, Cliff and Gina studied the bits of twisted, lightweight metal and wires, just as I did. I lifted my eyes and stared into Will's, noticing for perhaps the first time how dark a brown they were.

"Fli-Bi-Net," I whispered to him.

He'd found the remnants of a small drone.

* * *

Parke

"The poison delivery system self-destructed, as far as we can tell," Cliff said on the phone. "It was probably supposed to destroy the whole thing, but in this case, it failed."

"Well, now we know why it missed some of the prisoners," I said dryly. "Fli-Bi-Net's accuracy rate isn't the best." I thought for a moment before a shiver went through me. "You know, I think I understand what to do," I said.

"What's that?" Cliff demanded.

"Fight fire with fire," I said and hung up.

* * *

Cassie

Rob wasn't happy. Will mentioned to him again that his King ought to contact the water sprites. I think Rob saw the sense in it, although I wasn't privy to their conversation. As a result, Averill was scheduled to arrive at sundown.

It made me wonder what the original feud was about, but considered that I might never know; it appeared that Rob was more than tight-lipped about it.

When Averill arrived with his guards, he and Rob shut themselves inside my office for more than an hour. During that hour, the rest of us tiptoed about the house. Perhaps we were hoping for sounds of the argument, or a snippet of their discussion, but we heard nothing.

"Their conversation is mind-to-mind," Will said eventually and walked through the back door to get some air.

"They could be screaming at each other and we'd never know," Gina said.

Averill looked angry when he left; Rob didn't look any happier than his King. "We will send a message," Rob sighed when Averill disappeared into the cleft in the backyard. It healed itself with a snap, as if someone had zipped up the ground.

Chapter 25

* * *

Parke

"This will take everything we've manufactured up to this point," Frank Hillman explained to Randall Logan and me as we walked past a production line in his small factory.

Randall Logan, Paranormal Director of the Special FBI Division, nodded at Frank's words. Logan was a shapeshifter—what kind I didn't know. He was likely something large and nasty when he turned—large enough and nasty enough to command the vampire and werewolf agents in his division.

All of us were dressed in white suits and safety glasses as we walked through Frank's business. "We're loading the last of the facial recognition software," Frank informed us. "They'll be ready to go by tonight."

* * *

Cassie

Queen Re-Anne loved Southern cooking. She delicately cut into the chicken-fried steak Gina and I served, chewed her first bite and nodded her satisfaction.

A glass of sweet tea sat near her plate; she'd tried that first and was happy enough with it.

Rob, doing his best not to scowl, sat on the other end with Averill, who'd shown up for dinner when Queen Re-Anne said she was ready to talk.

Gina stole a glance at me; we stood near the doorway, ready to go to the kitchen if Re-Anne asked for anything. I knew Gina was about to explode from holding back her verbal admiration; Re-Anne's hair was so many shades of blue it defied imagination. If she moved, another shade emerged.

Her blue eyes, too, changed hues according to the lighting conditions. It confounded me that it was even possible.

Silence enveloped the table while Re-Anne enjoyed her dinner. Once her plate was empty, she lifted her eyes to Averill. "When you apologize to me and to your son, who is my consort, then I will agree to work with you and the others."

Uh-oh.

"I'd like you to do this," I said to both sprites as I pulled out a chair and sat at the table. "If they take the humans down, we're next, don't you think? They won't be happy until the entire planet is theirs."

"You could be right," Re-Anne agreed, tilting her head in a slight nod. "What do you think water might do to stem the tide?"

Of course she'd use water references.

"Uh, Rob can sense things in the ground," I stuttered. I felt as if I were making this up as I went along.

"And I can sense things in water."

"Is that, uh, water anywhere?"

"Yes."

"Okay, then can you sense water on a person?"

"That sounds disgusting."

"But what if it's necessary?" I said, the idea coming to me slowly.

"Only if it's necessary," she waved a hand while her hair went through several shades of blue.

"I think it's necessary," I sighed. "Everybody sweats. Do you think you can detect the poison in their sweat? Can you narrow it down like that?"

She blinked at me as if I'd grown a second head for a few moments. "If I combine my efforts with air," she sniffed.

Ohmygodohmygodohmygod.

* * *

"Prince Deverill refused to come home, once Re-Anne had her claws in him," Rob huffed later. Averill did apologize, although it was an angry apology, leading to an uneasy truce between him and Re-Anne.

I hoped Averill's efforts to bring air and water together had worked; he appeared to agree with water in that she and air together could find sweaty, on-the-run escaped prisoners.

Once that happened, earth and fire could take over, eliminating the problem. Before she left, water had given me a gift, however. In addition to the necklace, earrings and bracelet I wore, I now had a ring upon my right index finger. The blue stone looked as stormy as my emotions as I studied it briefly.

I'd gotten a cryptic text from Parke, too, but still hadn't figured out what it meant. He'd just said there was an experiment, that vampires would be out hunting after nightfall in the five affected states and that he hoped it would be enough.

I had no idea what *enough* encompassed, but as I had little information to go on, I didn't argue the point. Instead, I texted back, asking him what anyone intended to do about Fli-Bi-Net.

Trey's dept. moving in, he'd responded.

So far, nobody else had found any evidence left behind at the empty prisons. It had taken Will's ability to find what we had, and the rest of us to connect that to Fli-Bi-Net. The general public had no idea we had evidence linking the company to *Shakkor Agdah*.

Fli-Bi-Net had no suspicions that we'd targeted them—at least I hoped that was so. Panic had worsened; every hospital and medical clinic had taken measures to protect their employees and patients from contact with anyone who could be contaminated with the disease.

Governors and Mayors were busy distributing paper and electronic information on what to look for and what to do if someone were found with the disease. The President was also preparing to address the nation regarding the crisis.

The information was bleak; there was no known cure and anyone infected would die a painful death on their own. All a doctor could do for anyone affected was administer pain medication, keep the lungs as clear as they could and make the patient comfortable until they passed.

Every time I heard an update of confirmed cases, I clenched my fists in impotent rage and wished my fire demon could burn *Shakkor Agdah*.

"I am still looking, lady demon," Will appeared silently beside me. "I want them as badly as you do."

* * *

Parke

Time was running short. Two more days remained at least, before escaped prisoners started dropping like flies from the disease they carried. In that time, they could infect thousands, who could then infect thousands more. Reports of shootings came in by the handful; state and local police were on the alert everywhere.

Of course, some had been incorrectly identified as infected and killed outright, that's how bad the panic had become.

I was strapped into a military plane traveling to Alabama with Trey and Director Logan. We'd left a contingent of guards, human and paranormal, around Frank Hillman's business.

For now, he and his manufacturing concern were our best bet to combat what we faced.

National Guard troops had already been called out in most states. Tonight they would have a new objective, rather than merely running checkpoints into and out of any largely populated area.

In my home state, a special team of agents was silently surrounding Fli-Bi-Net's corporate offices and their manufacturing

Chapter 25

facility, both located in the Seattle area. Once the business was shut down and arrests made, I hoped they'd get needed information on where *Shakkor Agdah* was and how to get to them.

I also hoped Black Myth wasn't scattered throughout the country or worse, throughout the world. That could spell doom more than anything I could imagine, including what we now faced.

The military jet began to descend; I patted the jacket pocket containing my cell phone. I wanted to see Cassie or at least speak to her, but we had other things to do, first.

* * *

Cassie

The media had come up with a name for those infected—*Walking Death.* The reality of it was every bit as bad as it sounded. Part of me never wanted to see another news program in my life.

Another part reminded me that I was Princess of Alabama and needed the information. I couldn't get the images out of my head of medical personnel in protective gear pulling people into quarantined sections of hospitals so they could be treated.

A handful of churches were condemning the disease as an act of God and telling everybody whose fault they thought it was. If I remembered correctly, the same thing had happened during outbreaks of the plague.

Politicians, too, were still screaming that mass extermination was the best bet to ensure the safety of their state or constituency. The worst was a small number of militia groups who were gearing up to shoot anyone and everyone they thought could be an enemy. That encompassed anyone who didn't belong to their group.

In the eyes of all those people, whether believer, politician or militia member, open season on humans had been declared.

* * *

Parke

Daniel and his crew met us at the military base in Montgomery. Director Logan had cleared the way for them to be allowed on base. We had a long drive ahead of us, as did others Director Logan appointed.

If this failed, I expected martial law to be instituted in five states, with the surrounding states following suit quickly. The disease was spreading and to say it was terrifying put things in too small a perspective.

Chapter 26

assie

De-Leah had been convinced to cooperate quickly, I learned. Together, she and Re-Anne sent their people out, air carrying water sprites like floating soap bubbles throughout five states in search of human escapees. Once Re-Anne's sprites found someone whose sweat indicated they were infected, an alert was issued.

With her connection to Deverill, Averill's son, the coordinates could be passed to the earth sprites, who would come from beneath an escapee, as long as the infected one walked on open ground.

Once the infected one was pulled into the ground up to his knees, the fire sprites could take over.

I was grateful when Will said the deaths were instantaneous.

* * *

Parke

Thousands of tiny drones, armed with five minuscule tranquilizer darts each, lifted and buzzed away from the eighteen-wheeled behemoth we'd driven to the prison. We'd chosen this one for ourselves because it was where the remnants of Fli-Bi-Net's involvement was found.

Near other prisons, other trucks were releasing their supply of drones.

Each drone had enough power to fly for twelve hours.

We had twelve hours, therefore, to do as much as we could against this threat. All of us hoped it would be enough.

"Every time they dart a target, we'll be notified," Logan studied the tablet in his hands. "We'll have latitude and longitude. Vamps or National Guard will pick up the target, depending on who's closest. All the vamps are wearing GPS trackers so we'll know who's where."

"I can only imagine what level of trust that took," I mumbled. No vamp in his right mind would consent to wear a tracking device. It could get him killed.

"It's easily removed," Logan said. "That was the condition."

"Where will the targets be taken?" Daniel asked.

"Back to their prison. We've got some coming who will place returning prisoners in the infirmary. They'll be treated the same as those in a regular hospital until they die. We have to save face with the public as much as possible; I'm sure you understand that."

It sounded like the lie I knew it to be, but I didn't say anything. I wanted to be as honest as I could with the human population; Director Logan saw things differently. He answered to his superiors, however, and the President was one of them.

Being Chancellor at this moment didn't mean a thing in the face of human politics and politicians.

"We have our first," Logan crowed and held up his tablet. Nearby, a group of Logan's agents were huddled around a temporary military computer station. They began sending coordinates to the nearest cleanup team.

* * *

Chapter 26

Cassie

Numbers were transmitted by the fire sprites throughout the night; by five in the morning, more than sixteen thousand kills were reported. Throughout that time, I hadn't heard anything from Parke as to whether his experiment was successful or not.

"Take into consideration that many escapees in Colorado may have died in subzero temperatures," Cliff said. "I've heard they're finding bodies in daylight using helicopters."

"All the more reason to suspect escapees went looking for the nearest shelter," Will said.

"I was afraid you'd point out the flaw," Cliff gruffed.

"Merely the truth, master werewolf."

"We have little more than an hour before dawn where we are," Rob said. "In every state affected, sprites will continue to work until dawn. This is our contribution to the human races, in an effort to prevent what happened last time. After such an effort, we must rest and replace lost energy."

"My thanks," I offered a dip of my head to Rob, who suddenly looked embarrassed. "It was a gift to you as well," he whispered to me.

I had no idea why I deserved the gift. I resolved to ask him later—when I wasn't so tired I could barely see.

* * *

Parke

The vamps retired at dawn; the National Guard kept working. We still had two hours to go and we didn't want to waste any of that time. State troopers and other police departments had been pulled into the loop once dawn was imminent; so far, the effort had proved more successful than we thought.

Escapees by the hundreds were being transported back to their prisons, where government officials waited to question them while they received medical care. It had taken a heroic effort of coordination on the part of the State Department, the FBI, Homeland Security and dozens of other agencies.

It surprised me that all of it was done so swiftly, once I'd made the suggestion to go to Frank Hillman.

That's when I got the text from Cassie. Somehow, she, Cliff and Rob had worked a miracle on their end, employing the four sprite kingdoms to take down what they could by working together.

The grand total of escapees eliminated through their efforts was nearly twenty thousand.

I showed the text to Director Logan, whose eyes widened in surprise. "We won't have a full count, but according to what we have so far, that's almost forty out of the fifty thousand accounted for," he breathed. Handing my cell phone back to me, he walked away to make a call.

"Since when did water start speaking to the others?" Daniel whispered to me.

"No idea. I didn't know they were working on this," I stared at the message on my phone, terrified it would disappear forever, leaving us where we'd been before. "We're lucky," I said, "that everybody is watching for escapees and suspicious of anybody they don't know—and some they do," I added. "That doesn't mean we'll find all of them, but if we keep our guard up, at least we've eliminated a lot of the problem."

"I figure *Shakkor Agdah* won't like that much," Daniel shook his head.

"You're right. I hope they don't have a second wave to send against us. Frank won't have another batch of these drones ready for a couple of weeks. Parts have to be manufactured, and that takes time."

Chapter 26

"We need to find the bastards before they have time to send a second wave," Daniel said.

"Yeah. Any new information from your sources?"

"We have every Prince and Princess searching their state, looking for suspicious activity. Cliff has his people on the lookout, too. So far, nothing of consequence has been reported."

"I was afraid of that," I blew out a breath. "Fucking Black Myth."

"I second that."

* * *

Cassie

As tired as we were, our eyes were glued to the television screen as images of tranquilized bodies were hauled into prisons. Yes, we understood this was human damage control; bring in some of the inmates while telling the population the others died of the disease.

Either way, they'd end up dead. A national news program reported that perhaps ten thousand prisoners, spread across the four affected states, had been tranquilized and captured before they were transported back to a prison in their state. There, they could be given medical care during their final hours, to keep their suffering at a minimum.

"Every precaution is being taken by prison guards, medical personnel and national security, which is overseeing the operation," a television reporter said. He was dressed in protective clothing, although he was at least a mile away from the prison in Arizona. "I have a message from the President for any prisoners remaining on the outside; give yourselves up; food, shelter and medical treatment are waiting if you do."

* * *

Parke

I used to pull all-nighters in college. That was twenty years ago. I hadn't done anything like it in a very long time. My thirty-six-hour day was catching up to me. The trouble was, the only thing I could think about was pulling Cassie to me in a comfortable bed somewhere and falling asleep.

I was beginning to think Destiny was right; I should have done something else, rather than let Cassie go. She'd performed a miracle, in my opinion, by pitting the sprite armies against something that could threaten all of us.

In all my father's lengthy tenure as Chancellor, he'd never accomplished anything such as Cassie and I had the night before. The worry concerning what *Shakkor Agdah* would do in retaliation troubled me, but my brain was too tired and sleep-deprived to dwell on it for long.

"Word has it that newly-convicted prisoners will go to the private facility they're building here in Alabama," Director Logan was back. "Locals are scared the disease will linger in these state prisons."

"I can understand that," I said. "I wasn't aware that they'd voted to allow private prisons in the state."

"It's an emergency measure—they've agreed to six months, while the state facilities are scrubbed and sanitized."

"Sure. Whatever it takes, I suppose."

"I've reserved hotel rooms in Birmingham," Logan said. "For all of us. We'll get a few hours' sleep after the drones run out of juice, then have someone else pick up what they can so Hillman can refurbish them."

Hillman hadn't asked for that favor, but in my sleep-impaired state, I didn't argue. "I'll be ready for that room when we get there," I yawned.

* * *

Chapter 26

Cassie

Eating while you're dead tired wasn't my best choice ever, I decided as I stared at the breakfast sandwich on my plate. Willing myself not to gag, I lifted it to take a bite.

"Where do you suppose *Shakkor Agdah* is hiding out?" Gina asked before biting into her bacon, egg and cheese biscuit.

"I am having difficulty with that," Will said between bites. "In my estimation, they are hidden behind very thick walls and atop a very thick floor. If that were not the case, the earth sprite might find them," Will gave a respectful nod to Rob.

"They will place a shield about themselves when they go out, so air and water cannot find them as they did the humans last night," Rob said.

"How much magic do they have?" Gina asked Will.

"It isn't magic so much as power," Will replied. "The limits on their power are unraveling slowly. We must hope to find them before it unravels completely."

"How did those limits get there?" I asked.

"Their ancestors placed those limits, to keep the race in sync with others on this planet," Will said.

I blinked at him in sleep-deprived stupor—*their ancestors did that?*

"Then their ancestors were smarter than the current batch," Cliff huffed and bit off half his biscuit in one bite.

"Exactly," Will said. "Much, much wiser than these."

"So, thick walls and stuff, huh?" I went back to the previous topic. Somewhere, there had to be that sort of thing—didn't there?

"Yes. I suspect it may be fairly new construction, as older construction has a tendency to leak air or water after a while."

"Like how new?"

"Within the past forty years or so."

"Oh, well, that narrows it down," Rob snapped.

"We all need sleep," I held up a hand. "We'll discuss this when we wake."

* * *

Parke

I saw the breaking news on a television in the hotel lobby; the sight of Fli-Bi-Net's corporate office in Seattle burning didn't surprise me in the least. It was like them to destroy evidence by torching the building.

As for their manufacturing plant?

It imploded.

Just as if explosives had been planted at strategic points by a demolition team. Once Logan's people came close, it caved in on itself. Experts would be digging through rubble for weeks and still might not find anything.

Logan cursed under his breath for several minutes before turning and heading for the front desk.

For a moment, I considered getting a taxi to take me to Tuscaloosa, where Cassie was. I realized how foolish that was after a while and went to pick up my key card at the desk.

* * *

Cliff

I woke after three hours, with Will's words on my mind. He'd said it had to be recent construction and didn't leak; possibly built of thick concrete.

I went still for a moment.

Before his death, Blake Donovan and I had discussed the private prison being built in Alabama, as if the corporation building it already had prisoners lined up to move in.

Or clients.

Chapter 26

That big, concrete-lined hole in the ground that Blake and I had speculated about—*it was less than a hundred miles away.*

I was off the bed and running toward the kitchen, calling names to wake everyone as I went.

* * *

Cassie

"I know why they killed Blake and the other judge, and then came after Rob and me," Cliff said excitedly, thumping a stack of photographs onto the kitchen table.

"What are those?" Gina stifled a yawn.

"Aerial photographs of the private prison being built—before the state even had a chance to approve a private prison."

I turned the top photograph to face me, waiting for my brain to wake so it could absorb what my eyes were seeing.

"When were these taken?" I breathed.

"Eight months ago. They've had plenty of time to make improvements, since then."

Will studied the photograph over my shoulder. I could hear the heavy sigh as his breath fluttered the hair I'd tucked behind an ear.

"Yes," he said, his voice heavy with weariness and conviction. "They are there. Cassie," he gripped my arm and pulled me to my feet.

I am sorry filtered into my brain before his grip on my arm tightened and he flung both of us away.

* * *

Parke

At first, Cliff made no sense; I was mostly asleep when I pulled my ringing cell phone off the hotel nightstand and answered his call.

"What?" I croaked into the phone.

"Will. He took Cassie. I showed him photographs of the private prison they're building. I'm pretty sure he thinks *Shakkor Agdah* is there. He took Cassie and left the rest of us behind. Rob won't talk to me, but from the way he's acting, this won't end well."

"What the fuck?" I was awake, now. "Get on the road—now," I ordered. "I'll be heading that way as soon as I get dressed."

"It'll take an hour and a half to drive," Cliff growled. "I've ordered a police helicopter."

I blinked—he was right. "I'll call Director Logan and see if we can meet you there."

"Hurry," Cliff ended the call.

* * *

Zedarius

I hated myself. It wasn't the first time, either. The sprites knew—they'd seen it in the past, as they were immortal.

There was one sure way to destroy a pod of *Shakkor Agdah*.

It required a fire demon and one of my kind.

I'd stopped for a moment a short distance away from the edge of the concrete bunker. Yes, it looked like an empty, concrete-lined box from above.

Below that false bottom was *Shakkor Agdah's* headquarters. From where I stood, next to Cassie's unconscious form, I could feel the vibration of their combined shields around the perimeter.

They were certainly here.

I felt like the worst of betrayers for leading her to believe in me. For bringing her to this.

For rendering her unconscious.

For sacrificing her.

I wanted to fall to my knees beside her and weep my apology.

No words disturbed the stillness of the early morning; even the sun refused to look at me before I did this evil deed.

The greater good flashed through my mind and I gritted my teeth lest explosive curses pass my lips.

Chapter 26

Farewell, lady demon, I told her silently. *May your journey be peaceful to your next existence.*

Grasping her arm again, I flung both of us into the midst of shouting *Shakkor Agdah* before doing the necessary thing.

* * *

Parke

My ears were covered by noise-reducing headphones as the chopper Director Logan commandeered rushed us toward the private prison.

We were less than twenty-five miles away when the massive bloom of fire burst in front of us, causing our pilot to veer sharply away from his destination.

"What the hell was that?" Logan shouted into his microphone. I turned in my seat so I could see the huge fireball again; ahead of us, another helicopter was doing the same, flying away from the explosion to avoid the winds, smoke and subsequent percussion from the blast.

"Make a circle and come back around," Logan barked.

The pilot did as he was asked. I'd gone numb. A horrible, creeping fear now gripped my heart.

Will.

Cassie.

Explosion and fire.

Desperate, I sent what I could. *Cassie?* I begged.

She is gone, Will's voice answered.

* * *

Cliff

Rob looked guilty as hell.

"You knew this," I bore down on him. The Chancellor was inconsolable and refused to come back to the house. All he'd said to me, after his chopper landed a safe distance from the burning concrete hole, was if I saw the wizard again, to kill him.

"We all knew—all the sprites," Rob whispered as he hung his head. "To destroy *Shakkor Agdah* in large numbers, it requires a wizard—and a, uh, fire demon."

"Get out," I shouted at him. "Get. Out. Of. My. Sight."

Rob fled toward the backdoor. Moments later, I heard it slam behind him. He'd get back to his lying filth of a King in minutes, through a rift in the backyard. I threw back my head and howled my grief to the world.

* * *

Parke

The fire burned for two days. As it was contained within the concrete bunker, Director Logan prevented anyone from attempting to put it out.

When it died, the last bit of Cassie died with it. Only a blackened hole remained of *Shakkor Agdah's* headquarters. Everything was reduced to a fine ash that blew away with Alabama's winter breeze.

Several of us had come on a gray, bleak day in March to lay flowers. I'd had messages from all the sprite royalty. I'd ripped up every condolence note they sent.

They'd known all along. Cliff told me what Rob said. They'd led Cassie to slaughter, just as the wizard did.

The fucking, damned, betraying wizard.

To send me a mental message like that, right after he'd caused her death.

"We're here to say good-bye to Cassie," Gina placed a hand on my Prelim's arm. I'd begun to turn, I was so angry.

"Yeah." At least she'd stopped me before I destroyed my clothing.

Chapter 26

"Come," she pulled me toward the bunker's edge.

Chapter 27

C*assie*

My eyes adjusted to the near-darkness after what felt like forever. My mind was empty of thought until I realized it was empty.

Frantically, I scrabbled for memories—they were there, merely out of reach. I struggled to sit up from my prone position; beneath my back, it felt hard and uninviting.

I saw the bones, then.

A skeleton lay on a shelf across from the one I occupied. Beneath that shelf lay a pile of other bones.

A hand clapped over my mouth before I could shriek. For a moment, I struggled weakly against the arms that wrapped about me like bands of steel.

"Hush." The voice was gentle, at war with the strength employed to hold me down. "You're inside a crypt in New Orleans. It was the best place I could find to allow you to recover."

"Recover?" I hissed, turning my head to meet his eyes. "You fucking killed me," I hissed louder. "Get the fuck away from me. Never touch me again."

I could see his expression as he lifted his hands in surrender and stepped backward.

He'd hoped I wouldn't remember that part.

I did.

Now.

He'd meant to kill me all along. No wonder I'd felt ambivalent about him.

"The sprites knew," he said.

"So you're trying to shift the blame?" I sat up as best I could in the cramped, musty crypt.

"No, that's all my fault," he nodded, lowering his eyes.

"How the fuck am I here now?" I demanded. I'd died. I was sure of it.

"When your fire burned in that place for two days, I began to hope. With a spell from the controlling wizard, fire demons in the past just exploded into a fireball, destroyed whatever *Shakkor Agdah* were in the area, then dissipated immediately. You didn't dissipate. I'm still trying to work that out."

"Not a good enough explanation," I snapped. "You used me as your own personal incendiary device. You're a betraying asshole."

"I know." He considered my words for a moment before speaking again. "The task was quite difficult, but I was able to gather your sparks together—from the fire. I put you back together."

He sounded proud of himself.

"I'm going home," I slid off the shelf. My bare feet crunched on brittle human bones; he'd shoved a skeleton off the shelf I'd lain on before carelessly dropping me onto it.

"I will take you home," he offered.

Chapter 27

"Fuck you," I snarled and headed for the crypt's door.

* * *

Epilogue

Zedarius

Three days ago, I watched the lady demon walk out of the crypt in New Orleans. I should have insisted on taking her to a safe place; I let her go, instead.

It makes me ashamed, and I have not felt that emotion for years uncounted.

I sigh and consider the conundrum of the bigger picture, as humans in this day and age are fond of saying. I'd done what I thought necessary. It appears I have merely made enemies of allies, which will only aid Shakkor Agdah in the coming days.

No, I am not foolish enough to think we exterminated all of them. My hope is that we were able to cut off its head, at least, and part of the body.

Those remaining will be forced to regroup. I have much to do in that time, including the attempt to convince several to heal the rift between us and prepare for the next battle. They do not know the truth of things, as I do.

This Earth lies in a cluster of six, each not knowing the other exists—except for the very powerful among us. Many things are similar on each—countries, cities, laws and other human factors.

Earth One is weakest, with only humans and the faintest of paranormal stirrings upon it. Each subsequent Earth grows stronger in power and paranormal activity. Earth Six held the highest levels; it was destroyed when the powerful fought for supremacy.

Earth Five was next; those who survived the last battles on Six invaded Five when their world became uninhabitable. Those invaders quickly forgot why they'd traveled from Six to Five.

Five was destroyed, much as Six had been.

Earth Four, where I am, must be the last battleground. Should it be destroyed, the bridge between it and Earth Three must also be destroyed—to protect the weak living upon the last three Earths.

It is my duty to see to it, if it becomes necessary. I was taught this by my elder, who also taught me what he knew of the hidden histories.

Others of my kind are obligated to align with me should the destruction of the bridge be required.

I hope that time will never come.

The End